THE FOREST BEYOND

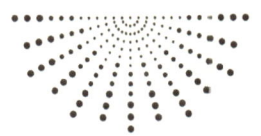

CHRISTINE DEYOUNG

Originally published under the title, Xylander: A Spirit Traveler Beginning

Ebook cover art designed by SelfPubBookCovers.com/ FrozenStar

Print cover design by www.mycreativepixel.com

❀ Created with Vellum

This is dedicated to my dad. For the writer in the both of us.

And in loving memory of my fur baby, Biscuit.
April 9, 2008-Jan 24 2015

By means of dreams or visions, young men and women used to acquire a guardian spirit to help them through the rest of their lives.

Lenni Lenape Tribe

PROLOGUE

𝒜ll she could see were tall, magnificent trees. Through the leaves, she could see the sky sprinkled with millions of stars like tiny silver sequins on a black dress. The full moon overhead painted everything around her in bright silver. A soft wind whistled through the trees, feathers of an owl rustled overhead, and a rabbit scurried away under the brush. The earthy scent of the rabbit floated along the ground like tiny brown wisps floating behind in its wake.

A robust masculine scent wafted over her, making the hair on her neck prickle. Her body stiffened while she searched for its source. Her heart sped up, sensing impending danger, and her muscles tensed in preparation to run or fight.

He stepped out from a clump of trees, and they stood frozen, sizing each other up. She kept her ground, staring into his ice-blue eyes. He was bigger than her. His muscles rippled under his fur when he moved. She would be no match against him in a fight, and if she ran, he would catch her.

Her heart raced, and she realized she was panting. She could smell his scent lifting off him in waves of red. It thrilled her yet frightened her. She wondered what he wanted.

She took a tentative step back and bowed her head in submission. He stepped to her right, and she countered with a step to the left. They circled one another, not wanting to expose their backs.

After assessing her, his body relaxed. A wave of relief washed over her, and she allowed him to step closer. His musk enveloped her, and sent a chill through her body, making her shiver. She closed her eyes and nuzzled her head into his chest. He smelled so wonderful, so intoxicating. He licked the side of her face and ear, and she forgot about everything else around her, falling deep into his spell.

He circled behind her while she basked in his scent. He grabbed her waist with his front legs and clamped her tight. Startled, she tried to pull away, but his grip was too strong. He bit down on her neck sending an electric shock down her spine to the tip of her tail. She reflexively arched her back and lifted her hips, giving herself to him as he unleashed his desire into her.

CHARLOTTE SAT STRAIGHT UP in bed, gasping for breath. Her heart pounded hard in her chest. Drenched in sweat, she untangled the covers wrapped around her legs. She took a deep breath and let it out slowly to calm herself, but immediately tensed again when she saw the clock's digital display: 6:55 a.m. *I'm gonna be late for school!* She threw the covers off and swung her feet out of bed, shaking the dream from her mind. She needed a cold shower to cool her blood and clear her head.

CHAPTER ONE

t school, Charlotte met up with her best friend, Lilly Locke. It was their sophomore year in high school, and they had been best friends and cheerleaders since the sixth grade.

"Hey, Lilly. How was your weekend?" Charlotte bounded up energetically next to her friend and Lilly's boyfriend, Evan, a senior.

"We went to a movie Saturday night." Lilly was quieter and more reserved than Charlotte, a perfect complement to Charlotte's high energy and enthusiasm.

"Oh, yeah? What'd ya see?" Charlotte shifted the books in her arms and looked around at the other students gathering around the front doors. She saw their friends Diane, Gina, and Mindy, all with their boyfriends, coming up the walk on the other side.

"We saw *Cocktail*, finally. You know, with Tom Cruise." Lilly raised her eyebrows up and down and gave her a knowing look.

"Hmmm . . ." Charlotte closed her eyes, imagining Tom Cruise standing in front of her. "Yeah, I saw that one last summer. I want to see *Young Guns*. There're a lot of hotties in that one." She winked at Lilly behind Evan's back.

The morning bell rang for them to enter the building and head to class. Lilly hugged Evan goodbye as they parted ways, and the girls walked to their first-period biology class.

"What did you do this weekend?" Lilly asked her as they took their seats.

"Oh, nothing much. Just church stuff." Charlotte shrugged and took out her book and notebook. She was between boyfriends at the moment. She glanced over at Lilly's hand where she wore Evan's class ring. She sighed. Charlotte wanted to wear a guy's ring like that, but, so far, she hadn't gotten the chance.

"Charlotte, dear, will you come here, please?" asked Mrs. Olsen, their biology teacher. She got up from her seat and walked to Mrs. Olsen's desk. "Will you run this note down to the office for me, please?"

"Sure, Mrs. Olsen."

Someone coughed into his fist, "Teacher's pet."

She turned in the general direction it came from and made a face.

When she stepped out of the classroom, she heard someone call to her. "Hey, Charlotte!" She turned to see it was Caleb, a senior football player.

"What are you doing out of class?" Caleb jogged up beside her.

"I'm running a note to the office for Mrs. Olsen." She gave him a big smile, showing off her dimples.

"Good. Then I'll walk with you." Caleb matched her stride as they walked down the hallway.

"Aren't you supposed to be in class?" She suspected he was skipping.

"Nope. Senior off period. I was on my way to the student center when I saw you, so I thought I'd say, hey." He had a great smile. She looked at his big brown eyes. They reminded her of two chocolate M & M's. She was really jealous of his long eyelashes.

"I saw your touchdown catch Friday. Congratulations." She looked at him as they walked down the outside corridor of the school and gave him a playful grin. He looked good in his tight jeans.

"Thanks! We should have had that last touchdown if Kale hadn't gotten called for holding. At least we beat the Rams." Caleb held the door for her as they entered the admin building. She caught a whiff of his cologne and inhaled deeply. She recognized the scent as her favorite.

"I know. The penalties nearly killed us. The refs were calling everything. They must have known it was a big rivalry game." She beamed a little at her knowledge of football jargon.

"Hey, I was wondering, would you like to go out with me this Sunday night?" Caleb looked at her with a hopeful smile.

They stopped in front of the office, and Charlotte turned to look at him as he reached a hand for the door but waited for a second to open it.

"Sure. That'd be great!"

"Awesome. I'll come by and pick you up at seven. I guess I'll see you at lunch then." He opened the door to the office for her.

"Thanks for walking with me, Caleb. I'll see you later." She gave him another smile and gently squeezed his bicep. She liked guys with muscular arms and shoulders. He flexed a little at her touch to show off for her.

"My pleasure." He saw her through the door and winked and waved at the school secretary inside and left.

"You should watch out for that one, young lady," Mrs. Crabtree, the school secretary, said. "He's a big flirt with everybody."

Charlotte handed her the note. "He's a nice guy, and you have to admit, he's cute." She turned to leave. She wished she had an excuse to stay out of class a little longer. She wasn't ready to go back and be bored.

"You have a good day, sweetie," Mrs. Crabtree called.

"You, too, Mrs. Crabtree." She opened the door, and with a quick wave, she headed back to class to dream about Caleb and his nice biceps.

When Charlotte stepped off the bus that afternoon, her dog, a blond cockapoo, waited for her on the front porch.

"Hey, Scuffy! You miss me?" She gave him a quick back scratch. He rolled over on his back, wanting a belly rub, too. She laughed and petted his belling then went inside.

"Mother. I'm home."

Her mother came around the corner from the laundry room. "Hey, hon. How was your day?"

"Oh, you know, typical Monday," She took a cookie from the counter. "I'm going for a walk before supper."

"Don't be late. I'm cooking goulash," her mother called after her.

After changing out of her school clothes, Charlotte headed out the back door toward the trails that led through the woods behind their house. Scuffy eagerly waited, his tail wagging. She had her sketchbook with her to make drawings of the different plants she saw.

She took a deep breath and smelled the fresh, fall air. Being in the woods gave her a sense of peace. She loved the quiet solitude of nature. She often dreamed of what it must have been like when the Indians lived in the woods of Arkansas. She imagined it as an easier and simpler way of life. She wished she knew what it had been really like back then.

She sat down on a tree stump and got out her sketchbook and pencils. She sat there for a minute looking at the tops of the trees swaying gently in the wind. She could feel her breathing match the rhythm of the breeze lulling her into a trance-like state. The fall was her favorite time of year. The temperature was perfect after the scorching hot summers. She loved the smell of the pine trees and drying leaves. It smelled like . . . *home*.

A movement caught her eye, and she spotted a cardinal. She loved the bright red color of the males. She looked carefully around to see if she could spot the female who was always near its mate. She wondered if all birds mated for life. *It would be really nice if I had a special someone,* she thought. Why was it that guys seem to come and go so quickly in her life?

Lost in her daydreaming, she realized she lost track of Scuffy and wondered where he had gone. She got up and walked further into the woods off the trail. A short way in, she came upon a small clearing of tall grass. She saw Scuffy running and jumping, supposedly chasing grasshoppers when, suddenly, he disappeared.

At first, she thought he ducked under the tall grass or fell into a hole. She remembered seeing Lilly fall in a hole once and giggled at the memory. Maybe she should follow him to check in case it was too deep for him to get out.

Suddenly, she was sucked forward like something grabbed the inside of her body and pulled her inside out. She felt the sensation of leaving her body. The pressure all around her released, and she felt like she was expanding out into the universe. A rush of sound and light came toward her, growing faster and louder, then passed through her. Her body compressed to a singular point, and with a *whoosh*, she was back. Everything happened in a matter of seconds. She stumbled forward and came to a stop.

What was that? Charlotte thought. She looked around wildly to get her bearings. Everything around her seemed to be the same. The trees, the grass, the clearing. *Where's Scuffy?*

She looked down to see she was wearing what could only be described as a Native American dress. *What the...? Did I fall and hit my head, and now I'm dreaming?* She looked at her hands, and they were tan, like the best tan she always tried but never got, regardless of how long she and Lilly laid out in the sun. On her feet were moccasins with beaded decorations. She felt her hair and pulled it around to see; it was longer and deep brown. She was confused and a little scared. *This can't be real. I must be dreaming and only thought I left my house to go for a walk.*

Someone called to her from the edge of the forest on the other side of the clearing. Charlotte looked behind her to see if there was someone else, but no one else was in the clearing but her. When she turned around, another Native American girl came out of the forest.

"Nahele, we need to be going," she said. *What did she say?* She wasn't speaking English, but somehow, Charlotte knew what this girl was saying.

"Nahele, did you hear me? We need to head back." *Nahele? Who is Nahele?* She felt she was in a trance. *This isn't happening, is it?* She looked down at her feet and saw a basket of what looked to her like a bunch of weeds and a few berries. The other girl marched toward her, grabbed her by the arm, and dragged her back from where she came. Charlotte quickly bent down, snatched the basket, and stumbled behind the girl. If this was a dream, maybe she should go along with it, and she would wake up, eventually.

Charlotte looked at the other girl more closely and noticed she was dressed the same with the same long, dark hair. She had big, brown eyes and the sweetest round face. Charlotte somehow knew that this was her sister, Hula, and Charlotte was called Nahele. Hula looked at her as they walked.

"Are you all right, sister?" she asked. "You look like you saw something to frighten you. Did you see a bear or panther?" Hula looked around checking for signs of dangerous animals.

"No. I am all right. I did not see a bear or panther. I must be tired from the sun and heat," Charlotte replied in someone else's voice. This voice was softer and melodic. It wasn't English either. She spoke the native tongue. Then, it came to her, *Wa sha zhe*. That's what tribe they were a part of.

"Are you afraid of your upcoming marriage to Tetonka?" Her sister giggled at the question. Charlotte stopped and looked at her sister.

"Marriage!" Charlotte exclaimed.

Her sister giggled again and said, "Do not pretend you have forgotten the marriage proposal from Tetonka."

Charlotte had a flash of Nahele's memory of her uncle, Wande, coming to her to tell her the news. "Tetonka has asked me if he can make you his wife, and I have said it is a good match."

Her heart sped up, and suddenly, she felt sick to her stomach. "I must rest for a minute." She sat down on a fallen tree afraid she was about to faint.

"We cannot wait much longer. It will be dark soon, and we do not want to be outside the village in the dark." Her sister looked worried. Hula placed her hand on Charlotte's cheek and told her she felt cool. Charlotte's throat felt dry, and she was having difficulty breathing.

"Here. Drink." Hula handed her a deerskin bag. Charlotte gratefully took a few sips and then some deep breaths to calm herself. For the first time, she noticed the forest had more sounds in it than she had ever heard before. More birds were singing, and more bugs were buzzing. She didn't recognize any landmarks either. It was also hotter than it had been before . . . *this*.

"Are you sure you know the way back?" This was too much for Charlotte to take in. *Where am I? Who am I? And what the heck is going on!?*

"Of course, I do! We have been walking these woods since we were babies. No more sitting. We must walk, now!" With a deep breath, Charlotte stood and gathered her strength. Maybe this was just some crazy, very realistic dream. If she played along, this would all sort itself out soon, she hoped.

CHAPTER TWO

They walked for a long time through the woods. Finally, after crossing a shallow stream, they broke through the edge of the tree line and entered a village of huts. The sun was setting low, directly at the end of the main road. In the center of this main road, stood a huge pecan tree. If two people stood on each side and wrapped their arms around it, their fingers would barely touch. She was in awe of something so old and sacred. It had to have withstood at least two hundred years.

Without a break in her step, Hula headed straight for the medicine woman's hut. Charlotte had to jog to catch up to her. At first, when she entered the hut, she couldn't see and had to stand in the opening to let her eyes adjust. A fire blazed in the center, and it smelled of herbs and spices.

Hula stood to the side slightly bowing, waiting for the medicine woman to acknowledge their presence. The medicine woman merely held out her hand, and Hula handed her the basket. When Charlotte didn't immediately offer hers, Hula looked at her, tilted her head toward the medicine woman, and said with her eyes, *Hand her your basket*. Charlotte looked at her hand, as if suddenly realizing she was carrying it, and handed it to the medicine woman. Then the medicine woman gestured for them to have a seat by the fire pit. She held a bunch of dried herbs in the fire until it caught. She blew out the flame and left the bunch of herbs smoking. She waved the smoking herbs all around the hut and around the two girls. She sat across from them, closed her eyes, and said something in a faint whisper. Finally, she gestured to Charlotte to come closer. She held Charlotte's face between her hands and stared directly into Charlotte's eyes for what seemed an uncomfortable amount of time.

"There is nothing wrong with this child that food and sleep will not cure. Now out." With that, she turned to her medicines and whatever she was doing before they walked in. The sisters exited the hut.

"Did you say something to the medicine woman about me?"

Hula turned to her sister and shook her head, confused. "No. I did not tell her about your episode in the woods. I do not know why she did that?"

Hula walked toward their family hut. Charlotte watched her walk away, confused. Suddenly, Charlotte's head began to swim, and she stumbled off balance. She clung to a nearby tree until the swimming in her head cleared.

Nahele's memories came flooding into her. Charlotte suddenly knew everything about who she was. She was a part of the Sky (*Tzi sho*) people, and those that lived on the other side of the road were the Earth (*Hun Ka*) people. They were all a part of the *Ni u kon ska* (People of the Middle Waters) or, as they were known by the French and Spanish traders, the *Wa sha zhe*.

She grasped the tree, breathing in sharp breaths. She looked around at the people moving about the village. No one seemed to notice her. Her heart thumped loudly in her chest as she tried to compose herself. Once her breathing slowed and her heart settled back into a normal rhythm, she walked to the hut she now recognized as hers.

Once inside the hut, she found Hula helping their mother, who was called Niabi, prepare the evening meal. She recognized her grandmother, aunt, and two small cousins who lived in the huts next to theirs. She recalled that their father, grandfather, and uncle were away with a hunting group.

She lit the fire in the pit in the middle of their hut while Hula unwrapped a roll of buffalo meat that looked like jerky and another roll of dried fruit. The five women and two children sat next to the fire to eat. Before eating, however, they said thanks to *Wah'Kon-Tah* (the Great Spirit) for providing their food and prayed for a safe return of their men from the hunt.

"Did you find the items the medicine woman wanted you to find today?" her mother asked. She was beautiful like her daughters. She had the same big, brown eyes that looked like a doe. Her hair was long and shiny. She wore a necklace of shells that their father had brought her from one of his trade trips. She also had many bracelets on each of her wrists.

Hula answered her mother, "We had to travel a long way to find what the medicine woman needed, but we found it and had no trouble on our way." She cut her eyes to Charlotte as Charlotte looked into the fire, lost in a daze.

"Nahele, what is on your mind?" her mother asked. Charlotte looked at her mother, blinking back into focus.

"I am worried about the men on the hunt," she replied, not wanting to make her mother or sister worry about her recent development.

"I am sure they will return home safely. Our men are strong and brave." Niabi patted her hand and looked lovingly at her daughter. "Are you thinking about your upcoming marriage?" she asked knowingly.

Charlotte looked down at her hands. She wasn't sure what to say. She was having a mixture of emotions at the moment. Everything about this experience was surreal. She was both excited and terrified. It felt real, not a dream. If it were real, then how?

"Something strange happened to Nahele when we were gathering," Hula interjected. Charlotte shot her a look of surprise and then quickly looked down. Now, her mother looked at her older daughter more closely.

"Are you all right, *Me nah?*" her mother asked.

"Yes, Mother. I am fine. It was a moment of disorientation. I am fine now," she said, not looking directly at either one of them for fear they might see that she was not exactly the person they thought she was. "I think I am tired and need to sleep." She got up and exited the hut to wash her hands and face in the stream.

The sun had gone down below the horizon, but the last rays of light still colored the sky. The night birds sang their evening songs, and the crickets and frogs chirped loudly. The smells in the air were of smoke and grass. As Charlotte neared the fresh spring, she could smell the wet earth and water. The spring water was cold and tasted clean and fresh. She washed the day's dirt and sweat from her face, hands, and arms.

As she walked back to the hut, she had an uneasy feeling that something was watching her. She stopped and listened more intently to the sounds around her. She slowly looked around and squinted into the woods. She could see a pair of glowing eyes watching her from the dark. She stopped and stood still letting her eyes adjust to the growing darkness. Finally, she was able to see that it was the face of a large dog or wolf. When she took a step toward it, it faded into the dark woods. She stood, staring at the spot where she saw it for a few seconds, then she decided she needed to get back to say the evening prayers.

❦

WHEN THE FIRST rays of light began to light the sky, the people in the village began to stir. Gradually, everyone exited the hut and faced the east to say their morning prayers.

"Look at us, hear us!
Heart of Heaven, Heart of Earth!
Give us our descendants, our succession,
As long as the sun shall move.
Let it dawn, let the day come!
May the people have peace,

May they be happy,
Give us good life,
Grandmother of the sun,
Grandmother of the light,
Let there be dawn,
Let the light come.*"

Charlotte opened her eyes and was surprised to find she was still in the Indian village. She wondered what was going on with her other life while she was here. Was it all happening simultaneously or had the future paused while she spent time in the past? She knew without a doubt that this had to be the past because the Native Americans of her day didn't live like this anymore. It was the life that she had always dreamed about. The air felt cleaner, and aside from all the natural noises of birds and bugs, it was peacefully quiet. But what was happening with her family in the future? Where was her other body during this time? She had so many questions. She had appeared in this reality without any knowledge of how or why it had happened.

Charlotte wondered if the medicine woman knew more than she let on. How could she ask her about what she was experiencing without alarming her or others in the village? What would the people think if they knew what was going on inside her mind? Charlotte decided she would go about life as usual for Nahele and watch and listen for any clues that might help her understand how and why this was happening.

About mid-morning, she sat outside her family's hut weaving a basket. She had completed three already. She was proud of herself for her new skill. It was a lot better than going to school and being bored.

She heard voices to the west and people rushed to the main road. *The men must be back from the hunt*, she thought. Her stomach did a flip. She felt both nervous and excited to see her father and her soon-to-be husband. She got up slowly, not wanting to be in too much of a rush. Her legs felt wobbly, and her knees were weak. *Did I eat breakfast this morning?* She was sure she did, but she felt light-headed as if she hadn't.

Hula ran up behind her, breathless. "Have the men returned?"

"The people are gathering in the west, and I hear their noises." Charlotte hooked her arm through her sister's pretending it was for sisterly affection rather than for support. "Let us go see what they have brought back." She smiled brightly for the first time in Nahele's body. She walked arm and arm with her sister toward the gathering of people and voices.

When they came into view of the new arrivals, she let go of her sister and stood with her eyes wide and her mouth slightly open. She had never seen so many tall men gathered together; not a single one of them could be under six feet tall. Those who were six feet were the short ones. Several were probably six and a half, and there were even two or three that would have measured at seven feet tall. She was in awe of such tall, muscular men. Up to this point, she hadn't noticed how tall the women were, but now she looked at them as well and noticed that they were tall for women. In this group of women, Charlotte would be average and maybe even a little on the short end. She had always felt too tall, especially as a cheerleader.

Hula looked at her quizzically. "Nahele, are you okay? You look as if you have seen a ghost?"

Charlotte quickly shook herself out of her stare and swallowed. Her mouth and throat had gone dry. She looked at her sister and smiled. "I am so impressed with the buffalo they have brought back." She needed to concentrate on her facial expressions and not keep drawing suspicion from her sister. She then looked back at the group of men to see if she could spot her father and Tetonka.

The men had paint on their face, arms, and chest. They wore jewelry around their necks and arms and even had pierced ears. They wore only a breechcloth and knee-high moccasins.

Many of the men talked amongst themselves or greeted their wives. Young boys, not old enough to go on the hunt, began to help unload the packs and take the horses to pasture.

Charlotte spotted a man moving past the other men coming toward them. He was her father, Chayton, beaming from ear to ear.

"My daughters! *Wah'Kon-Tah* has blessed me to look upon you one more day." He knelt on one knee before them and opened his arms for them to walk into his great big hug. Even though they were both coming of age to marry, he still wanted to hug them as his little girls, and they giggled into his arms as if they still were. She caught a whiff of his scent: sweat, sun, and buffalo. Then their mother appeared, and he stood to greet her. "And there is my beautiful wife," he said, embracing her a little more intimately.

Charlotte looked back at the crowd of men and saw a handsome warrior looking at her. When he saw her look at him, his facial expression softened, and Charlotte knew this was Tetonka. Her heart jumped, and her stomach flipped. He was an impressive man about six feet six inches. He had a strong face, high cheekbones, long prominent nose, and thin lips. He was slender in build with defined muscles. His arms were muscular and well defined. The lines of his shoulders, triceps, and forearms were distinct. Her gaze drifted down his body, and she felt her face flush hot. His chest was tan with powerful chest muscles. His breechcloth hung down low below his belly button. She could see the muscles in his thighs and the sides of his buttocks were taut. She quickly turned away before she could get any further with her thoughts. Out of the corner of her eye, she swore she saw him crack a smile at her reaction.

Next to him stood his warrior-brother, Kajika. He was an equally impressive man-boy. Both were between the ages of eighteen and twenty. He clapped Tetonka on the back and had a knowing smile on his face.

TETONKA STARED at Nahele long after she looked away. He thought about her always while he was gone. They hadn't talked much before he left, but he had been watching her for some time now. He knew from watching her and seeing the looks she gave him that he wanted to make her his wife. He had to step away quickly. Kajika was close on his heels.

"What's wrong, my brother? Afraid she will not accept you?" Kajika hadn't chosen a woman to be his wife, but instead, decided to chafe Tetonka for choosing his. They had been warrior-brothers (*kolas*) since they were young boys and came of age as men together. They spent many nights scouting the territory and held no secrets between them. They talked late at night beside the fire of what it would be like to be with a woman someday.

But now that the day was set, he found himself more and more anxious for it to arrive. He dreamed of seeing her alone in their hut. He hoped she would be willing to give herself to him, and he longed to touch her whenever he saw her. If she rejected him, it would kill him inside. He wanted to make her happy and provide for her as a husband should. The thought of his future with Nahele and building a family with her consumed his thoughts day and night.

"I am not afraid," Tetonka replied to Kajika. "I don't want her to think I am too eager, that's all."

Kajika made a *grmph* sound. "You need to show her who is boss and take control of her early." Kajika made a fist and waved it in front of Tetonka's face.

Tetonka stopped and turned to face him. "I will not treat my woman with force. I will treat her like the delicate flower that she is, and she will treat me with kindness and respect in return."

Kajika grunted again. "Women will be lazy if you do not treat them with force. They will not have your food ready when you come home at night and will deny you in bed."

"That might be the way you have seen it in your home, but that is not the way I have experienced it in mine. My father is a good man to my mother and has taught my brother and me to be the same. It is the same with horses, if you beat a horse, it will only be afraid of you and unwilling to obey, but if you treat it with gentleness and kindness, it will be loyal to you all its life."

He and Kajika had had this argument before, and Kajika never seemed to understand Tetonka's philosophy. Kajika's mother had died when they were young, and his father had taken on many wives over the years, so it seemed that Kajika didn't have the loving example of what a man should be like to his wife. This made Tetonka feel sad for his *kola*. Maybe he would understand more once he saw Tetonka and Nahele married.

CHAPTER THREE

*O*nce all the buffalo had been taken apart and set to dry or packed away, all the women went down to the stream to wash. The women stripped their clothes off and waded into the water. Some led small children in with them. The only males present were small toddling little boys. The little ones squealed at the cool water. Some of the younger girls giggled and splashed water on one another. After a sweltering day, elbow deep in buffalo blood and guts, Charlotte was relieved to be in the water.

She got out and made her way to the dry wrap she had brought. She wrapped the skirt around her waist, then she wrapped another deerskin around one shoulder and down under the other, tying it off to the side. She wrung her hair out and combed it long and sleek down her back. She picked up her wet skins and walked barefoot back to her hut.

Charlotte bent down to light the fire in their hut, then she heard a shuffling sound outside her door. She stood to see Tetonka standing outside. For a minute, they stood there looking at one another. Then she smiled, bowed her head slightly, and exited the hut to stand closer to him. She had to look up because he was a foot taller than her.

"You look well," he said in a low, husky voice. She wasn't sure she had the breath to say anything, so she nodded her head and smiled at him. "Would you like to take a walk with me?" He gestured toward the road. She nodded again and walked beside him.

They didn't touch, but they were very close to one another. Close enough that she could feel his body heat on her bare arm and shoulder. "I brought something back for you." He looked down at her and smiled proudly. She looked at him, scrunching her eyebrows together questioningly.

"Come. This way." He pointed with his hand toward the pasture. They walked around a few outlying huts to where the horses grazed. He took her hand to lead her directly toward a group of horses near the edge of the forest. He made soft cooing noises at the horses in order not to startle them and keep them at ease. He led her to a young mare. The horse was a mahogany brown, but the mane and tail were golden-yellow. He gently rubbed the horse's neck and looked at Charlotte. "This one is for you," he said, smiling down at her. Charlotte looked at him again, eyes wide with astonishment. Then she broke out into a big smile.

"You are most thoughtful, my love. She is a beautiful creature," she said, coming closer to her horse to stroke its mane.

HE SIGHED with relief to see that she accepted his gift. He couldn't stop staring at her as she admired the horse he had given her.

He thought Nahele was the most beautiful creature he had ever seen. It was more than her physical beauty, for there were many beautiful girls in the village, but it was the way she carried herself and how she spoke more with her eyes than her mouth. She moved gracefully in everything she did. Whenever he was near her, he watched her, drinking her in from head to toe. He longed for her so much so that his body ached with pain. He wanted to wait until they were wed to each other to make their union special, but it was still hard to keep from running his hands all over her as she was doing now to the horse.

When she looked at him, his insides seemed to melt, and, sometimes, he found it hard to think. He couldn't believe he was so lucky that she accepted his marriage proposal.

He remembered seeing her for the first time from across the fire laughing and talking with the other girls. He knew that she was the one for him. She didn't seem as timid as the others, but more reserved and thoughtful. He couldn't stand to be with a woman who talked too much. He had observed that from other girls and women in the village. He had witnessed women who nagged at their men and put them down, and he wouldn't be able to live with a woman like that. Somehow, he knew this wasn't in her nature, and he knew this was the type of girl he could love and protect all his life.

THE SUN WAS SETTING LOW, and soon the people of the village would gather around the great fire to hear the stories of the hunt and feast on the food that the hunters had brought back. Charlotte could smell the meat cooking over the flames from where they stood, and her stomach audibly growled. They looked at one another then laughed. Tetonka grabbed her hand. His hand engulfed her own, so tiny and delicate compared to his, and led her back to the main road in the village.

She was happy with this thoughtful man. He looked fierce and was a great warrior, but he had a gentle side to him that made her heart blaze with a passion for him. She was sad that she had to wait two more moons before her union with him. She hoped it would go by swiftly.

They came out onto the main road as the elders chanted their evening prayers to the setting sun. They knelt respectfully and lifted their hands in worship repeating the words of their elders. Then it was time to gather for the big celebration. He squeezed her hand one last time, bending his head down to hers. They touched foreheads, pausing to take a deep breath of one another's scent. Reluctantly, Charlotte pulled away. Tetonka went to sit among the men of the hunt, and she sat with her mother and sister.

She caught Hula looking at her with a big grin on her face. She knew what Hula was grinning about but wasn't going to say anything. Instead, she scrunched her nose and stuck her tongue out at her playfully making both of them laugh. They got a confused look from their mother.

Once everyone finished eating, the leader of the hunting party stood in the middle of the people next to the great fire. "We gather tonight to celebrate another successful hunt. Our brave hunters have brought back many buffalo that will sustain our people for the coming months in food and clothing." He gestured toward the hunters sitting together looking stoic and proud. Charlotte searched the group for Tetonka until she caught sight of him. He was already looking at her, his face neutral, but she could see in his eyes the care he had for her.

"We will share the stories the hunters have to tell us of how they brought down the great buffalo and celebrate their victories." The hunt leader sat down, and one of the older hunters got up to tell his story of the hunt. There was much laughter at the exaggerated moves and dramatic reenactments of the hunters. It was a wonderful time for all the villagers. The smaller children were bright-eyed as they watched the older hunters tell their stories, but as the night wore on, many of the young ones fell asleep in their mothers' laps.

When it came time for Tetonka to tell his story, Charlotte sat a little taller, so she could have a clear view of him. He was a great storyteller and actor. She had a flash of premonition of him telling their little children his hunting tales. She could see him making her and their children laugh at his antics before bedtime.

Tetonka had been a brave hunter. She gasped loudly when he told how he narrowly missed having a buffalo's horn rip his thigh open. She put her hand over her mouth as several people turned to look at her, and Tetonka gave her a slight wink in response. She was relieved that he hadn't come back injured. Suddenly, she was rethinking letting him go on future hunts, wanting him safe at home with her.

It was the life of the people, but Charlotte knew that the men were brave hunters and warriors. Many other Indian tribes that bordered their lands feared her people because they were formidable and difficult to defeat. Many had gone to war with the Spanish in recent years, and only a few never returned. The losses were much greater for the white man.

Her heart sank knowing that these people wouldn't be able to stay here much longer. But how much longer? Charlotte had no way of knowing what year it was now.

Tetonka finished telling his story, and the villagers yelled the hunters cry as he walked back to his seat among the other hunters. Charlotte sat looking at him with a big smile on her face. He sat down, wiping sweat from his forehead. He looked back at her and gave her a grin that made her heart skip. Yep, she didn't want to think about the far-away future right now, only the future that included her and Tetonka together.

Late in the night, the stories, feasting, and laughter finally died down. Those with young children had already gone back to their huts. She saw her parents walk hand in hand back to their hut. She hoped to see Tetonka one last time before going back. Hula hung around suspiciously. Tetonka appeared, coming from a group of men. He had been talking with his *kola*, Kajika. Charlotte hadn't spent much time around Kajika yet, but from their brief encounters so far, she wasn't comfortable with the way he looked at her.

Tetonka smiled and laughed. He took big strides with his long legs toward her. She must have been standing there with a goofy grin on her face because her sister nudged her hard in the side. Charlotte looked at her with a look that said, *What?*

Tetonka came to them and bowed slightly. "I thought I would walk you safely back to your hut," he said, giving Hula a somewhat annoyed look. Hula stood firmly by, smiling. Now Charlotte knew little sisters could be annoying, too. She sighed heavily as they turned to walk back.

Hula chatted nonstop about her favorite parts of the tales. She went on and on about Tetonka's story. Charlotte was happy when they arrived at her hut, and Hula went on in, not bothering to stay outside. She was thankful her sister at least had that much sense to give them a moment of privacy.

Charlotte turned toward Tetonka as he looked down at her. She wanted to run her hands all over his bare chest. It was right at her eye level, after all. His skin was dark and leathery from baking in the sun. She wondered if he was still that color under his breechcloth. Then she blushed at her sudden train of thought.

Tetonka took hold of her hands. "I am glad you came home safely," she told him, looking into his eyes. She could see the strain in his eyes of holding back what he wanted to do. She blinked her lashes at him teasingly. Suddenly, he grabbed her by the shoulders and pressed his lips to hers. She was shocked for a moment, but then melted and leaned into the kiss. But, before it could go on too long, he broke away from her.

Bowing to her slightly, he said his goodnight and turned abruptly, walking swiftly away. She let out the breath she had been holding and sighed contentedly. A wave of exhaustion swept over her. It had been a strange, yet exciting couple of days. What was she doing here? And why? Was she falling in love with this man? What was she going to do about getting back? She didn't have the answer to those questions, yet.

She went into her hut to lie on her mat. She laid her head down with a smile on her face. As she drifted off to sleep, Charlotte had visions of Tetonka in her mind and a smile on her face.

WHEN THE DAWN came the next day, Charlotte couldn't wait to see Tetonka. She quickly did her morning routine, said her morning prayers, then went out to look for him. She found his family's hut on the Earth side of the village. His mother told her that he had risen early to do the day's scouting and would not return until the evening. Her heart sank, but she understood that that was one of his responsibilities to the village, and she would look forward to seeing him in the evening.

All day long her thoughts were on Tetonka. She prayed he was okay, but then she knew that the scouting was not as dangerous as the hunting and not like it was when he went off to war.

By late afternoon, the women's work on the hides finished. Many of the women trailed back to their huts to prepare the evening meal for their families. She went back to the stream to wash her hands and face.

Hula came up beside her. "You look worried, sister," Hula said to her.

"I haven't seen Tetonka all day," she admitted.

"I am certain he is fine. He is a brave warrior and good at what he does. He will be back with the Dark Eagle," Hula said, washing her hands and face in the cold water.

"We should get back to help Mother with the evening meal," Hula said, helping Charlotte to her feet and walking with her back to their hut.

Her father sat by the fire smoking his pipe. "There are my beautiful daughters. How are you this fine evening?" he asked, smiling proudly at them.

"We are well, father," Hula said.

Charlotte kept her head down, not wanting her father to see the worry on her face.

"And how is my *Me nah*?" Her father looked at her lovingly.

She sat down next to her father and sighed heavily. "I am worried about Tetonka. He has been out scouting all day, and I have not seen him."

Her father put an arm around her and hugged her to him. "Why do you worry about him so much this day when he was out for many weeks during the hunt? Did he not come back healthy and strong?"

She knew he was right. She shouldn't be carrying on so. "I suppose after seeing him yesterday, I remembered how much I longed for him and looked forward to seeing more of him today," she admitted.

"Ah," her father said, looking over her head at his wife whom he still loved and longed for when he was away. "Young love is hard in the beginning, but once you are wed, you will settle into a routine and be content."

She thought it was easy for her father to say such things. He was a man always in the action, but a woman's duty was to stay behind and worry about her man not knowing what might happen to him.

"Come, have something to eat, little flower," her mother said, handing her a bowl of food that was a mixture of corn, beans, buffalo meat, and tomatoes. "You will feel better once you have eaten."

After she ate and helped her mother clean up, she went out to search for Tetonka. She thought she would check the horse pasture to see if his horse had returned.

Charlotte walked the way she remembered the previous night with Tetonka holding her hand. When she came to the pasture, she didn't see his horse, but immediately saw the horse he gave her. She tiptoed toward the horse, careful not to spook her. She spoke softly to the mare and ran her hand all along her sides and mane. She wished she had something to brush her properly.

Her horse lifted its head and snorted. Charlotte turned and found Tetonka leading his horse into the pasture. She sighed with relief upon seeing him and stepped carefully over to him.

When he saw her coming, his eyes lit up, and a tired smile broke his lips.

"I've been worried about you all day," she said, coming up to him.

He patted his horse on the rump to encourage it to go out to pasture and turned toward her. When she got close to him, he bent down and picked her up from behind her legs lifting her high above his head. She squealed with laughter. He looked at her with desire, as she leaned her head down to kiss him. He slowly lowered her down keeping his mouth on hers. But then, he quickly broke it off and turned her to the side to walk out of the pasture.

Charlotte was a little surprised at his sudden turn but walked with him back to the village. "Have you had something to eat?" Charlotte asked.

He nodded his head. "I had plenty of provisions with me on the scout today." Then he yawned. He looked bone tired.

"Did you see anything today?" she asked, holding his one big hand in both of hers.

He shook his head. "No. All was quiet." Then they fell silent as they walked toward her hut.

The sun had set long ago, and it was quite dark out with only a sliver of moon to light their way. They stopped in front of her hut and turned toward each other.

"I need to say good night here and get back to my own. I will be going out again tomorrow before dawn and need to get some rest," he said, looking down at her wearily.

"I understand. May the spirits guide your dreams and bring you safely back to me tomorrow," she said sweetly, rising on her tiptoes to give him a small kiss on the lips.

He smiled down at her and, once again, turned and walked away.

On the morning of the third day in the Indian village, Charlotte began to think this was her life now, and there was no possibility of going back. She was, no doubt, in love with Tetonka and didn't want to leave this place, but she was concerned for her life in the future. What was she to do? Maybe she should look for the medicine woman today and see if she could get answers from her.

She did her morning routine and asked Hula to walk with her to the medicine woman's hut. However, Hula reminded her they had promised to help their mother in the garden. Thinking that there would be time to see the medicine woman later, she joined her mother and sister in the garden.

Charlotte worked with them pulling weeds and putting the ripened vegetables in the woven baskets she had made. She had nearly forgotten her earlier intentions after a few hours working silently in the garden. She stopped to take a small break when she looked over and saw a wolf staring at her from the edge of the forest. It was a huge, beautiful animal with light brown fur. It sat there quietly panting with its tongue hanging out. When it saw her look, it stood and wagged its tail. It seemed as if it wanted her to come to it. She looked around to see if anyone else noticed the wolf. Out of curiosity, she got up and slowly approached it. As she got closer, she saw its eyes were a bright ice blue. They were strikingly bright. The wolf turned toward the forest and walked a little way in deeper. It stopped, however, checking to see if she followed. She continued into the forest to follow it, for it seemed it had something to show her.

CHAPTER FOUR

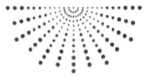

*C*harlotte jolted upright and gasped sharply. At first, she was confused and didn't realize where she was. A second later, she realized she was sitting in her seat in English II. All the students around her turned to look at her, and Ms. Parker stopped talking and looked directly at her.

"Are you all right, Charlotte?" she asked.

Charlotte searched frantically in her mind for what to say that could excuse her sudden awakening into this reality. "I remembered I forgot something in my locker. May I go get it?" She feigned importance and a need to get out quickly.

"Yes, make it quick, please." Ms. Parker looked annoyed at being interrupted in the middle of her instructions. Charlotte would have to get those from Lilly later. Speaking of, Lilly was staring at her, and Charlotte tried to give her a look that said, *Not now, later.*

Charlotte slipped out the door and closed it gently, then leaned back against the cinder block wall of the hallway. Her head was spinning. *What happened?* The last thing she remembered was following that wolf with the intense eyes, then... *here!*

She walked as calmly as she could to the girl's bathroom and ran cold water over her hands and wrists. She stood staring closely at her face in the mirror. She looked, but she still felt disoriented. She was here in her school as Charlotte McAfee, but in the back of her mind, she still felt like Nahele back in her village. It was almost like her mind was in two places at once. Like remembering a dream after waking, and it still lingers in the back of your mind.

She looked more closely at her eyes. They seemed different somehow. What was it? But, before she could lean in closer to look, someone came into the bathroom, and she quickly looked down at her hands and pretended to finish. She needed to get back to class.

Briefly, she thought about going to the nurse and complain about being sick, but then she felt guilty for lying. She needed to figure out what happened to her and find out what happened in this world. She couldn't afford to get behind in her school work. She needed to talk to Lilly.

Thank goodness English was the last class before lunch. When the bell rang to leave class, Lilly was right beside her before she could stand up out of her seat. "What happened to you?" Lilly asked in a harsh whisper. "You haven't been yourself all week and then, suddenly, in class, you jerk to life like you just got here."

"Really? Is that what it looked like?" They walked slowly down the hallway to their lockers, letting the other students clear out ahead of them. They were always among the last ones to the cafeteria line anyway. "What exactly did you see or was unusual about me this week?" Charlotte asked, tentatively.

"Charlotte, you're usually a chatterbox that I can't get to shut up. You're always laughing and flirting with everybody, but the past few days you've been like . . . sleepwalking," Lilly looked worried for her friend.

"Sleepwalking, huh?" That explains how she felt. But what was it? "I'm not sure I can explain what's been happening." She wasn't sure how much to tell Lilly, but if she couldn't tell Lilly, who else was there to talk to?

They stepped into the crowded cafeteria and took their place at the end of the line. There were two lines in which to choose. The left line was always the designated meal for whatever day of the week it was, and the right line was for the standard cafeteria version of a hamburger and soggy fries.

"What's for lunch?" Charlotte asked.

"It's Thursday, so it's taco salad day." Lilly looked at her concerned again. "You don't remember what day it is?"

"Not until you told me just now."

"So, you've been sleepwalking through your life the past couple of days and don't remember what day it is. What do you remember?" Lilly was gearing up for her best deductive reasoning skills.

"If I told you what I had been experiencing the past couple of days, I'm not sure you would believe me. You would probably call my parents and tell them I needed to see a shrink or something." She wasn't sure she had much of an appetite right now. She needed to figure out what was going on. Maybe she was going crazy. Maybe she hit her head and had been in a coma-like state. *Does that even happen?* She felt around her scalp for bumps or sore spots.

"What are you doing?"

"I'm checking my head for any bumps in case I hit my head, and I've been walking around with a concussion."

"A concussion! Here, let me see." Lilly reached to feel Charlotte's head for her.

"What's the matter? Charlotte got lice?" *Oh, no.* Charlotte knew that voice, and he was the last person she wanted to see her like this and start stupid rumors. It was Kale. At six feet four inches and 225 pounds of solid muscle, he was the biggest sophomore football player, heck, probably the biggest period. Although there had been big guys in the past, they had graduated now, and Kale was left to rule the field and anyone else he darn well pleased.

For some reason, Charlotte always had an internal radar for where he was at all times. There seemed to be this unspoken magnetic connection between them that they danced around. Today, that connection seemed to be broken, and he managed to sneak up on her unaware.

Lilly dropped her hands quickly, and Charlotte straightened and turned to look at him. Putting on her happy face, Charlotte said, "No,

Kale. I don't have lice. I think I might have bumped my head, and Lilly was checking for me to make sure I didn't have a big bump." She tried to blow it off like it was nothing.

"Well, that explains how you've been acting lately. I kept trying to get your attention, and you ignored me more than usual. I usually get a response out of you eventually." Kale grinned mischievously. It was true. Kale was always saying something to her or throwing something at her to get her attention trying to distract her from class.

"I'm fine, Kale. Thanks for asking." Charlotte turned her back on him and gave Lilly a face that meant, *Make him go away*!

Lilly quickly put in, "Bye, Kale!"

Instead, he took a step closer to Charlotte and whispered into her ear. "Why don't you go out with me Saturday night? I could make you forget whatever it is inside that pretty little head of yours."

A cold shiver ran down her spine. She flashed back to the previous year when they had tried to date. She remembered how happy she had been to be with him. But then, the jealousy began, and when her parents could hear him screaming at her through the phone, they made it very clear it was time to break it off. She was heartbroken. A part of her still liked Kale, but he had a scary side that told her to stay away.

Without turning, she replied, "Sorry, Kale. I have plans. Maybe some other time."

Kale stepped back and glared at her back for a few seconds before he turned to go outside and join his football buddies.

Lilly and Charlotte finally got through the food line and found seats that other students vacated to mill around in the courtyard until lunch was over.

"Well, now that you're back in the land of the living and not walking around like a zombie, we need to talk about next week's plans for Homecoming," Lilly said, putting aside Charlotte's little dilemma, for now, to concentrate on more important matters.

Homecoming, Charlotte thought. It was the busiest week of the year, especially for the cheerleaders. They had to paint signs for all the spirit days, make goody bags for all the football players, and plan the big pep rally.

"This year's theme is The Old South," Lilly informed her.

"Who came up with that theme?" Charlotte hoped it wasn't her, and she didn't remember. *Gone with the Wind* was one of her favorite books.

"I think it was the seniors who voted for the idea." Lilly pushed her taco salad around on her plate. "The student council will take care of the voting for the court on Monday."

"I guess we need to get volunteers to do the class skit." Charlotte knew who was going to oversee that... her. Talk about turning on her Southern charm. She was going to have to muster as much energy as she could to get people to work on the pep rally skit and posters.

"We also need someone to get the supplies for the hall decorations." Lilly looked at her hopefully. As if she didn't have enough on her plate already. *What was Lilly doing?*

As if reading her mind, Lilly said, "I have a student council meeting this afternoon after cheer practice, then maybe you can come over to my house, and we can talk more about what's up with you."

"Actually, you need to get me caught up on what Ms. Parker said today when I so rudely interrupted everything." Charlotte was still a little embarrassed about her sudden outburst in class. There was no telling what else she had missed out on while her consciousness was away. Lilly suddenly looked tired as they got up to put their trays away. Neither had eaten much. It was time to go to world history, which was a snoozefest anyway. Charlotte bet no one had noticed one bit that she had been out of it during that class. She was sure she looked like that all the time during that class.

"I'll catch you at cheer practice, and we can talk more about what we're going to do for a skit," Lilly said, picking up her books and walking to the door. Charlotte had a sinking feeling she was the one who was going to have to come up with that idea, too. Better get her head in the game and shake this craziness about Nahele and Tetonka. But in her heart, she still wanted to go back there, wherever there was, if she could. Or maybe, it was all a silly daydream in her head.

"There it is again! You had that look again!" Lilly stood in front of her accusingly.

"Shh," Charlotte looked around, "not so loud. I don't want everyone else thinking I'm losing my mind."

"Sorry." Lilly turned back around but then whispered, "What happened then when you got that look?"

"I was thinking about it." Charlotte didn't know how else to explain it.

"It? What is it?"

"That's what I'll have to explain later. Right now, we don't have time, and we have to get to class." She wasn't sure how exactly to explain to her friend what it was, as she wasn't sure herself.

"Okay, but in the meantime, try not to think about it. Okay?" Lilly looked at her for reassurance.

"Okay, got it. No thinking, only doing." Now Charlotte was mocking her, but in the back of her mind she still felt connected to them and knew she wasn't going to be able to ignore them for long.

AT ONE O'CLOCK THE next day, the announcement was made to dismiss the football team and cheerleaders. Charlotte still wasn't sure how she could explain her situation, but she felt she had to talk to someone.

She was already seated when Lilly plopped down beside her on the bus. "Whew! It's finally game time," Lilly said. "I thought this day would never end." Charlotte got the feeling that Lilly knew the conversation they were about to have, but somehow was dreading it.

"Okay, out with it," Lilly finally demanded.

"Well, I'm still not sure how to explain it, and I still think you're going to call me crazy. But, I need to talk to someone about it and maybe talking about it out loud will help me sort it out," Charlotte admitted. Lilly didn't say anything but let her continue.

"I was walking in the woods behind my house with Scuffy when, suddenly, he seemed to disappear," she tried to explain.

"Who disappeared? Scuffy?" Lilly was confused already.

"Yes, Scuffy. Anyway, I thought maybe he had fallen in a hole, so I went after him. That's when I felt something suck me forward. I remember stumbling forward like I missed a step up or something. When I came to a stop, I looked down, and I was in the body . . . of an Indian girl." Charlotte looked sheepishly at Lilly to see her reaction. As she suspected, Lilly looked at her like, *are you kidding me?*

Charlotte continued before Lilly could say anything out loud. "I'm serious! I thought I was daydreaming, but when another Indian girl, who was my sister, by the way, grabbed me, I felt it for real. We also walked for several miles back to the village, and believe me, it was real."

"Okay, you're right. I do think you're crazy," Lilly admitted.

Charlotte sighed heavily. She knew this was going to be hard, but now that she had said it out loud, she had convinced herself of the fact that it was real rather than dispel it.

"Look," Lilly was making an effort to be open-minded. "What other proof can you give me other than you telling me that it *felt real* to you. Who were these people? Are they people living now?"

Charlotte had to admit, she was going to have to come up with some compelling evidence to support her story, or no one was going to believe her. "After I got over the initial shock of being someone else, her memories came to me. I know the people are from the *Wa sha zhe* tribe, and they're from a long time ago. It wasn't present-day."

"So, you're not only telling me that you were suddenly transported into someone else's body, but you also went back in time?" Lilly was having a difficult time with this as much as Charlotte did when it first happened to her. "Sounds like something straight out of Twilight Zone to me."

They sat there for a few minutes contemplating that possibility. Then they looked at each other and burst out laughing. Okay, so maybe she did bump her head.

"What's so funny? Someone tell a good joke?" One of the other cheerleaders popped her head over the seat in front of them.

"It's an Algebra II joke. You wanna hear it?" Charlotte said.

The other girl wrinkled her nose and made a gagging sound. "No thanks," and turned back around.

Lilly and Charlotte looked at each other again and burst out laughing. But when things quieted down, Charlotte felt unsettled. What other proof could she give? Maybe if she did some research to find out who these Native Americans were, she could convince Lilly of what she was saying was true. She leaned her head against the window and watched the countryside whiz by. The land she saw as they drove by had changed so much in the last two hundred years. *What happened to all the people who once lived here?*

CHARLOTTE'S MOTHER knocked on her bedroom door. "Charlotte you need to get up."

Charlotte pulled the covers over her head. "But, Mother, it's Saturday, and I want to sleep in."

"Come on, Charlotte. You need to go to your brother's football game. He goes to your activities to support you; now you need to go to his game to support him."

Charlotte seriously doubted Tad or Ryan went to her events to support her. She kicked back the covers with a huff and sat up. Rubbing her hands over her face, she tried to clear her head. *What was I dreaming?* It was something to do with Nahele and Hula, but not Tetonka. *He must be away again.*

Shrugging off her nighttime dreams and early morning fog, she got up to see if she could find breakfast.

Back at the school football stadium, Charlotte found a spot at the top of the bleachers. It would be a comfortable spot for Lilly to see her. Lilly's younger brother, Jordan, was the same age as her brother Ryan, so they were always together again at their little brothers' events.

Lilly came up the steps. Lilly sat down beside her and wrapped her arms around her knees. "I've been thinking about what you said, being the Indian girl, do you think it could be a past life memory?"

Charlotte thought for a moment. "Maybe. That would explain the time difference."

"Where did this happen again?" Lilly seemed more curious now.

"Do you mean where did I zone out or where did I go?"

"Both. I suppose."

"I *switched*, I guess you could say, in a clearing in the woods behind my house. But, I think I was still in the same area. It was all still woods, so, who knows." Charlotte shrugged thinking back. "Hey! Do you think you could come with me to check it out?"

Lilly thought for a minute then replied. "How do you know it won't happen again? What if we get out there and we both go through? How will we get back?" Lilly panicked at the prospect.

"I don't know for sure. But you said that my body was still here going through the motions. Our *shadow-selves* will still be here going through life as normal." Charlotte tried to sound helpful. "Besides, I think it has something to do with the dogs, too."

"Dogs? You said something about Scuffy, but was there another dog?" Lilly had an unhealthy fear of strange dogs and getting attacked.

"When I was on the other side, I followed a wolf that came to me, and it disappeared like Scuffy did. Then I woke up in the middle of English class." She came to this realization for the first time.

"So, you think that the dogs had something to do with enabling you to switch back and forth?" Lilly was beginning to doubt this story again.

"That's the way it seems. I'm trying to tell you what happened the best I can and get a handle on all of this as well." Charlotte was a little exasperated at the complexity of her dilemma.

"Okay, so if we go out there without Scuffy, you think we'll be okay?" Lilly wanted to be reassured.

"That seems to be the case. So, you want to come back home with me after this? We could go back and trace my steps," Charlotte tried to sound more confident than she felt.

"All right, but remember if something happens to me as well, this was all your idea." Lilly wanted to be a good friend and stick this out with her so that she could hopefully solve this mystery.

37

More cars pulled into the parking lot. "Uh-oh. It looks like the football players are here to go over last night's film." There were guys on the team that she didn't mind looking at—good eye candy—but then there were those who always had a smart remark to ruin her day and who she would rather avoid. Lilly turned around to look. Maybe if they stayed still, they could get a good look at the guys walking to the field house without them noticing, and they could bask in the pleasure of seeing them without having to exchange words.

"Oh, there's Caleb. He's so cute," Lilly said with a little gleam in her eye.

"Hey! You have Evan!" Charlotte was only partially accusing.

"I can still look and appreciate," Lilly whined. "But, don't tell Evan, okay."

"My lips are sealed." Charlotte ran her fingers across her lips.

"Oh crap, don't look now but guess who pulled up." Lilly ducked down a little as if she could hide a bit more. Charlotte knew who she meant—Kale. She had to admit he had the body of a god, but his attitude ruined everything.

Unfortunately, he did see them and came straight over to the fence to talk. "What are you two babes doing out here?" He leaned on the fence attempting to strike a pose.

"We're here to watch our little brothers' football game." Charlotte beamed a big smile at him. She couldn't stop herself from teasing him.

"Did you see the hurt I put on them last night?" Kale smacked his bicep as a show of his muscular might. Charlotte expected him to kiss each one of his biceps next.

"Uh, we sure did," Lilly said sarcastically, struggling to suppress her laughter.

"I got knocked out there for a little while. I don't even remember the third quarter." Kale rubbed his head while flexing his biceps for them some more. The girls looked at each other and rolled their eyes.

"Oh, wow! That sounds terrible. Did you go to the doctor to have your head examined?" Charlotte gave Lilly a look out of the corner of her eye, suppressing a giggle.

"Nah, I'm good. Takes a harder hit than that to crack this thick skull." He knocked on his head.

"I'll say." Lilly bumped Charlotte with her shoulder.

"Charlotte, did you get the lice out of your hair?" Kale jabbed at her.

"Yes, I did. Thanks for asking, Kale." Charlotte flipped her hair back and tossed her head. She winked at him for added effect. When she did this, Kale looked dumbfounded. His eyebrows went up slightly, and his mouth went slack, but then a slow, boyish grin spread across his face as if he had been given a promise to Disneyland.

He dropped his voice deeper to sound sexier. "Have you reconsidered my offer for tonight?"

"You better get in there, Kale. Coach will be looking for you." Charlotte continued to smile at him coyly.

"You know how to reach me if you change your mind, Charlotte. I'll see you ladies later." He puffed out his chest and stood a little taller. When he turned to leave, Lilly and Charlotte couldn't hold it any longer and burst out laughing. Kale didn't look back but gave it a little more strut in his walk as they watched him walk away.

LATER THAT DAY, Lilly and Charlotte walked through the woods to the clearing. The grass was knee-high. "What if there are snakes?" Lilly suddenly thought to ask.

"It's too cool for snakes this time of year. They've gone underground," Charlotte said, distractedly.

"Are you sure?"

"I'm sure, Lilly."

Lilly kicked something with her shoe and bent down to pick it up.

"Hey! You found my sketchbook." Charlotte walked to Lilly to retrieve her notebook. "I forgot I had it with me on Monday. I must have dropped it when I switched." She thumbed through it, checking for any damage.

"So, this must be the spot." Lilly looked around expecting an

Indian to pop out of the woods. It appeared the same, and they looked down at themselves to make sure they were still the same. When they decided they were okay, they began to walk around, looking for anything out of the ordinary.

"I don't see a hole or a portal or anything." Charlotte was a little disappointed.

"Yeah, everything looks perfectly normal," Lilly agreed. "What now?"

"How do you feel about a long walk?" Charlotte wanted to retrace her steps as she remembered it to see if she could find evidence of the village.

"I don't know." Lilly looked hesitant. "How far are we talking?"

"By my estimates, it normally takes me about twenty minutes to walk a mile through the woods. We walked about an hour and a half to two hours one way." Charlotte knew it was asking a lot since they would have to walk all that way back as well.

"I don't think I'm ready for that." Lilly looked skeptical. "Besides, we don't have any water or food. Aren't we supposed to have supplies when we go out for that long?"

"You're right. We're not prepared. Maybe we can plan better and try again tomorrow."

"Uh, I think I have something to do tomorrow." Lilly didn't find hiking through the woods for three to four hours appealing. She had about all she wanted of it as it was right now.

"Okay, we'll go back." Charlotte was disappointed, but she understood. Not everyone was as crazy as she was about hiking through the forest, but she knew she didn't need to do it alone. There weren't as many dangerous animals in the woods anymore as there were two hundred years ago, but it still wasn't smart to go out alone.

"Let's go back. I think we've had enough for today." Charlotte turned to head back. Lilly let out a sigh of relief. She was a good friend, but she did have her limits.

CHARLOTTE OPENED her eyes still lying in bed. It was Sunday morning. She had slept restlessly all night dreaming she was in the Indian village. *Why can't I get this out of my head?* She rubbed her eyes with her fists.

A thought suddenly occurred to her, and she sat straight up in bed. What if she was experiencing these things to affect some change in the past? *Am I supposed to do something to help these people?* She knew from her history lessons that eventually life wasn't going to be good for any Native people in this state. From what she could remember, most of them were forced to move to Oklahoma. She was fairly certain none of them were still in Arkansas. How many had died struggling to remain and fight for their land here?

She needed to talk to Lilly and go to the library to do some research. She needed to know more about what happened to these people. She also needed to confirm the fact that she was in Arkansas when she was with the Natives and what time in history it was. *The date may be more difficult than the place*, she thought.

Her dad knocked on the door interrupting her thoughts, "Charlotte, you up? You need to be getting ready for church."

"Yes, Dad," Charlotte replied, getting out of bed. "I'm getting in the shower now." She would have to think about this some more. Maybe this was happening to her for a reason.

That afternoon, after church, Charlotte stepped out onto the back porch.

"Hey Scuffy? Did I interrupt your nap?" Charlotte brushed the leaves off his back. "Do you think you could take me back?" She wasn't sure if he even understood. When he turned and went down the steps out into the woods, she supposed he had understood what she wanted. She quickly followed him.

They didn't go back to the clearing. They had only gone a short way into the woods when she saw him blink out. *So, it's not about the spot.* It was her dog initiating the process. She followed closely behind, this time, preparing herself for what was to come.

CHAPTER FIVE

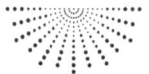

*C*harlotte opened her eyes and looked around. She stood deep in the forest. How far was she from the village? She circled around looking to identify any landmarks or trees. She listened to the sounds around her. She froze when she realized the birds weren't singing, and the insects were silent. She quieted her breath so she could listen more intently.

She heard an animal snort behind her, and she turned around slowly. About thirty feet from her was a huge black bear. Its nose twitched, smelling the air for her scent. It raised on its hind legs sensing that she was either a threat or would make a great meal. She looked at its long claws on its massive paws. Terror struck her heart, and she found it difficult to breathe. She had no idea which way would lead her back to the village, and this massive bear would surely outrun her in seconds. It let out a huge roar, giving her a clear view of its enormous teeth. Saliva dripped down its teeth and lips.

If she was to survive at all, she had better think quickly. But before she had time to work anything out, the bear landed on all fours and began to charge. Pure instincts kicked in as she rounded and sprinted as hard as she could. She dodged trees and ducked under limbs with surprising quickness. She pumped her arms and lifted her knees as best she could. She could hear the bear crashing through the brush after her.

Then, out of the corner of her eye, Charlotte saw another flash of fur. *Oh no, not another one*, she thought. But then she heard a bark and a growl. While still running, she turned her head back to get a look at the new animal. It was her wolf. The wolf that had led her back to being herself. She didn't waste any more time thinking about it. She took advantage of the momentary distraction that the wolf had given her. The bear stopped momentarily when the wolf intercepted it, but it was back in hot pursuit.

Charlotte could see the edge of the village ahead through the trees. She hadn't been far after all and was heading in the right direction. Just when she thought she was going to break free of the trees, her foot caught on a root, and she landed on her knees. Trying not to stop, she scrambled on all fours, struggling to get purchase under her feet to upright herself again. The wolf barked and growled, doing its best to throw the bear off course.

When she cleared the trees, a group of men from the village rounded the huts, bows and arrows at the ready. They must have heard the bear roar. She ran past the men, seeking to put them between her and her pursuer. When she was behind the last man, she whirled around to see the bear galloping out of the forest.

When the bear saw the men, it skidded to a stop and reared up again on its hind legs. It opened its mouth to release another roar, but before it could get a sound out, it became a pincushion with six arrows all over its chest and throat. It fell to the side with a thud, and a last huff escaped its nose.

Charlotte looked down at her wolf panting next to her. She collapsed to the ground and wrapped her arms around its neck, burying her face in its fur. She cried and whispered thank you to her animal guardian. When she lifted her head, the wolf licked the tears from her face.

Afraid the men might turn and shoot it next, the wolf turned and bolted back into the forest. She stayed crouched on the ground and stared after the spot where it disappeared into the brush. She then turned to see that the men had indeed witnessed her moment with the wolf and were regarding her with awe. They seemed to realize that the wolf had saved her and that it must be her animal spirit guide. They all nodded their heads in respect and admiration for such an honor.

Charlotte stood and looked past them at the bear. She walked cautiously toward it now, still and lifeless. She knelt by its side and placed her hand on its neck. She said a prayer out loud and mourned the loss of its life and prayed to *Wah'Kon-Tah* to guide its spirit in the afterlife. All the men followed suit saying prayers of loss and mourning. When she had paid her respects, she stood to leave. She looked at each of the men who had come to her rescue. She nodded and cast her eyes down in gratitude and honor for coming to her aid. As she began to walk away, one of the men caught her arm.

"We will make a fine skin for you from this bear," he said. Again, Charlotte bowed her head in appreciation for their bravery and protection. The bear had intended to make her his next meal, but now it would serve many of her people in many more ways. She headed back to the village in search of her family as the men began to drag the carcass away to strip it for all its parts.

She reeled from her adrenaline rush back as Nahele. *What an entrance that had been.* She thought about how unpredictable it was whenever she made the switch. There would be no guarantee as to where she would be when she switched back. Maybe if she chose times at early morning or late at night, she might be able to switch at times of sleeping or waking. But then, other than this last time, it hadn't been times of her choosing, but whenever the dog or wolf had appeared and led her away. She hoped she could figure out a way to make the transition less risky in the future.

As she approached her family's hut, she saw her sister sitting outside the entrance doing her beadwork. Charlotte was suddenly exhausted as her adrenaline rush crashed. She fell to her knees beside her sister and wrapped her arms around her neck.

"What happened, sister?" Hula asked, wrapping her arms around Charlotte's torso in confusion.

Charlotte didn't have the strength to pull away. She buried her face in her sister's hair, and said, "I came across a bear in the woods; some men from the village shot it." That was all that she had the strength to tell her. Hula gasped and held her tighter recognizing the close call her sister had had.

Tetonka sprinted toward them calling for Nahele. She lifted her head from her embrace with her sister to see fear in his eyes. She pulled herself up but was spared from taking a step as Tetonka grabbed her fiercely in his arms.

"I heard from the men that shot the bear that it was you the bear was after," he said, squeezing her so tight she had trouble breathing.

"I am fine, aside from my heart almost beating out of my chest. But now, you are about to squeeze the life out of me."

He realized his strength on her and released his hug. She took a sharp breath in, then hugged him back.

He held her out at arm's length examining her face and body. She had a few scratches on her arms, and her knees were dirty and scraped, but otherwise, she was whole and alive. He hugged her again this time, careful not to squeeze the breath out of her.

"Ahem!" Someone cleared his throat behind her back. Tetonka released her, so she could turn to see who it was. Her father stepped out of the hut.

"What's this I hear of a bear?" he asked.

"Nahele came across a bear in the woods, but before it could make dinner out of her, men from the village brought it down." Hula rushed in, eager to tell the tale.

Her father took a step toward her placing his hands on her shoulders. "I am glad to see you are all right, and you were able to escape his intentions." Her father looked at her with a mix of humor and concern. It was a part of their way of life to be this close to danger, but it didn't mean they were any less grateful when they survived. She wrapped him in a hug as well, finally able to relax and appreciate her near miss.

"We will go see to the butchering of this bear and make sure we get the best parts to bring back and celebrate," her father said, slapping

Tetonka on the shoulder, indicating he intended to take the man-boy with him.

Hula and Charlotte watched them turn and walk away. Charlotte was proud to have such wonderful, caring men in her life. She loved them both so much.

After they disappeared through the village, their mother approached with a basket of fresh vegetables. "What are you two staring after?" she asked, looking from one to the other.

"Oh, I am sure Hula will tell you the whole story," Charlotte said with a half-smile toward her sister.

"Well, come help me prepare for tonight's feast gathering and tell me all about it." Niabi ducked into the hut and the girls followed in behind.

LATER THAT EVENING, the people gathered next to the Mother Tree in the center of the village. A massive fire blazed as all the men of the community sat around it in a full circle. The women sat behind the men. Charlotte sat behind and in between her father and Tetonka. Her mother was directly behind her father, and Hula was on her mother's other side. The food that was prepared for the feast was placed around the fire. The Peacemaker chief of the Sky clan came to the center of the circle and addressed the people.

"My people. Tonight, we honor *Wah'Kon-Tah* in song, dance, and feast. May you walk the Red Road and one day when you walk the Milky Way, may *Wah'Kon-Tah* welcome you home with all our ancestors!" The members of the tribe yelled and cried out in warrior fashion in agreement.

"Now we will observe the traditional dance of our people." The Sky chief stepped aside as the dancers dressed in all their traditional splendor began to dance to the beating drums in a circle around the fire. Another group of elders chanted their songs honoring *Wah'Kon-Tah*. The people watched intently the movements of the dancers. The drums, singing, and dancing filled Charlotte's heart with joy. She hoped that one day she would learn the dances of her people and bring her family honor as she worshiped Wah'Kon-Tah.

She couldn't help but stare at Tetonka's back. She admired his sleek muscles and big frame. As if feeling her gaze on him, he turned slightly to look at her. She blushed a little and looked down. He broke into a big smile and turned back around.

When the dancing and singing had come to an end, the medicine woman entered the circle with her smoking herbs and waved it around all the people sitting around. She chanted her medicine words that only the medicine people knew.

When she made the full circle, she gestured to the food that had been near the fire and blessed by the dancing and singing. The first wives of all the men went to retrieve the bowls of food that they had brought to the feast. They placed the bowls in front of their families then sat down with them as each man shared the food with his family.

Tetonka shared the meal with them tonight because her father had invited him as an honor and tribute to his future son-in-law. Once they were married, they would leave the Sky clan and join the Earth clan where Tetonka's family lived. She would miss seeing her mother, father, and sister daily, but she knew that they would still be in the village, and she could visit them anytime she desired.

While the adults continued to eat, drink, and talk, a few of the children got up to play in the outer regions of the circle of people. Charlotte saw a boy about five years old with his little sister who looked about two. The brother was careful with his younger sister and entertained her, making her squeal and giggle. The boy pretended to be a buffalo and allowed his sister to slay him. She thought the children were beautiful. The little girl had long black hair all the way down her back and the prettiest brown eyes. She had a perfectly round face with cute pouty lips. Charlotte longed for the day when she would have children with Tetonka. She hoped they would have one of each. She knew that having a boy would make Tetonka so proud, but she also knew that having a little girl would steal his heart. Either way, she looked at the children and smiled, looking forward to the day with eagerness.

"Nahele, did you hear me?" Tetonka was saying.

Charlotte jumped slightly. "I'm sorry. My mind was off dreaming."

"I said, I have something for you." Tetonka reached into his pouch slung across his shoulder and chest. He pulled out a necklace and gestured to place it over her head.

"You made this for me?" she said in surprise. She looked at it draped around her neck and stroked it. It was made of the twenty long claws from the bear that had tried to swipe them across her neck earlier that day. She shuddered a little at the thought of what those claws could have done to her if they were still attached to their owner.

"I thought you deserved something as a reminder of your bravery in outrunning the bear, and how *Wah'Kon-Tah* allowed you to stay here with us taking the bear instead," Tetonka said with a little choke in his voice.

"Oh, thank you, my love. I shall wear it with honor and pride and always think of you who made it for me." She looked at him with her big brown eyes. She blinked them at him sending a communication to him that she couldn't say with her words in front of her family. He flushed a little, and his Adam's apple bobbed up and down as he swallowed hard getting the full translation.

Interrupting their private moment, the Sky Chief came back to the center of the circle and addressed the people once again. "As the Dark Eagle begins to set, let us lift our voices to *Wah'Kon-Tah* in tribute to all his creation." He got down on his knees and lifted his hands toward the setting sun. The people did as he did, and they said their evening prayers.

When they finished, everyone stood and began to talk among themselves. Her father went over to join a group of men to smoke the peace pipe. Her mother picked up the bowls to take them back to the hut.

"I guess I'll walk you back to your hut again," Tetonka said a little sheepishly.

"Oh great! I wouldn't want a great big bear to get me in the dark," Hula said, skipping ahead of them a little. Tetonka and Charlotte rolled their eyes and turned to follow her. This time Tetonka reached down and grabbed her hand. They had walked only a little way when he stopped and turned her to face him.

"My heart would stop beating in my chest if anything should ever happen to you, my love," he said to her, holding both her hands in his. "I realized this as soon as I heard the news about the bear, and I could hardly breathe until I saw that you were all right."

"I feel I would do the same if anything should happen to you as well," she admitted. "I worry about you every day that you are away from me and not near enough for me to touch you."

"I shall always do my best to return to you. It is with you that I belong, and I can't wait for the day when I shall call you my wife." He pulled her a little closer to him.

Charlotte was about to raise up on her toes to kiss him when Hula cleared her throat next to them. They turned to see her standing with her arms crossed and her head tilted to the side. "I thought you were walking the both of us back?" she said, a little annoyed. Charlotte imagined Hula would be glad when they were wed, too, so she didn't have to be a witness to all their mushiness.

Tetonka and Charlotte sighed heavily and turned to walk back to the hut. Once they arrived, Hula went in while Charlotte paused to look at Tetonka.

"Thank you for the lovely necklace again," she said, lowering her eyes seductively. She enjoyed teasing him that way, especially when she saw the reaction she got out of him.

He bent down to kiss her, soft and sweet. But before she could enjoy it for too long, he broke it off and said goodnight. She watched him as he faded into the darkness, her eyes lingering on his backside for as long as she could see it.

THE NEXT MORNING, Charlotte woke to find Niabi poking the fire. "Good morning, my beautiful one." Charlotte stretched and rubbed her eyes.

"Where's father?" she asked, looking around.

"He has gone with Tetonka and others to the trade post. They will be gone for a few days."

Charlotte's mood sank, and she slumped back down on her pallet. It wasn't the same if she knew she wouldn't see Tetonka for a while.

"Don't be so sad. You need to get used to these days. He will have to leave the village many times."

"Why don't you ever go with father on his trips?" Charlotte asked.

"I did before you were born, but now I stay behind to take care of you and your sister. I took you a few times when you were little, but I don't think you would remember. When you are wed to Tetonka, you can go with him if you choose to."

That seemed to cheer Charlotte somewhat, and she got up to do her morning routine. "I'll go to the stream to wash and be back to help you with the morning meal." She ducked out of the hut and inhaled a deep breath of the morning air. The air smelled fresh tinged with a bit of smoke. She felt refreshed as if the oxygen here were richer. The air was still warm, but it would be fall soon. *Two more moons,* she thought. *Will it ever pass fast enough?*

As she walked to the stream, she spotted her wolf standing and wagging its tail at her. *I suppose if I want to pass the time, it'll go faster as myself.* Charlotte changed her direction to follow the wolf.

"I need to give you a name, so I can call you if I need you." The wolf came to her and sat in front of her as if waiting to be knighted.

She thought for a minute then said, "How about Bear Killer?"

The wolf curled its lip a little and gave a tiny growl.

"Oh, you don't like that one. Well, I guess you didn't kill it." She gave it more thought. "What about Bear Chaser?"

The dog shook its head slightly.

"I know, Barkley!" The wolf gave a little bark in approval and wagged its tail. "Come on, Barkley. Take me back to the future," Charlotte said, giggling a little as they left.

CHAPTER SIX

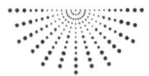

"Charlotte are you listening?" Lilly was saying.

Charlotte blinked her eyes, straining to focus. She stood in the courtyard outside the school building. School hadn't started yet.

"I'm sorry, what?" She turned toward Lilly.

"Oh, good. You're here. For a minute there, I thought you were lost in the past again," Lilly said, looking relieved.

"I was. I just switched back," Charlotte admitted.

"You were!" Lilly stared at Charlotte for a minute wide-eyed then said slowly, "Seriously?" But before she could ask her any questions, the morning bell rang, and they headed off to first-period.

"You have to tell me later. Right now, I'm glad you're here to help me with all this Homecoming stuff." Lilly went over all the things that needed to be done again. They had already talked about this, but it was time for action; Lilly wanted to make sure they stayed on top of everything.

One thing was for sure, this week would help pass the time and get her mind off the past and her thoughts about Tetonka. Her feelings for him were growing stronger every day. It was getting harder to separate the two minds of Charlotte and Nahele. *Who am I?* Was she Charlotte pretending to be Nahele, or was she Nahele pretending to be Charlotte? Or was she both? If she found it hard to know who she was, she could say things that were out of context at the time. What would they do to her if she said something about the future? The Natives did have a different view of the Spirit world and nature. Maybe they would be more receptive to her situation than the people here in the future. Although her friend Lilly was making an effort to be open, she doubted she could trust anyone else with this knowledge. She needed to do some research and possibly contact the medicine woman to see if she could give her any more information.

The more time Charlotte spent back there, the more she understood their ways. If she kept going back, maybe she could find out why this was happening. For now, she needed to focus on this week and all the Homecoming stuff. It might be a while before she could get away again.

"How was your date with Caleb last night?" Lilly asked as they settled into their seats.

"My date?" Charlotte had forgotten that Caleb had asked her out. *Oh, no. I must have been like a zombie,* she thought.

"Let me guess, you don't remember," Lilly whispered.

All Charlotte could do was shake her head. What was she going to tell Caleb?

Just then a knock came at the door to the classroom, and Mrs. Olsen went to answer it. Charlotte could see Mr. Hughes, the principal, standing just outside the door. A few minutes later, Mrs. Olsen came back, escorting someone into the classroom.

"Class," Mrs. Olsen said, "This is a new student at our school. This is Brock Van Houten." She said his last name slowly, looking down at his schedule to make sure she got it right. "You can have a seat over here for now." She gestured to a seat one row to the right and two seats up from Charlotte.

From the moment he stepped into the classroom, Charlotte's eyes went big and round, and her mouth fell open. She was interrupted from her state of awe when a paper wad hit her on the side of the face. She looked over to her left to see Kale glaring at her from the other side of the room. Lilly, also next to her in the row to her left, looked wide-eyed as well. She shot Kale a glare that meant, *mind your own business,* then looked down at her desk.

Looking down and pretending to look over her notes, Charlotte cut her eyes to look at him again. He was extremely tall, probably a couple of inches taller than Kale. He was slimmer than Kale with clearly defined muscles tight against his shirt. He had thick black hair about shoulder length, pulled back in a short ponytail at the nape of his neck. He had a dark tan as if he spent a lot of time outdoors.

She caught a glimpse of his eyes as he nervously glanced her way. Her heart jumped to her throat. They were a gorgeous blue surrounded by dark lashes and dark eyebrows. Suddenly, she found it hard to breathe.

Mrs. Olsen wrote notes on the board. Charlotte usually paid close attention and wrote down detailed notes, but today, her focus was lost entirely. She tried to scribble something on her paper, but her mind felt fuzzy.

She kept her head down but stole glances at him occasionally. Poor guy was so tall he had to sit sideways under the desk because his knees wouldn't fit under it. He caught her looking at him, and she quickly looked down. She had an uncomfortable feeling that he was still looking at her, but she was afraid to look.

When the bell rang to end class, Charlotte gathered her things quickly to make it to his side.

"Hi. I'm Charlotte," she said, venturing to be casual and friendly. "Would you like me to help you to your next class?" She secretly hoped it was with her.

"Sure," he said looking down at her with a mixture of amusement and astonishment.

"This is my friend Lilly," she said when Lilly joined them. "We're cheerleaders."

"Oh, I get it," he said, recognition dawning on him. "You're like the welcoming committee. I thought you were offering because you might be interested in me."

Charlotte blushed a deep red at this. "Well... " for once, she was at a loss for words and looked down embarrassed that he had called her out like that.

"Can I see your schedule?" Lilly took over momentarily while Charlotte was caught off guard. "I see you have geometry next. We're in Algebra II across the hall. We can walk you," she said, handing back his schedule and looking at Charlotte to see if she had recovered.

She had, but now she looked up at him staring right at his face.

"Is something wrong? Do I have something on my face?" He swiped a hand down his face, checking.

"No, I'm sorry," she said again, this time turning up her charm and lowering her eyes a little as she tilted her head. "I was deciding what shade of blue to call your eyes."

"Oh," he said, curiously raising his eyebrows. "And what did you decide?"

"I'm not sure yet. I may have to get a closer look later." Now it was Brock's turn to blush.

"Ahem, okay! We better get going. The class is down this way," Lilly said, leading the way down the hall.

When they arrived in front of their next classrooms, Charlotte turned to Brock. "I guess we can meet out here after class and see where you go next."

"Can't wait!" he said, giving her a wink and ducking into his classroom.

After he had disappeared, and they turned into their classroom, Lilly caught Charlotte by the arm. "Really? You didn't wait five seconds to flirt with the new guy!"

"I'm sorry. Last I heard you were taken and I'm not. What's the harm?" Charlotte said, nonchalantly taking her seat.

"Well, don't you think you put it on a little thick?" Lilly said, making an excuse for her overreaction.

"Okay, I'll tone it down next time," she relented. The rest of the class period she couldn't wait for the bell to ring so she could see if he had any more classes with her.

As it turned out, they had the same English class, but he had shop mechanics and carpentry when Charlotte had Spanish and typing. They had world history but at different class times and their athletic period was the same, but he would be with the boys while she worked out with the girls.

For lunch she didn't want to be overly pushy, so she let him go off with the guys he had already met when Coach had introduced him around. Lilly noticed Charlotte wasn't as talkative as usual during lunch.

"What's wrong?" Lilly asked.

"Huh? Oh, nothing. Only thinking," Charlotte said, picking at her food.

"Are you thinking about the new guy?" Lilly said, teasing.

"Well, a little. What do you think about him?" she asked, deflecting it from her.

"Oh, he's cute. He's going to give Kale a run for his money I bet." Lilly looked outside to see if she could see the jocks hanging out at their usual spot.

Caleb came up beside Charlotte and straddled the bench where she sat.

"Hey, Charlotte! How's it going?" he asked, full of smiles and energy.

Uh-oh, she thought. *I wonder how bad I screwed up our date.*

"Pretty good, Caleb. How about you?" she said, only giving him half her usual charm.

"Not bad. I had a really good time Sunday night. I asked if you had a date for Homecoming this Friday, but I never got an answer?" Caleb looked a little confused but not upset about what must have been her weird behavior. She prayed he didn't ask her any questions about their date that she couldn't remember.

She looked at Caleb and his big puppy-dog eyes. "No, Caleb. I don't," she had to admit. How could she resist those eyes?

"Great! Would you like to go with me?" he asked, lighting up even more.

"Uh, sure," Charlotte accepted, feeling somewhat confused as to why he would ask her out again. She hoped she hadn't done something she would learn about later and regret.

"Awesome!" he said, jumping up from his seat. "I guess I'll meet you after the game, and we'll go to the dance."

"Can't wait!" she said, halfheartedly.

When he practically skipped outside, Lilly leaned over the table. "Wow, Charlotte. What was that?"

"What do you mean?" Charlotte pretended she didn't know what Lilly was referring to.

"You know what I mean. If he hadn't been so excited to ask you, he would have noticed you weren't enthusiastic about going out with him."

"I can't remember anything about our date Sunday night," Charlotte admitted.

"It must not have been too bad since he asked you out again."

Charlotte felt a little sick to her stomach about lying to Caleb and pretending she remembered their date. It was a horrible feeling knowing you did something that you couldn't remember doing.

"Besides, it's only to the dance. Since you're a cheerleader and he's a football player, you're pretty much busy during the whole Homecoming thing anyway. There's not much of a date when you're meeting after the game at the dance." Charlotte suspected that Lilly knew what was on Charlotte's mind but decided not to push it.

At the end of the day, announcements were made regarding who the representatives were for the Homecoming court. Lilly was chosen as one of the three for the sophomores, which meant she would be busy with the court and leaving even more stuff for Charlotte to do.

Charlotte didn't get much of a chance to talk to Brock the rest of the week. She did manage to enlist his help to put up hall decorations. His height came in handy for putting up the streamers. He looked in her direction every day in biology class, and she would always smile and say "Hi." He would smile back at her and say "Hey" back. In

English class, she was always aware that he was there. He sat on the other side of the classroom, but she would sneak a peek at him occasionally. He seemed always to be looking at her, or she sensed when he was looking at her and that made her turn to look at him. She caught him looking at her in the hallway one time, and it looked like he was about to approach her to ask her something. But someone else got to her first, and when she looked back to see if he was still there, he had left.

❧

FRIDAY, Charlotte was busy with other students all day preparing the gym and didn't attend many of her classes. Before she knew it, it was time for the homecoming pep rally. She stood nervously on the sidelines of the basketball court as the student body noisily crammed into the bleachers. She watched the crowd of faces for Brock, but she didn't spot him. As the gym filled up with more bodies, the noise level reached a deafening pitch.

The football players paraded in while the band played the fight song. She noticed Kale kept his eyes on her whenever she was on the court. She searched the student body again for Brock. He had to be in the stands with all the other students. Sitting down, he didn't stand out as much over everyone else. He must have sat toward the top of the bleachers out of her eye level because she never saw him. She wondered if he was watching her. She secretly hoped he was, but if she messed up, she hoped he wasn't.

After the Homecoming Queen was announced and everyone cheered, the students rushed out of the gym to go home and change. Charlotte stayed behind to get ready for the football game. She was jealous of those who were going home to get dressed up and be with their dates.

During the game, Charlotte found herself searching the stands for Brock again.

"Charlotte!" Becca, the cheer captain, yelled.

Charlotte had been staring into the stands. She looked to her captain and noticed the other cheerleaders dancing to the team fight song.

She quickly picked up the routine and danced. Her captain gave her an annoyed look, and she finally turned her attention to the game instead of the stands.

Finally, the game ended. They beat the visiting team 42 to nothing. Fans rushed the field to stand with the football players and cheerleaders as they sang the alma mater. Only then did Charlotte remember she still had a date with Caleb, and she searched for him among the crowd. She didn't see him either. She assumed he went to the fieldhouse to shower so he could meet her as soon as possible in the cafeteria.

Charlotte joined Lilly and Evan as they walked from the field to the cafeteria. They brought clothes to change into in the girl's bathroom, and the DJ was already blaring music that thumped through their chests. She watched all the couples as they came in, got their picture made in front of the Homecoming backdrop, and then went off to dance. She kept watching the door for Caleb to walk through at any minute. After an hour, it looked like all the football players were in attendance with their dates. Finally, she decided to join the group in the center and dance with her friends. She hoped to see Brock. If he was there, it would have been impossible to miss him, since he would be taller than most everyone else.

"I thought you had a date!" Evan had to yell over the music.

"I did. But I haven't seen him," Charlotte yelled back.

They danced to several of their favorite songs: Def Leppard's *Pour Some Sugar on Me*, Guns N' Roses' *Sweet Child O' Mine*, Whitesnake's *Is This Love*, Robert Palmer's *Simply Irresistible*, Aerosmith's *Angel*, Bon Jovi's *Bad Medicine*, Van Halen's *When it's Love*, and AC/DC's *You Shook Me All Night Long*. When Def Leppard's *Love Bites* came on, Charlotte decided it was time to take a bathroom break.

When she exited the girl's bathroom, someone slammed her back against the wall. She looked at the person two inches from her face.

"Kale! What are you doing!" He pressed her hard against the wall and had his knee wedged between her legs. He had a hand on each of her wrists effectively nailing them to the wall.

"You know you want me, Charlotte," Kale said, roughly. She caught a whiff of alcohol on his breath.

"Kale, you're hurting me!" She tried to squirm out of his crushing embrace. She was no match for his strength, especially a full-on body press. He pressed his mouth to hers and forcefully opened her mouth with his tongue. For a few seconds, Charlotte gave in to the kiss. Visions danced through her mind, reminding her of when they had dated, and she had been so excited to be with him. Eventually, she came to her senses and tried with all her strength to push him off. She only managed to push him about an inch, but it was enough to break the kiss.

"Kale! This isn't right! What are you doing?!" Charlotte was furious, even more so because she was powerless against him. What she wouldn't give to have a bat or something, so she could hit him. She choked down a sob. A part of her still had a terrible crush on him, but it was ruined by the fact that, deep down, she knew he was no good for her.

Kale stopped and stared at her, his eyes intense. Then he pushed off her with a growl and turned to the outside doors, throwing them open with both hands, banging loudly. Unfortunately, the music was playing so loud no one else heard it. She stood stunned, struggling to breathe air back into her lungs. Someone came around the corner to go into the bathroom, so she quickly recovered herself and went back to the dance floor.

Charlotte found Lilly and yelled into her ear, "Do you think Evan could give me a ride home?"

Lilly looked at her and mouthed, *Now?*

She nodded her head, *yes*, and made her eyes pleading. Lilly took pity on her since her date never showed.

Lilly probably thought Charlotte was quiet on the ride to her house because she had been stood up by Caleb. Maybe he decided she was a boring date after all and changed his mind. But Lilly didn't know about Kale assaulting her. Charlotte decided to keep that to herself for now.

It had been a long day. She was confused about all that had happened. She found herself thinking about the new guy, Brock, a lot. He was good looking and tall. She loved tall guys, not to mention those blue eyes with that dark hair. He was a dream come true. Then, there was Kale and what he did to her tonight, and the mysterious disappearance of Caleb. She wanted to sort it out in her mind, but she was too exhausted to run her mental wheels over it.

CHAPTER SEVEN

*C*harlotte slept past noon the next day. She walked out onto the back porch wrapped in her favorite blanket barefooted. Scuffy hurried to her, wagging his butt. She squatted next to the dog and rubbed him on the head and neck. She thought about going back to the village, then she felt the switch.

She found herself on her knees looking down into the creek. The water was calm and smooth as glass. She looked at the reflection shining off the water. The mirrored water revealed a beautiful Indian girl reflecting back at her. Charlotte admired the girl's long hair and round, brown eyes. She had delicate features with soft, brown skin. Then she realized, *that's me—or, rather, Nahele.* Charlotte hadn't seen what Nahele actually looked like until now. She admired the girl's beautiful features and had to admit, she was a little jealous.

The face of a tall Indian man appeared over her shoulder. Startled, Charlotte fell back on her rump with a gasp. She looked up to see Tetonka looking down at her, smiling.

He squatted next to her and said, "Don't worry. It's just me." He held out his strong hand to help lift her up. She took it and smiled into her lover's eyes as he helped her stand.

"I came to give you this for tonight's celebration dance." He presented her with a beaded headband. It had a single, tall feather attached to the back. "It was my grandmother's."

Charlotte took it and inspected it. "It is lovely."

Tetonka reached for the headband again. Charlotte allowed him to take it and place it on her head. "Beautiful," he said as he looked at her with the added adornment.

Charlotte leaned over the water once again to see for herself. Her heart swelled, and a lump formed in her throat, realizing what an honor it was to be given something that had belonged to his grandmother, now gone.

She turned back to Tetonka as a tear slipped from the corner of her eye.

Tetonka reached up and wiped the tear with his thumb, then leaned down to kiss her gently on the lips.

Charlotte's whole body sighed as she leaned into the kiss. Tetonka wrapped his arms around her drawing her firmly against his warm body. She felt heat radiating from his skin as she inhaled the warm scent of his masculinity. She could stay locked in his arms, their lips glued together like this forever.

Someone coughed behind them, and they jerked apart. Tetonka and Charlotte turned to see Kajika standing a few paces away with his arms crossed over his chest. Charlotte noticed the stern look on his face and wondered why he looked at them that way.

"It is time to get ready," Kajika said. Then he quickly turned and walked back to the village.

Tetonka turned to Charlotte again. "I'll see you at the dance." He kissed her gently on the forehead then followed Kajika back to the village.

Charlotte stared after him. She took a deep breath in and let it out slow and long. Her heart skipped a beat as she thought of his warm body pressed against hers, his strong arms wrapped around her, and his lips firmly pressed to hers. She touched her lips as if she could bring the feeling back to them. *Why did their kisses always seem so short?* she wondered.

Shaking herself out of her reverie, she walked back to her hut to prepare herself for the dance.

Her people were celebrating with some members of a neighboring village who had come to share news of their people in other areas. It was customary to honor guests with a feast and dance celebration. Once everyone had formed a big circle around the fire outside the Peacemaker's hut, the drummers began banging on their drums. The dancers, who included most of the younger members of their village, began stomping their feet and circling the fire. The women formed an inner circle going clockwise, while the men formed an outer circle going counterclockwise.

Charlotte kept her eyes on Tetonka as he did with her. Her heart beat to the rhythm of the drums as the other members of the tribe sitting around the outside of the dancers chanted. A peace pipe was passed around to the older members who were sitting. The air filled with smoke from the fire. Charlotte could feel the heat from the fire lashing out at her as she jumped and kicked in the custom of her people. The air smelled peculiar, and it made Charlotte feel light-headed. As the dancing, chanting, and smoking continued, Charlotte began to lose herself in the ritual.

She lost track of Tetonka as the bodies around her began to blur. She swayed and turned, feeling the powerful rhythm of the dance possess her body and soul. She swung her arms out, twirling until she felt as if she was flying. Slowly, she felt herself floating up into the air. She no longer felt the ground beneath her feet and felt light as air. A cool breeze lifted her high above the heads of the dancers. She looked down, and she could see everyone dancing and chanting below her. She wasn't afraid, so she allowed the feeling of flying envelope her as she hung weightless and unnoticed by the people below.

After a while, she realized she had no body. She looked carefully at the individuals dancing below her, and she saw Nahele dancing with the others. *I must have left Nahele's body.* Charlotte thought with alarm. She was still in Nahele's time, but she was no longer in Nahele's body. She panicked. She felt herself falling. She braced herself for the impact that was about to come.

Charlotte sat straight up in her bed gasping for air. Her heart raced and sweat clung to her body. Had she been dreaming or did she switch back to her body? She looked over at the clock to see that it was past midnight. She flopped back on her bed and stared up at the ceiling. She tried to remember every detail of the previous day. She was sure she had been Nahele, but something in the dancing had loosened her hold in Nahele's body, causing her spirit to release. Happy to be safely back as herself, she closed her eyes and tried to sleep. She dreamed of dancing around the fire and watching Tetonka all night.

CHAPTER EIGHT

*C*harlotte never got a call from Caleb explaining why he ditched her. That had never happened to her before, but she tried not to be too upset about it, since her heart hadn't been into the date in the first place. Monday and Tuesday were uneventful. Everyone seemed to be "hungover" from the extreme excitement the previous week.

On Wednesday, when she got home from cheer practice, she saw an unfamiliar car parked in the driveway. As she got out of her friend's car, her dad came out the front door of the house.

"How do you like your new car?" her dad asked with a big smile.

"My car?!" she said, hitting an octave higher than usual.

"Yeah, I know it's not brand new, but it'll do for your first car."

Charlotte inspected it. It was a 1986 white Ford Tempo with blue interior. She got in behind the steering wheel to check out all the gadgets inside. It was manual lock and window which meant she had to turn the crank to roll the window down and would have to lean over to unlock the passenger side door from the inside. It was a two-door, which also meant anyone wanting to sit in the back had to push the seat in front forward and climb in behind. It had a cassette player and an FM radio. But, the most important thing, it meant she no longer needed to rely on anyone else to give her a ride to places. She could drive herself where she needed to go or even give other people rides.

"Want to take it for a test drive?" her dad asked.

"Absolutely!" Charlotte said, getting the keys from her dad and starting the car.

She pulled onto some neighborhood streets and tried to stay off the main highway as much as possible. On one of her turns, she spotted a group of guys she knew playing basketball in the driveway. She cranked her window down and stuck her hand out.

"Hey, guys! Look at my new car!" she yelled, waving excitedly.

"Charlotte look out!" her dad yelled with a firm grip on the dashboard in front of him and pressed his right foot into the floorboard on an imaginary brake. Because her attention had been momentarily distracted, she had veered off the road and drove onto someone's front lawn.

"Oops!" she said, coming to a stop. Luckily, she didn't hit anything and didn't do too much damage to the grass. She was able to back up gently and get back on the street.

"I think that's enough for today. Let's get home for supper," her dad said, probably sounding calmer than he felt.

"Sorry, Dad. I promise I'll be a better driver than this. I won't do that again," she pleaded, hoping this didn't mean she would have to wait even longer to be driving on her own. Her sixteenth birthday was Saturday, so officially she wouldn't get to drive alone until Monday. That gave her a few more days to drive with either her mother or her dad chaperoning her and build their confidence that she would be capable of going on her own.

FOR THE PAST SEVERAL DAYS, she tried to find Caleb to figure out what happened. But every time she asked about him at lunch, she was told he had gone back to a classroom to do make-up work, or they simply didn't know where he was. She thought it was odd that he would avoid her like that after he was the one who asked her out then didn't show. It seemed very strange.

Her friends were bringing dates to her sixteenth birthday party, which meant she needed one, too. She wanted to ask Brock, but she felt maybe it was still too soon to go there. There was this other guy who had been flirting with her a lot in typing class, so she decided it wouldn't hurt to ask him. His name was Jacob, and he was a junior. He didn't play football, but he played basketball and baseball.

When Charlotte asked him to come, he seemed excited. "Great! The party is at my house at five, Saturday," she told him.

"Excellent. Do I need to bring anything?" Jacob asked.

"Nope. Only yourself. It's not going to be a big group of people. Only a few of my friends," she explained.

"Got it. I'll see you Saturday then," he said, and they went their separate ways.

Come Saturday around 4:45, Lilly and Evan arrived early.

"Happy birthday!" Lilly said, coming in the door.

"Thanks, Lilly!" Charlotte said, taking a gift from her and letting them into the house.

"Oooh, the cake looks delicious!" Lilly said, licking her lips. Then she had to smack Evan's hand as he attempted to swipe his finger through the icing. Charlotte laughed as she went to answer the door again.

At about 5:30 p.m., her mother said, "Why don't we go ahead and open presents." There was no sign of Jacob, but Charlotte tried not to be worried. She opened Lilly's present first; she gave her a book about Native Americans.

"This is awesome, Lilly. Thanks! I can't wait to read it," Charlotte said, hugging her. Everyone looked at one another wondering why in the world she would be happy with a book about Native Americans, but, of course, Lilly knew, and that's why it was so special.

"Who wants cake?" Charlotte's mother asked.

"I do!" Evan volunteered first. Lilly punched him on the shoulder. "What? She asked; I answered," he said, giving Lilly a hurt look and rubbing his shoulder. Everyone had cake, ice cream, and punch, and then Charlotte sent everyone down to the basement to play pool or video games.

"I'll be down there in a second." Charlotte waved everyone down. There was still no sign of Jacob.

"What are you going to do?" Lilly knew that Charlotte was concerned about why Jacob hadn't shown up.

"I'm going to call his house to see if something has happened," she said. "You go ahead. I'll be down in a minute." Lilly shrugged her shoulders and did as she asked. She found Jacob's home number in the phonebook and called. His mother answered on the second ring.

"Hello?" Mrs. Wood answered.

"Mrs. Wood? This is Charlotte McAfee. Is Jacob there?" She held her breath.

"No, dear. He went out hunting with one of his friends early this morning and hasn't gotten back. Can I take a message?" Mrs. Wood said sweetly.

"Well, I had invited Jacob to come to my sixteenth birthday party tonight. He hasn't shown up, so I was a little worried why he wasn't here." She felt a little dejected.

"Oh, my!" Mrs. Wood replied, "I didn't know he had other plans this evening. He went out with that Kale fellow, and they haven't gotten back."

Kale, Charlotte thought. That was mighty suspicious.

"Maybe I should send Mr. Wood out to go find them in case they've run into trouble. I'll be sure to have him call you as soon as he gets in. This isn't like him, and I'm terribly sorry that he's done this to you on your birthday," Mrs. Wood apologized.

"It's all right, Mrs. Wood. I hope he's okay."

Charlotte hung up the phone and sat staring into space. She secretly prayed Kale hadn't been stupid enough to do something to Jacob. Maybe he hadn't gone to such extremes as violence and had taken him out there to keep him distracted so that he would miss the party. She was also beginning to understand what might have happened to Caleb as well. She was going to get to the bottom of this and figure out precisely what Kale was up to. Who did he think he was disrupting her dates like this, especially after what he did at the dance? She was beginning to get fed-up with his behavior.

The rest of the evening, she tried to enjoy hanging out with her friends. She laughed as her guests challenged each other playing *Donkey Kong*. Lilly and she played *Frogger*, and everyone had a turn at *Mario Brothers* on her brothers' new Atari. They played pool and watched *Back to the Future* on the VCR. Charlotte tried not to think about the fact that here she was on her sixteenth birthday, and she was the only one without a date.

THE NEXT DAY, Jacob called to apologize. He said he and Kale had gone to a new place several miles out to go deer hunting. At some point, Jacob noticed that Kale wasn't near him anymore. When he got to where Kale had parked, his truck was gone along with Kale. Jacob had to walk five miles before his dad drove by and picked him up. Charlotte was glad to hear Jacob was okay, but Kale was going to have some explaining to do.

To make up for missing her birthday party, Jacob invited her to a hayride he was having at his farm with his church youth group the following weekend. She accepted and quickly forgave Jacob for missing her party.

Jacob picked her up in his truck and drove her back to his family farm. There was a large group already gathered around a fire in the yard.

"Let me help you get out." Jacob rushed around to the passenger side of his truck that was jacked-up higher than a normal truck. She smiled and appreciated him going out of his way to please her and make up for missing her birthday party.

Soon after, Jacob's dad pulled up in a tractor pulling a cotton bale cage. It was the kind Charlotte had seen leaving the cotton fields full of loose cotton on its way to the cotton gin. It had green wire sides at least eight feet high from the inside.

"How are we going to get in that?" Charlotte asked.

Jacob grinned at her. "We climb." He then leaped up grabbing the side and climbed it like a ladder. He straddled the top and held a hand down to her. "Here, I'll help you over."

Charlotte wasn't sure about the climbing at first, but once she got her foot in one of the holes, it was like climbing a very tall chain-link fence. Jacob gave her a hand to steady her as she swung a leg over the top, then she carefully climbed down the other side. Jacob didn't bother climbing down; he jumped from the top landing on the wooden floor with a loud thud.

Once everyone had climbed in and claimed a seat either on a hay bale or on the floor, Jacob's dad began pulling them along through the fields. Occasionally, he crossed over some rickety bridges with no railing on the sides. Charlotte was afraid the bridges weren't built to hold the weight of the trailer and every time they had to cross one, she held her breath waiting for the worst to happen. Unfortunately, on one of the crossings, the back tire of the trailer slipped off the side of the bridge, tilting everyone to one side. Charlotte screamed along with all the other girls inside.

Instantly, Jacob was up and over the side to help direct his dad to maneuver the trailer wheel back onto the bridge. Charlotte's heart was in her throat as she envisioned herself tumbling over the side, trailer and all, into the deep ditch and muddy water below. She breathed a big sigh of relief once the trailer had cleared the bridge and was safely back on solid ground.

Just as Jacob was about to climb back into the trailer, some pointed out a opossum scurrying away. Jacob snatched it up and, having the good sense given to all teenage boys, decided to throw it into the cage with all the already overly excited teens inside. Hysteria ensued. Charlotte found herself climbing the back of boy next to her that she didn't even know in an effort to put some distance between herself and the animal. The opossum hissed like a cat.

"Jacob! Get that thing out of here!" someone yelled.

Laughing, Jacob climbed the side of the cage and jumped down to the floor. He scooped the animal up and tossed it over the side. Charlotte winced when she heard it hit the ground with a loud thud. She hoped Jacob hadn't hurt it. It wasn't its fault that it happened to be in the wrong place at the wrong time. It was probably much more afraid for its life than she was.

When they finally got back to the farm, Charlotte was a little more than relieved to be out of the cage. She had expected a nice quiet hayride through the countryside, singing corny songs or telling ghost stories. She hadn't bargained for a near-death experience and an attack by a wild animal. Okay, it hadn't been that dramatic, but in the moment, it sure felt that way.

While they roasted s'mores over the fire, Jacob asked, "Have you ever been cow-tipping?"

"No," she answered him suspiciously while licking sticky marshmallow from her fingers.

"Ah, you have to experience cow-tipping at least once in your life." Jacob pulled on her arm in the direction of the cow pasture.

Jacob led her around the farmhouse to a picket fence. He helped her climb between the wooden boards into the pasture.

"Here, let me help you." He took hold of her elbow to help guide her around cow patties. She was thankful for his efforts to keep her boots clean. As they went further into the pasture, she could make out the shape of a cow.

"Doesn't this hurt them?" she asked, not sure that this was a smart idea.

"It wakes them up is all," Jacob said. "They sleep standing up. So, when you run up on their side, they fall over. Watch." Jacob let go of her and took off at a jog and hit the cow perpendicularly. The cow gently crumbled to the side.

He jogged back over to her, "See. No big deal. Now you try."

Charlotte wasn't sure about this. She looked around for another cow standing nearby. She spotted another one several feet away. She gathered herself and took off at a leisurely jog like she saw Jacob had done. But before she could get halfway there, Jacob called out to her.

"Stop! Come back! That's the bull!" As soon as Jacob yelled, the bull turned his massive head toward her. It gave a big snort at about the time it registered in her brain what Jacob had said. Jacob caught her and grabbed her by the arm. He pulled her behind him in the other direction running as fast as he could. She felt like her feet were barely touching the ground trying not to trip and fall and be trampled by the bull.

When they got to the fence, their momentum carried them over it, and they flipped over the top. When she looked back over the fence, the bull hadn't even given pursuit, but instead had watched them run away.

She slumped down on the ground, "I think I've had enough excitement for one night."

"All right, I guess it's time to drive you home." Jacob extended his hand to help her stand.

The ride back to her house was quiet. Charlotte thought Jacob was sweet and gentlemanly, but she wasn't feeling a strong connection. She thought if he didn't call her again for another date, that would probably be for the best.

As they topped the middle hill of her street, they saw long lines of white toilet paper floating down from the trees in her front yard. "Uh-oh, looks like someone paid your house a visit tonight," Jacob said as he pulled to a stop in her driveway.

Charlotte sighed. It seemed the excitement wasn't going to end yet. She thanked Jacob for driving her home and got out to assess the damage. When she looked down, there was a full can of shaving cream in her driveway as if someone had dropped it and ran. As she bent over and picked it up, an orange Bronco pulled into her driveway. Charlotte knew that Bronco. It was Kale.

She pretended to spray his Bronco with the shaving cream, but within a split second, he jumped out of the vehicle and grabbed her from around her back pinning her arms to her side. He yanked the can out of her hand and sprayed the shaving cream in her hair.

"Kale! Not my hair!" she screamed. He let go of her, jumped back in his truck, and drove to the top of the hill at the dead-end in front of her neighbor's house.

Charlotte realized she needed to get the shaving cream out, so she ran to the outside water hose. She washed the shaving cream out of her hair, but she also wanted answers from Kale. She ran up the hill all the while shaking her head of excess water.

Kale and her neighbor, Isaac, stood outside his Bronco when she came to a halt. Unfortunately, she had made herself dizzy by shaking her head while running at the same time, causing her to lose her balance and collapse to the ground.

The guys looked at her. "What have you been doing tonight, Charlotte?" Kale asked with a smirk on his face.

"I should be asking you that question, Kale." She decided to remain on the ground for now.

"Ah, nothing much. Just hanging out here with my buddy, Isaac." Kale gestured toward her neighbor.

"I don't suppose you know who toilet-papered my house tonight do you?" She stood slowly and dusted off her jeans.

"Nope. I pulled up when you tried to put shaving cream on my Bronco. Do you know what that stuff does to the paint job?" Kale said and then spit to the side.

Eww, she thought, *chewing tobacco is so nasty.* "I wasn't going to do it. I was only pretending." Charlotte smiled her sweet and innocent smile while squeezing more water out of her hair. This got Kale's attention. "And I don't suppose you had anything to do with the fact that my date ran out on me Homecoming night and then my date for my birthday just happened to get 'stranded.'" She added air quotes to the last word.

"I have no idea what you're talking about. But I'm sorry to hear about your misfortune recently. Maybe you're not going out with the right kind of man." Kale made a move to get closer to her.

At first, she was a little stunned. She took a step backward not sure what he was going to do next.

"Don't worry, sweetheart. I don't have any more shaving cream. Why don't you come take a ride with me, and I'll show you a good time?" She allowed him to get close enough to put his arm around her shoulders, but then a cold chill went through her, and she quickly shrugged him off.

"Sorry, Kale, but I've had enough adventure for one night. I need to go home and get to bed." She quickly turned on her heel and walked down the hill. She felt Kale's creepy stare on her as she walked away.

"You should stop fighting it, Charlotte. Eventually you know it's me you want," he called as Charlotte descended.

CHAPTER NINE

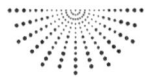

*C*harlotte was getting accustomed to spending time as Nahele on Saturdays. This time, she woke up early to head out back and follow Scuffy into the woods.

When she switched to Nahele, she gathered food supplies and wrapped them in a deerskin cloth. She walked to the horse pasture to find Tetonka with his brother, Takoda, and Takoda's kola, Nayati.

They were securing supplies to the horses when Tetonka saw her walk up.

"Good morning," Tetonka greeted her with a big smile that melted Charlotte's heart. Every time she saw him, he took her breath away.

He stepped toward her and took the food bundle from her to add to his horse's pack. He swung up on his horse with a grace that astounded Charlotte, then reached his hand down to her to hoist her up behind him.

She wrapped her arms around his strong torso as he led the others out of the pasture. Takoda carried long sticks that were to be used as fishing poles.

Tetonka let his horse take a leisurely pace as they followed a thin trail to a nearby lake. Charlotte didn't recall ever going to this lake before from Nahele's memory. She was excited to be spending the day in Tetonka's presence.

When they reached the lake, Tetonka swung down first then reached up and grabbed Charlotte by the waist. He lifted her off the horse and gently placed her on the ground as if she was as light as a feather. Charlotte suspected he was trying to impress her a little by making it seem easier than it was; either way, it worked.

She watched the three young men secure a long, woven strand of buffalo hair to the end of the sticks, then tie a small metal hook at the end of the strand.

"Where did you get those?" Charlotte asked, wondering how they had metal in this time period.

"We traded for them at the last trading post," Takoda answered, looking at her with a wide grin. He looked especially pleased with himself to have a new "invention."

Nayati dug in the soft earth near the lake and pulled out long, slimy worms placing them in a small pouch. After he was satisfied with the number of worms for bait, he handed one to Tetonka and one to Takoda, and they worked them onto their hooks.

Charlotte noticed Nayati pulled one particularly long one and broke it in half, placing one half on his hook and the rest back in the pouch. She wrinkled her nose a little at this.

She was glad they hadn't looked to her to do the fishing. They had invited her along for company. She had promised her mother she would gather some herbs and plants to bring back so that it wouldn't seem like a total waste of her day.

The young men stripped down to only their breechcloth and waded into the cool water. Charlotte spotted a large rock jutting out a little over the water and made her way to it. She climbed the side carefully, then stepped to the edge, sat down, and hung her feet out to dangle into the water.

She watched the men stand still as trees in the water, patiently waiting for a small tug on their lines. She soon realized that this might take a while, and their patience and ability to stay so still was impressive.

She leaned her hands back on the warm rock and lifted her face to the warm sun. She closed her eyes, drinking in the warmth and the lazy feel of the day around her. She focused her attention to the sounds of the lake. She heard the edge of the water lapping gently against the dirt shore. She heard a myriad of bugs buzzing, zipping to and fro. She could hear the wind blowing through the tall trees that surrounded the lake. The long branches full of leaves swished back and forth in a silent dance.

She felt something touch her knee, and she opened her eyes and looked down. It was a delicate blue damselfly, not to be confused with the larger dragonflies that were also darting here and there. Charlotte sat very still watching the damselfly and admired its bright hue of blue. It amazed her that nature could produce such a striking color. To her, natural colors were greens, browns, yellows, and reds, but blue seemed to be a special color reserved only for a special few creatures in nature.

Eventually, the damselfly decided it had other things to do, and it lifted off and zoomed away. Charlotte tried to see where it flew to, but it was too fast for her eyes to follow.

Just then, Tetonka jerked his line up hard, pulling a big catfish out of the water. He grabbed the line and held it up for Charlotte to admire.

"That is a big one," Charlotte said, admiring the muscles in Tetonka's arm as he proudly held his catch up for her.

Tetonka walked out of the water and secured the fish in a basket that was submerged in the water. That way, they could fish for hours without the fish dying and rotting before they made it back to the village.

As Tetonka walked back out into the water, Charlotte admired the way his muscles flexed with every movement. His body was so very lovely. He had nice broad shoulders punctuated by prominent shoulder muscles. Long lines of muscle rippled along the back of his shoulders and down the length of his spine.

His leg muscles flexed as he lifted his thighs high to walk through the deep water. He waded out into it until the water was well above his waist. Charlotte admired his deep tanned chest and strong, lean arms as he threw his line further out into the deep water. His face was relaxed and pensive, as he stood like a stork, hovering over the water, waiting to strike at just the precise moment.

She watched in quiet bliss until she felt her eyelids grow heavy. The warmth of the sun on her skin and the hum of the sounds around her lulled her into a drowsy sleep. She laid back on the rock to take a quiet nap.

She was startled awake by cold water, splashing on her. She sat up to find Tetonka, smiling at her, taking aim with another bladed hand above the water. She immediately jumped down from the rock.

Her breath caught in her throat, momentarily, at the shock of the cool water compared to the heat of the rock. She returned a splash at Tetonka, who splashed her again with such a big wave that it went completely over her head.

But before she could shake the water out of her eyes to return the favor, he lifted her up out of the water and brought her back down, dunking her under. She shot up out of the water, sputtering and spitting. Realizing her hair was matted over her face, she leaned back down in the water, coming up with her head bent backward so the water would pleat her hair straight back. Now she could see where her attacker had gone. He stood over her, grinning.

She didn't want him to think he could dunk her and get away with it, so she dove under the water to grab his legs. She lifted his legs, buckling his knees, causing him to fall back into the water. Before he could get his legs under him again, she jumped on top of him, pushing his shoulders back down under the water as soon as he tried to come up for air.

Not wanting to be outdone, he wrapped his arms around her waist and rolled her back into the water, submerging her once again. Realizing this could go back and forth forever, she decided to surrender herself and wrapped her arms around his neck.

He settled his arms around her waist and squatted under the water, leaving only their head and neck above the water.

Charlotte smiled at him, and he smiled back.

"I take it you are finished catching fish, because if you are not, we likely just scared them all away."

He nodded proudly. "While you were sleeping, we caught quite a few fish."

Charlotte looked around for the other two men and found them sitting on the shore, eating the food she had packed for the day.

"Aren't you hungry?" she asked.

"Famished," he said, then planted a big, wet kiss on her lips.

Charlotte slipped tighter to him, opening her mouth to him for a long, hot kiss. They were interrupted by a big splash over their heads. They turned to see that Takoda had thrown a heavy rock in their direction, just at the right angle to douse their heated moment.

Charlotte sighed. They were always being watched and chaperoned it seemed. Tetonka took her hand and led her out of the water. She wrung her hair out and sat on the ground to dry out. Takoda handed her some food, giving her a teasing grin. She stuck her tongue out at her future brother-in-law and took the food.

This was the most peaceful and serene day she had ever had, and she wished it would never end.

CHAPTER TEN

*C*harlotte parked her car in the school parking lot, got out, and shut the door. Immediately when she did so, she realized she made a huge mistake. Not only had she locked her keys in the car, but her keys were still in the ignition, and her car was running.

How could I be so stupid! she said to herself. *Crap, when this gets around school, they're never going to let me hear the end of it.* She walked over to the gym and found her uncle, the head football coach, in the athletic office.

"Hey, Uncle Tommy," Charlotte said as she came in warily.

"Hey, Charlotte. How are you this morning?" her uncle asked, smiling.

"Well," she said, hesitating, "I locked my keys in my car, and I need to call Dad, so he can come unlock my door."

"You don't need them right now, do you? It can wait until school is out, surely," he said.

"Well, there's another problem. The car is still running," she said, turning her face down.

"What!" her uncle looked at her then burst out laughing.

"Shhh," she said. She didn't want anyone else to overhear about her stupid mistake. "It was an accident, and now I need Dad to come unlock it," she said pleadingly.

"Okay, okay. I'll call him for you, and we'll fix it. You go on to class, and I'll bring your keys to you. What class do you have first?" he asked, composing himself a little better.

"I have biology with Mrs. Olsen. Thank you, Uncle Tommy!" she said, giving her uncle a hug and quickly heading off to class.

She got to her seat as the tardy bell rang. Lilly leaned over, "Cutting it kind of close, aren't we?"

"I'll explain later," she whispered back. Charlotte sneaked a peek over at Brock. He was looking at her. She smiled at him, and he smiled back.

"Today, we're beginning a new unit on genetics. Who knows what DNA stands for?" Mrs. Olsen asked, breaking them out of their smiles at each other. What she wouldn't give to go out with Brock. She sat doodling on her paper thinking about what it would be like.

"Charlotte? Do you know?" Mrs. Olsen asked.

"I'm sorry?" she said, looking up suddenly.

"I asked if you remember where the DNA is located in the cell?" Mrs. Olsen repeated.

"Oh, yes. In the nucleus," Charlotte answered, embarrassed that she was caught off guard. Luckily, she remembered that one.

Before the end of class, her uncle brought her keys. She hoped he hadn't told anyone else about what she did, but unfortunately, he told a few of the other coaches, who told a few of their players, and of course, she was the talk of school by lunchtime.

"Have you heard the rumor going around about you today?" Lilly asked her at the lunch table.

"Yeah, that I locked my keys in my car while it was still running," she answered embarrassed.

"Well, that, but there's something else they're saying," Lilly said.

"Uh-oh, what now." Charlotte stopped her fork midway to her mouth worried about what she was about to find out.

"The rumor going around is that you got drunk this weekend," Lilly said, not believing it.

"What! That's ridiculous! You know I don't drink!" Charlotte's voice got louder with each sentence. "Why would they possibly be saying that about me?" She was utterly flabbergasted at what people in her school would say about one another regardless of the truth or facts to support the rumor.

"Someone said they saw you when you got home from Jacob's hayride. You fell flat on your butt and had trouble walking," Lilly said, looking to her for an explanation.

All Charlotte could say through gritted teeth was, "Kale!"

"What about Kale? What did he do?" Lilly asked confused.

Charlotte filled her in on her suspicions about Kale, what he did to her at the dance, and their little encounter Friday night.

"Well, that explains a lot. It would be like him to start a rumor like that about you," Lilly said, much to her relief to find that her best friend hadn't started drinking alcohol underage.

"I can't figure out what his deal is. Why's he going to so much trouble to interfere with my dates and spread rumors about me that aren't true?" Charlotte asked, pushing her tray away from her. She was no longer hungry.

"Do you remember doing something to him that might have made him angry at you?" Lilly asked.

"Not that I know of. If I did, it was unintentional." Charlotte sat racking her brain thinking of what might have happened to bring this upon herself.

"Well, not to add insult to injury, but I heard something else today you're not gonna like," Lilly said. Charlotte was afraid to hear any more at this point and braced herself for Lilly's next statement. "I heard Susan asked Brock out, and they're going to the Halloween party together this weekend."

This was the worst news ever. Charlotte was crushed. She put her face in her hands and sighed heavily. If he had heard the rumors going around about her, he probably had the wrong impression of her. Now that someone else had gotten to him before her, she probably lost any chance she ever had of getting a closer look at those gorgeous eyes. This was turning out to be a miserable day.

Suddenly, she wanted to go home and bury her head under the covers.

"Are you okay?" Lilly asked. The bell rang to end lunch.

"I suppose I have to be, right?" Charlotte said, getting up from the table. "What else am I to do? I guess I could go back to the past and live the rest of my life there. At least there, I have a man who loves me, and we're getting married."

"Wow! You haven't told me about this." Lilly perked up catching up with Charlotte as they walked to class.

"Yeah, we haven't had much time to talk about that aspect of my life lately," she said whispering.

There was still the possibility that she had a purpose for switching into Nahele. She needed to do some research. Before Lilly and Charlotte went their separate ways, Charlotte asked, "Do you think you could go with me to the library this weekend?"

"Yeah, sure. Are you driving?" Lilly asked.

"Yep! I'll pick you up Saturday. Thanks, Lilly," she said, hoping all the rumors from today would blow over quickly.

"A BUNCH of us are going over to Gina's house tonight. Are you coming?" Evan asked her Friday morning before school.

"I'll be there!" Charlotte said, glad that it was finally Friday. The rumors from the beginning of the week quickly went away thanks to Lilly counteracting by telling people the truth. But it still didn't stop the jabs about her leaving her keys in the car while it was still running. She would have to live with that one, but hopefully people didn't believe the rumor that she had been drunk. One person in particular —Brock. He had seemed a little more distant the past couple of days. She saw him with Susan a few times, but he didn't smile near as much around her as he did when he saw Charlotte. Maybe there was hope there after all.

That night, Charlotte drove carefully out to Gina's house. When everyone had arrived, someone suggested mixing flour and water in a bucket. The result was a dough that they scooped out and threw at one another or on-coming cars. Swept up with the group, Charlotte went along as they trekked through the dark woods to the main highway. They hid in a ditch next to the road. When a single car came by, they jumped and tossed their handful of dough at the vehicle. With twenty plus clumps of dough hitting a vehicle in rapid succession, it sounded like gunfire. It must have scared the driver into a heart attack. Luckily, the car kept on going down the road. If it stopped, they didn't have time to find out. After the dough hit the vehicle, a man in a house across the highway came out onto his porch and cocked his rifle, pointing it in the air.

Without seeing if he planned to aim it at them, the mass of teens took off scrambling through the woods. Charlotte ran for her life. The trees whipped by as she ducked and weaved her way through the forest. She felt others running beside her, but she miraculously outpaced them. She had to lift her knees high so that she wouldn't stick in the mud. As they neared the edge of the forest, she began to slow down and finally breathe.

Once everyone made the clearing, they broke down laughing hysterically.

"That was close!" Someone said next to her. Charlotte turned to see it was Brock.

"Hey! I didn't see you here," she said, looking around to see if Susan was nearby. Before she could say anything else, Susan walked out of the woods and came up beside Brock.

"Oh my gosh! That was crazy!" Susan said, smiling up at Brock.

"Yeah, I would've hated to have been that driver. I probably would've slammed on my brakes and knocked heads if that had been me," Brock said, looking more at Charlotte than at Susan.

Gina walked up. "Hey, we're going to walk over to the cemetery. Come on!" Charlotte didn't want to get in between Susan and Brock, so she jogged ahead to the front of the group as they headed to the cemetery.

Charlotte knew she should feel creeped out by being in a cemetery on Halloween night, but she felt oddly at peace. Her house backed up to a cemetery, and she would often accompany her dad on his frequent jogs around it. At least there was a full moon out that made roaming around the countryside at night a little more visible.

She walked along one of the rows reading the names when Brock came up beside her.

"You know in the Philippines, families gather in the cemetery and hold reunions. They play games, sing songs, eat lots of food, and even play Karaoke," he said.

Charlotte looked over at him. "No, I didn't know that." She smiled at him then looked over her shoulder. "Where's your date?"

"Oh, she's over there acting like she's freaked out and wanting to cling to me for protection. I had to get away before she started digging her claws into me," he said almost in a whisper.

Charlotte cringed at the thought of Susan getting her claws into him, in more ways than one. "Not having any fun?"

"Oh, it's all right," he said, coming to a stop in front of a large monument. "This one's old. It says born in 1824, died in 1888. This person died a hundred years ago," he said in awe.

"What's your idea of fun?" Charlotte couldn't help but ask.

"I like hiking, a little mountain biking, camping out in nature, but not this creeping around and vandalizing things," he said, putting his hands in his pockets and looking up at the silhouettes of the treetops. "I'd rather be camped out sitting by a fire with a small group of friends."

"That's more my style as well," she said, suppressing her excitement. "I have a great trail area in the woods around my house, and I hike out there all the time with my dog."

"Really? That's awesome. Any cool places to see?" he asked.

"There's this great cliff lookout area that I like to go to and look over the trees and out over the hills and daydream," she said, dreaming what it would be like to be out there with him.

"Hey! There you are! I lost you," Susan said, coming up to Brock and hooking her arm through his.

Taking this as her cue to leave, Charlotte said, "I think I need to head back now. Don't get lost you two." She pretended not to care that they were together and hoped Susan didn't think she was moving in on her territory, even though deep down she wanted to.

She found her way through the dark back to Gina's house. When she walked in, she saw a few couples had stayed behind to watch the horror movie, *Friday the 13th: Jason Lives*, and were making out on the couch. She made a U-turn and went to the kitchen instead. She poured herself a Coke when someone came in behind her.

"Well, look who's here all alone," Kale said.

Charlotte turned around and leaned her hip against the counter. "Hello, Kale. I decided that it was pointless to come here with a date since you would probably find a way to sabotage that, too." She eyed him suspiciously over the rim of her Solo cup as she took a sip.

Kale pretended to be offended. "What? Me? I assure you; I have no idea what you're talking about." Despite his words, he grinned like the Cheshire cat.

She lowered her drink and took a deep breath deciding if she should engage him in his ploy or ignore it. He walked toward her, backing her into the corner of the kitchen counter.

She raised her drink at his chest. "Hold it! Don't come any closer to me." She darted a look around to see if anyone else was nearby to rescue her.

Kale raised his hands. "Ah, come on, Charlotte. Just one little kiss. You remember how good it was, don't you?" She could see him lusting after her with his eyes, and she almost gagged.

The front door opened as several teens walked into the house, talking and laughing. Kale turned his head to see, and Charlotte quickly side-stepped him. Not giving him a chance to grab her or corner her again, she slammed her cup down on the counter and grabbed her purse. She walked out the front door as Brock and Susan came in. She ducked her head down so Brock couldn't see the tears flooding her eyes.

Brock turned to her as she brushed past him and watched her stomp down the driveway toward her car. She didn't want to see Brock and Susan together anymore tonight. It was too depressing, and with Kale cornering her, she was ready to get out of sight. As she slammed her car door, she heard someone call her name, but she didn't look back to see who. She turned the car on and threw it into reverse. She felt like she couldn't get out of there fast enough before tears streamed down her face.

❧

THE NEXT DAY, Charlotte picked Lilly up to go to the local library.

"Where'd you go last night? I tried to find you when we got back from the cemetery, but someone said they saw you leave." Lilly looked worried for her.

"Oh, I decided I'd had enough. Sorry, I didn't say goodbye." Charlotte started to feel a little depressed again, remembering the events of the previous evening.

"I understand. I saw Brock and Susan, too. If it makes you feel any better, I don't think he's that into her."

"Yeah, a little. But Susan sure seems hung up on him. I can't blame her," she admitted.

"It won't last long. You mark my words. She won't last long with him."

Charlotte hoped so. But, with her track record lately with dates, she was afraid to make the effort and fail. Maybe she should just admire him from afar. That way, she wouldn't be so crushed when it ended badly.

At the town public library, they asked the librarian where they could locate information on Native Americans. "Are you doing this for a school project?" The librarian asked.

"Yeah, something like that," Charlotte said.

"Well, I'm afraid we don't have anything other than children's books. You may need to go to ASU's library if you're looking for more in-depth material. You won't be able to check anything out. You'll have to stay and write down your research there at the library," the librarian said.

"Okay, thanks for telling us. We'll go there and check it out." Charlotte grabbed Lilly's arm and directed her out of the library.

After driving the extra twenty miles to Arkansas State in Jonesboro, they had to ask directions twice to find the library. The library was bigger than any they had ever seen before. They were used to their little high school library and the town library that were both mostly one big room.

"How are we going to find what we're looking for in here?" Lilly looked wide-eyed and a little intimidated.

"We ask," Charlotte said, walking confidently toward the information desk. "Excuse me, sir, where can we find books on Native Americans who might have lived in Arkansas?"

"You'll need to look in the card catalog under subjects. Most of the texts will be on the second floor," the college library aide said, looking a little annoyed that young high school students were interfering in his library.

They found the section they were looking for and began pulling promising texts off the shelves. They found a large table nearby to spread everything out and began reading through the books for any information they could find.

"How do you spell *Wa sha zhe?*" Lilly asked.

"I think it would be W-a-s-h-a-z-e," Charlotte answered the best she could.

After looking through a list of tribes in the encyclopedia, Lilly said, "I don't see any tribe listed with a name like that."

"Well, that's a native pronunciation. Maybe the French, who came in contact with them first, wrote it down differently," Charlotte said.

"French doesn't have a 'W' in their language," Lilly said.

"Excellent! I'm so glad you took French, and I took Spanish. How do you think they would have spelled it?" Charlotte was glad to have a good friend like Lilly right then.

"The word, *Oui*, starts with an *O* even though it's pronounced like a *W*, so let's look at anything starting with an *O*." After Lilly looked through the list again, she said, "How about this? Osage."

"That may be it. It would be like the Europeans to distort the names and pronunciations," Charlotte sighed, dejectedly.

"It says here that their known territory was from the Missouri

River in the north, the Mississippi River in the east, the Arkansas River in the south, and an undefined area in the plains of Nebraska, Kansas, and Oklahoma," Lilly read for her.

"That would cover Northeast Arkansas." Charlotte was relieved to hear. "Does it say anything about where they had villages?"

"It says that one of their earliest villages was the *Marais des Cygnes*, or Marsh of the Swans, near the fork of the Osage River. I saw a map here somewhere. . ." Lilly sifted through several of the open books. "Here it is. That's almost in the middle of Missouri."

"Maybe that was their large population area, but from what I know from Nahele, they're living in an outpost village that guards the edge of their territory," Charlotte said.

Lilly read more about their descriptions. "They were described as the tallest Native Americans anyone had seen," Lilly added.

"Oh yes! They are! A few are over seven feet tall. It's like being in a village of giants." Charlotte was excited to tell Lilly about her new people and tears came to her eyes realizing how much she missed them.

"There's a quote here from Washington Irving, you know, the guy who wrote, *The Legend of Sleepy Hollow*," Lilly said.

"How do you know that?" Charlotte asked, raising her eyebrows.

"It says so right here. Anyway, he's noted as saying that they were the finest looking Indians he had ever seen."

"What else does it say?" Charlotte leaned in closer to look over Lilly's shoulder.

"It says that there were two bands, the Big Osage and the Little Osage. Except, that doesn't refer to their height, it was a misunderstanding in interpreting their hand signals. The Big Osage called themselves the 'Top of Tree Sitters' and the Little Osage were the 'Down Below People,'" Lilly read for her.

"There it is again. Another label put on a people because they didn't correct a misunderstanding of their names." Charlotte sat back down in her seat with a huff.

"Well, then we have established that this is their territory, and now we have a name for the tribe in writing. What else are you looking for?" Lilly was proud of her skills thus far in the discovery.

"I would like to know what time frame I'm in, so I can figure out what happens to them. I don't know if I'm to help them with something or why this is happening." She felt like there were still so many questions to be answered.

"You'll have to give me more clues from what you have heard at the village to narrow down a time frame. As to why this is happening, I came across something else over here." Lilly reached for another small book under the pile. "The librarian brought this over thinking it might help with our research, *Indian Medicine Power.*" She thumbed through the first few pages. "It doesn't have anything specific to the Osage but listen to this. This is from Quetzalcoatl, a prophet-king of the Toltec Indians in southern Mexico. He talked of a time when there would be a different white man (or woman)," she added, "'who wore the feet of doves and would work with the Indians to build a new and better world of peace, love, and brotherhood.'"

"The 'feet of doves'? Could that mean people of peace?" Charlotte asked.

"I don't think it's a literal description." Lilly smiled. "There's more. The author quotes a Chippewa man as saying, 'We feel that we are the traditional keepers and protectors of the Earth Mother, and we feel that there is coming a time when there is going to be a major cleansing and changing of things.'"

"I don't think I'm going to be able to affect that big a change. That's not referring to one person, but a group of people. What does that have to do with medicine anyway?"

"I don't think the Native Americans referred to medicine in the way we do as in healing a wound or curing a sickness. I think they refer to medicine as spiritual power or even religion," Lilly said.

"Okay, I can see that. But I still don't see where you're going with this," Charlotte said, still confused.

"I'm getting to that. He quotes Sun Bear, 'I tell them that the start of it is that they must first learn to walk the earth with a good balance.

That means you have to learn to relate to each other and to the Earth Mother and learn to live in real harmony with her.'"

"I can certainly agree with that. From my experiences so far, the People are religious and harmonious with all the plants and animals around them. They pray for everything, and take no more than necessary," she said, but then added, "However, they've been taking more for fur to trade with the French and Spanish. That could be a beginning of a downfall for them."

Lilly was still scanning through the pages, using her speed-reading techniques to catch meaningful phrases or words. Then she said, "This says that most Indians believed in reincarnation and that many of those slaughtered by the Whites in the early times could be reborn as today's youth." She looked up with big eyes at Charlotte. "That could be you!"

"That seems possible as to why I can experience Nahele's past life. Maybe I'm in a hypnotic state when it happens, and I'm re-experiencing my former life." Charlotte had to sit and think about this while Lilly kept reading.

After a few minutes of silence, Lilly suddenly blurted, "Listen to this!" making Charlotte jump because she was deep in thought. "I'm paraphrasing here, but this says they didn't believe in time in the linear sense, but that the past, present, and future all occur simultaneously by raising their level of consciousness through visions or dreams."

"I've tried meditating before as a way of raising my consciousness. I think that was what I was doing before all this happened. I didn't intend to, necessarily. I was looking at the tops of the trees watching them sway and letting my mind and body get into that rhythm," Charlotte said, thinking back.

"Really? I didn't know you did that." Lilly sounded surprised.

"Yeah, well, I haven't done it much, and it's not something I go around telling people," Charlotte admitted. "Honestly, I don't think many people around here are ready for that kind of thing."

"What kind of thing?" Lilly asked.

"You know, meditating and higher consciousness. We live in a strong Bible-believing, God-fearing, and repent or go to Hell area. Most people would claim I was worshiping the devil without attempting to understand what it's about."

"I suppose you're right. It's out of the norm for around here." Lilly had to admit she didn't quite understand it all herself, but she was interested now and wanted to learn more. "If you were watching the trees and meditating, could that also hypnotize you?"

"Yes, they're the same thing. Meditation is clearing the mind of all unnecessary thoughts and relaxing the body. It can feel hypnotic. There doesn't have to be anyone there with a deep voice giving you subconscious instructions. It's a state of mind," Charlotte informed her.

"So, you could have meditated yourself into a hypnotic state and reconnected with a past life?" Lilly questioned, summarizing.

"I suppose so. But that still doesn't explain the role of Scuffy and Barkley." Charlotte felt there was more to what was going on than they had discovered so far.

"Barkley?" Lilly asked, ready to laugh.

"That's another story. I'll tell you about it on our way home. Maybe it's time to head back," she said, reluctantly, wishing they had more time.

"It's too bad we can't check this book out. I bet it has a lot more to tell us," Lilly said, looking the book over. "Maybe I can write the ISBN down and order it or get it at the bookstore."

"That's a great idea. Why don't you do that while I gather the rest and take them to the return rack." Charlotte felt they had made a little progress but not enough.

Back in the car, Charlotte began to tell Lilly more about her experiences as Nahele.

"You could have been killed by that bear! How scary!" Lilly stared at Charlotte while Charlotte drove them home.

"I know! It was terrifying, especially after I had time to think about it. I also couldn't have escaped without help from Barkley." She shuddered at the memory of it all.

"What if you did die while your consciousness was with Nahele?

What do you think would happen then?" Lilly brought up a great question.

"I have no idea. That's why I need to know more about what's going on and why." She felt frustrated. "I have a feeling the medicine woman may know more than she's letting on. I need to go see her, but I haven't had the chance yet."

They sat quietly in the car, thinking and sorting out in their minds the whole situation.

Lilly agreed that she would continue reading and researching to find out more about the Osage and what happened to them. Charlotte needed to know if any significant event occurred and if her time was around that event that she might need to prepare for. Which meant that she needed to figure out what timeframe she was in as Nahele. She also needed to see if the medicine woman could give her any more information as to how this was happening. There was still a lot of mystery around this whole phenomenon. At least she felt confident Lilly believed her now. She was relieved to have someone on her side who she could talk to and work with to figure this out.

CHAPTER ELEVEN

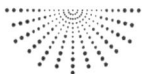

*T*he next afternoon after church, Charlotte mulled over everything that Lilly and she had discovered at the library. *The past, present, and the future all together? Reincarnation?* She didn't know what to think about it all. She decided to go to her room and read the book Lilly had given her for her birthday. At the time she got it, Lilly didn't know the specific tribe that they needed information about. This book was one about Native Americans in general: their culture, their rituals, and their spiritual beliefs.

At some point, Charlotte must have fallen asleep, and she began to dream:

She walked in the forest following someone, but she couldn't make out who. The edges of her vision were fuzzy as if she was in a fog and the only part that was clear was right in front of her. She walked softly, not making a sound. She stopped behind the person she followed still unclear about who it was. She could see beautiful, vibrant colors radiating from this person. All the colors of the rainbow surrounded him or her. The colors sparkled and flared out in all directions. Charlotte wanted to speak but found she couldn't make

her mouth move. All she could do was watch and wait to see what would happen next.

Then a bird flew gently from the sky and landed on the outstretched hand of the person. She could see now that it was a woman with long dark hair dressed in a long white gown. The flowing gown blew around her legs, but Charlotte felt no breeze. The bird was a white dove. It, too, had iridescent colors sparkling from the ends of its feathers. The woman began to sing to the bird. It was the most beautiful song Charlotte had ever heard.

The bird spread its wings and flew away as the woman stretched out her hands to the sky. The sky was the most magnificent blue Charlotte had ever seen. It was clear and blue for as far as she could see. The woman continued to sing lifting her hands to the sky. Tiny sparkling snowflakes began to float down, even though there were no clouds. The snowflakes also sparkled with brilliant colors radiating out from their delicate white patterns. The snow began to cover the ground, but it wasn't cold. It covered the area filling Charlotte's heart with the most peaceful and loving feelings she had ever felt. She felt entirely at peace and nothing but pure love for the whole universe.

The woman began to sing softly and lowered herself down to the snow-covered ground that felt soft as a multitude of cotton balls. She laid herself down in a peaceful sleep now humming with her beautiful voice. Charlotte could feel the humming sensation in her chest, vibrating her inner spirit. She, too, began to feel sleepy, and the scene before her began to blink out in darkness as she closed her inner mind to a deep and pleasant sleep.

BROCK COULDN'T STOP THINKING about Charlotte. The moment he saw her that first day when he walked into class, her beauty immediately struck him. He was haunted by the feeling that he had seen her somewhere before. He wracked his brain all day battling in his mind where he'd seen her. That night, as he laid awake thinking about her, it dawned on him. He had seen her face in a dream. It had come to him in a flash, but that flash vision of her had burned itself into his mind. Now, he felt more than ever that she was the girl for him.

He loved watching her at school. Her mouth especially intrigued him. He loved her smile and the way her mouth moved when she talked. He could sit and watch her forever. A part of him didn't want to disturb the delicate balance he had built these past few weeks. He was afraid that if he did ask her out that it would shatter the perfect image he had built up around her.

She seemed to exude energy, and it was hard not to catch her enthusiasm whenever he was around her. He loved the way her eyes lit up every time she looked at him. If they did start dating, he hoped that he could make this one last. He couldn't stand another lousy breakup right now. Besides, if this relationship did go south, how could he stand looking at her every day at school and them not being together. He quickly shook himself of that thought and tried to be positive. This time wasn't going to be like the last.

Saying a little prayer, he looked up her phone number in the phone book and dialed the number. He held his breath for the first ring.

CHARLOTTE WOKE SOMETIME LATER and looked outside to find it was dark. *How long have I been asleep?* She looked at the clock, and it read 8:30 p.m. Why had her parents let her sleep this long? They must have thought she needed the rest. Her stomach growled, and she realized she missed supper.

She opened the door to her bedroom quietly, not sure if anyone was still up. It was quiet in the living room. She could see the blue flicker from the TV in her parents' bedroom, so they were still up watching TV in bed. She tiptoed to the kitchen to see if they saved her any food from supper. Sure enough, her mother had wrapped a plate full of food for her and left it in the fridge. She warmed it in the microwave and sat to eat at the kitchen bar when the phone rang. She was right next to it, so she quickly picked it up.

"Hello?" she said.

"Hello? Is Charlotte there?" asked a deep voice.

"This is she. Who is this?" she asked.

"This is Brock. I hope I'm not calling too late," he said, tentatively.

Charlotte's heart suddenly went to her throat, and her hands shook. *Oh my gosh! It's him!!* she practically screamed in her mind. She took a deep breath before answering.

"No, not at all. I took a late nap and just woke up. I'm afraid I'll be up awhile now that I've thrown my sleep schedule off." Charlotte laughed a little, sounding as calm as possible.

"Well, good. It sounds like I called at the right time then," he sounded more confident.

"Well, sort of. I warmed a plate of food my mother left me from supper and was about to eat."

"Oh, I can call back at another time then if you want me to," he said, hurriedly.

"Oh, no! That's okay. As long as you don't mind me chewing in your ear for a little bit." She then had visions of chewing on his ear but quickly ran that out of her mind.

"I don't mind at all. Go right ahead. I hope you don't mind. I looked your number up in the phonebook. I knew your uncle's name, so I thought your phone number was the other McAfee listed."

"I'm a little shocked to hear from you," she confessed, hoping she wasn't being too honest. "I thought you were going out with Susan."

"Who, Susan? No. That was one date. I said yes to her, so I had an excuse to go to the party. I don't think I could go out with her long term," he said.

"Really? Why's that?" she asked with food in her mouth.

"She's too high maintenance for me," he told her.

"High maintenance? What does that mean?" She wanted to know so she could be the exact opposite.

"Well, how should I put this? She's clingy for one. And then, she talks way too much. It's the kind of talking that goes on without her caring whether the person she's talking to is listening to her or not. I bet she talks like that to herself when no one else is around to listen to her."

Charlotte almost choked on her food at that.

"Are you okay?" he sounded worried.

"Yeah, I'm okay. You made me laugh right when I swallowed," she choked out. She drank some water to clear her throat then said, "I'm better now. Continue. This is good."

"Well, she's also fairly picky about getting dirty or worried about breaking a nail. I can't handle a girl like that. It would drive me crazy. I feel sorry for the guy who does go out with her long term. She'll probably have the guy carrying her on his back and waiting on her hand and foot," he said.

"I see. I know she's fashion conscious and always picture perfect. I don't think I've ever seen her wear the same outfit twice. But I've known her for a long time. I've known most everyone at school since kindergarten. It's nice having a fresh face in town," she said, smiling dreamily across the phone.

"Why, thank you. I wash it every day," he said, aiming to be funny. It worked. She giggled, maybe a little too enthusiastically.

After a brief pause of awkward silence, Charlotte asked, "So, why did you call?"

"I got tired of waiting for you to make the first move, and I thought, since I'm the guy, I needed to step up and do it myself," he admitted.

"Oh." She was a little dumbfounded at this and didn't know what to say immediately.

"I hope I'm not being too presumptuous," he said, a little concerned.

"Nice use of vocabulary!" Charlotte said, feeling a little more confident.

"Thank you. I've got the dictionary right next to me wanting to make an impression." He made her giggle again, but a little more naturally this time.

"You're good. I bet you broke a lot of hearts when you moved away. By the way, where did you move from?" she thought to ask suddenly.

"I moved here from Oklahoma," he said.

"Oklahoma, huh? What part exactly?" she asked, suddenly more alert.

"I don't think you would have heard about it. It's a small town called Pawhuska in the middle of Osage Indian territory."

Charlotte did choke this time and gasped for air.

"Are you okay? Do I need to call an ambulance?" he said worriedly this time.

"No," she squeaked out. "Give me a second." She tried to stop coughing and swallow some water. Her eyes watered, and she reached for a paper towel to wipe her eyes and mouth. After she felt like she could breathe easy again, she squeaked, "I've heard of the Osage Indians."

"Really?! I'm impressed. Hardly any outsider ever knows about the Osage," he sounded both impressed and curious. "What have you heard?"

"Well," what could she say, she'd been living off and on as one for the past two months. "I had to do some research on them recently for a project." She thought that was closer to the truth without having to reveal too much.

"I'm an open book, baby. Ask me what you want to know, and I'll tell you. If I don't know, I can ask my mom. Her grandmother was a full-blood Osage, which makes me one-eighth Osage. I was born on the reservation, so I know a lot about them, or at least, I think I do. Either way, I can help you with what you want to know."

This was good. Maybe he would be a useful source of information for her to find out what was happening, but she didn't want to reveal too much, too soon. She needed to be careful how she approached this.

Her dad came into the kitchen, "Charlotte, it's getting late. You need to get off the phone."

"I know, Dad, but I took a late nap, and now I'm not sleepy." She tried giving him her most innocent look.

"All right, thirty more minutes and that's it. Then you need to try to go to sleep. You've got school tomorrow." He turned and went back to his bedroom.

"Who was that? Do I need to let you go?" Brock asked.

"It was my dad. He said I have thirty more minutes. Then, I have to try to go back to sleep."

"That's if you don't get bored with me before then and decide to hang up," he said, half-jokingly.

"Well, get your dictionary back out so you can impress me some more," she said, laughing. He laughed too, and she realized she loved his laugh. She wished she could see him right now. She would like to be looking into his gorgeous eyes and smile.

"I tell you what. Why don't you put together some questions that you still have about the Osage and go out with me next weekend, and I'll give you all the answers you want," he said charmingly.

"Oh, smooth. That's the best pick-up line I've ever heard," Charlotte said, beaming from ear to ear. Then she remembered, "Oh wait! Friday night is our last football game, and then Saturday night I'm hosting this year's Miss Harvest Queen pageant. I'm the reigning queen and will be passing my crown on to this year's winner." She said this last part with exaggerated importance dripping with sarcasm.

"Oh wow! I didn't realize I was speaking with royalty. Maybe I should be addressing you as 'My Lady' and bowing in your presence," he said, catching on to her sarcasm.

"Please don't get the wrong impression. It's a little pageant that the Future Business Leaders of America began putting on last year to raise money for our events that we go to in the spring. It's not that big a deal." She tried to play it down and hoped that he wasn't going to mistakenly put her in the same category as Susan now.

"Well, for someone as beautiful as you, I bet no one stood a chance of even coming close," he said.

She blushed a little and was glad that he couldn't see her now. She suddenly realized they were off from the original, more important issue of going out on a date.

As if reading her mind, he said, "Well, then the next week basketball season starts, and I'll be playing on the team."

"I'll be there cheering you on from the sidelines!"

"That's if Coach puts me in."

"He'd be stupid not to, as tall as you are?"

"Well, I'm the new guy, so he's not sure of what I can do yet. So, I need to make a good impression if I want to get any real playing time."

"I'm confident you will. How could you not? If you want, you could come over here to my house and work on your shot. We have a basketball hoop in the driveway," she said, hopefully.

"That'll work. We'll have to hang out together at school until we can find the time to go on a real date. How's that sound?"

"Umm, it sounds like you're asking me to be your girlfriend before we've even gone out," she said, more excited on the inside, but not wanting to push it.

"Well, I'm willing to give it a try if you are?" he said without hesitating.

"That was fast. But, okay! Never accuse me of turning down an adventure or jumping in with both feet!" she said, as her heart raced once again.

"Fantastic. That's my kind of girl. Always willing to try new things and not afraid of an adventure," he said happily.

"That's me. It's like you know me already!"

"I'm looking forward to getting to know you more. I guess I'll let you go now so you can get some sleep," he said, being polite.

"I think I'm gonna have a tough time doing that now," she said, excitedly.

"Drink some chamomile tea. That's what my mom does when she has trouble sleeping," he suggested. She wondered if it was going to be hard for him to go to sleep tonight as well.

"Thanks for the tip. I'll have to see if we have some. I guess I'll see you tomorrow then," Charlotte wished she could call Lilly right now and tell her the news.

"You're welcome. Sleep tight, sleeping beauty," he said in his deepest and sexiest voice.

"Good night, prince charming," she said, giggling softly. They hung up. She was so excited. She practically skipped to her bedroom and forgot to look for the chamomile tea.

CHAPTER TWELVE

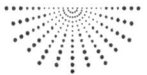

*T*he next morning, Charlotte bounded up to Lilly and Evan in the courtyard before school. "Well, someone sure is happy for a Monday morning," Lilly said, eyeing her suspiciously.

"Evan, can I talk to Lilly privately for a second?" she said, trying to control her enthusiasm.

"Sure. I'll be over here." He walked over to a group of guys who were huddled together a few feet away.

Charlotte tugged Lilly's arm and pulled her a little further out of earshot. "You're never going to believe what happened last night!" She tried to whisper the best she could but could hardly hold back.

"Okay, try me. After what we've been talking about lately I can only imagine," Lilly said, catching on to her energy.

"Brock called me last night!" she beamed.

"And?" Lilly waited.

"Well, two things. First, he asked me out!" Lilly and Charlotte squealed and jumped up and down together, and the group of guys and Evan turned to look at them.

"And..." Charlotte said, quieting to a loud whisper, "He's one-eighth Osage Indian."

"No way!" Lilly exclaimed too loudly. Again, the guys turned to look at them. Evan looked concerned, and she could tell he wanted to know what was going on. Charlotte wondered what Lilly would say to him.

"Yes, way! I never thought to ask him where he moved from. He's from Oklahoma and was born on the Osage Indian reservation," she said excitedly, finally relieved to share her news with her friend.

"That's so strange. What are the chances given the things that have been happening to you, and then your dream guy happens to come to our school who might be connected to this in some way?"

"It is a strange coincidence." She thought for a second. "But, the best news is, we haven't been able to nail down a specific day to go out since, Friday is the last football game, Saturday is the pageant, and, next week, basketball season starts."

"Really? So, what did you decide?" Lilly asked curiously.

"He asked me if in the meantime if I wanted to hang out at school and what-not until we could find a day to go out on a real date!" she said, practically jumping up and down.

"Oh wow! That was fast," Lilly said looking at her with big eyes.

"I know! I think it might be good this way. Take some time to get to know one another hanging out and doing normal stuff like you and Evan." She looked up dreamily.

Once it seemed the initial excitement had calmed down, Evan thought it might be okay to approach them, "Is it safe to come back now?"

"Yeah! Brock asked Charlotte out," Lilly announced.

"Congratulations. And this is something you had to tell without me around?" he said looking slightly hurt.

"Oh, you know. Girl stuff first. Don't feel hurt. We still love you, too," she said nudging him in the shoulder.

"Yeah, yeah. Save it for your new boy-toy," Evan said, putting his arm around Lilly.

The bell rang for them to go to class, and Charlotte skipped ahead of them eager to see if Brock was already there. He was standing outside the classroom, waiting for her.

"Hey, you!" he said as she came up to him. He opened his arms to hug her, and she slid into his side like they had always greeted each other this way. He gave her a quick squeeze then asked, "Did you get any sleep last night?"

"Eventually," she said looking up at him. He was so tall. He kept his arm around her shoulders, and they looked at each other smiling.

"Ahem, well. Congratulations you two. Now we should probably get into class before the tardy bell rings," Lilly said, walking in ahead of them.

Brock still had his arm around her as they entered the classroom, but then he pulled away to let her go to her seat as he went to his. Charlotte risked a quick glance over at Kale. His eyebrows were scrunched down, and his nostrils flared. He reminded her of a bull in a bullfight, getting ready to charge the red cape of a Troubadour. Her heart raced. This could mean big trouble. She suddenly realized she should probably warn Brock about him. She had a terrible feeling in her stomach, dreading what she knew was going to have to happen.

She looked over at Lilly, and the look on her face meant she had come to the same conclusion. They both knew there was going to be trouble.

AFTER ENGLISH CLASS, Charlotte told Brock that she had an FBLA meeting during lunch. "I promise, beginning tomorrow, we'll have lunch together." She gave him a quick hug and headed off with Lilly to Mrs. Cannon's room. Brock watched her bound away full of energy. Brock headed toward the cafeteria to grab lunch, feeling the same exuberant energy. Before he opened the door to the cafeteria, someone shoved him from behind.

"Hey! Watch it, man!" he said as he turned around to see who the offender was. Kale stood behind him with a few of his buddies in tow.

"I think the one who needs to watch it is you, hippie," Kale barked. He sized Brock up, but remained a couple of feet away, to hopefully lure him back away from the door and out into the courtyard.

"I have no idea what you're talking about, dude," Brock said not wanting to invite more aggression from this guy. He seemed to be gearing himself up for a fight.

"I saw you with your arm around Charlotte this morning. You need to be warned about her," Kale folded his arms across his chest which allowed him to push his biceps out in a way that made them look bigger in an attempt to intimidate Brock further. It didn't work. Brock wasn't afraid of this guy. He had dealt with guys like him before. He knew he could hold his own but getting in a fight at school wasn't on Brock's agenda.

"What do I need to be warned about?" Brock asked curiously, but seriously doubting the validity of what was about to come out of this guy's mouth.

"Charlotte's my girl. Everyone knows that. She belongs to me and no one else." Kale's face was red with anger.

Brock was surprised. "Does she know that? Because she's free to be with whoever she wants. She didn't say anything to me about being taken." Brock stood straight in front of Kale, putting his hands in his front pockets to show he didn't intend to take the bait to fight. This struck a nerve with Kale. His face went a slightly darker red, and his jaw muscles clenched.

"She's mine," Kale growled. "She doesn't know it yet. But there can be no one else for her but me." He poked Brock in the chest and gave him a little shove. Brock took a step back but didn't let it show that he was starting to get angry as well. One more shove and he might not be able to contain himself.

"I think you need to get your story straight. She doesn't belong to you or anyone. You can't own someone, and they have to want to be with you." Brock stared back at Kale, giving him a look that meant he wasn't going away.

Kale stared back at him. Brock could see he was deciding how far he wanted to play this. Brock clinched his fists in his pockets, preparing himself for a fight, but he wasn't going to throw the first punch, just the last.

"This isn't over between us. This is just getting started. You wait.

She'll come around and see that I'm the only one who's man enough to be with her." Finally, Kale turned away with a loud snort.

Brock watched him strut away with his two goons close behind. He heaved a heavy sigh of relief to see him walk away.

He had to admit, that brief encounter troubled him. Well, Brock didn't scare away so easily, and he found it a challenge to get to the bottom of this little dilemma and find out what was really going on.

He didn't see Charlotte again until after basketball practice. Charlotte had finished with cheer practice about an hour earlier but stayed behind and waited for him. She was reading a textbook sitting on top of the concession stand counter in the gym lobby when he came out of the locker room. Before he let her know he was there, he looked at her for a few seconds. She sat cross-legged on the counter with her head bent down over her book. She had one elbow on her knee with her fist holding up her cheek. Seeing her facial features from this angle, he admired how beautiful she was.

"Hey, you!" he said, feeling his heart skip a beat at the sight of her.

"Hey!" She brightened up with a big smile and jumped down from the counter to skip up to him. She wrapped her arms around him for a big hug then quickly pulled back.

"Eww, sweaty!" Charlotte stepped back, scrunching her nose and wiping her hands on her sweats.

"Yeah, sorry about that." He laughed.

"No worries. I have to take a shower when I get home, too." She beamed at him.

She grabbed her athletic bag and walked out to the parking lot with him. "So how was the rest of your day?" she asked. He watched her walking next to him and could see her ponytail swinging back and forth as she bounced up and down. For some reason, he thought that ponytail was sexy. If he stepped back a little, he could watch her walk from behind and get a good look at her perfect butt, swaying back and forth, too. She looked amazing in her tight sweats.

Brock tried to decide whether to tell Charlotte about his encounter with Kale. He decided he wouldn't tell her the details of what he said but tell her that something happened. "Do you know that guy, Kale?" he said.

She stopped beside her car and turned quickly, "Oh no! What did he do now?" The look on her face said she was a little afraid but also angry.

"So, you've had problems with him before?" he asked, closing the gap between them.

She leaned back against her car as he came to stand right in front of her and put his hands on her hips. She let out a big sigh to calm herself for a second before she began. "Apparently, I've done something to him to make him angry with me. He's interfered with the last two guys I had dates with. I was going to warn you about him, but I haven't had a chance yet."

"Well, he got to me at lunch today," Brock informed her.

"Don't believe a word he says," Charlotte said, looking at him, apparently frustrated.

"I didn't," he said, looking down at her and pressing his body harder against hers. He could feel her breasts pressed against him. He suddenly didn't want to talk about Kale and his accusations.

"What did he say exactly?" She cocked one eyebrow up questioningly. He thought that was the cutest look he had ever seen.

"It's not important," he said, getting closer to her mouth and lowering his voice to a whisper. She wrapped her arms around his neck pulling herself a little higher to reach him.

"I assure you, I'm completely innocent," she whispered before his lips found hers. He caught her lower lip and sucked it gently. He worked his lips around hers, flicking his tongue teasingly. He cupped his hand to the back of her head while his other hand wrapped around her lower back and pressed her harder into him.

He felt her body go limp, and she let out a deep sigh. She moved her hand up his neck and popped the ponytail tie freeing his long hair. It was slightly damp with sweat, but she didn't seem to mind as she ran her fingers through his thick hair.

After a few minutes of what felt like pure bliss, he pulled away from her an inch. "I suppose we better head home, or our parents are going to come look for us."

She looked mesmerized, and her eyes were out of focus. "I, uh, yeah," was all she could manage to say.

"Are you going to be okay to drive?" He looked at her amused. He stepped back to give her more room to breathe.

"I'm okay," she said, shaking her head slightly and straightening. "You're quite good at that. I think I'm the one who needs to watch out for you. You're gonna put me under some spell and have complete control over me."

He laughed at this. "I promise. I won't make you do anything you don't want to." He smiled at her mischievously.

She stepped up to him and put her hands on his chest. "Why do I have a feeling I would enjoy whatever you wanted me to do?" It was her turn to smile mischievously.

He cleared his throat as a couple of things ran through his mind. *Oh no, too far*, he thought. "I'll call you tonight before bed. Is that okay?"

"I'll be waiting!" she said, giving him a quick hug then turned to her car. He was tempted to pull her back in for another long kiss. Then she turned to him again and stretched her arm out to him. "Oh, you might want this back." He reached out to her hand and took the rubber band she had pulled free from his hair.

He smiled and took it from her. "Yeah, Coach isn't too happy about my hair and said I need to get it cut if I want to play on his team."

"Awww... that's too bad. I was looking forward to playing with it some more." She gave him a slightly hurt look that he knew she was using to tease him.

"He gave me a deadline of when I have to get it cut, so I'll hang on to it until the very end for you." He winked at her.

She gave him a big smile and got into her car. He was sorry to see her go but looked forward to many more days after this. After all, it was only their first day together. There would be plenty of time for more and, hopefully, when he was a little less sweaty and in need of a shower.

❧

CHARLOTTE LAID in bed staring up at the ceiling. She kept replaying the kiss with Brock in the parking lot. The moment he pressed her against the car and touched her, her mind went to mush. She couldn't stop thinking about his lips. Her heart sped up again, and her palms began to sweat thinking about him. He had smelled of sweat with a faint whiff of cologne, and it had been intoxicating.

She closed her eyes and sighed dreamily again. It was a good thing he had her pressed against her car or she might have melted to the ground. She remembered feeling his hard body through his T-shirt and his hips pressed against hers. She loved coiling her fingers in his sweaty hair.

Charlotte was so excited and euphoric that likely she wouldn't get to sleep anytime soon. Their conversation over the phone hadn't been long but had been full of flirtatious remarks. She mentioned to her parents that she was seeing someone new, but they didn't ask much.

A thought suddenly occurred to her. What had Kale told Brock? Was it about her reputation around school? She had never had a steady boyfriend for longer than a couple of weeks. She had been out with a lot of guys, but nothing serious. Kale had been her last really serious attempt and it was because of his quick temper that she broke it off with him. It hurt her to break up with him like she did, but she also had enough sense to realize when to walk away from a potentially dangerous relationship.

Charlotte tried to count the guys she had had dates with in her first few years of dating. *Okay, so there have been a lot, and all of them a date or two.* Maybe she did have a reputation.

She hadn't thought about Nahele since yesterday. The marriage was set to take place at the end of the month. A flush of butterflies filled her stomach. Getting married meant—sex. Should she intrude on that private part of Nahele and Tetonka? If it was her past life, it was already her life to experience. But, if she was an outsider sent to make an impact in the life of Nahele, then was it her place to be there during such an intimate time?

109

Charlotte mulled this over in her mind. She tossed and turned and couldn't fall asleep. Finally, around midnight, she threw the covers back and went out onto the back porch. Scuffy was curled up in the corner, but when she slid the sliding-glass-door open he jumped up to greet her. She squatted to pet him. What was this connection they had? Why was he able to help her switch back and forth? What was she even doing? Why wouldn't someone tell her more?

She decided the only way to get the answers she needed was to keep going back. Maybe this time she would understand more of what was happening to her.

CHAPTER THIRTEEN

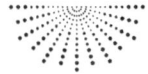

*C*harlotte woke to hear the morning prayers of the people. Niabi stirred the fire in the hut as she rolled over and sat up. "Good morning, little flower." Her mother smiled sweetly at her. She looked around the hut. Her grandmother moved around, and her sister rolled her mat.

"Do you want to go down to the stream with me, sister?" Hula asked. Charlotte had missed her sister. She didn't realize how much she had missed them.

"I will go with you, sister," Charlotte said and began rolling her mat and put it away. They walked silently to the stream. Charlotte was still barefoot; the grass felt wet and soft underneath her feet. It was cooler now, and the air felt more like autumn. The leaves were still green, but she knew they would soon turn yellow and red. The mourning doves softly cooed.

Their mother had asked them to gather some roots to bring back for breakfast, so after washing their faces and scraping their teeth with the reeds, they filled their baskets with the roots. When they turned to walk back, Charlotte hooked her arm into her sister's, and they walked pleasantly arm in arm back to the hut.

When they returned, their grandfather was back from saying the morning prayers and sat by the fire, smoking his pipe. Grandmother gathered bowls while their mother took the roots from them and put them in a kettle already boiling over the fire. Their aunt entered the hut with her smaller children who immediately clung to Grandmother's legs. Father and Uncle soon joined them, and with everyone present, they whispered their thanks to *Wah'Kon-Tah* and quietly ate their morning meal.

Only after everyone had finished eating did anyone speak. Her father spoke first, "Nahele, after you finish with the bean harvest this morning, I have permitted Tetonka to give you riding lessons on your horse."

Charlotte nodded her head to him and quietly said, "Thank you, Father."

Then her uncle said to her mother, "Soon, Tetonka's family will be presenting this family with gifts of food, and we need to make sure we have stored enough food to present back to them. Have we set this aside, sister?"

"Yes, I have stored it away carefully. I would like to have a fresh deer kill to add, and we will add some beans from the harvest today. We have stored plenty of corn for the marriage feast as well as in our winter stores. We were truly blessed with a bountiful harvest this year." Her mother sat with a straight back looking beautiful as ever. She glanced at Charlotte and gave her a wink and a tiny smile. Charlotte smiled back, tears coming to her eyes as she thought of not living in this hut any longer with them.

What if Tetonka's family wasn't pleasant to her? What if they didn't like her? She knew deep down that her worries were unwarranted, but she couldn't help having some doubts and concerns as the time came nearer.

CHARLOTTE HURRIED through her section of the bean harvest. She was anxious to see Tetonka. Her mother prepared a meal sack for her, and she bundled her mat. They would take the next few days away from the village. It was unusual for her parents to let her do this with Tetonka before their wedding had occurred, but she wasn't going to complain. If they approved of the idea, then she wasn't going to argue. Not every girl in the tribe got to learn how to ride a horse, of course, not every girl had a horse. She was blessed to have a healthy mare as a gift and the opportunity to learn to ride.

She hurried to the pasture where she was to meet Tetonka. As she came around one of the huts and saw the pasture area, she saw Kajika standing with Tetonka. They were talking and gesturing to the horses. Her heart sank. She didn't know why she didn't like Kajika or why she didn't trust him. He hadn't done anything to her specifically but being around him made her feel uncomfortable. If he was going to be with them during her riding lessons, then she understood why her family had allowed this adventure. Kajika was probably going along to keep them separated at night.

She walked a little slower toward the pasture now and lowered her eyes as she approached the two men.

"I'm glad you could come." Tetonka greeted her. She came to stand close to Tetonka and put a little more distance between Kajika and her. The two men smiled at her as if they had been talking about her.

"Good to see you, Nahele," Kajika said as he bowed his head slightly to her.

Charlotte tried to smile and swallow her reservations. If she was to be Tetonka's wife and Kajika was Tetonka's kola, she had to get accustomed to him being around. Warrior-brothers swore a blood oath to one another to always watch out for one another in times of war and hunting. It had been Kajika, after all, who had diverted the buffalo from goring Tetonka's leg at the last buffalo hunt.

She looked at Tetonka, "When do we start?"

"For the rest of the afternoon and evening, we are going to sit in the pasture and be like a horse among the horses," Tetonka said.

This sounded ridiculous to her. She understood that Nahele's people considered all animals as if they were their brothers and sisters, but she wasn't sure how acting like a horse in the pasture with the horse was a way to learn to ride.

As if reading the look on her face, Tetonka explained, "The horse must feel that you are one with him. He has to get to know you on the same level as a horse. A horse cannot understand as a man understands, so the man resides with the horse to understand him."

"Here, let us set our blankets at the edge of the pasture, and while we are becoming one with the horses, we will explain more," Kajika said as he held out his hand for her to give him her bundle. She first looked at Tetonka to get his approval; he nodded, so she handed Kajika her bundle and followed him to the area he intended.

They laid their blankets out side by side and hung their food bundles on nearby trees slightly away from the horses. She imagined that this was to keep the horses from sniffing out their food and taking some for themselves. The two large men sat on each side of her cross-legged, facing the horses, casually grazing.

"Your horse must get used to your scent and recognize you so that when you come near, it will trust you and bond with you," Tetonka began to explain.

"We will also be watching your horse to see how she interacts with the herd." Kajika took over, "Is she a leader or a follower? Does she nip at the other horses or is she patient with them? By observing your horse, you can begin to understand your horse's temperament, and if she will be a gentle horse to train or a difficult horse that will require more patience."

Charlotte began to understand the logic of this and settled in to watch her horse and observe how she interacted with the others. After a short while, some of the other horses began to wander closer to them. They grazed and worked their way closer. She could see that the horses' eyes were watching them, and their ears would turn toward them, even though, their heads didn't move.

The three of them sat quietly watching for quite some time, and her legs began to cramp in the sitting position. She suddenly stretched her legs out, and some of the horses closer to them jumped causing the others to spook as well and run to the other side of the pasture.

Tetonka laughed, "It is important not to make sudden moves. They can spook easily if they are not used to you." He leaned toward her,

"Always approach them gently and make soft noises to make them feel at ease. Here, I will show you." He got up and held his hand down to her to help her up. They walked toward her horse quietly. Tetonka made sounds as she kept one eye on him and one eye on her horse. She mimicked his actions while also watching her horse's reaction.

Her horse lifted her head and swiveled her eyes and ears in their direction. Tetonka laid a hand gently on her side while he comforted her. He gestured for Charlotte to come alongside her horse and around to her head. "Here, rub the nose and let her smell you."

She did as she was told. The horse nudged her gently. This wasn't their first meeting, but it was a longer greeting than the last time she had seen her horse.

"Have you thought of a name for her?" Kajika asked. She hadn't heard him walking behind them, and he startled her.

"The color of her mane and tail remind me of the silk in the corn stalk, so I will call her Cornsilk." Both Tetonka and Kajika nodded their heads in approval.

"It is a good name," Tetonka said.

"Did you spend a lot of time with your horse?" she asked, looking at Tetonka.

"Yes, before we are to become scouts, we are sent out into the woods alone with our horse. When a scout is out for many sleeps away from the village, it is important to make a strong bond between horse and scout," Tetonka answered, looking at her but remembering his experience fondly.

"After spending many days and nights alone with your horse, the two can communicate from mind to mind with one another and make moves without a sound," Kajika added. "This also becomes important during buffalo hunt when horse and rider have to move quickly and make quick decisions."

She didn't plan on riding her horse in a buffalo hunt. She wanted to be able to ride her horse and go with Tetonka on some of his trips. She also felt that one never knew whether an emergency might call for a woman to leave the village when the men were away. That is why some women were trained to ride, shoot a bow and arrow, or other necessary defenses when they were left alone without the men in the village.

"Let's return to our blankets and light a fire. We will tie our horses close by, so they will sleep close to us tonight." Tetonka led her back to the blankets while Kajika gathered the reins of their horses.

TETONKA LIT the fire while Charlotte took a small kettle to fill with water. She took time to wash and relieve herself. When she turned to walk back to the blankets, Kajika was standing not too far behind her watching her with a strange look on his face. She stood still for a second wondering how long he had been standing there. She didn't look down from his stare this time and gave him a look that meant she wasn't going to be intimidated by him. He backed off then, and she walked around him.

She made a mental note to stay close to Tetonka and not get caught alone with Kajika again. She handed Tetonka the kettle and sat down as she watched him prepare the meal.

Kajika returned and sat across the fire from her. She was relieved that he didn't sit close to her. She didn't want to say anything to Tetonka. There wasn't anything to tell him except her suspicions. It could be that she imagined things, and it would change once she and Tetonka were rightfully married.

They ate silently chewing their food like the horses. Afterward, Kajika said that they needed to take the horses down to the water. She made sure Tetonka was going as well before she made a move to follow.

"The rider needs to become the *itancan,* or leader, of his horse much as there is a leader in every herd. Once the horse accepts the role of *waunca,* or imitator, then the horse will look to his itancan for guidance and direction," Kajika explained as he handed Cornsilk's reins to her. Each of them walked in front of their respective horse, showing the horse who their leader was.

Once at the stream, Tetonka said, "The itancan is responsible for checking for danger at the water before he takes a drink. Once he takes a drink, the rest of the herd will follow." She watched as Tetonka knelt, cupped his hand full of water and took a sip. Then he allowed his horse to take a drink. When he finished, he stepped back to let her practice. She held her horse's reins behind her and drank as Tetonka had done. Then she allowed Cornsilk to drink. Cornsilk seemed to take her lead with ease. Charlotte had observed that she was a gentle and patient horse. Tetonka had most likely seen this in her horse before getting it for her as a gift. A high-spirited horse would have been too risky for her to ride as an inexperienced rider.

When this lesson was complete, they walked back to the small camp they had made at the edge of the pasture.

"If you pay attention to your horse's reactions and noises, they will alert you to the slightest danger or change in your surroundings," Tetonka said, taking a seat next to her on his blanket. She had recognized this before. Horses were attuned to the noises in the forest, and if anything sounded out of the ordinary, they would either stomp their hooves or snort loudly. "Many scouts' lives have been saved because of an early warning by their horses," he said.

Charlotte took all this in with quiet patience and nodded her head in understanding now and then. She was a fast learner, but she had a feeling tomorrow would be different and more difficult. As the night darkened, they settled on their blankets. They were arranged in a semi-circle around the fire. Tetonka was at her head while Kajika was at her feet. She didn't think Kajika would do anything to her with Tetonka present.

"It is a tradition for hunters to tell stories at night around the campfire. There is a story among the old hunters," Tetonka began. "A long time ago, a hunter went out to kill a deer. He saw a deer in the brush but didn't have a good shot. Patiently, he followed the deer until it was more visible. He quietly aimed his bow and arrow and released it. The arrow missed the deer, but it hit a tree, turning the arrow and hitting the deer in the back. The hunter hadn't realized he had hit the deer until he tracked it down and found it dead in the woods."

"I have a better story than that," Kajika retorted. "One time, a hunter shot a deer, and the arrow went clean through the deer shooting another one beyond it. So, he killed two deer with one arrow."

"Listen to this story," Tetonka continued, attempting to outdo Kajika. "When I was a young boy, and I was not yet old enough to hunt, I was in charge of taking care of the horses by taking them to the water. My uncle had shot three deer on his hunt, but he was not on his horse and needed it to bring back the deer. He sent me to fetch his horse. I was running alongside an embankment when I saw ahead five deer running in my direction. I quickly hid down in the embankment waiting for them to pass so that I could jump out and scare them. As they came by, I jumped and yelled like a bear. Instead of jumping and running away, all five of them fell down dead. So that day, we brought home eight deer."

"That is not true," she said, straining not to laugh. "You need to be careful. The snakes have not yet gone underground, and they will jump out and bite you for telling an untruth."

"It is true. I would not tell an untruth while the snakes are still out." Tetonka said to her, giving her his most honest look.

She smiled at him, reserving her judgment, but looked at him with admiration. She felt she could look at him always and listen to his stories, true or not. She was lost in thought, looking at him when Kajika startled her by speaking again.

"I have another story. This one is serious. Have you heard of the demon animals?" he asked, looking at her.

She shook her head, and he continued with his story. "Legend tells that there is a hill that stands alone on a level plain with no other hills around it. It was known that demon animals lived there because of the bones of all the animals that they devoured were scattered about the entrance to their cave that was hidden under this hill. No man or animal had ever beaten them, and any man or animal that they pursued was sure to be caught and killed. The only thing the demon animals feared was water."

There was complete silence around the fire as Kajika told his story, and Tetonka and Charlotte sat listening intently. "Then one day two young hunters were tracking deer when they came upon this hill. They immediately recognized the hill as the one where the demon animals lived. So, they quietly began to retrace their steps, hoping they wouldn't be discovered. But, it was too late. They were discovered, and the demon animals began to chase them. The two hunters knew that if they could get to the water, they would be safe. As they plunged into the water, the demon animals reached out to catch them and missed. The demon animals let out a terrible roar at having missed the two hunters and vowed that if anyone came near their hill again, they would never get away and would surely be eaten. Now many years have passed, and the location of this hill has been lost, but now and then there are stories that hunters went out to hunt and never returned. It is believed that the demon animals caught these hunters. Sometimes, you can even hear their cries in the middle of the night when they hunt, for they do not come out during the day. That is why many hunters will only camp at night near water."

Having finished this story, Kajika looked at her proud of himself. She didn't know what to think of this story and was a little frightened that it might be true. She looked at Tetonka to see if he believed it, and he only gave her a shrug as if to say he didn't know if it was or not.

For a while, the three of them sat quietly around the fire deep in thought, listening to the sounds of the forest. She had to admit the story disturbed her a little bit, and she felt a little jumpy whenever a screech owl called somewhere deep in the forest. She rolled onto her back and stared up at the stars in the night sky. There were so many more to see without the invention of electricity in this time. The sight was both beautiful and frightening.

Eventually, she felt her eyelids getting heavy, so she snuggled under her bearskin. Tetonka and Kajika did the same. Tetonka looked at her questioningly with his eyes. Apparently, he understood that Kajika's story had spooked her, and he looked at her concerned. She gave him a reassuring smile and closed her eyes. She didn't think she would be able to sleep, seeing images in her mind of demon animals watching them from the shadows.

CHAPTER FOURTEEN

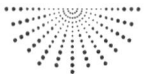

*C*harlotte felt she had just closed her eyes for a second when she heard the mourning doves cooing. She heard someone stirring around and opened her eyes to see Tetonka putting more wood on the fire to cook the morning meal.

When he saw her awake, he smiled and said, "Good morning. Did you sleep well?" He kept his voice low, even though she noticed that Kajika was not on his blanket. She assumed he was at the stream, getting water in the kettle.

"After hearing Kajika's story last night, I did not think I would be able to sleep, but I suppose I was so tired from the day's activities that I finally slept," she said, smiling back at him.

They looked at one another intently and didn't hear Kajika return until he dropped the kettle of water noisily next to the fire making her jump. She looked at him, and he smirked down at her as if he was happy to have startled her.

"I hope you got lots of rest. We will have a grueling day of riding today," Kajika said as he sat down. Tetonka prepared the meal and handed some to each of them. They sat silently as they ate not looking at anyone or anything in particular. She was excited to get to her riding lessons today, but she had an uneasy feeling in her stomach.

She didn't know why she felt this way, but she didn't trust Kajika. He made her uncomfortable whenever he looked at her, and she felt that there was something sinister in his eyes. So much of her communication with Tetonka was through looks and body language that she thought she was especially attuned to reading other people's body language. She could tell a lot about a person in a few short minutes of watching someone and looking in their eyes. Her instincts told her that Kajika wasn't all what he seemed to be, and this worried her greatly.

The first lesson of the day still didn't include getting on the horse. Charlotte was beginning to wonder if she would ever actually ride Cornsilk.

"The next lesson we will work on involves touching your horse," Tetonka instructed her. "Run your hands all over your horse gently as if brushing her. This is so that she gets used to you, learns to trust you, and will be willing to let you ride her." Tetonka took hold of her hands and guided her hands along her horse. They worked down the horse's neck, around her shoulders, down her front legs, then back up to her chest, along her sides, over her hips, and down her back legs. The way Tetonka helped her sent chills down her spine and after a moment, she forgot they were paying attention to the horse. She felt Tetonka's breath on her neck, and when she turned her head to look at him, her face was inches from his. They paused. Her breath caught in her throat; her heart pounded against her chest. She lowered her eyes to his lips and looked at his mouth.

Kajika coughed behind them and they jerked out of their trance. "I think that is enough for now. Let's move on to lesson three," he said.

Tetonka backed away from her. She took in a deep breath unaware of when she had stopped breathing. She kept looking at Tetonka dreamily. Kajika grabbed her by the shoulders and roughly turned her toward her horse.

"Every good rider and horse learn to communicate with one another silently without making sounds from your mouth or gestures with your hands," he said as he placed the reins in her hands. "Look at your horse, and with your mind, tell her to walk toward you."

She looked at him confused. Kajika stood back and folded his arms across his chest, and Tetonka stood next to him looking a little more patient and encouraging. If it weren't for Tetonka, she would have given up on this idea of riding her horse and gone home a long time ago. Kajika seemed to be getting more and more agitated as each lesson progressed. For a horseman, he wasn't very gentle or patient.

She let out a huff and turned toward her horse. She let go of the reins and stood about ten feet directly in front of Cornsilk and thought with her mind, *walk*. After a moment's pause, Cornsilk took one step. She raised her eyebrows in surprise at this, but then Cornsilk stopped. She softened her face and thought, *go on, walk*. Cornsilk then took another step. This time, she kept her face encouraging, and Cornsilk continued to walk toward her until she reached out and rewarded her with a pat on her nose.

"Good," Kajika said. "Now, keep working at it with different thoughts such as stop and backup." With this, he turned to leave her to work. Tetonka hung back for a second, gave her a reassuring smile, then he too left to let her practice.

It didn't take long for her to figure out that it wasn't that Cornsilk was reading her mind. The horse picked up on her eye movements and tiny physical indications for what she wanted her to do. She had a sudden new appreciation for the intelligence of these magnificent creatures. She was lost in her "communication" with Cornsilk when Tetonka came back to tell her it was time to take a break. She let Cornsilk graze as she followed him back to the blankets for mid-day prayers and meal.

"You are doing well," Tetonka said as he held her hand and looked down at her.

"It pleases me that you say so and are here helping me. I'm afraid I would not have stayed if Kajika was my only teacher," she confided in him.

"I know Kajika can be a bit hard at times, but he is a good rider and knows how to handle his horse," he said.

She merely nodded her head and looked down as they sat down to pray and eat.

After they had rested for a little while, Tetonka helped her up and said, "Now you need to learn how to get on your horse." This excited her for that meant she was closer to riding.

"Put your left hand on your horse's withers here, but don't pull or use force. It is only to maintain balance," Tetonka said as he helped her get into position. She was glad that Tetonka was instructing her on this part. "Now plant your left foot and swing your right leg."

When she tried to do so, they realized her long skirt hindered her. Before they realized what was happening, Kajika took out his knife and knelt in front of her. He moved her feet apart then plunged his knife into her skirt in between her thighs and ripped downward. She let out a startled scream, but she was prevented from moving by Kajika's firm grip on her waist. Then he quickly turned her around, shifted her feet apart again, and did the same thing to the back. He stood up from her then and slid the knife back in its sheath.

She turned around and surveyed her skirt. It was ruined. She looked at Tetonka to see his reaction. At first, he had a look of shock and concern, but then, after a second, he shrugged and said, "Now do it."

She swung her right leg tentatively. Well, it gave her the motion she needed. Maybe later she could sew the inseams and make long riding pants.

Tetonka went back to instructing her. "Practice swinging your right leg without putting it on the horse. You want to have enough swing that it brings your left foot off the ground."

She swung her leg a few times, each time kicking her leg higher and higher. On about the fourth swing, she forgot to keep a hold of her horse for balance, and her left foot came off the ground sending her flying backward and landing hard on her back. She laid there stunned and out of breath for a moment. Tetonka rushed to her side concerned. Kajika burst into laughing so hard that he was doubled over at the waist.

When she could breathe again and got over the shock, she giggled. Seeing that she was all right, Tetonka laughed as well. They laughed until their sides hurt. Tetonka helped her up and dusted her backside off.

When he could stop laughing, he finally said, "Let's do it again. This time keep a hold of your horse and hook your ankle onto Cornsilk's back."

She did as she was told and on the third swing, she swung high enough to hook her foot over her horse's back. But, Tetonka hadn't told her what to do after that, and she hung there stuck. Again, the men laughed, watching her struggle with what to do. Tetonka could have helped her at this point, but he was too busy laughing, and now she was getting a little annoyed. To make matters worse, Cornsilk walked forward as she hopped on tip-toe with one leg hanging on her back. Tetonka didn't let her go far, however, and helped her out of her awkward situation.

She glared at him, her face flushed with heat. When he looked down sheepishly as if to say he was sorry, she allowed herself to laugh as well. When things calmed down once again, Tetonka told her how to hook her arm once her foot was up and pull herself onto her horse.

She tried once more, this time she wrapped her arm around Cornsilk's neck. She struggled to get upright, but she finally did it. She sat there looking proudly at Tetonka and Kajika. They nodded their heads approvingly.

"Now that you are up there, you need to find the spot that feels comfortable. You must squeeze your knees behind the horse's shoulders to maintain your balance." Tetonka helped her move into the correct position. "Do not kick your horse with your heels or hit her in any way. If you are gentle, your horse will understand your subtle movements and understand what you want her to do."

She sat high on her horse. She felt she was too far up and almost on her neck, but as she shifted her hips forward, Cornsilk walked forward. Tetonka walked alongside her, guiding the horse and her.

"Now to stop, lean back a little." When she did so, Cornsilk stopped. "She has already been trained with a rider, so she is a good horse for a beginner," he said.

"When you want to go faster, you can click your tongue, and when you need her to slow down or stop, pull back gently on the reins. Never pull too hard and hurt her neck. She will learn to trust you and do whatever you ask if you are careful with her."

She nodded her head and practiced doing all the things he said. Tetonka let her have a few practice rides up and down the pasture.

"Now, it's time to take a little ride with the horses," he said. With this, he swung onto his horse. Now that she understood how hard riding could be, she was amazed at how easy he made it look. Of course, his long legs and stronger body was a huge advantage over her. She didn't notice when Kajika got on his horse, but he was there right alongside them.

"Follow me and do not be in a hurry." Tetonka led the trio, with her in the middle and Kajika behind.

They went out of the pasture onto a small buffalo trail that the men used to get to some of their hunting camps. They kept it at a steady pace. She was beginning to get a feel for how her horse moved and matched her movements until she felt like they were one complete animal instead of two. Soon, however, her legs began to cramp, and the lack of a saddle began to chaff her inner thighs.

They came out of the woods into a little clearing. They were at the top of a small hill with a creek running alongside the left and a pond several hundred feet off to the right. As her horse took a step downward, something happened to spook her, and Cornsilk took off running to the right off the path. Charlotte didn't know what to do. She wrapped her arms around her horse's neck struggling to stay on. The ground was uneven, and she was afraid that her horse would step in a rabbit hole and go down. If that happened, her horse would inevitably break a leg and possibly crush her underneath. They were heading straight for the pond, and Cornsilk didn't show any signs of slowing down. She completely forgot everything Tetonka had told her and hung on for dear life. She squeezed her eyes shut and braced herself for a cold plunge into the water, but her horse slowed to a stop. She opened her eyes to see that Tetonka had run up beside them and grabbed Cornsilk's reins to stop her. Once she could pull herself to a sitting position again, she let out a big sigh of relief.

"I thought I was going for a swim," she said, looking gratefully at her rescuer.

"What happened to cause your horse to run?" he asked.

"I'm not sure. There was a sudden noise from behind, and the next thing I knew, we were racing down the hill toward the pond."

Tetonka's expression turned to anger as he looked back up the hill toward Kajika. Kajika hadn't moved from on top of the hill. He sat resolutely on top of his horse looking down at them. She saw the way Tetonka looked at him and realized that it must have been Kajika who spooked her horse.

Tetonka led her horse back up the hill. When they got back to the trail, he said, "Maybe that is enough for today. Let's walk back now. Kajika, you lead this time." He gestured to Kajika as he gave him a stern look.

Kajika didn't seem to notice, and turned his horse around, and led them back to the pasture. She eased back into the slow swing of her horse's gate and thought about the incident. Had Kajika intended to harm her? Maybe he wanted to give her a quick lesson on how to handle a runaway horse. She knew it happened occasionally and a rider needed to know how to handle a horse that got spooked, but she felt that it was a little devious to surprise her like that, especially since she was still so new to riding. Her suspicions of him were growing more profound, and she felt her instincts were screaming at her to pay attention.

She was relieved when they arrived back at the pasture. Tetonka quickly swung off his horse and came to her side. "Next time, we will have a lesson on how to get off your horse, but for now, I will help you down."

She was grateful for this and let him grab her by her hips and lift her down off the horse. When her feet touched the ground, however, he didn't let go of her but held her to him for a few seconds.

"Are you sure you are all right?" he asked into her hair.

"Yes, I'm fine. I was a little scared at first, but I'm okay now. Are you?" she asked, realizing his body was a little more tense than usual. She looked at him to see his jaw muscles clenching. He turned to look in the direction Kajika had gone to release his horse. His eyes squinted, and his mouth pressed firmly. He was unhappy with Kajika at the moment. Then he looked down at her again, "Our lessons are finished for now. Go gather your blanket, and I will walk you back to your hut."

She let him take the horses to graze as she walked to her blanket to roll it up. She could hear Tetonka saying something to Kajika, but it was too low to make out his words. She could hear the tone and the gruffness, however. Kajika had finally stepped over the line, and she was relieved to hear Tetonka standing up to him. She would be glad to get back to her hut and rest, away from Kajika for a while.

❧

CHARLOTTE WAS SORE ALL OVER. When she sat down, she moved extremely slow.

Her father looked at her and smiled. "How were your riding lessons?"

"They were well," she said. In truth, she felt she had barely begun when Tetonka told her to head home. But, now that she knew the basics, she could slip over to the pasture and work with Cornsilk whenever she finished her other duties. Besides, she was glad to have some distance from Kajika. She wondered what Tetonka had said to him.

"We shot two deer on our hunt yesterday," her father told her. "We will have plenty of food for the wedding feasts and lots of gifts for the family members."

"Speaking of deer, we have some hides to work on and make you a new skirt," her mother said, nodding her head at her torn one.

"It is not ruined. I plan to sew the inseams to make some riding pants for myself," she informed her mother.

Niabi raised her eyebrows, "Riding pants? I have never heard of such a thing. Where did you get that idea?"

Charlotte swallowed quickly and worried she might have slipped in revealing something unknown to her people. She hoped they wouldn't ask any further questions.

The family looked at one another and shrugged their shoulders. "I would like to see these riding pants when you are finished. I might want some for myself," her grandfather put in.

"Grandfather, you do not need such things. You can wear your regular buckskins like other men. Riding pants would be for women who want to ride a horse." She laughed a little at her grandfather's innocence.

"Hmm," her grandfather responded.

"If they turn out well, maybe it is something we can add to our trade items with the white man. I hear their women want to learn to ride as well," added her grandmother.

She was pleased that they had accepted her idea and hadn't asked any more questions. Now, all she wanted was to lie down and go to sleep. But first, she desperately needed a bath. "Sister, will you go with me to the water to wash?" she asked Hula.

Hula nodded and came to help her stand when she saw that she was struggling. "Maybe we can go by the medicine woman's hut first and see if she has an ointment to rub on your sore body."

She smiled at her sister for being so thoughtful and welcomed the chance to see the medicine woman again.

They walked side by side to the hut when Hula spoke, "How was your experience with staying out under the stars with Tetonka?"

"Kajika was there as well, so it was not only the two of us," Charlotte informed her.

Hula must have seen the look on her face because then she asked, "But, what happened?"

She looked sideways at her sister and sighed. She didn't want to say bad things about people, and she could be imagining things with Kajika. On the other hand, she needed to confide in someone, and Tetonka probably wasn't the best one for that.

"I have a strange feeling whenever I am around Kajika," she said.

"Oh?" Hula responded. When she didn't ask any further, she decided to say more.

"I think he did something to spook my horse, and it took off out of control before I had enough experience to know how to handle it." This got Hula's attention, and she turned to look at her. "Of course, Tetonka came to my rescue and stopped the horse before we took a plunge in the pond."

"Thank *Wah'Kon-Tah* that he did. Were you frightened?" Hula asked.

"I was terrified. Tetonka did not look happy with Kajika afterward. That is why he sent me home, and we will work on more at another time," she added.

"I see," Hula said looking down as they continued to walk. "Maybe it was an accident, and you have nothing more to worry about."

"I hope that it was. I would not like to see trouble between me and Tetonka's kola. I know it would hurt him if we did not get along."

They came to the medicine woman's hut and entered quietly. She was mixing something in a bowl when they entered. They waited patiently for her to address them.

"What brings you two to see me?" she asked, somewhat more pleasant than they were used to from her.

They looked at each other puzzled. Then Hula spoke, "My sister is sore from learning to ride her horse, and we were wondering if you had an ointment to soothe her."

The medicine woman smiled and continued to stir the contents of the bowl, "What do you think I am mixing for you right now?"

They looked at one another with wide eyes and then looked back at the medicine woman. She put the ointment in a swatch of animal skin and wrapped it. "Put this on where you hurt after you wash in the water. It will help you relax and sleep better tonight."

"Thank you," she said taking the package and bowing to her.

"You can call me, *Onaiwah*," she said, looking directly at Charlotte, who looked at the medicine woman bewildered for a moment while she stared back at her patiently. "That is all," she finally said, dismissing them. They had no choice but to exit the hut and walk to the water.

"I wonder how she knew," Hula whispered to her.

"She is a medicine woman for a reason. I suppose the spirits talk to her and tell her the things she must do before it happens," she suggested.

"That may be true. It must be nice knowing what is about to happen," Hula said.

"I don't know. For some things, I would not want to know was about to happen. Like someone's death, for instance," she added.

"That is true as well. But I would not mind knowing who I am to marry and how many children I am to have someday," Hula said.

"It will all happen at the right time and when *Wah'Kon-Tah* thinks you are ready." Charlotte put her arm around her sister as they continued to walk to the water.

Charlotte knew all too well about some things that were going to happen, but she still didn't know anything specific about these people. One thing was for sure, Onaiwah had to know what she was. How could she not know if she knew such trivial things as preparing her ointment ahead of time? She resolved to see Onaiwah the next chance she got.

She washed in the water and felt much better afterward. Hula helped her rub the ointment over her legs and arms. She was surprised at the places that were sore considering how little she had been on the horse. She couldn't imagine how she might have felt if they had spent a full day riding.

As they walked back to the hut, Charlotte spotted Barkley at the edge of the forest. "You go on ahead," she told her sister. "I will meet you back at the hut."

"Are you sure?" Hula asked looking at her worried.

"I will be fine. I will be right behind you." She gave her sister a quick kiss on the cheek and watched her walk away to make sure she didn't see where she was going, and then Charlotte turned to the spot where she saw Barkley.

CHAPTER FIFTEEN

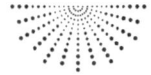

*C*harlotte woke up in bed. Her head felt stuffed full of cotton. It pounded at her temples like a gong of a huge grandfather clock. She slowly turned her head to see the time. She had to squint her eyes to focus and read 7:00 p.m. She threw back the covers and moved to sit up slowly. Her whole body ached, and her stomach lurched a little when she sat up. She sat on the side of the bed, attempting to move her thick tongue around in her mouth to unlock it from the sticky sour stuff that coated it. She needed a drink and some aspirin.

She gingerly walked to the kitchen and found her mother sitting at the kitchen table.

"You're up! How do you feel?" she asked.

"Like I've been mummified," she croaked out. She sounded awful. She must have been sick these past couple of days. That was probably a good thing, considering it was her shadow-self that had been here, and Brock might have noticed her acting strangely.

"How long have I been out?" she asked her mother.

"You've been asleep most of the time since you woke up sick Tuesday morning," she replied getting up to put a hand on her forehead. "Your fever is down. I'll make you some tea. Do you feel like eating?"

"I'll try the tea first and see how that goes. I could use some aspirin though." She sat down at the kitchen table and rested her head in her hands. Maybe she should have stayed as Nahele a day or two longer until this body had recovered fully. Then she thought to ask, "What day is it?"

Her mother didn't seem to think it was out of the ordinary since she had been sleeping so much. "It's Wednesday night. Your dad and brothers should be getting back from church soon."

Okay, so she still had time to get better before the football game Friday and to be fully present to emcee the pageant on Saturday. "Has anyone called for me?"

"Lilly came by yesterday to drop off your books and missed assignments, and I think that new boy called, but you were too sick to talk. Who is this new guy?" her mother asked as she set the tea down in front of her then sat beside her.

"His name is Brock. He moved here from Oklahoma last month." She took a tentative sip. It felt warm and wonderful going down her throat. "He asked me out last Sunday, and we only got to be together Monday after practice before I got sick."

"I hope he isn't sick, too." Her mother connected the dots quickly.

She hoped he wasn't either. What a horrible way to begin a dating relationship. It seemed to be her luck as usual.

The phone rang, and her mother answered it.

"It's for you," she said, handing her the cordless phone.

"Hello?" she said in an uncharacteristically deep voice.

"Charlotte? Is that you?" Brock asked.

"It's me. Unless a demon has possessed my body." Charlotte tried to clear her throat and ended in a coughing fit.

"Oh, you sound horrible."

"Gee, thanks. It's a good thing you can't see me then because I'm sure you would run away screaming."

Brock laughed. "I've been worried about you since yesterday when you didn't come to school, and then when I called last night, your mom said you were too sick to come to the phone."

"I'm sorry to do this to you right when you ask me out. How are *you* feeling?"

"Now that you mention it. My head has been hurting all day, and I'm sore all over. I thought it was from basketball practice."

"Uh-oh. You better get your mom to take your temperature."

"Yeah, I guess you're right. I'll do that and call you back to tell you what she says. Are you feeling any better?"

"Well, I got out of bed for the first time in two days. I'm not certain yet either. Maybe I can give you a better report when you call me back."

"Sounds fair. I'll call you back in a few minutes."

"Okay."

"Oh, and Charlotte?"

"Yeah?"

"I missed you."

"Aww, thanks." She couldn't help but break into a big smile.

"Okay.... talk to you in a minute."

"Okay."

They hung up. Her mother looked at her ready for a full report about the other end of the conversation she heard.

"He said he's had a headache too, and now he's going to have his mom check his temperature. He's gonna call me back to let me know."

"It must be flu season already," her mother said looking worried. That probably meant the whole family was about to get sick. Better now than closer to the holidays. They had spent several Christmas's in the past with the entire family too ill to enjoy opening presents.

A few minutes later, Brock called back to say he did have a fever, and it looked like he wouldn't be at school tomorrow either. She told him she would likely be out another day as well.

"You haven't given me your phone number, so I can call to check on you," she said.

"Oh well, in that case, you got a pen? It's 9-5889. Got it?"

"Got it."

"Sorry to hang up on you so soon, but I need to go lie down." Brock suddenly sounded more tired.

She told him she would call him tomorrow to check on him, and they hung up. She hoped they got through this and still wanted to see each other in the end.

Then the phone rang again. This time it was Lilly.

"I'm glad to hear your voice, even though you sound like you smoke a pack a day." Lilly chided.

"Mother said you brought my schoolwork over. Thanks."

"No problem. You seemed out of it."

"To tell you the truth, I haven't been myself the last couple of days, if you know what I mean." Her mother had left the kitchen, but she still didn't want to say anything to raise any suspicion.

"Oooooh," Lilly replied.

"Yeah, so at least I've spent the past two days not knowing I was sick." Charlotte couldn't tell her all that she had been experiencing over the phone.

"What are we gonna do with Brock when you switch?" Lilly asked, realizing how awkward it would be.

"Good question. We probably need to come up with a game plan to prepare for the next time."

"Do you know when that'll be?"

"I never know when I'm going to switch until I do. But there doesn't seem to be anything pressing I need to do over there until a few more weeks. By then, maybe we'll have figured out a way to tell Brock."

"Do you think that's a good idea?"

"I don't know. If we continue to date, I don't see how I can avoid it. Besides, he's part Osage. Of all people, he might understand the most."

"Maybe. I would still take it slow, though, and don't rush into telling him yet. See how this relationship pans out first."

"You seem to know me so well."

"Well, I've seen several guys come and go. You never stay with anyone longer than a couple of weeks."

"Why am I the last person to suddenly realize this is my m.o.?"

"Really? You didn't know that?"

"Not until recently. I had an epiphany, you might say."

"No kidding? Well, it's true. But you seem to be more into Brock than I've seen you with anyone else in a long time."

"That's good to hear. I do like him. I think he might be getting sick, too. I have a curse on me or something."

"You don't have a curse. You'll get through this, and then we can concentrate on your other agenda."

"Thanks, Lilly. At least I have a great friend like you. I don't know what I'd do without you."

"Glad to know I'm appreciated. Get better soon, so you don't leave me to cheer at the football game without you."

"Got it. Lots of orange juice and sleep."

Saturday, Charlotte called to check on Brock. "How are you feeling?" She hadn't seen him for almost a week and wished she could visit him at his house, but then it was probably too soon to make that move.

"I'm better. Dr. Mom here says I should be in the clear by tomorrow."

"That's great news. I can't wait to see you." She smiled into the phone.

"I heard I missed quite a game last night."

"I'll say. It was like watching warriors in a battle. Guys left the field all bloody and bruised. It's a wonder no one was sent to the hospital."

"Sounds like any normal Friday night football game."

"Well, this one was ten times worse. The Newport police had to be called to break up the fight in the end."

"Yikes, that is bad."

"It was also freezing. We didn't do as much cheering as usual and stayed huddled on the sidelines."

"That's probably why they lost then. You didn't give 'em enough pep juice."

If Brock had been sitting next to her, she would've punched him playfully in the shoulder. Instead, she had to settle for "Hmpf."

"I hate it that I can't be there tonight," he apologized, changing the subject.

"I think you would be bored after a while anyway."

"Me, bored? Watching a bunch of pretty girls parade across the stage with the prettiest one of all at the mic for me to watch the whole time? I don't think so."

She blushed a little. "Another guy, Tanner, is helping me emcee. You probably know him. He plays basketball. You two are about the same height."

"Oh, yeah! He and I have a bet for the basketball season to see who will get the most dunks."

"Well, that will be fun to watch."

"That is if we get much playing time. Neither one of us is a starter, so it depends on how much coach puts us on the court."

"I think you will. Like I said before. You've got to show Coach Foster what you can do, and he will put you out there."

"I hope so. But he seems to favor his starters a lot and gives them the most attention during practice."

"You need to *wow* him when you do get a chance to play."

"First, I need to get my health and strength back. Our first game is next week."

"Then maybe I should let you go and get some more rest. I need to get ready for tonight anyway."

"Okay. I'll call you tomorrow afternoon."

"Can't wait!"

Charlotte was glad her mother and she had gone dress shopping several weeks ago. So much had been going on lately and then with her being sick, it would have been a crisis if she had to find a dress last minute. The dress she wore as the returning Miss Harvest Queen 1987 was her favorite color, a cobalt blue. It was made of satin taffeta with the puffiest sleeves she had ever worn. It had a low neckline and fit perfectly to her waist and hips coming to a point right at her knees. Looking at herself in the mirror, she thought she looked like a blue petunia. She decided to wear her hair in a bun topped with her crown. Her only jewelry was a pair of dangling rhinestone earrings. She looked simple, yet elegant. Perfect for a returning queen and not over the top that would overshadow this year's contestants.

Once the pageant was underway, Tanner and she took turns announcing the contestants. It was her turn to announce the contestant when Susan walked on the stage. Charlotte noticed that she was so nervous she could hardly make her mouth smile. Her lips quivered going from a smile to frown. That happened to inexperienced girls sometimes. She felt almost sorry for her.

Susan left the stage, and Tanner began announcing the next contestant. "Contestant number nine is Miss Kensey Harris, daughter of Ronnie and Mitzi Harris. She is a sophomore this year and very active in school..."

Charlotte's attention began to drift. Her mind drifted to her last encounter at the Osage village. *The medicine woman knew what I needed before Hula and I came to see her. She told me to call her, Onaiwah.*

"Kensey is a cheerleader and plays softball in the Spring..."

What's up with Kajika? Why does he seem so hostile to me? Is he hostile or is he jealous?

"She is in National Honor Society, Who's Who Among American Sophomores, Student Council representative..."

I wish I could be with Tetonka right now. He makes me feel safe. But what about Brock? I like Brock, too.

"Please give one last applause for Kensey Harris."

It was Charlotte's turn to announce the next contestant, but she was staring off into space. Gradually, everyone turned their attention to her. The girl on the stage stood in place, wavering nervously, waiting to be announced. Tanner nudged her to get her attention back to the pageant. She blinked and realized everyone was waiting for her.

She cleared her throat and began reading off the card for the next contestant, "Contestant number ten is Miss Bailey Page..."

After the pageant was over, Charlotte posed for several pictures with all the winners and some of her friends who had participated. She plastered a smile on her face trying to hide her embarrassment inside. Finally, when it seemed all the flashing cameras had ceased, she went backstage. Lilly was waiting for her in the wings.

"Oh my gosh, I thought you had switched out in the middle of the pageant. I was about to freak!" Lilly said in a harsh whisper. She grabbed her by the arm and pulled her to a quiet corner. "Are you okay?"

"Yeah, I'm fine. I didn't go anywhere. My mind drifted off, and I wasn't paying attention to my next turn." She had been standing for hours. "Can you get me some punch? I need to sit down."

"Oh, sure! Be right back." Lilly scurried off to the drinks and refreshments set out for the people working backstage.

When she got back, she handed her a cup of punch and sat beside her. "Are you sure you're okay?"

"Yeah, I'm fine. I started thinking about other things and spaced out." She flitted her hand in demonstration. She slumped a little in her chair, something she rarely did after years of discipline to always sit with a straight back.

"I'm glad it didn't go on longer than it did. I was ready to jump up there and pull you backstage." Lilly put her hand on her shoulder to comfort her.

"Thanks, Lilly. I'm glad you are watching out for me. It's good to know I can count on you." She managed a weak smile for her friend. "Now, I'm ready to get home. I think my face muscles will be sore tomorrow from all the smiling I've done tonight."

SUNDAY AFTERNOON COULDN'T GET THERE FAST enough. Charlotte didn't hear much of the preacher's sermon that morning and lunch dragged on too long. She had just woken from her Sunday afternoon nap, when Brock called right on cue.

"So, what're we gonna do tonight out on our first big date together?" Brock asked.

"Have you ever cruised the strip?" Charlotte asked.

"Can't say I have, yet."

"Well, come pick me up, and I'll show you!" She told him how to get to her house and to give her an hour to get ready. She didn't need that much time, but she wanted to make sure she was perfect for him.

Brock drove up in a black Ford F150. It looked brand new; either that, or he took good care of his truck. She saw him pull into the driveway, called bye to her parents, and dashed down the front steps. He hopped out and met her on the passenger side.

"Hey, you!" he greeted her.

"Hey!" Charlotte slid her arms under his letterman jacket and sighed as he wrapped her in a hug. He was warm and smelled wonderful. She would have been perfectly content to stay there wrapped inside his jacket with him the rest of the night. Eventually, they broke apart to get into the truck. He let her in the passenger side, but she slid over to the middle so that she could sit next to him. He got in and roared the truck to life.

"Where are we headed, boss?"

She gave a short laugh at this and said, "Turn east on the highway."

"You got it."

The strip began at the Wendy's next to the Twin Movie Theater. "That's the first turn-around spot. Then we drive down Kings Highway. We used to turn around at the Dog-n-Suds on the other side of the railroad tracks, but now they're building a new overpass, so we have to turn around at the gas station next to Pizza Inn," Charlotte informed him.

"And all you do is drive back and forth to see who you pass?" he asked a little confused.

"That or some people find a place to park and sit out on their hoods watching to see who drives by. I usually park in front of the hospital."

Whenever Charlotte saw someone she knew, she leaned over to Brock's horn and honked and waved. Several times she had Brock stop in the middle of the road to talk to people.

"People stop and talk in the middle of the road?" Brock asked again.

"Everyone knows this is the strip on the weekends. The locals avoid it because they know it will be stop and go. My dad hates it. Having fun?" she asked.

"Anything with you." Brock put his arm around her and squeezed her tighter to him. She snuggled into him, getting a whiff of his cologne. She wanted to melt right there next to him; he smelled so wonderful.

They cruised up and down a couple more times when an orange Bronco pulled to a stop beside them. "Uh-oh," she said, but before she could explain, Brock already figured out who it was.

Kale leaned out his window, "Let's see whatcha got under that hood!" Kale revved his engine.

"Where to?" Brock responded.

Kale and Brock idled next to each other, preparing to race down a dark and deserted road.

"I don't like this," Charlotte said as she scooted over to the passenger seat and buckled her seatbelt. "Brock, why are you doing this?"

"Somebody has to stand up to this guy. He can't keep throwing his weight around, thinking I'm going to cower in the corner." Brock looked over at Kale while revving his engine. They eyed one another to see who would make the first move.

"Brock, please don't do this. What if we get hurt? What if we get caught?" Charlotte pleaded nervously.

"I got this, Charlotte."

Kale floored the gas pedal, and Brock responded.

For a few seconds, no one moved forward. Both trucks spun their wheels before grabbing the pavement. The trucks lurched forward, and Charlotte was slammed against the seat. She squeezed her eyes shut and prayed silently.

They were neck and neck at first. The speedometer climbed over 120 mph. She spotted a blue flash out of the corner of her eye.

"Cop!" she screamed. Up ahead was a crossroad.

"Turn left here!" she shouted, pointing to the left.

Brock slammed on the brakes and took the turn. She screamed as the truck turned on two wheels. "Turn into that driveway there!" She pointed again.

Brock screeched into the driveway. He cut the lights and the engine.

They sat still for a minute, afraid to breathe in case the cop could spot them by their breath. Charlotte slowly unbuckled and scooted back next to Brock. "Do you think he saw us?" she whispered.

Brock was looking over his shoulder to see if they were followed. "Kale kept going straight. I think the safest choice would have been for him to follow Kale. Unless Kale turned somewhere else after we did." He turned to look around. "Where are we?"

"This is my uncle's driveway," Charlotte told him.

Brock swung around to face her. "Coach McAfee?"

"The last time I checked, he was the only uncle I have here in town," she said, cracking a little smile.

Brock looked at her and pulled her closer to him. "You're so damn beautiful," he said as he pulled her into a kiss.

She melted into him and the kiss. All thoughts immediately left her brain. There was nothing else in the world but his lips, strong arms, and heavenly smell.

They were so engrossed in one another that they didn't see her uncle come out of the house and walk toward the truck. He knocked on the driver side window making Charlotte scream at the top of her lungs.

"Ah!" Brock ducked his head and cupped his right ear with his hand. He reached down with his left and rolled down the window.

"And what do you two think you're doing? You can't sit in your own driveway and make out?" Charlotte's uncle looked both amused and concerned.

"Uh, well...we were ...we pulled in here because we thought we were being followed and were waiting until it was clear," Brock stammered.

"Uh, huh. Well, it looks clear to me now. I think it's time for you to take Charlotte home." Coach McAfee smiled broadly as if he couldn't wait to inform Charlotte's parents about this.

"Please, Uncle Tommy, don't call Mom and Dad. We'll head straight home, I promise," she begged.

"I won't. But, now that I see who you're going out with, I'll be sure to keep my eye on him at school." He patted the rim of the window and looked Brock dead in the eyes.

"Yes, sir," Brock said humbly as he started the truck.

He backed up carefully and turned up the road.

"I hope you don't get in trouble for this." Brock looked at Charlotte warily.

"I won't. Sorry for screaming in your ear," she apologized.

"You've got some lungs on you; that's for sure." Brock put his arm back around her and squeezed her tight again. She snuggled back into him and enjoyed what little time she had left next to him before they arrived back at her house.

TUESDAY EVENING STARTED the basketball season. Charlotte had to be at the girl's game that played before the boy's game. Traditionally, the cheerleaders didn't cheer for the girls' game, but her school had a long-standing tradition under Coach Dillingham for state champion girls' basketball, so the cheerleaders began to cheer during the second half of the girls' game. For the opening game, the girls' team crushed Nettleton 65 to 25.

After the girls' basketball teams cleared the court, the boys' basketball teams jogged out onto the court in single file. They wore their warm-up suits and started out with a lay-up drill. The combination of exercises they went through was like watching a dance routine. One of the players must have been directing when they moved from drill to drill, but it was subtle. One minute they were working on lay-ups, the next minute they weaved in and out, passing the ball around. After this display of agility, they pulled their warm-up pants off by grabbing them in the front and yanking forward. They had snap buttons down the side that allowed them to pop off quickly. Charlotte thought this was sort of sexy and watched Brock carefully when he did it.

To begin the game, the announcer announced the starting line-up. The starters sat on the bench while all the other players formed a double line for each of them to run between and give high-fives when their name was called. The cheerleaders extended the line and did jumps and cheered for each of the players. Charlotte was sad to see that Brock wasn't one of the starters, but she hoped he got some playing time. He was still recovering from being sick, so it was probably best he didn't play the whole game anyway. He did glance over at her during this time and gave her a little wink, so she knew he was watching her from the corner of his eye. She most definitely would be watching him.

The game started with a jump ball in the center. Tech's tallest starter, Liam, easily tipped the ball to Jacob, who dribbled the ball while the other players set up in their play positions. The cheerleaders began their cheers, and the gym became loud and full of excitement.

At halftime, the score was Tech 25, Nettleton 23. The cheerleaders stormed the court with jumps and cheers and set up to do their half-time cheer. When they finished, the drill team took over the court and did their routine. After this was over, it was time for the basketball players to come back out onto the court and do some more warm-up shots.

During the warm-up, a stray ball rolled toward Charlotte, and Brock ran over to pick it up. He whispered a quick, "Hey!" and she giggled back as he jogged back on the court to take more shots. He only played a little bit the first half, but she hoped he would see more play time during the second half.

The loud buzzer rang to signal time to clear the court and start the second half. This time, the team that got the ball first was determined by the position arrow. It was Nettleton's ball first. The play action went back and forth with each team setting up to shoot the ball. A foul was called on Liam when a Nettleton player was shooting under the basket. This gave the Nettleton player a chance at the free-throw line. When all the players lined up along the box, a buzzer sounded to indicate a player was switching in. Brock was substituting in for Liam. Charlotte's stomach did a flip.

The Nettleton player missed the shot, and Brock rebounded the ball. He threw it to Jacob, the point guard, and they ran down the other side of the court to set up a chance to score on their goal. The ball was passed around from player to player while other team members tried to get open and make a clear shot. Jacob passed the ball to Brock, who was standing close under the goal, and he easily laid it up for two points. Charlotte cheered at the top of her lungs doing a high kick and yelling, "Go, Brock!" He didn't look at her, but he had a little grin on his face.

The lead switched back and forth. As Nettleton would score, they would be up by two points. Then, Tech would take the ball and score a 3-pointer and be up one point. By the end of the third quarter, it was Tech 36, Nettleton 35. It was going to be a close game to the very end. The teams gathered around the coaches during the brief pause between quarters to wipe the sweat out of their eyes and drink some water. The cheerleaders bounded onto the court to do a quick cheer, followed by Nettleton's cheerleaders doing the same. Then the buzzer sounded again for the fourth quarter to begin.

Brock was back on the bench, and Liam was back in the game. The refs called more fouls, and more players saw time at the free-throw line. Nettleton pulled ahead 44-38. Coach Foster called a time-out to talk to his players. When the team came back on the court, they set up a man-to-man defense. Tech scored two more points to pull it within four. Nettleton was moving the ball around when Liam was called for a foul. This was his fifth foul, and that put him out of the game. Brock was sent in to take his place. Charlotte's nervous energy went higher.

Nettleton scored two points, and Brock stepped out of bounds to pass the ball to Jacob so that he could dribble it into play. Tech set up their offense. Jacob couldn't find a teammate open, so he took a 3-pointer and made it. Two minutes left on the clock. Nettleton took the ball and dribbled to their basket. They passed the ball around ticking time off the clock. Their guard passed it to the center, and he went up for two points. Brock fouled him when he was shooting. Nettleton made the basket and got a chance at the free-throw line. He missed! Brock rebounded the ball and quickly threw it to Jacob to run it down the court. Tanner sprinted down with him, so Jacob tossed the ball up to him, and Tanner dunked it in. Tech's fans went wild! Everyone was on their feet cheering.

Nettleton called another time-out with less than thirty seconds on the clock. The score was 48 to 45 Nettleton. Charlotte bit her nails. The gym was loud and hot, but all she could think about was Tech winning the game. The buzzer sounded to end the time-out, and the players stepped back onto the court.

Nettleton had the ball. They passed the ball around again wanting to take time off the clock, but suddenly Jacob reached in and stole the ball. He ran down the court and set up to take the 3-pointer. He was fouled while shooting, but he still made the shot, tying the game. Now it all came down to Jacob at the free-throw line. The gym went quiet on Tech's side, but Nettleton's side tried to yell and break his concentration. Jacob took a deep breath and dribbled the ball twice in front of him. He squared his shoulders and paused to concentrate on the goal. He lifted the ball up into shooting position and gracefully released it into the air. The ball sailed a perfect arch toward the goal and sunk into the net without touching the rim.

The gym went wild! Nettleton quickly grabbed the ball and threw it in to a player standing at half-court. He then threw the ball way into the air in the hope of a lucky last-second shot to win. He missed the goal as the buzzer sounded to end the game.

Tech won! Everyone jumped and cheered. Charlotte was so excited. It had been a great game to start off the season. She couldn't wait to congratulate Brock. As all the cheerleaders ran onto the court, she ran to Brock and hugged him around the neck.

"Yay! We won!!" she yelled. Brock grinned from ear to ear.

AFTER CELEBRATING FOR A TIME, the teams went back into the locker rooms as the fans gradually left the gym to go home. Charlotte waited in the lobby for Brock to change. He came out wearing his warm-up suit over his uniform. She ran to him again and put her arm around his waist. "That was a great game!" she exclaimed.

"I only scored two points," Brock said a little dejected.

"I know! And I screamed my lungs out cheering for you when you did," she beamed at him. "You were also important in rebounding and passing the ball to the right players at the right time, so it's not all about how many points you make."

"You're definitely a cheerleader. You always look on the bright side and cheer people up," he said, looking down at her with admiration.

She bounded a couple of steps to prove that her bouncing energy and enthusiasm also made her a great cheerleader. They left the gym and Brock walked her to her car. When they got close enough to her car to see it, they saw that someone had written in shoe polish all over her windows.

"SLUT" was written in big bold letters across her front windshield. Along with a few other choice words on the side windows. They had whited out her headlights and taillights.

"Oh, my gosh! You've got to be kidding me!" was all Charlotte could say. Her excitement from moments before deflating.

"I wonder who's responsible for this?" Brock asked.

"I'll give you three guesses, and the first two are for practice," Charlotte said. She stood in front of her car with her hands on her hips looking suddenly drained of all her energy.

Brock looked the car over to check for any structural damage. He didn't see any further harm. "Go ahead and start the car and see how well you can see out the windshield."

Charlotte did as he instructed. The car started fine, but her visibility was obscured.

"I'll go back to the gym and get some wet paper towels to clean this off," Charlotte said and ran back to the gym.

Brock stood outside her car looking around to see if he could spot any other evidence to indicate who might have done this. He couldn't get over why someone would do this to her. He had heard whispers from other students at school saying dreadful things about Charlotte, but all the rumors seemed like petty gossip and jealousy. He had never witnessed Charlotte being rude or impolite to any other students in school. She smiled and hugged lots of people and made everyone she was around feel noticed and happy. One person, in particular, came to mind.

Charlotte came running back, and he helped her clean the windshield off. They concentrated on a spot for her to see and wiped off the headlights and taillights the best they could. She would have to wash it with soap and water later.

"Do you need me to follow behind you on your way home?" Brock asked.

"No, I think I'll be all right. But I could use a ride to school tomorrow, since I won't have time to clean this in the morning before school."

"I'll be there bright and early," Brock said as he gave her a hug and a kiss.

He wished they could stay there a little longer, but it was a school night, and he needed to get home and shower. He worried about her as he watched her pull out of the parking lot and drive down the road toward her house. Brock turned in the other direction and headed to his home, wondering how he could put an end to this assault on his girlfriend.

CHAPTER SIXTEEN

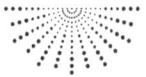

"Charlotte, I've been meaning to tell you that my family is going to Oklahoma for the week of Thanksgiving," Brock announced to her a few weeks later.

"Oh, no! That means I won't get to see you for a whole week?" She stuck out her lower lip and gave him her best puppy-dog eyes.

"And, I don't know if we'll be able to talk on the phone. It depends on if my grandparents have their line fixed."

"Ugh, how am I ever going to survive!" Charlotte hammed.

Brock nudged her with his shoulder and said, "I think you'll live." She could tell he, too, wasn't looking forward to being away from her. They had grown close over the last few weeks. She had never been with the same guy for this long, and it was nice being with him at school every day.

"To be fair, my family is going to visit my uncle Jimmy over Thanksgiving," she finally admitted.

"Oh, so you were going to make me feel bad for leaving you when you were going to be leaving me anyway," Brock teased.

"I had to let you know how much I'd miss your presence!" She smiled at him then gave him a small kiss on the cheek.

The bell rang to end lunch.

"Hey, Lilly," Charlotte said, "wait for me a sec will ya?"

"Sure," Lilly said as she said goodbye to Evan.

Charlotte hugged Brock bye as he went off to his next class.

"I need to ask you a favor," Charlotte said.

"Sure, what's up?" Lilly asked.

"Well, after Thanksgiving break, I need to switch for a while," she whispered.

"Ooooh," Lilly responded. "What do you want me to do?"

"Well, since Brock still doesn't know about it, and I'm not ready to tell him yet, I need you to run interference for me when I'm my shadow-self," Charlotte informed her.

"Okay, I'll do my best. It's not going to be easy."

"I know. I'm not sure how you're going to do it either but stay close by and tell him it's my time of the month or something and that's why I'm acting strange."

"Oh, that's a good idea. Guys get all freaked out when you tell them that, and I'm sure he won't think anything of it."

"Let's hope not. Hopefully, I can find a way to tell him soon, so we don't have to play these games around him."

"Yeah, I'm not very good at covering for people. I get nervous and my parents, especially, always know when something is up if I'm not telling them the truth."

"Let's hope you get good at it in a couple of weeks. I appreciate this, Lilly." Charlotte hugged her friend.

"You have to tell me all about it when you get back. This is the big event isn't it?" Lilly said looking at Charlotte.

"Yeah, I have to be a part of this. I feel it." She got butterflies in her stomach thinking about it. Charlotte hoped she was doing the right thing. She still had a week to think about it in case she changed her mind.

CHARLOTTE'S MOTHER'S only brother and his wife with their five-year-old son lived in an old farmhouse at the top of a big hill, or some might call it a small mountain. The road leading to their house was so steep that Charlotte was always afraid their vehicle would flip over backward as they went up. Once they got to the top, their home was somewhat secluded with only farmland all around.

When the Thanksgiving feast was finally ready, her grandpa announced, "It's time for everyone to gather around the table to say a prayer before we eat." Everyone gathered around the food laid out on the table and held hands. "Russell, will you lead us in prayer?"

Charlotte's dad led the family in a short prayer giving thanks for all their many blessings, for the food, and for the opportunity for everyone to come together as a family. Everyone said, "Amen," in unison and dug into the food on their plates.

After everyone had eaten, her dad and grandpa settled down in the recliners to watch football, while her mother, grandma, and her aunt put leftovers away and cleaned dishes. Tad, Ryan, and her little cousin, Jason, went outside to play.

"Charlotte, would you like to come outside," Uncle Jimmy asked.

"Sure," she replied jumping from the couch to walk outside.

The temperature was cool, but pleasant. The sky was a beautiful blue with only a few puffy white clouds floating by. The temperature was warm enough to play outside without a jacket, but, come sundown, it would be chilly.

"I wanted to get out of the house and get some fresh air and talk to you for a minute, see how things are going with you," her uncle admitted.

"Oh, well, I'm doing great. I've been seeing someone," she said, wondering why he had a sudden interest.

"What's he like?"

Charlotte sighed heavily and looked like a star-struck love puppy before she answered, "Oh, he's tall, dark, and handsome..." She looked at her uncle, and they laughed again.

"Does he treat you good?" her uncle asked, sounding protective.

"Yes, he's a perfect gentleman. He plays basketball, and it's been fun watching him play so far."

"That's good. Maybe I'll come down and catch a game or two." Her uncle preferred basketball over football as his sport to watch.

"You didn't ask me out here to talk about my love life, did you?" she asked, still feeling like there was something else he wanted to say.

"No, I mean, I do want to make sure everything is going all right with you, but I do have another reason," her uncle said, leaning against the fence and lighting a cigarette. He stood silent for a minute as if deciding what to say next. "Do you remember hearing a story about your grandma making a single red rose grow and bloom on a rose-bush in the middle of winter?"

"Yes, I've heard that story a few times. I was little when I first heard it, so I wasn't old enough to think anything about it." Charlotte looked at her uncle wondering where this was going.

"Well, it seems that Grandma has a gift for helping plants grow healthy and ripe with her touch," her uncle explained.

"I thought that meant she had a green thumb, you know, like she was a good gardener."

"Well, there's more to it than that. A good gardener can't make a rose bloom in the middle of winter."

She could see his point. She waited to hear more.

"Has your mother ever indicated to you any special abilities that run in our family?" her uncle asked, blowing smoke into the air.

She thought for a second, "If she has, I may have been too young to understand what she was talking about. She hasn't said anything to me lately."

"Yes, well, it goes back to your great-great-great-grandmother who was a Cherokee Indian from South Carolina. She traveled to Arkansas with her husband in the 1850s. It was said that she had special abilities and each generation from her has had someone with something special." This was news to Charlotte.

"What do you mean, *special*?" she asked carefully.

"Ah, good question. Well, it varies. Your mother has an ability of premonitions—of things that are about to happen, then they do. However, when this happened to her as a teenager, she didn't want her ability. She was too afraid of knowing something terrible was about to happen, so she's worked hard to block it, I think."

"You can do that?" She was shocked to be hearing this for the first time.

"If she still gets them, she doesn't say anything about it. Would you like to know about mine?" he asked, looking at her.

Her eyes widened in astonishment. She never expected this. Why hadn't she thought of a family connection to what was happening to her? "What can you do?" she asked, a little breathless.

"I get visitors… spirit visitors," he whispered.

They stood at the fence watching a neighbor's horse casually grazing in the middle of a field contemplating what this meant.

"What do they say?" she finally spoke.

"Sometimes it's not always clear. They tell me something and then later when a certain event happens it suddenly makes sense. The prophecy that I was told, in light of something else happening, come together."

"How often has this happened?" Charlotte asked wide-eyed.

"Not often. Maybe a handful of times since I was a teen." Her uncle looked casual as if this revelation was normal for everyone.

"Does it scare you?" she asked.

"When I see them, they look like a regular person. It's the sudden appearance out of nowhere that catches me off guard."

"Have you seen one recently?" Understanding starting to sink in.

"I did a few weeks ago. It was an Indian woman, very beautiful. She had long dark hair and big brown eyes. She was wearing a buck-skin dress."

Charlotte gasped and put her hand over her mouth.

"What? You recognize her?" Her uncle turned to look at her, curious to know what she knew.

She asked instead, "What did she say?"

"She said, 'talk to your niece.' You're the only niece I have. I had a feeling it was about our family abilities when she said it, but that was all she said." Then he looked at her more closely, "What has happened to you?"

She wasn't sure she wanted to tell him everything, yet. Where should she begin? "That Indian woman that you described, I think I know her," she began.

"And?" Her uncle stood waiting.

"Her name is Nahele, and she's an Osage Indian who lived somewhere around here a long time ago."

"And how do you know this?" Her uncle asked patiently.

"Well, it seems that I can leave my body somehow and go into her body and experience her life in the time it happened." She looked at her uncle to watch his reaction.

"When did this begin?" He was much calmer and accepting than Charlotte expected.

"A couple of months ago, I was out with my dog in the woods, and I thought I saw him disappear. When I followed him to see where he went, I was sucked out of my body and into hers in the past." Telling her story always gave her the goosebumps.

"That's quite an ability. But you were able to come back?" Her uncle suddenly looked worried.

"Yes, in her time there's a wolf that guides me back to this time. I only stay for a few days, and then I come back here." Then she thought to ask, "Have you ever heard of anything like this happening before?"

Her uncle shook his head slowly, "No, I haven't. This is more powerful than anything I've ever heard of. Most of the abilities are psychic in nature. Clairvoyance, clairaudience, clairsentience, that sort of thing."

"I don't even know what that is?" Charlotte felt overwhelmed.

"I can explain it to you some other time. First, we need to find out more about your purpose in going to this time and place."

"Yes!" She perked up suddenly, "That's what I have been struggling to figure out. I've been back and forth several times now, and there doesn't seem to be anything out of the ordinary occurring, that I can understand, as to why this is happening." Charlotte's heart sped up, hoping that her uncle could help her finally.

"There has to be a reason," her uncle confirmed, "Like when a spirit appears to me, it's to give me a directive about something important."

Her heart raced, and she was excited to know that someone else understood her and could help her. "Uncle Jimmy, I'm so glad you said something to me. I've been struggling with this wondering what to do. I've told my friend Lilly about it, and she and I have been working to find information in the library, but, so far, we've come up empty."

"What do you make of the dogs' role?" he asked.

"Well, my guess is they're my guides. They know when I'm needed in one time or another and lead me away when I need to switch." She didn't want to tell him about how her wolf had also saved her from being mauled by a bear. He might worry more about her.

Her mother stuck her head out the back door, "Charlotte, what are y'all doing back there?"

"Now that you've told me about Mom, I wonder if she still gets some premonitions," Charlotte said, smiling at her uncle. "It makes me wonder how much she knows but never tells us."

"You're right. It makes it hard to sneak around behind her back," her uncle winked at her.

"Coming, Mother!" Charlotte called.

Her uncle put a hand on her shoulder as they turned to go back in the house, "I'll see what I can find out on my end. In the meantime, please be careful. That time was much riskier and more life-threatening than it is now. Write to me and keep me updated, and I'll do the same for you. Sound good?"

"I will. Thanks, again, Uncle Jimmy. It means a lot to me knowing more about this now." She walked back with her uncle to the house, feeling more confident and relieved to hear that she had a family connection to the things that were happening to her. If this was a special ability that ran in her family, then she was confident that there was a purpose in what she was doing.

THEY DROVE HOME on Saturday after Thanksgiving. When her dad pulled into the driveway, he came to a sudden stop half-way. Everyone in the van sat staring at the sight in front of them processing what they were looking at. At the other end of the driveway close to the garage doors, was a blackened burned spot. After looking at it for a little while, it suddenly dawned on her.

"My car!" Charlotte yelled.

She jumped out of the van and went to inspect it. After moving around the burn spot, she could see where the rubber from the tires and the red glass from the taillights had melted to the concrete. Her dad parked the van and came to inspect it as well.

"What the heck happened here?!" he said. Her dad's face turned red hot that almost matched his red hair and his pale blue eyes blazed. She instinctively moved a couple of steps away from him.

Charlotte was so shocked that she couldn't think of anything to say. Why would someone burn her car? Her mother went to the front door and found a note. She walked back to the driveway and handed it to her husband.

"What's it say?" Charlotte asked.

"It's a police note, saying they towed the remains of the car and left a number to call when we got back in town," her dad told her, sounding angrier by the second. The neighbor across the street came out of his house and walked over to talk to them.

"I'm sorry you guys weren't here when this happened," Larry said.

"Did you see who did this?" Her dad asked. Charlotte sensed he was trying to control the rage inside him and not lash out at innocent people.

"I saw a blaze go up and came out to inspect. I didn't get a good look at the kids in the truck; I had to run back in the house to call the fire department. Whoever did this piled several bags of leaves over the car then set it on fire."

Charlotte was over the shock now, and tears filled her eyes. All her hopes of independence gone up in smoke. She couldn't hold it back any longer and cried.

Her mother put her arm around her and whispered, "Come on, honey. Let's go inside and let Dad figure this out."

She followed her mother back into the house. *Why would anyone do this to me? What did I do to deserve all this?*

She needed to lie down. She took a quick peek out the window a little later and saw a police car pull up in the driveway. She hoped they would find who did this. But what good would it do to find them? They couldn't bring her car back.

She flopped backward onto her bed and laid there staring at the ceiling. She tried to remember what she had left in the car, a few cassette tapes: Air Supply, the latest Chicago tape, and Huey Lewis and the News. Thankfully, the rest of her tapes were in her cassette case still sitting on her bedroom floor next to her stereo. That would have been a bigger disaster replacing all her music, not to mention the self-made tapes recorded from the radio.

In the kitchen, Charlotte heard the phone ring. A few seconds later, her mother knocked on her door and said it was for her.

"Hello?" she answered.

"Hey, you," Brock said.

Her heart melted with relief to hear his voice. Before she could get any other words out, she cried right into the phone.

"Oh, no, Charlotte? What's wrong? Are you okay?" Poor Brock. That was no way for her to start the conversation on the phone.

"We... got...home...and found...my...car...burned!" she choked out through sobs.

"What!" Brock almost yelled.

All she could do was continue crying. When she felt she had cried enough, she wiped her tears and blew her nose.

"Sorry, I had to get that out," she apologized.

"This is horrible, Charlotte. Have you called the police?"

"They left a note on our door to call when we got home. Dad's out there talking to them now. Our neighbor reported it."

"Did he see who did it?" Brock asked.

"No, he saw the tail end of the truck going over the hill, then he had to run back in and call the fire department." She stifled another sob.

"Charlotte, I'm so sorry about this. Do you need me to come over?" She could tell he wanted to be there with her.

"I don't think it would be a good time right now. My dad is quite mad, and I don't want him meeting you for the first time when he's angry like this," Charlotte said, disappointed that she couldn't see him.

"I understand. I don't want him meeting me under these circumstances either."

"When did you get home?" she asked, thinking it best to change the subject.

"A moment ago. I ran to the phone as soon as we got in," Brock said.

"I'm so glad you called. I've missed talking to you and can't wait to see you."

"Same here. How was your visit to your uncle's?" he asked.

Charlotte wished she could tell him about her conversation with her uncle, but she wasn't sure how he would respond. As they talked, she began to feel a little better.

"I guess I'm going to need you to pick me up again for school," Charlotte's eyes began to sting with tears again.

"I'll be there bright and early. Don't worry, Charlotte. We'll find out who did this."

CHAPTER SEVENTEEN

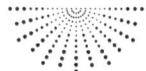

*C*harlotte was relieved when it was finally Monday again. Her stomach did a flip, and her heart skipped a beat when she caught sight of Brock's truck pulling into the driveway. She skipped down the steps to greet him. She was especially relieved to wrap her arms around him and sighed into his chest.

"I missed you, too," he said, bending his head and whispering into her ear.

"I'm so glad to see you," she said looking into his beautiful blue eyes.

"It was a lonely week without you," he admitted, gazing down at her, appearing as relieved as she was to be reunited. "Did the police find out anything?" he asked.

"Well…." She stepped back a little but kept her hands on the front of his shirt.

"Uh-oh. What now?" he said, suspecting something had happened.

"I was wondering. Do you think it could be…" she started, but Brock cut her off.

"I've thought about that too," he admitted. "But we don't know anything for certain. I think it is best we play it cool for now and see if he gives anything away."

Charlotte nodded in agreement as he opened the door for her, and they rode to school.

They rounded the corner to the courtyard and spotted their friends. Lilly and Evan walked up to them, "Hey, you two. Did you have a good break?" Lilly asked, but when she saw Charlotte tear up and begin to cry again, she asked, "What? What happened?"

Charlotte told them everything she knew, which wasn't much. She was without a car again. "I'll need a ride home after school today," she said, looking hopefully at Brock.

"Of course," he said bringing her in for a hug again.

At least, now she had a steady boyfriend to give her rides and to watch out for her while someone was out there plotting awful things to do to her. Things were getting out of hand. Burning her car had graduated into criminal activity. She wondered how far, Kale, if it was him, was willing to go.

Charlotte felt uncomfortable as they walked into biology class. She didn't even want to look in his direction, but she noticed Brock did, and the look on his face meant he had a few plans of his own. She needed to tell him she didn't want him to take revenge out on Kale. It could make matters worse. Besides, what if it hadn't been him.

Mrs. Olsen began class, and she tried to drown out her thoughts and concentrate on school.

CHARLOTTE WAS glad to be back at school, not because of school itself, but because it meant she got to be with Brock. She loved walking down the hall with his arm around her shoulders. After practice that evening, he drove her home. He pulled into the driveway and cut the engine. He showered off this time after practice so that he wouldn't be offensively sweaty and stinky in the truck. She ran a hand through his slightly wet hair.

"I like your haircut," she said, looking at him dreamily.

"I was wondering when you were going to say something," he

added looking at her carefully. They were inches apart from each other and had other things on their minds besides hairstyles.

He leaned in to kiss her, and she wrapped her arms around his neck. They kissed one another, exploring one another's body, then she realized that at some point they were going to have to draw the line.

"Stop," she said breathlessly.

He stopped kissing her and looked at her face, his eyes slightly unfocused.

"I don't want to tell you to stop, but a part of me knows that I need to," she said reluctantly.

He sat looking into her eyes for a minute slowly coming to his senses. "I want you so bad, Charlotte."

"I know. I want you, too. But how far are we willing to go? How far is too far?"

"I think that's up to you," he said.

"Up to me?" she questioned, pulling back from him a little. "You want to go all the way?" She was a little confused and surprised at his willingness.

"Heck, yeah. Every guy wants to go all the way. It's in our nature."

She sat looking at him for a second. He shifted uncomfortably in his seat.

"I'm sorry, Brock. I'm not ready. Besides, I don't want it to be a reckless decision of passion in the front of a truck. I want it to be special without fear someone will catch us." She couldn't believe she was even admitting to that much.

"I understand. I want the same thing. I don't want a one-time thing to ruin the rest of our lives," he admitted, cooling down now.

Charlotte swallowed at this thought and felt like an ice bucket had been dumped on her.

Through the fogged windows, she could see the front porch light blink on and off. "That would be my mother signaling for me to come in. She's watching us through the window."

Brock wiped part of the windshield off and looked at the porch. He could see a silhouette in the side window by the door. "Tell your mom I said 'Hi,'" he grinned.

"I guess I need to introduce you to my parents soon, huh?" she said.

He looked at her and touched her face lightly with his hand. "I'd like that." Then he kissed her gently on the lips.

He got out of his truck so that she could slide out on his side. She gave him one last hug and said, "Goodnight. Do you wanna pick me up in the morning?"

"I'd like that, too," he said as he got back in his truck. She waved goodbye as she headed up the steps, and he backed out of the driveway.

Later that evening as her family was going to bed, she wrote a letter to her uncle Jimmy.

Dear Uncle Jimmy,

I am writing to you, Monday night, December 1st. I wanted to let you know that after I write this and put it in the mailbox, I'm going to switch back to the past for a few days. I don't know what time I'm in or for sure where I am geographically, but I will try to find out. I thought it would be best to let you know in case anything happens. I have several questions that still need to be answered.

Do you know of anything historically that would be of significance for me to influence?

Maybe you can call upon a spirit visitor to give you more information. I don't know if it works that way for you, but it might be worth a try.

Thanks for being my confidante. I will write back with more news when I am myself again.

Love always,

Charlotte

She walked outside to the mailbox and placed her letter inside. Scuffy was waiting for her as if he could sense when she intended to switch. She knew by now that her spirit would leave her body and go to Nahele's and this body would go back in the house and go to bed and continue life as usual on autopilot. She scratched Scuffy on the head and said, "Okay, boy, I'm ready."

CHAPTER EIGHTEEN

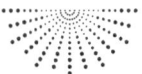

$\mathcal{T}$he late afternoon sun was just above the tree line when Charlotte brought back a basket of squash and peppers from the garden. The pumpkins would be harvested in the next couple of weeks. A messenger came to the hut to announce the arrival of all the family members of Tetonka. She went to the nearby huts of her grandparents, and aunt and uncle to tell them the wedding guests would soon be arriving. Her family stood outside their hut when they saw Tetonka's family walk toward them with armloads of food and gifts. She was nervous. This part of the ritual involved the families and not Tetonka and her.

Her Uncle, Wande, greeted the visiting family, "Welcome to our family hut. Please come in. A fire is waiting."

He directed them into the hut and invited them to sit around the fire. Hula and Charlotte were the last ones to enter. They stayed relatively out of the way and watched and listened to what their elder family members said.

"It is good that you have received us," Tetonka's father began.

The family said prayers and the food was passed around. After the meal, her father got out his pipe and lit it. "With this peace pipe, we welcome the family of Chaska and their gifts." He took a long puff on the pipe, then handed it to Chaska who also took a puff and passed it on to the next male. The women sat outside the men quietly observing.

When the little cousins got restless, Hula and Charlotte quietly took them outside the hut to let them play. "How are you feeling, sister?" Hula asked.

"I am happy that this day has finally come. I am having trouble not seeing Tetonka right now. I want to run to wherever he is and be with him," she admitted.

"Do you know where he might be?"

It was customary for the bride and groom not to see one another for the three or four days before the marriage union and allow the families to get to know one another.

"He could be anywhere way out in the woods far away. I would have no way of knowing where to look for him if I tried." She was worried and a little sad.

"Don't worry, sister. I am certain he is well. He is probably thinking of you just as you are thinking of him at this time."

The families sat together quietly talking well into the night. When it came time for Tetonka's family to leave, everyone bid them a good night and watched as they walked back across the middle road to the Earth side of the village. Tomorrow, it would be her family to walk to Tetonka's side of the village and return the favor.

The third day was a repeat of the first day, with Tetonka's family coming back to the Sky Clan side of the village. Day four was the main event. The women in her family spent all day bathing her, decorating her, and putting her in her best dress. At mid-afternoon, she stood outside her family hut with all her possessions as the women in Tetonka's family raced to her hut to claim something that belonged to her.

She got on Cornsilk, and her father led her horse across the village toward Tetonka's hut. She had butterflies in her stomach, and she was so nervous she could hardly hold onto the reins in her hands. She couldn't wait to see Tetonka. She barely noticed all the people lined up along the way as they smiled and threw tiny winter flowers over her as she passed. All her family members walked behind. She could see tears in her mother's eyes as she walked to her right. Her grandparents walked arm in arm behind her horse smiling proudly, no doubt remembering the day of their wedding union. Hula was beside her mother looking more sad than happy.

Her uncle, aunt, older cousins and their families, and her younger cousins all followed the parade as they wound their way through the village. When they came within sight of Tetonka's family, she saw they were gathered around the hut that Tetonka had built to be their own. When her horse came to a stop, Tetonka emerged from the hut.

Her heart leapt. He was in his finest buckskin pants and a buckskin shirt. He had an eagle feather in his hair, dangling earrings, a bone necklace, and armbands. His clothing had been decorated with delicate beads, but her attention was on his facial expression. He looked like he was holding back a mixture of emotions: happy, sad, proud, nervous, excited...

He walked to her horse and reached up to her. She swung her leg over Cornsilk as he caught her by the waist, helping her down. They stood for a moment looking at one another, pleased to be within arm's reach once again. Then he turned toward his family and said, "Father, Mother, Uncle, Aunt, Grandfather, and Brother, I present to you my wife, Nahele. May she bless our family as she has blessed my heart."

Everyone in attendance as witnesses cheered and celebrated. They went to the main hut of the family and had a marriage feast to feed one hundred. Tetonka and Charlotte sat side by side, not eating much, but watching the others around them enjoy the time in their honor. Their minds weren't there, but on each other, waiting for the appropriate time to go to their hut. They touched casually, and their looks lingered. She smiled shyly at him as if this was the first time she had ever been around him. Tetonka acted clumsy and nervous as well, fighting to calm the storm that was building within him.

Their families laughed at the tales they shared about them when they were younger. She saw Tetonka blush when his grandmother told of how he was particularly fond of his mother's breast and was a difficult toddler to wean. She was horrified at the telling of how she played with her boy cousins naked in the mud. It seemed that everyone had a favorite story to tell about one or the other.

Then Kajika spoke and told the story of teaching her to ride her horse, and everyone laughed except Tetonka and Charlotte. He conveniently left out the story of how he spooked her horse, but that was just as well. As the evening wore on, Kajika came by to wish them well. Tetonka nodded his head in gratitude but didn't have much to say to his warrior-brother. She sat stoically beside him, not letting her true emotions for the man be revealed.

At last, Tetonka's father stood and gave a final speech of goodwill for the couple. He blessed them for many years of life together, the making of many children (and the trying to do so, which brought lots of hoots and shouts of laughter), and good health and fortune in the making of their home. When he nodded to Tetonka that he was finished and gave his consent for them to leave, Tetonka stood and offered her his hand. Charlotte placed her hand delicately in his and rose feeling shaky and weak. Tetonka held her hand to his chest and led her away from the family who were still smiling proudly at the newly married couple.

CHARLOTTE HAD a constant smile on her face. She swept the hut that was the home for the two of them. She kept the fire going and prepared the meals when Tetonka came home from scouting. Both their families had shared some of their stores of food and supplies that would hopefully last them through the winter. Tetonka had mentioned that he would like to go on one last hunt for deer or buffalo before the first snow fell to ensure that their provisions would last.

At night, they made love to one another, exploring each other's body and discovering new things every time. She had no idea that it could be this wonderful. Her heart jumped for joy every day when he came home and during the day, she missed him so much her heart ached.

She went to the garden to help bring in the pumpkin harvest and the last of the squash. It would be the last of the vegetables from the garden for the year. There were still other food sources in the forest that would be gathered from time to time, like nuts and winter berries. Everyone had plenty of animal hides to stay warm.

When it rained, the people stayed in their huts huddled around the fire. They would visit neighbors or other family members and spend the day inside telling stories and playing games. It had only been a couple of days since their marriage union when they had one of these cold and rainy days. Tetonka decided to stay in, knowing that any intruders to their land wouldn't go far in this weather.

They went to his father's hut to enjoy time with his family. She was still getting used to being with his family instead of her own. She was more quiet than usual and felt unsure of what to do most of the time around her new mother-in-law. She opted to be close at hand whenever Mahpee instructed her to do something.

They finished their evening meal, and the family settled in to tell stories. She helped Mahpee wash the bowls and put them away.

Chaska told a story, "Some time ago, a hunting party had been away from the village for many moons. They had traveled over many mountains west of here. When the hunting was complete, the leader announced to the hunters that they would be leaving at dawn. But when dawn came, and the hunters were about to break camp, the leader ordered his young scout to go and fill his kettle with water. The young scout said, 'Great Leader, the spring where we found the water is a long way off, and you have ordered our men to break camp and leave for home. If I go for water, the return will be delayed. Can it wait until we come to a stream along our way?'

"Instead, the leader ordered his men to put down their burdens and wait until the young scout returned from the spring with water. Seizing his vessel, he hastened to the spring that was on the other side of the mountain a way far off. As the boy approached the spring, he saw a beautiful woman sitting to the side of the spring in the grass dressing her hair. She wore a white buckskin dress. The woman appeared not to look at him, and without taking further notice of her, he dipped his vessel in the water and took leave to return to his leader.

"He walked past the beautiful woman, but after a few steps, he stopped. Normally, he was loyal to his leader and would hasten to return, but there was an unusual power about this woman that kept attracting him to go back. He was suspicious that she was not a real woman, but the urge was irresistible. He was undecided for a time because his orders to promptly return to his leader drew his mind away, but her influence was greater, and he was drawn to her against his better judgment.

"He returned to her spending a brief time talking to her. Afterward, he hastened back to camp with the water for his thirsty leader. Upon return, the leader seized upon the vessel and drank and passed it to the officer next in rank. Then the young scout whispered hastily to the leader telling him of the woman by the spring. After a minute's thought, the leader said to his men, 'My thirst is not yet quenched. Drink the water in the vessel, while I go to the spring and drink some more. Wait here until I come back.

"The leader approached the woman cautiously. She invited him to sit beside her as she began to tell him of things that had not happened but were to come. This frightened the leader, and he quickly left to return to his men. When he returned to camp, he ordered his men to march with the greatest speed possible. This they did, keeping up the pace until sunset and darkness came when they were obliged to camp for the night. Nothing unusual happened through the night, and after an undisturbed rest the men marched again before sunrise and traveled at the same pace that they did the day before. They traveled in the same way on the third day and the fourth, as though fleeing from imminent danger.

"On the morning of the fifth day, as the sun was rising, the leader ordered his men to resume the march but to travel at a moderate pace, as he believed that the danger which necessitated their flight was passed. He was yet speaking when a warrior spoke to the leader and said, 'Great Leader, there sits a woman not far from here.' 'Bring her to me,' the leader said. The leader spoke kindly to the woman, advising her to go home, but she refused to do so. For a long time, the leader talked to her, but neither arguments nor threats could break her determination to follow the men. Thus, prompted by the fear of personal harm by supernatural means for the wrong that he had done the woman, he ordered his men to treat her with respect, and he not only took care of her himself but ordered his men to refrain from violation of her innocence.

"The leader and his men resumed their journey and in time reached home with the spirit woman. She made her home with the leader, who treated her as a member of his family and accorded her all the honors due from a father to a daughter, and she conducted herself in the manner of a chaste woman.

"There came a time when a young man of the Wa-sha-zhe division was taken with an uncontrollable desire to make the spirit woman his wife. She accepted his courtship and in time became fondly attached to him. Then when each knew that one could not live without the other, they agreed to marry according to the custom of the people. The parents and the relatives of the young man sent many valuable presents to the leader, who was now looked upon by all the people as the father and protector of the woman. The father and mother accepted the presents and shared them with their relatives. Then, after a time, the adopted relatives of the young woman dressed her up in the finest clothes they could find, and they had her taken to the young man with presents that greatly outnumbered those that were made by the relatives of the young lover. Then the woman and the young man sat together in the midst of their relatives and ate together, and all knew that the two were married.

"Many children were born to the couple, and the mother and all the children were known to possess the power of prediction, talking with spirits, and other supernatural powers**."

CHARLOTTE LAID STARING at the walls of the hut and watched the shadows cast by the fire. Tetonka and she had left the family hut soon after all the stories had been told. She loved lying in his arms as he curled her into him every night. How could she ever think about leaving this?

But then, she heard the story about the Spirit Woman and believed it was connected to her somehow and that she was there for a purpose. She was torn. Here she had everything she had ever dreamed of, but in the future, she had Brock. How could she choose? She knew she needed to get back to being herself, but there she had to go to school, deal with people who were vandalizing her property and threatening her, and a wonderful boyfriend who she could only kiss and hug. She wondered what would happen if she did choose to stay long term. If her body in the future was on autopilot and not her true self, she had a feeling that it was vital for her to get back to that body and not stay.

Charlotte thought again about the story she had heard. Her Uncle Jimmy said that special abilities were passed down from one of her ancestors who was Native American. This woman had apparently been Osage, but she wondered if they shared an ancient ancestor as well. *What abilities did he say? Prediction, talking to spirits, and others?* She wondered what other abilities there were besides those that he had not mentioned.

And what of her purpose? Life here seemed to be relatively care-free. She knew all too well the dangers of animals, but they were not a constant threat. What of the white men that she knew were coming? She knew the Cherokee would be driven west in what would become the Trail of Tears. Did that involve them coming through here? She should pay attention more in her world history class. It would seem her next move then was to dig into some history and find out what she should be looking for.

"Are you still awake, my love?" Charlotte asked as she laid curled next to Tetonka.

"Hmmm?" he groaned.

"Forgive me, but I wanted to ask something," she said, as she rolled over to face him. Tetonka opened one eye questioningly, so she continued. "What does the land look like further out when you go out scouting?"

Tetonka opened both his eyes now and tried to focus, "Why are you asking this now?"

"I am sorry. I haven't traveled much outside the village, and after hearing the stories tonight, I got to thinking about what else lies beyond here."

Tetonka rolled onto his back pulling her toward him as he did. She propped herself on her elbow, so she could look into his face. "To the east a few valleys from here the land flattens, and there are not as many trees but an abundance of grasses It is where we have hunted many buffalo. There are two small creeks lined with trees, but once you cross over and continue for half a day, you will come to a river that the French call the Saint Francis."

It was strange to hear him speak words familiar to her as Charlotte. This is all Charlotte needed to confirm the location as the same as her present-day home, but she wanted to hear how much more he knew.

"What of the Marsh of the Swans?"

"It is further north and west. Many of our people think that we need to move back to the northern tribes. They think we are not safe staying here anymore. Some of the more eastern tribes are closing in toward the Great River, and some fear they will cross over soon and enter our territory."

"What do you think?" Charlotte asked.

"I think we should stay and fight for our land. Many moons ago in the spring, we caught some white men hunting on our lands, and we drove them away. Some say that there are more and more coming, and we will not be able to keep fighting them off. More *Wa sha zhe* bands live closer to the *A kan sea* River and have been killing and stealing from the white men. I think they are right to defend themselves, but others of our tribe here think that *Wah'Kon-Tah* is not happy and will punish them for all their killing."

"Thank you, my love. Sorry to have disturbed your sleep." She kissed him lightly on the cheek as he closed his eyes.

She laid her head down on Tetonka's chest. This was useful information for her and something that she needed to think about. Soon, she felt Tetonka's breathing slow, and he snored softly. When she was certain he had fallen asleep, she tiptoed out of the hut to find Barkley.

CHAPTER NINETEEN

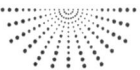

*C*harlotte walked into the courtyard at school. When Lilly spotted her, she broke away from Evan and ran to her, "Hey, Charlotte. Are you back?" Lilly whispered even though she got to her before Evan could hear.

"Yeah, I'm here," she said, sounding disappointed.

Lilly looked back to see how far Evan was, although he was walking toward them. "That was the longest you've been gone," she whispered before Evan approached.

Changing her tone, Lilly asked, "So, did you get any rest yesterday after the basketball tournament this weekend?" Lilly gave her a questioning look that only she could see. Evan put his arm around Lilly. The look on his face suggested he felt he was missing out on something but didn't want to ask.

"Sure." Charlotte gave her a forced smile.

"Where's the boyfriend?" Evan asked.

Charlotte shrugged her shoulders. She didn't feel entirely present. Evan jerked his chin indicating for her to look behind her. When she turned around, Brock had rounded the corner from the parking lot and was walking toward them. She shook herself a little and took a deep breath.

"Hey, you," Brock beamed at her.

"Hey." She smiled brighter coming into his hug.

Lilly watched her carefully, and when she saw her face and smile, she sighed with relief as well.

"Hope you're feeling better," Brock said, looking down at her.

She looked at Lilly for help. The only thing Lilly could do was raise her eyebrows and lift her shoulders slightly. She had to assume she had stuck to their story.

"Yeah, I'm much better," she said, a little hesitantly, trying not to look at Brock directly. She hoped she would have a chance to catch up with Lilly privately soon. Lilly looked at her as if she was thinking the same thing.

They continued with small talk until the morning bell rang, and then walked toward their first-period class.

Lilly was able to fill her in once they got to Algebra II second period. They had cheered a basketball tournament in Jonesboro Thursday through Saturday. She had gotten more and more absent-minded as the week progressed. Lilly told Brock that she was on her period and wasn't feeling well. He seemed to understand and didn't question her mood.

"You got really spaced out by Saturday. You would just sit and stare. You know how someone looks when their mind is somewhere else, but usually, if you click your fingers in front of their eyes they snap out of it, but you wouldn't. I kept close to you and felt like I was your seeing-eye dog."

"I'm sorry, Lilly. I guess now we know that I shouldn't stay gone longer than two or three days."

"I would hate to imagine what you'd get like if you stayed longer than a week."

She nodded her head. "The truth is, even though I'm here with you now, I still don't feel a hundred percent. Maybe it's harder for me to recover when I'm gone longer as well."

They were interrupted when Mr. Dodds asked Charlotte to put one of the homework problems on the board. She looked at Lilly in desperation. When Mr. Dodds turned his head, Lilly quickly handed her her homework paper, and Charlotte copied it onto the board. When she finished, she returned to her seat.

"Excellent, Charlotte. Class? Does anyone have any questions about how Charlotte solved this problem?" Mr. Dodds continued. She had no clue what she was doing, but it would be suspicious if she raised her hand to ask him to explain it after she wrote it on the board. She needed Lilly to catch her up on homework as well it seemed.

After English class, Brock had his arm around her as they walked to the cafeteria for lunch. "Are you sure you're okay?" he said looking down at her.

"Yeah, I'm fine. Why?"

"Well, you were quiet last week. I got kind of worried about you."

Charlotte nodded her head. She wished she could tell him the truth. "I'm sorry. I guess I get that way when it's my time of the month. I withdraw into myself." She hoped it was a believable excuse.

Brock seemed to buy it when he said, "Well, I can deal with that rather than angry moods that some girls have when it's their time of the month. I worried it had something to do with our conversation last Monday."

She panicked a little racking her brain back to last Monday.

Brock sensed she had forgotten and said, "You know, in the truck after I took you home…"

Realization dawned on her, "Oh, yeah. Sorry. I can hardly remember what I ate for breakfast this morning much less what happened a week ago. But, no. It had nothing to do with that." She gave him a reassuring smile, hoping she looked convincing. A pang stabbed her in the heart, remembering all she had done with Tetonka during the last week after she had denied Brock. She felt sick to her stomach feeling she had cheated on him. How would he react if he knew?

"Hey, listen. I was wondering if you wanted to see a movie this Thursday. We have another basketball tournament here this weekend, but I thought we could go out during the week." He opened the cafeteria door for her to walk in.

"Sure! That sounds great! What do you wanna see?" She asked, welcoming the chance to be alone with him for a little bit.

"That depends. Do you like comedy, drama, action, or horror?" They stood in the lunch line, and she turned to look at him walking backward as the line moved.

"I like any of it depending on what mood I'm in. But, I think I'm in the mood to see a comedy. I need something lighthearted and funny right now."

"Then how about *Twins* with Arnold Schwarzenegger and Danny DeVito? I've heard it's supposed to be funny." Brock didn't care what they went to see. He wanted to be alone with her in the dark.

"Sounds like a plan to me!" She beamed at him and gave him a quick kiss on the lips. She quickly turned away before he could catch her for more.

Thursday after school, she went home to freshen up before Brock picked her up at six. Her mother knocked on her door. "Come in," she said.

Her mother pushed open the door and stepped in. "I wanted to check on you and see how you're doing?"

Charlotte looked at her a little confused, "Why?"

"Oh, nothing. How are things between you and Brock?"

"Great!" she said.

"You two seem to be hitting it off. I wanted to make sure you're making wise choices." Her mother sat on the end of her bed. *Great*, Charlotte thought, *not this talk right now*. Out loud, she said, "We are, Mother. You don't have to worry about me. I'll be fine."

"Okay, well. You have a curfew at eleven o'clock tonight. Don't be late, and I mean in the house before eleven, not in the driveway sitting and 'talking' past eleven."

She got the idea. "Okay, Mother. I got it."

Charlotte expected Brock to pull up in his black truck, but instead, he pulled into the driveway in a metallic blue muscle car. When she got to the driveway, Brock waited for her to open her door. "Whose car is this?"

"This is my dad's car. He let me borrow it for tonight," he said proudly.

"I know nothing about cars. But I love the color," she said. At least it had a bench seat in the front, so she could sit next to him.

"I thought you'd like the color. It seems blue is your favorite, right?" He looked at her teasing her with his eyes.

She giggled and nudged him a little. "You got it Blue-eyes!"

"It's a 1972 Chevrolet Impala. My dad bought it from the original owner and has kept it in great shape ever since." To drive home his point, he revved the engine a little more than necessary as they topped the hill. It was loud. She supposed it sounded what a muscle car from the seventies was supposed to sound like.

Since it was a weeknight, the theater was practically empty. She suspected this was what Brock was aiming for. They sat at the back anyway. When the lights went down, Brock casually draped his arm around her shoulders, and she snuggled a little closer to him. She wished the armrest in between them was movable, it was going to be digging into her side all through the movie.

The movie had barely begun when Brock leaned down and kissed her. It was as if he had been starving and was finally allowed to eat. She melted into him and was intoxicated by his warmth and smell. He explored her mouth, neck, and ears with his lips while running his hands through her hair and under her shirt. She did the same to him, but that was where they kept it. The next thing she knew, the theater lights came on, and the movie was over. They hadn't watched a single scene, but their private time together was more than worth the price of admission.

As they walked out of the theater, Charlotte felt disoriented like she was coming out of a deep slumber. She excused herself to the bathroom before heading home. When she got a look at herself in the mirror, she was shocked. Her hair was a mess, and her makeup rubbed off. She had mascara smudges under her eyes. She tried to put herself together the best she could, hoping Brock didn't notice or care at this point what she looked like. When she exited the bathroom, Brock smiled brightly at her, so she guessed he didn't mind.

The parking lot was almost empty as they walked toward Brock's dad's car. Brock had parked it away from the main group of cars so that no one would put a ding in it. When they approached the car, both of them stood there staring at it with their mouths open for a few seconds. The windows were smashed in, all the tires slashed, and the paint was scratched all over.

Brock put his hands on the sides of his head, "Oh my god! My dad is going to kill me!"

Charlotte grabbed hold of him because he looked like he was about to collapse to his knees.

"Who would do this!" Brock yelled. After the initial shock, full rage set in.

She was still in the shocked phase. She held onto Brock until he shook her off to circle the car and get a look at all the damage.

"This'll cost a fortune to repair! Go call the police and then call my dad!" he yelled.

Charlotte ran back to the movie theater hoping they hadn't locked up for the evening. The manager let her use the phone in his office. She dialed Brock's dad first; then she called the police.

When she got back to Brock, he was still circling the car and fuming. Since his dad was twenty minutes out, the police got there first. While Brock talked to them, she found a curb to sit on and waited. As she sat there, she realized she should have called her mother, too, to tell her she might not be able to make it home before curfew.

Finally, Brock's dad arrived driving Brock's truck. When he stepped out, she realized she hadn't met him yet and hated that it had to be under these circumstances.

"Are you Mr. Van Houten?" one of the police officers asked.

"I'm Alexander Van Houten," he said, offering his hand to shake with the officer. Then he got a closer look at the car. He ran a hand through his dark hair that looked a lot like Brock's. He wasn't as tall as Brock, but he had the same basic build. She noticed that they both stood the same way and carried themselves similarly.

177

"Any idea who might have done this to your car, Mr. Van Houten?" the officer asked.

"I have no idea," Alexander stood and shook his head in disbelief at what he was seeing.

She decided to get up and speak to the officer. "My car was burned the week of Thanksgiving. It could be the same guy or guys who did this." Brock looked at her now with sympathy and came over to put his arm around her. She shivered from standing out in the cold for so long.

"Did you file a police report?" asked the officer.

"Yes, with the Paragould police."

"Well, I'm afraid for now, unless the theater has a security camera set up pointed in this direction, there may not be anything we can do. We'll tow it for now and dust for fingerprints, but I can't make any promises we'll be able to catch these guys."

Brock's dad nodded his head and signed off on all the paperwork. Brock walked her to his truck and helped her get in. He got in on the passenger side, opting to let his dad drive home instead.

When Mr. Van Houten got in the truck she thought to introduce herself, "I'm sorry, we have to meet under these circumstances, Mr. Van Houten."

"Please, you can call me, Alex," he said, still polite enough to smile at her as he started the truck.

At first, everyone was quiet, thinking about the car. She finally spoke again, "Brock, do you think it could be Kale?"

Brock sighed heavily, "I have no idea. It's a guess at this point. It can't be random that someone burns your car in your driveway and then seeks out my car, or rather my dad's, all the way here in Jonesboro and damages it." Then he slammed his fist down on the inside of the car door. "I don't understand why someone would go to so much trouble to do such things to someone. What do they want?"

They were silent for a few more seconds, then Alex interjected, "I'm reminded of a story that one of the elders told when we lived on the Osage reservation. 'There once was an old Indian. His little grandson often came in the evenings to sit at his knee and ask the many questions that children ask. One day, the grandson came to his grandfather with a look of anger on his face.

"Grandfather said, 'Come, sit, tell me what's happened today.' The child sat and leaned his chin on his grandfather's knee. Looking up into the wrinkled face and the kind eyes, the child's anger turned to tears.

"The boy said when he went to the town with his father to trade the furs he had collected over the past several months, he was happy to go because his father said that, since he had helped him with the trapping, he could get something for himself. Something that he wanted. The little boy was so excited to be in the trading post. He hadn't been there before. He looked at many things and finally found a metal knife! It was small, but a good size for the little boy, so his father got it for him. Here the boy laid his head against his grandfather's knee and became silent.

"The grandfather, softly placed his hand on the boy's head and said, 'And then what happened?' Without lifting his head, the boy said he went outside to wait for his father and to admire his new knife in the sunlight. Some town boys came by and saw him, they got all around him and said bad things. They called him dirty and stupid and said that he shouldn't have such a fine knife. The largest of these boys pushed him back, and he fell over one of the other boys. He dropped his knife, and one of them snatched it, and they all ran away, laughing.

"Here the boy's anger returned, 'I hate them, I hate them all!' The grandfather, with eyes that had seen too much, lifted his grandson's face, so his eyes looked into the boy's.

"Grandfather said, 'Let me tell you a story. I too, at times, I have felt a great hate for those who have taken so much, with no sorrow for what they do. But hate wears you down and doesn't hurt your enemy. It's like taking poison and wishing your enemy would die. I have struggled with these feelings many times. It's as if there are two wolves inside me, one is white, and one is black. The white wolf is good and doesn't harm. He lives in harmony with all around him and doesn't take offense when no offense was intended. He will only fight when it's right to do so and in the right way. But the black wolf is full of anger. The littlest thing will set him into a fit of temper. He fights everyone all the time for no reason. He cannot think because his anger and hate are so great. It is helpless anger, for his anger will change nothing. Sometimes, it is hard to live with these two wolves inside me, for both of them seek to dominate my spirit.'

"The boy looked intently into his grandfather's eyes, and asked, 'Which one wins Grandfather?'

"The grandfather smiled and said, 'The one I feed***.'"

They sat silently again letting the story sink in. "So, you're saying that whoever is doing this is letting his black wolf control him?" Charlotte asked.

"That, but more importantly, which wolf are you going to feed?" Alex said, staring straight ahead at the road, letting the question rest on both of them.

She had to admit, Alex had handled the damage to his car much better than Brock had, or even her dad had when her car was destroyed. But she knew he was right; she wouldn't let things like this make her angry and fill her with hate. The person who was doing this to them was the one who had the problems and was only letting their inner black wolf get out of control.

"I see your point, Dad," Brock finally said. "But I'm getting more concerned about Charlotte's safety. What if the next time he decides to harm her personally?"

Charlotte hadn't thought of this and looked wide-eyed at Brock. He patted her hand to reassure her, and then Alex said.

"You two are going to have to be extra careful where you go and not put yourselves in vulnerable places where someone could sneak up on you and attack you. You need to let me know if you see anything suspicious."

When they pulled up to her house, it was 11:30. Her mother was waiting for her by the window.

"Mr. Van... I mean, Alex, could you come speak to my mother about why I'm home past curfew?" she asked politely.

"Sure," Alex said and got out of the truck. Brock got out to let her out on his side.

"I'm sorry our night got ruined like this," he said, looking down at her and searching her eyes.

"It wasn't all ruined." She smiled at him and gave him a firm kiss but didn't let it go on for too long since her mother and his dad were talking a few feet away. By the time Charlotte climbed the stairs, Alex was saying goodnight to her mother.

"Goodnight, Charlotte," Alex said politely, nodding.

"Goodnight, Mr. Van Houten," she said as she watched him descend the stairs.

She turned to her mother. "I guess he explained everything?"

"Yes, he did. I'm glad you're okay. Let's go in and go to bed. It's late." Her mother put a hand on her back and followed her inside.

⁊⁊

A WEEK LATER, she arrived home from school and found an envelope on her dresser addressed to her. She sat on her bed and opened it.

December 11, 1988

Dear Charlotte,

I did some research on the history of Arkansas that might not be in any of your school textbooks. Of course, De Soto came to the Arkansas area in search of gold in 1541. His Spanish regiments slaughtered many villages they came across. They also brought several European diseases with them that nearly wiped out all Native Americans that were living in Arkansas at the time.

The natives either recovered or other tribes moved to the area over the next 130 years, and the next European contact came with the French explorers Marquette and Joliet in 1673. In 1682, La Salle claimed the area for France naming it Louisiana. There was an Arkansas Post established along the Arkansas River in 1686. The Spanish took over ownership of the Louisiana Territory in 1762, but the French continued to run the post and maintain relations with the Indians. As a matter of fact, by that time it was common for many Indians to have intermarried with the French.

Of course, you know the American Revolution occurred from 1775 to 1783. In 1803, the United States purchased the Louisiana Territory from

France, who had taken over possession once again in 1802. Thomas Jefferson sent Lewis and Clark on their expedition in 1804. They started in St. Louis and went north on the Missouri River. Arkansas became a territory in 1819 and a state in 1836. By the 1840s, most of the Eastern tribes had been moved to Indian Territory in Oklahoma.

Once you can give me a more specific time frame, I will do my best to narrow down any other historical data I can find. I may have to resort to a more non-traditional form of research and investigate by asking locals who might have information passed down through ancestors.

Please be careful and keep me updated.

Love,

Uncle Jimmy

Later that evening, after everyone had gone to bed. She slipped outside to find Scuffy.

CHAPTER TWENTY

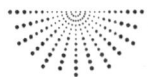

*C*harlotte sat on the floor, carving out pumpkins. She was in Tetonka's parent's hut helping his mother. She was beginning to feel more comfortable with them. They were patient with her and seemed to like her well enough.

Tetonka entered the hut and unloaded his armload of firewood. "A Black Robe man has come to visit the village," he announced.

Charlotte looked at Tetonka surprised. "A missionary?" she asked.

Tetonka nodded his head.

"Where is he?" she asked again.

"He has been welcomed into the Peacemaker Chief's house. He wants to speak to the people who want to listen to him."

She looked at him for a moment, studying his reaction. It could be an opportunity for her to get some more answers. "Will you go with me so that I may listen?"

Tetonka looked at her confused. "Why do you want to listen to a Black Robe?"

She didn't want to upset him. "I am curious about any news he might have outside the village. You said that many white men and other tribes are getting closer to our territory. Maybe he will have some news about people coming from the east."

Tetonka thought about this for a minute, then he nodded. "I suppose it won't hurt to listen to what he has to say. But, I'm not going to conform to his religion." He turned a stern look at her. "All white men fight over their religion as if they are undecided as to what even they believe. I do not need a white man to tell me how to walk the Red Road. I am only accountable to *Wah'Kon-Tah*. I do not need a white man in black robes to tell me how to live." Tetonka seemed adamant about this. She had never heard him talk about such things. Maybe that would be a conversation for another time.

She turned to her mother-in-law asking for permission. Mahpee nodded her head, allowing her to abandon her task for the moment and see the missionary who had come to their village.

When Tetonka and Charlotte approached the Peacemaker Chief's house, it was already overflowing with people from the village. "I do not think there is any room left for us," Tetonka said, turning to leave.

She caught his muscular arm and said, "Please, I would like to see him." She pleaded with her eyes, hoping Tetonka couldn't say no to her.

"All right," he huffed. He grabbed her hand and began to push his way through the people. They came to the edge of the circle where many of the elders from the village were seated smoking the peace pipe and listening to the words of the missionary. He was speaking in French and had an interpreter with him who looked to be from one of the northern tribes.

She looked around the circle and was surprised to find her father, uncle, and grandfather among the men sitting around the missionary talking. Her father spoke, "What news can you give us of our old friend, Pierre Chouteau?"

The missionary nodded after the translator interpreted the question, "Monsieur Chouteau has traveled south to the *A kan sea* Post to maintain peace with the *Wa sha zhe* bands there. They are killing and stealing and refusing to abide by Spanish law. Many want to continue trade with your people, but others are afraid that you will be too violent and untrustworthy."

When the interpreter finished translating the men around the circle exchanged looks to assess the acceptance of what the missionary was saying as true or not. Some had heard, as Tetonka had told her, that the bands close to the *A kan sea* river were becoming more violent and troublesome. It put their group of people in danger, even though they weren't taking part in the crimes.

She whispered a question in Tetonka's ear for him to address the missionary through the interpreter, "What is the White Chief in the east called?" Tetonka didn't know why she would ask such a question, but he did as she asked.

The missionary looked curious, too, as to why such a question would be asked, but he replied, "The White Chief in the new United States of America is called Thomas Jefferson." This narrowed down the time for her, and her heart sped up at the news. She then leaned over to Tetonka and asked her next question, "Who claims this land under their Chief? Is it the White Chief in the east?"

The missionary shook his head, no and then said, "The Spanish Chief still claims this land, although there is talk of the French taking it back." When she heard this, she nearly cried out in joy. She needed to ask one more question.

"White men name the days, months, and years. What do you call this day?"

Again, the missionary was surprised to hear such a question because the natives were never interested in such things and few even knew such things existed. Nevertheless, he was happy to supply the answer. "It is the 20th day of the month October, in the year of our Lord 1801."

She never thought she would be able to solve this vital mystery. Tetonka looked at her confused and a little concerned as to why she would ask such a question and where she even heard of such things. She bowed her head to hide her reaction, but on the inside, she was jumping for joy.

Others in the group began to ask other questions, so she leaned toward Tetonka and said, "We can go now. I have heard enough."

Tetonka seemed to be relieved to leave the stuffy hut and get on with other more important things rather than sit around and listen to a foreign white man in a silly black robe talk about things that didn't seem to matter to him. Once they were free from the crowd that surrounded the hut, he turned to her with a questioning look.

She looked at him, making an effort to look innocent, but he stopped walking, and she assumed he wanted an explanation. What could she tell him that would settle his mind and seem reasonable? "I remember hearing stories from my grandfather when I was young of how the white man counts the days. I didn't know if it was true or not, so I wanted to ask him if he knew the name of today."

Tetonka looked intently at her for a minute then asked, "And why did you want to know about the White Chief in the east?" She swallowed hard and felt her palms go sweaty. This would be a harder one to explain away. Finally, she settled on an explanation that she hoped wouldn't frighten him.

"I have had dreams of the White Chief in the east. He will force us to move from our lands, and if we do not obey, many of us will be killed or starve to death." She kept her face calm and looked deep into Tetonka's eyes as he looked into hers. He looked at her as if he was trying to read a hidden omen written on her face. Finally, he must have been satisfied that what she told him was the truth.

"This is grave news indeed. Should I bring it up to the elders?" Tetonka asked.

She looked down, thinking. She didn't want to alarm the People too soon, yet she knew that it could save a lot of lives if she could convince them to leave this village and move further west. She looked at him again and said, "I do not want to tell the elders yet. Let me see if the spirits give me more visions so that I will understand when it is the right time to give them this news."

This seemed to satisfy Tetonka. He looked at her one last time, then took her hand and walked with her back to their hut. She wondered what he thought of her receiving information from the spirits in her dreams. That wasn't exactly the truth, but she felt it was as good an explanation as she could give that would be acceptable to her people. There were many stories of members of the *Wa sha zhe* who received dreams and premonitions. Charlotte hoped that they would accept her as no different.

She also hoped that it wouldn't frighten Tetonka and make him distant toward her. She decided she wouldn't push the topic and would let Tetonka reflect on her words and come to her when he was ready to hear more.

She returned to her work next to Mahpee. She sat quietly contemplating what her new information meant. It was December 20th in Charlotte's world, that meant this time was two months behind as well as 187 years. It seemed like a random amount of time, and she assumed it had to do with the events that brought her and Nahele together, rather than a round figure in time that she stepped back into. Charlotte couldn't wait to get back to Lilly and tell her the news, and she would tell her Uncle Jimmy when they came to visit for Christmas. But in the meantime, she couldn't help but want to stay a few days to enjoy sleeping with Tetonka. As Charlotte worked silently, a big grin crept across her face.

CHAPTER TWENTY-ONE

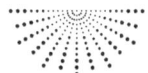

*C*harlotte finished the last of her semester finals and drove her mother's Lincoln Continental home. It was Christmas break and she looked forward to having two weeks free from school. She bent toward the steering wheel and peered up toward the sky. It looked like a storm was coming. From the look of the clouds, it seemed they might be spending the night in the basement.

She usually looked forward to Christmas, but this year she felt something was missing. Maybe it was because she had gotten used to having Brock around, and he would be away again during a major holiday. She didn't know what to do with herself. She was usually so busy with school, cheering, doing stuff with Brock or Lilly, that a holiday was a shock to her routine. Maybe it would give her an opportunity to be Nahele again for a few days without feeling like she was missing out on something here.

When she entered the house, she smelled something wonderful cooking.

"Mmm, what smells so good?" she asked, coming up beside her mother at the stove.

"I'm baking some cookies and pies to get ready for the holidays next week," her mother said as she stirred something with the blender.

"Are you sure it's going to last until next week? You'll have to hide it somewhere so that the boys won't eat it all before then."

"What do you mean hide it from the boys? You will eat it all, too, if I let you." Her mother gave her a knowing look.

Charlotte grinned at her, consenting.

"Your dad and I are going to a Christmas party at the church tomorrow. I need you to stay here with your brothers."

"Okay. I don't have any plans anyway." She sat down at the bar suddenly saddened by the truth of it.

"Good. I wasn't sure if you and Brock had made any plans."

"He's going to New York with his family this week." She hung her head down to emphasize her disappointment.

"Don't look so pitiful. He'll be back, and you two can spend time together. Sometimes it's good to have some distance every once in a while. You don't want to be together so much that you get on each other's nerves."

She supposed her mother was right, but for the life of her, she never thought Brock would ever get on her nerves. But, she couldn't say the same for Brock.

A few days later, on Christmas Eve, Charlotte and her family had just finished eating when they heard the tornado sirens from the nearby fire station. She sighed as everyone filed down into the basement to wait out the tornado warning. While they huddled together in a small section of the basement, they sang all the Christmas songs that they could think of. When they ran out of those to sing, her grandpa led them in a few folk classics that she loved to hear. These were songs that had been passed down through the generations orally. One of her favorites was about a man named Rosenthal and a goat.

She thought of the Osage people. They had no written language. That was one of the criteria she had recently learned in her world history class that qualified a group of people as civilized. So, by that definition, the Osage people were either not a civilized people or were not living in a civilization. Probably both. But, the People had a rich history of oral traditions and rituals that they observed. They had a religious belief but did not have a centralized government as defined by Europeans. Therefore, the Osage were classified as savages in the Europeans' eyes. *If only they had realized how wrong they were*, she thought.

Finally, the storm died down, and her dad determined that it was safe to go back upstairs to open presents. While everyone was occupied, her uncle caught her in the kitchen getting a refill of hot chocolate.

"Have you had any new developments lately?" her uncle asked, remaining cryptic.

"I have." She turned to him with a big grin of satisfaction. "A missionary visited the village, and I was able to ask him the date. It is two months behind here, so if I went back today, I would be in October 24, 1801."

Uncle Jimmy looked at her astonished. "That's great news. It would seem that your new 'friends' are years away from any real danger."

She sighed, and her smile faded, "Maybe not according to any historical records."

They were quiet for a little while watching Jason play with his new toys and Tad and Ryan play with him. Then her uncle said, "What's it like over there?"

She looked at him thoughtfully. "Wonderful. It's peaceful; no one is in a hurry to be anywhere. The nature seems to be more alive. It's as if the land itself hasn't been spoiled or corrupted. Imagine. No pollution, no machines, no electricity."

"I would think you would have a challenging time roughing it like that in the wilderness," her uncle assessed.

"Well, I'm not out on my own. I have a whole village of people, and we all take care of each other." She lowered her voice when she saw her mother look in her direction. "I'm also married."

Her uncle turned to look at her surprised. Charlotte could see the wheels turning in his head as he looked at her. She smiled and looked down embarrassed at what she knew he was thinking.

"Is he good to you?" he finally asked.

She looked up. "Oh, very. He looks out for me and has taken good care of me. He would protect me with his life at whatever cost. He is gentle and would never intentionally harm me."

Her uncle seemed satisfied with this and let the rest of the questions he had go for the moment.

That night, she was given the task of getting Jason to sleep so Santa could come.

"Santa won't come if little boys are still awake," she told her five-year-old cousin. His eyes were big, and he didn't look the least bit sleepy. She tried to keep him quiet by telling him to listen carefully for reindeer hooves on the roof. By lying completely still and listening, he eventually fell asleep.

The next morning, Charlotte was awakened by Jason shaking her. "Charlotte, can we go out there now?" She raised up and rubbed her eyes.

"We have to make sure your parents are up, so they can see your presents, too."

Jason didn't want to wait any longer. He ran out of the bedroom toward the living room squealing. Charlotte dragged herself out of bed. Unless her parents had Brock wrapped up with a big red bow, she would be back to bed within the hour.

THE LAST WEEKEND IN DECEMBER, Tech participated in the Arkansas Indian Classic Basketball tournament held at Arkansas State University. It had been an exciting tournament, and Tech was now in the finals.

Lots of students were coming into the gym. Many had been at the earlier games, but others waited to come once they made the finals. Tech's side of the gym was filling up fast. Charlotte looked into the student section and saw Kale glaring down at her. She hadn't had much contact with him over the past few weeks, but she was always worried he was going to surprise her somewhere.

Before the game started, she needed to go to the bathroom. She grabbed Lilly to go with her.

"How was your break?" Lilly asked as they walked toward the bathrooms.

"Good. Brock was gone all last week, so I was fairly bored," Charlotte said.

Lilly looked at her knowingly and asked, "So, I guess you went *elsewhere* for a little bit?"

She looked at her and gave her a tiny grin. "Yeah, I did." Then she remembered, "Oh, and I got a date for you."

Lilly looked at her confused. "A date? But I'm dating Evan."

Charlotte stopped and looked at her a second before she realized their confusion. She burst out laughing and said, "No. I mean a time date that Nahele is in."

"Oh!" Lilly laughed with her. "So, when is it? Or was it?"

"It would be October 31, 1801, if I switched right now," Charlotte said.

"Wow! That's so wild." Lilly thought about it, then said, "I guess now we know a timeframe to look for."

"Yeah, I've already had this conversation with my uncle, and he concluded that there wasn't anything major in the historical records to indicate something we needed to prevent. But, I'm convinced it's something that won't be in the regular white man's records."

They washed their hands in the sink and heard the buzzer that meant they would be announcing the players soon. They rushed out of the bathroom toward the court.

"I guess we'll have to talk about this later!" Lilly yelled as they ran between the bleachers. Lilly was ahead of her, so she didn't see when Kale reached a hand out from under the bleachers and pulled Charlotte under.

"Kale! Let me go! I'm supposed to be out on the court!" Charlotte tried to shake off his grasp, but his hold on her was too firm. She grimaced realizing she would see bruises there tomorrow.

"I need to talk to you first," Kale said gruffly.

Charlotte stopped struggling. "Make it quick, please." She tried to stay calm.

"I know what you are, and I know what you've been doing." Kale looked down at her glaring into her eyes.

Her breath caught in her throat. She looked at him frightened. Kale grinned down at her wickedly.

"You've been a naughty girl, Charlotte."

"Exactly what are you talking about, Kale?" She narrowed her eyes at him, daring him to say it out loud.

"You know what I'm talking about, Charlotte," Kale said, certain he was on the right track. "And when we get back to school after break, I'm going to tell everyone that you're a witch."

Okay, maybe he did know something she didn't want him to, or perhaps he was still fishing to get a reaction out of her. "I assure you, Kale. I have no idea what you're talking about." She tilted her chin up to him in defiance.

"We'll see about that next week. When everyone finds out about who you truly are, you'll be shunned by everyone and no one, not even Brock, will want to be around you anymore."

This struck a nerve with her, and suddenly tears stung her eyes. She didn't know why she was letting Kale goad her on like this, but she admitted that this had been a concern of hers deep down. She decided not to satisfy him by crying in front of him or saying anything more that might incriminate her, so she turned on her heel and ran to the sideline. She got there before the referee tossed the jump ball.

Lilly looked at her asking, *where did you go?* Charlotte shook her head as if to say, *not now.* It was hard enough to get her head back into the excitement of the game. She fought back the tears.

AFTER THE GAME, Brock and Charlotte headed to a New Year's Eve party with some of her friends from church. They stopped by her house to let her shower and change, then they drove to Crowley's Ridge College where everyone was meeting in the gym there.

Brock noticed she was quiet and seemed to be distracted. "Are you okay, Charlotte? You can't be that upset that we lost the tournament; we did get second."

She turned toward him as if he had startled her out of deep thought. "Oh, I'm not upset about that. It was a great game." She didn't want to tell him about Kale. It would only bring up more questions that she wasn't ready to answer yet.

"So, what is it?" Brock wasn't convinced.

Charlotte shrugged her shoulders buying time for her to come up with a good excuse. "I don't know. I guess I get a little sad at the end of a year."

"Really?" Brock looked amused.

"Well, yeah. It's been a good year. I hate to see it go. Besides, I always get a little scared, thinking about the new year to come."

Brock didn't know what to say to this. He turned his head slightly to look at her, but then turned his attention back to the curvy road.

She thought she should explain. "The future is so unknown. It's kind of scary to think about the things that might change. I get comfortable with the way things are and don't want the good things to change."

Brock understood her now. "I can see your point. I don't like good things to change either. But, I also have the hope that good things will only get better." He smiled at her. "I was unhappy about moving here. It was a big change for me. I was leaving things that I had known all my life to go somewhere I knew nothing about or any of the people who lived here. But, I found you almost the moment I got here and look how great that's been."

This cheered her somewhat. "I'm so glad you moved here, Brock. I didn't realize how lonely I was until you and I got together. I get so excited to see you every day that I can, and I always feel like the time I do spend with you is never enough."

Brock made the turn onto the campus, and she directed him toward the gym. They pulled into a parking space, but Brock waited to turn the engine off. He turned more toward Charlotte to look at her while he spoke.

"Is that all that's on your mind?" He put his arm around her to comfort her.

She looked down at her hands in her lap. She had a lot of things on her mind right now, but none of them she could share with him. She looked back at him and smiled. "Yeah, I guess that's all. Maybe I'm a sentimental douche."

Brock hugged her tightly. "I don't think you're a sentimental douche. I think that makes you sweet and a special part of who you are."

She pulled back from him a little. It was the complete opposite opinion of her than what Kale had expressed earlier. "You think I'm sweet?" she asked, feeling a sting in her chest.

"Of course, I do, Charlotte. Why would you think you're anything less?"

She searched his eyes in the dim light. She wanted to tell him everything. "It's that no one's ever told me that before, and with people always writing terrible things about me on my car and vandalizing my property, after a while, I begin to feel like I must be this horrible person that people hate, and there must be something about me that makes them want to hurt me." She found herself fighting back the tears again.

"Charlotte, don't let those people get to you. Those people who are targeting you are doing so because they hate themselves, and they're jealous of the beautiful and sweet person that you are."

Brock put his hand under her chin and lifted her head, "Charlotte McAfee, I think you're the most beautiful person both inside and out, and I'll do everything I can to keep those who say otherwise away from you." He could see the tears welling in her eyes and to keep the tears from forming in his own, he kissed her to emphasize his point.

They held one another in the cab of the truck. Charlotte relished the feel of his warm body next to hers. She could feel the thump of his heart against her chest. He smelled wonderful, fresh from his shower after the game. His breath was hot on her ear when he broke the silence. "I really don't want to go inside."

"Me neither," Charlotte said.

"But I suppose we should."

"Yeah, I suppose."

Brock released her from his embrace and opened the door. The cold from outside blasted over her, bringing her back to the present. It was a fitting reminder of how different her love life was with Brock than with Tetonka. She wanted more with Brock, but her conventional upbringing said it was wrong. She tried to tell herself that what she had with Tetonka was totally separate, but a part of her felt that a major reason for her returning to the past was to experience what she couldn't have here in her present.

A guilty pang hit her in the gut again thinking about what Brock would think if he knew. Would he be angry? Would he understand? Or would he abandon her like Kale said he would if he knew the things she was doing behind his back.

She tried to push those thoughts from her mind as she sat with all her friends and played games. At midnight, someone called out the countdown, and everyone kissed the person they were with. It was the first time she had ever had someone to kiss on New Year's Eve. She hoped that the superstition would come true, and it meant that they were going to have a happy year together. But deep down, she feared this happiness wasn't going to last forever.

CHAPTER TWENTY-TWO

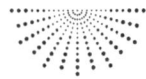

*N*ew Year's Day, while everyone slept in late, Charlotte snuck out the back and followed Scuffy into the woods. She assumed her shadow-self would go back to bed and sleep like everyone else.

The harvests were in, and all the food had been stored away for the winter. The village messenger went around to the huts announcing that a game of shinny (an early version of Lacrosse) would be played. Once word got around about the game, the players set out to make their Lacrosse sticks or dig out ones they had stored away from previous years.

Anyone was allowed to play, men, women, and children. The only rules were that men couldn't hurt women and children, and women couldn't harm children. The men, however, were brutal with one another.

Charlotte opted to find a relatively clear space with an unobstructed view to watch. A few other women who were either pregnant or with small children also sat around her to watch what they could for a while. The end of the game was only decided once everyone mutually agreed they were too tired to go on. Some told of games lasting from sun up to sun down for three days in a row. Older men who could no longer play would sit near the goal areas to keep track of scores.

Once the play area was established, and everyone had their sticks, the players gathered together. Team captains were chosen, and they subsequently picked their teams. The teams then selected a color that meant each member had to paint that color on their face so that they could be identified as either teammate or opponent. She noticed that Tetonka had red on his face, and Kajika wore black.

An elder placed the ball in the center of the field and quickly ran out of the way. The two teams lined up several paces away from the ball. When the elder gave the signal, several brave individuals rushed toward the ball to take possession. Elbows were thrown, and men were knocked down right at the start.

A red team member took possession and tossed it in Tetonka's direction. He caught the ball in his net and ran to the opponent's goal to try to score. A black team member came running at him head on, but before he could get too close, Tetonka tossed it to another team member who caught it and ran around the opponent. He was then blindsided by a black team member, and he lost the ball.

Black team scooped the ball and ran in the other direction. The ball was tossed back and forth between black team members several times, but then a red team member intercepted it and put it into play, going back in the other direction.

The play continued this way back and forth for most of the time. When one team got close to the opponent's goal, an opponent team member would be there to block the goal and keep it from going in. Then the play would shift to the other goal and all the players would race one another down to the other side jockeying for possession of the ball or fighting to make their opponent drop the ball.

The men played extremely rough. They would trip one another with their sticks or by sticking their feet out. The women would do the same to the men, even though, the men couldn't trip the women. The women, however, had no problem tripping other women. The children playing were all at least older than eight years old; most of them were boys. They were critical players because if they got the ball, no one was allowed to hurt them, so they could quickly run to the goal. However, the older members were crafty in using their sticks to hit the younger players' sticks to make them lose the ball and regain possession.

The women who played looked like they were having fun, and she noticed that there were several who were running back and forth, but hardly ever touched the ball. Those were the ones enjoying themselves and laughing at all the antics that the others pulled on the other team members. The men, on the other hand, were serious. Several had bloody lips or noses and scratches or bruises from being punched. More than once she winced when someone came up bleeding.

After about an hour of play, someone finally scored a goal for red, and all the red team members cheered and yelled the warrior's cry. This incited the black team members to play even harder to be the next to score a goal.

Tetonka jogged over to her. She had a container of water for him when he got thirsty. He drank heavily from it, kissed her quickly on the mouth, and ran away, smiling. She watched his muscular, lean body run away admiring the muscles flexing in his long legs. She sat back down with a big smile plastered on her face. Some of the women on the sidelines were helping their men by yelling instructions or giving them warnings of opponents about to jump out at them. After a while, she found herself yelling as well to get the ball or watch out! She wished she could play; it looked like a lot of fun.

Then she had a sudden wave of nausea and realized she needed to eat. She brought a bundle of food for Tetonka and her when he wanted to take a break. Another woman sitting close to her was nursing a baby with a toddler still clinging to her side. She admired them silently envisioning herself in that position one day.

Tetonka ran back to her and plopped down on the ground beside her. "Are you enjoying the game?" he asked, breathlessly. He was sweaty despite the chilly temperature. She handed him something to eat, and he chewed it down hungrily.

"I am having a wonderful time," she smiled back at him. His breathing quickly returned to normal as he rested on his side propped by his elbow while eating and drinking. The play continued regardless of some members taking a break. When they rotated back in, others would sit out and take a break. There was no timing, no time-outs, no referees to call fouls. Although, a few times she wanted to yell foul but quickly caught herself because there was no such thing.

When Tetonka finished, he kissed her once again, picked up his stick, and ran back into play refreshed. Charlotte admired his cunning in the game. He was swift and agile, moving around the trees and running effortlessly. She noticed that Kajika was always close by, but instead of being his helper, he was his opponent, and they fought one another more fiercely than any other. She supposed this was playful fighting between warrior-brothers, but they were so rough with one another. If one didn't know they were kolas to one another, one might think they were fierce enemies sworn to kill one another.

The sun was getting low in the sky, and some members were sitting out longer and longer. Many of the women were out of the game by now and were either resting on the sidelines or had chosen to go back to their huts to prepare a meal. All the young boys were still out there. They either had lots of energy or didn't want their older peers to see them give out too soon.

She saw that Tetonka had the ball again and was running zig-zagged toward the goal. It looked like he might score when suddenly Kajika stepped out in front of him, swung his stick at Tetonka's face, and knocked him out cold on the ground.

Charlotte screamed and jumped up, running to her fallen husband. When she got to him, he was already coming to.

"My husband! Are you all right?" she knelt at his side.

He tried to get up, but she put her hand on his chest and shook her head telling him to wait. He looked at her as if he couldn't focus on her clearly and dropped his head back to the ground.

She saw a red whelp forming on the side of his head above his temple. She looked at Kajika who was standing over him. He only looked a little concerned. She narrowed her eyes at him as if to say, *you didn't have to do that.* He got the reprimand, shrugged his shoulders, and walked away.

"Come, my love. I think it is time to end for today." She helped him sit up slowly. Then putting his arm around her shoulders, she helped him stand up. "Let's go to the stream and wash before we go back to the hut."

He grunted his consent as they hobbled over to a secluded area of the stream. She helped him sit down by the creek to remove his knee-high moccasins. When she tried to help him remove his breechcloth, he pushed her hand away so that he could do it. She looked at his face a little hurt that he didn't let her attend to him.

When he saw her face, he said, "I am all right." Then he smiled pleasantly at her.

When he waded into the water, she decided she would join him. Charlotte removed her dress and moccasins and followed him. The water was colder now. She moved slowly until she reached him with the water up to her waist.

She shook uncontrollably. Tetonka looked back at her with a big smile. He wrapped his arms around her as if to help warm her up, but then holding her tight he fell to the side, dunking them both under the water.

She came up gasping for air and sputtering, shocked by the sudden cold. Tetonka held her down to keep the water at shoulder level, crouching under the water. Gradually, her body adjusted to the temperature, and she stopped shivering. He pulled her to him tighter, and she wrapped her long legs around his waist, pressing herself against his chest. Now he was smiling at her with an altogether different intent behind his eyes.

She gently touched the swollen red bump on the side of his head, and he winced a little. She looked at it with her lips pressed tight together, and he watched her carefully. "It's not that bad. I'll survive."

She looked him in the eyes and smiled knowingly. "I know you are tough and think that nothing will ever hurt you, but you are still a mortal man capable of injury."

He squeezed her a little tighter. "With you in my arms, I feel like I am invincible and could survive anything." Then he planted his lips on hers. They kissed as the sun's rays hit the glistening water, and it turned the sky shades of pink and purple. He moved his mouth to her neck, and she sighed with pleasure. Their body heat pressed together helped them forget the frigid water as they caressed each other. Eventually, they grudgingly got out of the water and put their clothes back on. Tetonka held her hand as they walked in the dying sunlight back to their hut.

CHARLOTTE WOKE to a warm fall day. Tetonka had already left the hut. She sat up and stretched her body. She felt a sudden wave of nausea and quickly laid back down. She needed something to eat, but before she could eat, she needed water, which meant going to the stream.

She carried the kettle to the stream. This part of the stream was a different area than where she was used to going from the Sky clan side. Other women were also filling their kettles. She didn't recognize anyone. It was odd living in the same village she had always been in but feeling she was a stranger on this side.

The custom of the people was that a Sky clan member always married an Earth clan member. She had been born in the Sky clan and married into the Earth clan, whereas, her mother had been born in the Earth clan and married into the Sky clan. It ensured that neither group outgrew the other, and there was a balance of power between the two. The Sky clan members were the Peacemakers, and the Earth clan members were the Warriors. Hence, the reason Tetonka and his family were primarily scouts and would be warriors if the elders determined to wage war. The men from the Sky clan could be warriors as well but would negotiate peace and sit in on council decisions as they grew older.

Charlotte carried the kettle full of water back to her hut and set it aside to light the fire. Once she had a good fire going, she placed the kettle over it to warm. She checked the stores of food. She chose some dried meat and corn mash. Once the water was warm but not yet boiling, she scooped some in a small bowl. She put the meat and mash in the warm water and stirred it to make a gruel. They had no utensils, so everything was either drunk from the bowl or scooped with the fingers. She did a little of both.

She washed the bowl out and placed it back with the others. They didn't have many items in their hut, but it was just the two of them. She suddenly felt nauseous again and ran out of the hut. She threw up everything she ate outside. *Well, so much for that*, she thought. She covered it with dirt and went back in. Now, she felt sleepy again and decided to lie down. She must have dozed off because she opened her eyes a little later and it was already noon.

Charlotte tentatively set up again. She hoped she wasn't getting sick with something. She knew the dangers of disease in this time. There weren't many cures for the people. The medicinal plants they knew to use were only partially effective for the common sicknesses that the people contracted. But if any of them were exposed to a disease from the white man, it could be fatal.

Panic suddenly struck her. *The missionary who had been here, did he bring something to the village?* Her heart pounded, and her breathing sped up. *Calm down. You're making yourself panic for no reason*; she tried to tell herself. She began to hyperventilate. She put her head down between her knees and took a few deep breaths. Now she felt light-headed. She rolled onto her back and laid on her mat staring at the ceiling of the hut. This was silly. She was letting her imagination get ahead of her. Maybe if she got out of the hut and walked in the fresh air, she could regain her sanity and stop panicking.

She walked outside the hut. She took a deep breath of fresh air. Feeling better, her stomach grumbled. She decided instead of making a meal for herself again she would go over to her family's hut and visit them. It was easier to share a meal with family rather than eat alone.

CHARLOTTE ENTERED her parent's hut and found her mother and Hula preparing a meal. When Hula saw her walk through the door, she immediately jumped up and embraced her.

"Nahele! I am so happy to see you!" her sister squeezed her a little tighter than usual.

She hugged her back relieved to be with her family again. "I thought I would come visit and share the mid-day meal if you wish." Her mother also came to her and hugged her. It felt so good to be in her mother's arms again, and for an instant, she wished she was a little girl again so that she would be under her parents' protection and never have to worry about the things adults had to take care of daily.

Her mother and sister welcomed her to sit next to the fire. This time she chose to nibble on some dried meat and not overeat. Her mother gave her a tea to wash it down, and it helped soothe her stomach.

"Is there any news you might have for me?" Charlotte asked to make conversation.

Hula was always one to talk, and this sent her into a tirade of the ins and outs of other members of the Sky Clan. Who was to be married to whom, and who was mad at who for some silly reason. Charlotte barely listened; she was just happy to be in the company of her mother and sister.

She caught the eye of her mother, and Charlotte gave her a small smile. Her mother knew she wasn't listening to Hula either. They exchanged a look of understanding and patiently waited while Hula ran down all the latest gossip. Then she heard her say something about the missionary visit.

"What did you say?" Charlotte interrupted.

"I said the missionary wants to take a group of men to visit the Big Osage village at Marsh of the Swans. Father, Grandfather, and Uncle have volunteered to go."

She thought about this for a minute. "When did they say they would be leaving?"

"They plan to leave two sleeps from now," Hula informed her.

"What does the missionary want by taking a group to the Big Osage village?" she asked. This could be something she could investigate from her own time.

"I think there is talk of moving our people back to the big village for safety. Some say white men from the east will be coming across the Great River soon, and we will not be able to hold them off." Hula looked at her to see her reaction.

She nodded her head. "Tetonka told me the same thing. He believes we should defend ourselves and strike anyone who trespasses on our territory, but I have tried to tell him that there may be too many for us to attack." She looked at her mother to see her reaction. Her mother looked thoughtfully into the fire. She nodded her head as well.

"I am afraid you may be right, *Me nah*. We have enjoyed a time of peace here, but from what I have heard of the southern bands, they are stirring up trouble that is going to reflect on us even though we are innocent." Niabi looked at her daughters. "The French have always been good to us and have maintained good relations with us, but the Spanish and English have waged war with many other tribes in the east and the west. They will be looking toward our land next, and we are caught in between them. I am afraid we will not be able to hold them off for much longer."

Charlotte thought this was insightful of her mother. "What if the elders choose not to move but fight instead?"

They sat contemplating this issue for a minute. They were interrupted in their thoughts by her grandfather entering the hut. When Charlotte saw him, she stood quickly to greet him. However, when she did so, she got light headed, and her vision became black around the edges. When she swooned, her grandfather was quick to catch her before she fell.

He lowered her back to the ground, *'Me nah!* Are you not well?" Her grandfather looked down at her concerned.

Charlotte rested for a few seconds, regaining her sight as the blood made it back to her head. "I am well now." She tried to smile at him. "I must have jumped up too quickly to greet you and went faint for a moment."

Her mother and grandfather exchanged looks. Hula was at her side with more tea. "Would you like another sip to drink?"

She graciously took the tea from her sister and sat up regaining her strength. When everyone continued to look at her with concern, she smiled at them and said, "Really. I am fine. I got up too quickly. I am better now." She didn't like seeing them worried about her.

After she finished her tea, she looked at her sister. "Is there something I can help you with today?" She wanted to get out of the smoky hut again and get some fresh air.

"I was going to collect some more firewood for the hut if you would like to come with me?" her sister replied.

"I would love to come with you." This time she got up more carefully. She kissed her grandfather gently on the head, and she followed her sister out of the hut.

Once out in the fresh air, she breathed in deep once again and felt her head clear. She hooked her arm with her sister's and walked with her to the village woodpile. They reached the woodpile and began to gather sticks. Hula wore a bracelet their father had given her, and it fell into the pile when she reached for some wood.

Hula reached into the woodpile to retrieve her bracelet and immediately pulled back screaming. Charlotte looked over at her to see what happened and saw Hula gripping her right wrist staring in shock at her hand. When Charlotte got a closer look, she saw two puncture wounds in the flesh between her forefinger and thumb. Horror gripped her heart as blood trickled down Hula's hand.

"We must get you to the medicine woman!" she said, helping her sister up. Hula kept a grip on her wrist as Charlotte helped hold her while walking briskly through the village to Onaiwah's hut.

When they entered the hut, Onaiwah turned to see the two frightened girls. Onaiwah took one look at Hula's hand and knew instantly what had happened. She directed them to sit by the fire. She knelt to examine the wounds more closely.

"Did you see the snake that did this?" Onaiwah asked.

All Hula could do was shake her head. The wound area was already swelling and flushing with fever.

"She dropped her bracelet down into the woodpile and reached down to retrieve it," Charlotte began to explain.

"Likely, you startled it when the bracelet fell in, and your hand was the next target for its anger," Onaiwah answered.

"I know not to dig into the pile and only to take wood from the top, but I reacted when it fell," Hula said, trembling. She fought back the tears as best she could.

Onaiwah took a string and tied it tightly around her wrist cutting off the blood flow and hopefully any toxins that might go to her heart. She turned to prepare some herbs when Hula began to convulse.

Onaiwah changed her course of action. "It's going to have to come off," she said, placing a knife in the fire.

"Come off? What come off?" Charlotte cried, panicking, even though she wanted to be strong for her sister.

"Hold her arm steady for me," Onaiwah instructed her. Charlotte was to Hula's left; she wrapped her right arm around her sister in a hug. She held Hula's arm straight and down at the elbow but then buried her face into her sister's shoulder and began to cry. Onaiwah took the knife from the fire and, lifting it over her head, came down as swiftly as she could, cutting the hand off at the wrist. Hula screamed, then fainted.

Onaiwah wrapped the stub with a cloth packed with some moss in between the layers to absorb the blood. She fastened it tightly with another string.

"Lay her down over here," Onaiwah instructed, gesturing to her pallet in the corner. "You go find your father while I attend to her." Charlotte didn't want to leave her sister, but she knew that her parents needed to know what happened.

Charlotte rushed out of the hut not sure where her father might be. She came upon one of the elders of the village. "Have you seen Chayton?" she asked. The old man gestured toward the stream, and she took off at a full sprint.

She saw her father's back as he washed off his hunting knives. "Father!" she screamed not waiting to get close enough to touch him. He whirled around immediately on alert at his daughter's fear.

"It's Hula," she said breathlessly. He ran toward her catching her by the shoulders.

"What happened, *Me nah?*" he said, keeping his voice calm until he could learn the full situation.

"She's...been...bitten...snake..." Charlotte gasped in between breaths.

"Where?" her father asked.

"Medicine woman," she got out still gulping air. That's all her father needed to know. He took off at his full speed which was twice as fast as Charlotte could go; he had much longer legs and stronger muscles. He was already inside when she came to the door of the hut. She had to pause outside the entrance to catch her breath. She felt light headed and queasy to her stomach. She could be going into shock herself over the excitement and sudden exertion. The last thing she remembered was thinking she needed to sit down then everything went black.

When Charlotte opened her eyes, she tried to bring them into focus. She was lying on Onaiwah's pallet where Hula had last been. "What happened?" she asked, struggling to sit up.

"There, there. Lie back down. Your father took your sister back to their hut. She will be okay. It will take some getting used to after losing a hand, but it is much better than losing her life as she almost did." Onaiwah handed her a cup of tea. "Here, drink this. You know it as Sassafras." Charlotte began to take a sip then realizing what the woman said nearly spit it out at her.

"What did you say?" Sassafras was one of Charlotte's favorite plants.

"It's not what we call it here with our people," Onaiwah said, sitting calmly next to her.

"But, I'm one of your people, why would you say that?"

"I have known before I sent you and your sister several moons ago what would happen to you and who you would bring back with you on that day." Onaiwah searched her eyes and rested her hand lightly on her shoulder.

"You sent me out there to get those plants so that I would make a connection?" she asked. "How did you know? What is happening to me? I have so many questions?" Her mind was suddenly reeling from months of doing this all on her own.

"I don't have time to answer all your questions now. I sent for your husband to get you. You need to rest now. You will have a little one soon." She said this last part with a big smile. Again, Charlotte's eyes went wide with the second shocking bit of news since she fainted. Suddenly, she needed to lie back down.

Tetonka burst into the hut looking all around like a wild man. When his eyes landed on her, he rushed to her side. "My love, what has happened?" he asked only slightly out of breath.

"She is fine. It is her sister who brought her here. I'm afraid we had to cut her sister's hand off after an adder snake bit her." Onaiwah looked bereaved at what she had done.

Tetonka looked back at Charlotte. "But, why are you lying here and not Hula?" he asked, catching up on the day's events.

"She can tell you all about it while you carry her home. She will be all right. But, she needs lots of rest right now." Onaiwah smiled slightly, despite the horrible events that led them to her. "Here, take this medicine with you, and when you are feeling better, my dear, come back and see me, so we can talk." She handed her a small packet of herbs she had put together then turned to her fire.

Tetonka scooped her up like a small child and carried her out of the hut. Charlotte nuzzled her face into the crook of his neck, smelling his strong scent. She lifted her lips to his ear and whispered, "You are going to be a father soon."

He stopped and looked down at her, his eyebrows raised in astonishment. Realizing what she meant, he squeezed her into him a little tighter then took long strides back to the hut.

CHAPTER TWENTY-THREE

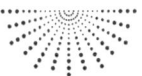

*T*etonka carefully laid her down on their pallet. He pulled the bearskin over her before turning to the fire and lighting it again. Charlotte snuggled under the skin, watching him. She was struggling with so much emotion. Her sister had lost a hand and would have to deal with that for the rest of her life. On the opposite end of the emotional spectrum, she just found out she was pregnant. Everything she had always dreamed of was coming true.

Charlotte observed Tetonka as he lit the fire. She could tell that many things were going through his mind as well. He turned to look at her and caught her smiling at him. He paused for a minute, and a big smile slowly spread across his face. He scooted closer to her. He looked down at her and caressed the side of her face.

"You look more beautiful today than I have ever seen." He looked deeply into her eyes. She saw tears welling in his. He leaned down and kissed her tenderly on the lips. She reached her hands over his neck and pulled him closer to her.

When he finally raised up, he asked, "Is there anything I can do for you?"

She shook her head, "I am fine. I have had plenty of tea today. I will need to go to the stream soon, but, for now, come lay beside me."

She opened the skin for him to slide in beside her. It wasn't cold outside, but the snuggling together under it felt more intimate. He snuggled her into his chest and wrapped his arms around her. He smoothed her hair with his big hand while he rested his chin on her head. Finally, he asked, "What happened to your sister?"

She told him everything that happened. She shuddered into his chest, and he squeezed her a little tighter. Tears that she tried desperately not to release flowed anyway. Tetonka remained quiet and patient until her tears ran out.

She lifted her face toward him, and he kissed each of her cheeks wet with tears. They smiled at one another, feeling a bliss that they never realized was possible.

He rolled to the side, spooning her into him. He nestled his mouth next to her ear. "I love you so much," he whispered.

"And I, you," she said, smiling pleasantly.

"I will take care of you and this baby. My heart is full of joy to know you will be the mother of my child."

Charlotte sighed and almost cried again.

He ran his hand down to her belly as if he could protect it more. She placed her hand on his. His hand was so big; it covered the whole area below her belly button. She couldn't feel anything down there yet, but now that she knew that she was pregnant, she was more conscious of her body. Her body was already displaying changes. Nausea in the morning, dizziness, and the extra exhaustion she realized were all early warning signs that she had missed.

Charlotte was so happy and full of joy; she never wanted this moment to end. They laid there holding one another for a little while until her bladder urges couldn't be ignored anymore. Since she had to go to the stream again, she offered to get water for the kettle. Tetonka was afraid for her to go out alone at this moment, so he insisted on going with her.

They walked out of the hut, holding hands and smiling from ear to ear. The sun was setting low, casting a golden glow across the ground and sky. Charlotte was so full of joy that she felt the nature all around her was celebrating with her. At the edge of the forest, she saw

Barkley panting with his tongue hanging out. She turned to walk toward him. Tetonka had never seen him before and jerked her hand back to prevent her from going any further.

Charlotte turned to Tetonka and said, "Do not worry, my love. This is my spirit guide. I would like you to meet him." Tetonka looked worried and uncertain of the danger. "Come. You will see," she encouraged him. He hesitated a few more seconds, then, keeping a firm hold on her and guarding her body slightly with his, he allowed her to approach the wolf.

When they approached the wolf, she knelt and reached her hand toward Barkley. Barkley happily approached her and licked her palm. She looked at Tetonka, who was still standing next to her uncertain. "See. He protects me as you do. He is the one who saved me from the bear."

Tetonka realized he owed this wolf his gratitude. He knelt as well and scratched the wolf behind the ears.

"Thank you, my friend. I trust you will look out for her when I am away."

Barkley gave a sharp bark and wagged his tail enthusiastically. Then Tetonka did something unexpected. He placed his hand on her stomach and addressed the wolf. "I will honor you as well at the birth of our firstborn."

The wolf seemed to understand what this meant and put his paws on Tetonka's shoulders and licked his face. This surprised Tetonka, and he fell over backward with the wolf on top of him. He laughed heartily, and the two of them playfully wrestled along the ground. Charlotte thought this was the most amazing sight she had ever seen, and it warmed her heart to see the two of them together.

THE NEXT DAY, Charlotte decided was the day she would talk to the medicine woman, Onaiwah. Why she had finally decided to reveal herself to her, she didn't know. But, now that she knew that Onaiwah had known all along, a part of her was angry that Onaiwah had waited this long to say something. Maybe she had a reason for keeping her secret. Perhaps Charlotte had to discover some things on her own, but now she would wait no longer.

After she kissed Tetonka bye for the day and settled her stomach with some tea and nibbles of cornbread, she made her way to Onaiwah's hut. She was nervous and excited to talk to her. She found her palms sweating, and her heart raced. She was almost scared about what more she would discover.

Charlotte quietly entered the hut and looked around. Onaiwah was sorting through her supplies when she turned her head toward her. She smiled brightly and gestured for her to have a seat by the fire.

"Would you like something to eat or drink?" Onaiwah asked.

She shook her head, "I have already had my morning meal. I have to be careful, or it will come back up." She grinned, slightly embarrassed.

Onaiwah bowed her head knowingly. She sat next to Charlotte and took her hands. She turned more toward her as she sat studying her palms. Then Onaiwah rubbed her thumbs across Charlotte's palms, closed her eyes, and muttered a prayer under her breath. Charlotte tried to sit as still as possible patiently, waiting for her to finish.

After several minutes, Onaiwah stopped and let her head drop down. At first, Charlotte worried she had fainted, but then she slowly lifted her head. Her eyes were misted over as she looked softly into Charlotte's eyes.

"I am certain you have many questions for me," Onaiwah said quietly. "But first, let me tell you a story.

"Many moon cycles ago, at a time when our people had first come to the land, The Moon gave birth to a special daughter. She was the daughter of the Moon and the White Buffalo, and she was called the Rainbow Spirit Woman. She was given extraordinary gifts that would be passed down through her sons and daughters for all time. These gifts were to be used wisely to help all the other people of the tribes during their journeys here on the land. Each of her sons and daughters would receive a special gift, but only those who were most worthy would receive the greatest and most cherished gift of all, that of Spirit Travel. These special children of the Moon and White Buffalo would be able to separate their spirits from their body and travel across planes of time and enter the body of someone who would be called a receiver. The receiver did not have to be a descendant of the Moon and White Buffalo, he or she only had to have a heart willing to receive.

"The Rainbow Spirit Woman wanted to give an additional gift to these special children called the Spirit Travelers. She took a piece of the sky carried to her on the wings of a white dove and placed it in the eye of the Spirit Travelers so that those who identified them would know that they were special indeed. The sky is a symbol of wisdom and peace, so by placing a part of the sky within the Spirit Travelers, they would be gifted with wisdom and seek peace at all costs.

"The Rainbow Spirit Woman also saw a need for her special children to be guided and protected, so she instructed some of the animals of the land to assist the Spirit Travelers in their journeys. These animals also received a piece of the sky so that they too may be identified and held in special honor. Those animals came in many forms: some were birds of many kinds like the falcon or owl, some were horses, some were great cats, and some were wolves or their descendants, dogs. These animals would always be near their Spirit Traveler to guide them between planes of time and help protect them in times of danger.

Whenever a Spirit Traveler needed guidance, they could call on their animal spirit guide to assist them, and while the Spirit Traveler's spirit was gone, the spirit animal served to protect the shadow-self until their spirit returned. The bond between Spirit Traveler and spirit guide is strong, but a Spirit Traveler would have many spirit guides to guide them throughout their lives, and if ever a spirit guide gave his or her life to save their Spirit Traveler, they would receive the highest honor of eternal life among the stars.

"The Spirit Traveler may travel to many lives all throughout their lifetime and live the life of a hundred in the time of only one. Sometimes, their journey was unknown, and their purpose would only be revealed at a time when it was needed. Other times, the journey was for growth and understanding so that the Spirit Traveler could become strong in their abilities. . ."

She paused for a moment as if telling this story was taking enormous strength from her. "Close your eyes, child. I will teach you how to reach out to your other self."

Charlotte did as Onaiwah asked. "Now look into your mind for your shadow-self."

At first, her mind was blank. She took a deep breath and let it out slowly relaxing her mind and body. A tiny light began to grow as if she was seeing it far away. The light grew bigger until it appeared to her in her mind like a window. She could see through the window and saw herself sitting on the couch in her living room. "I see," Charlotte whispered.

"What are you doing there?" Onaiwah asked.

"I'm watching TV."

Onaiwah didn't ask what that was, but continued, "Who is there with you?"

"My mother. We are watching old Elvis Presley movies. We love watching those together."

"Good, good. Now, if you wanted, you could place yourself back there fully, or you can check in from time to time. But if you concentrate, you can move back and forth between here and there more freely. You do not always need your spirit animal to guide you, although they will always be available to you when you need them."

Charlotte nodded her head in understanding. She could feel the connection, and she could make it stronger if she wanted to. It felt like all she had to do was step through the window, and she would be there.

"There is one thing I must warn you about—" Onaiwah began, but before she could finish, someone rushed into her hut with a hunter who had been injured.

The spell Onaiwah was under broke. "I am sorry, my dear, but we will have to continue this another time," as she promptly attended to her new arrival.

Charlotte was confused at the sudden interruption. She needed to know more. There was a warning? After all this time she was finally getting some answers only to be cut off. She wanted to shake Onaiwah and demand more answers, but she could only watch as Onaiwah attended to the injured hunter.

She finally decided she didn't want to be in the way, so she stood to go. "Thank you, Onaiwah." Onaiwah turned to her and bowed her head toward her, and Charlotte turned and exited the hut. She would be back.

CHAPTER TWENTY-FOUR

*I*t was Saturday before school was to start back for the Spring semester. Brock called and asked if Charlotte wanted to go for a hike.

"I thought you'd never ask!" she beamed into the phone.

"Great, because you have to tell me where to go. You're the expert around here. I'll be there in thirty minutes."

They hung up, and she quickly dressed for the hike. The temperature had dropped to the mid-forties, but if she dressed appropriately, it was still comfortable enough to be outside. She put on her new hiking boots she got for Christmas. Then she packed some snacks and drinks. She wasn't sure how long they would be out, but she wanted to be prepared this time in case they went on a long hike.

Twenty-five minutes later, Brock pulled into her driveway. When Charlotte didn't come immediately out, he thought it was about time he met her at the door instead of expecting her to come running out the door as soon as he drove up. He bounded up the steps two at a time and knocked on the door.

Charlotte's little brother, Ryan, answered the door. Instead of saying "Hi" to Brock, he yelled, "Charlotte! Your boyfriend's here!" Then he opened the door further for Brock to step in.

"Hey, man!" Brock said to Ryan, offering to give him a high-five. Ryan slapped his hand as hard as he could then took off running into the living room.

Her dad appeared next. "Hi, Brock. Come on in." Brock noticed her dad wasn't smiling at him, but his voice was pleasant enough.

"Thanks, Mr. McAfee." Brock suddenly felt nervous.

Brock was spared from having to sit, however, when Charlotte came out of her bedroom. As soon as she saw him, her face lit up, and he ultimately forgot about her dad.

"Hey!" she said hugging him. "I'm ready!"

"Where are you two off to?" her dad asked.

Charlotte turned to her dad beaming. "We're going to do some hiking in the area," she said.

Her dad grimaced a little. "In this cold?"

"Yeah, Dad. It's perfect for hiking. Besides, I have the best winter coat and boots on the market."

This made her dad smile, since it was his company's coat and boots that she was wearing. "Okay. But don't wander off too far and get lost and keep track of the time."

"Sure thing, Dad!" she called as she dragged Brock by the hand out the door.

Charlotte instructed Brock to turn left on the highway away from town instead of their usual turn to the right. About a mile down the highway, she told him to take another left. Now they were on a curvy, gravel road. They drove down this road for several miles before she instructed him to turn again. It was an even smaller dirt road. It was only about another mile down when she told him to pull off into a cul de sac next to a path winding through the trees.

Brock parked the truck and walked around to grab her hand. They headed out on the trail leading away from the road.

"I have a question!" she announced.

Brock was slightly taken aback. "Okay..." he smiled down at her.

"I was wondering if you knew where the name, Van Houten came from?"

"Wow, that's random," Brock chuckled.

"Well, I don't mean to be rude. But ever since you were introduced as a new student in class, I've wondered where it came from. It isn't a regular name that I've heard often—or ever." She turned a bright smile to him.

"Well, as a matter of fact, I do know it's origin, and you're not the first person to ask about it. It's Dutch. My dad's lineage, obviously. Our original ancestor came from the Netherlands and first settled in the state of New York."

"Cool, I didn't know that," she said, holding his hand and almost skipping along beside him as they walked the trail. "If your dad is from New York, how did he meet your mom from Oklahoma?"

"My dad went to Oklahoma State University to get a degree in Agricultural Technology. He met my mom there when she was a nursing student. Van Houten literally means, 'from the forest.'"

At this, Charlotte stopped and swung around, "Really? That's so cool! How apropos!"

"It is, isn't it. I know another one you'll like. Xylander. It means woodsman or man of the woods."

"Oooh, I do like that. Zeeelaaander." She sounded it out. "That would be a great name for our first child! Xylander Van Houten, which would literally mean woodsman from the woods...Ha!"

It was Brock's turn to stop cold in the trail.

When she turned and saw the look on his face, she said, "Just kidding!" and laughed.

When Brock's heart beat again, he continued to walk with her. "Where are we headed anyway?"

"Just up here." She continued to lead him up the trail. They came out of the clump of trees onto a rock jutting over a sharp drop off. "This is the spot I've wanted to bring you to for a long time now."

"Yeah, this is nice. Good call." He looked out over the cliff that was now over the treetops. He could see down below a small stream meandering through the trees. She motioned for him to sit down next to her.

He sat down on the ground on his left hip, his right knee up, and his right forearm rested on his knee. If she could make a mold and cast a stone statue of him, she would love to look at him like that for the rest of her life.

She leaned into him to get a closer look at his eyes. After studying them for a few seconds, she said, "I've decided your eyes are a topaz blue with flecks of green. It gives them sort of a turquoise color from further back." Their faces were inches apart. She could smell his warm breath and knew he was seconds away from touching her lips.

"Your eyes are a golden brown, more like amber. You have flecks of green as well and a streak of light blue right there." He pointed to a section on her right eye. He was leaning in for a kiss when she suddenly straightened.

"A what?" She leapt up and took off, running for Brock's truck. His momentum had already moved forward so when she vacated her spot, he fell into empty space, kissing the air.

"Hey! Where are you going?" He called to her watching her run down the hill toward the truck.

"I have to see something," she called over her shoulder as she ran. She got to the passenger side of his truck and turned the side-view mirror so that she could see her face. She leaned in close to look at her right eye. Sure enough, there was a small line of light blue that she had never noticed before.

Brock caught her at the truck. "What happened? One second you were there and then the next thing I know you're running away from me," he said slightly out of breath.

"When you were on the reservation, did you ever hear stories about Spirit Travelers?" Charlotte asked.

He stood scratching his head a second, "I think. I vaguely remember something about a Spirit Woman. There were lots of stories about Spirit People, Dreamers that predicted the future, and people who came back from the dead. My mom might be able to tell you more." He looked down at her with one eyebrow raised. "What's this about, all of a sudden?"

"Is your mom off work today? Do you think I could talk to her?" she asked, rising up on her toes.

"Yeah, she's home today. I suppose I could take you home and introduce you," he said still confused about this sudden turn of events.

"I promise I'll explain everything. But first, I need to talk to your mom to see if she remembers any stories about Spirit Travelers." She had her hands flat against his chest looking at him.

Before she could get away from him again, he wrapped his arms around her and planted his lips firmly on hers. She melted into his arms and circled her arms around his neck. His lips were soft, and the way he moved around her mouth drove her to want more. She would have liked to have stayed there a little longer, but she broke it off.

"This is important. I promise. I'll make it up to you." She smiled at him, a little out of breath.

"Okay. Hop in." He sighed. She could tell he was a little dejected about their change of plans.

Charlotte jumped in the truck and scooted over to the middle. Brock walked around to the driver's side and got in. As he started the truck, he looked at her and said, "I'll give you this: you keep me guessing. There's not a boring moment with you."

She snuggled in close to him and rested her hand on his thigh, smiling excitedly. It would be wonderful if his mom could give her some answers, and she could come clean with him. She couldn't keep him in the dark much longer.

They pulled into his driveway ten minutes later. He got out of the truck and helped her down from his side. "You have no idea how much this means to me. I promise. I'll make it up to you," she repeated.

Brock opened the door to the house holding her hand. "Mom! You here?" he called.

"I'm in here," she replied from somewhere in the house.

As they stepped into the living room, Brock's mom came in from the kitchen, wiping her hands with a towel. "Oh, you brought company. Please, excuse our mess. I wasn't expecting anyone."

"Don't mention it, Mrs. Van Houten. I'm sorry for showing up without notice," Charlotte said, straining to contain her excitement. It could turn out that she didn't know anything, and Charlotte would be back to square one.

"Mom, this is the girl I told you about, Charlotte," Brock said.

"Please, call me Olivia. Can I get you something to drink?" she asked as she shook her hand.

"I'll take some water," she said politely.

"Are you sure? I made some sweet tea," Olivia encouraged.

"In that case, I'll have some tea," Charlotte said, looking at Brock.

"Me, too," Brock put in.

"Good. Have a seat, and I'll be right back." She went back to the kitchen.

Brock led Charlotte to sit down on the couch. When he sat down, his knees were a lot higher than the edge of the sofa. He rested his elbows on his knees and looked down at his feet. Charlotte ran her hand across his back, comforting him and trying to ease her own nerves.

Olivia came back and handed them their drinks. "Why do I have a feeling that this visit has a purpose?" she said as she sat across from them in a recliner.

"Well, Mrs. Van Houten... Olivia, Brock has told me your grandmother was a full-blooded Osage." Charlotte said a silent prayer that she was doing the right thing, and they wouldn't kick her out of their house calling her crazy..

"Uh, hmm," Olivia nodded her head.

"Well, I have a special interest in the Osage and was wondering if you remembered a story that they used to tell about a Spirit Traveler?" Charlotte glanced nervously over at Brock. He was still sitting forward but was looking at her eagerly waiting for where this was going.

"A Spirit Traveler? Yes, it seems I do remember something. It was said that a Spirit Traveler was one whose spirit or soul could leave their body and enter the body of someone else. But it wasn't a body that would be in their present time, but someone from the past or future." Olivia looked intently at her.

"Was there a way to identify a Spirit Traveler?" Charlotte asked already expecting the answer.

"Those who had green or brown eyes with only a small section of blue." When Olivia said this, Brock scooted away from Charlotte a bit and turned more to look at her questioningly.

Charlotte looked from Brock to Olivia and said, "Mrs. Van Houten, do you mind looking at my eyes?"

Olivia came close to her and knelt in front of Charlotte so that she would be at her eye level. She looked at Charlotte's eyes, then gasped. "What are you saying?"

Charlotte took a deep breath and closed her eyes for a second. *Please be okay with this.* "I'm a Spirit Traveler," Charlotte admitted out loud.

They sat for a moment, no one breathing or blinking. She wanted to give them time to absorb this information and waited until one of them was ready to speak.

Brock finally spoke, "But those stories aren't true. Those are just stories. Right, mom?" He looked to his mother for confirmation that this was all a joke. This couldn't possibly be real. Olivia sat back on her heels still looking thoughtfully at Charlotte. Charlotte tried to remain still and calm while they processed this news.

"Charlotte, how did you hear about Spirit Travelers?" Olivia finally thought to ask. Brock turned to her to hear her answer.

"I heard it from a medicine woman in an Osage village. She spoke in riddles, and it wasn't clear to me what she was telling me at the time. But then earlier, when Brock told me that he saw a blue streak in my eye, it dawned on me what she was saying." She was still holding back waiting for the next question.

"Where was this Osage village? There are no others now outside the reservation in Oklahoma."

"I believe it's about twelve miles from here somewhere on Crowley's Ridge," she answered.

"You believe? But how did you get there?" Brock asked.

This was the key question she was waiting for them to ask, "I am guided there by my Spirit Animal and I *switch* from being me to being an Osage girl named Nahele." She waited for their reactions.

Brock and Olivia looked at each other then back at her. "Nahele?" Olivia whispered. After a few more uncomfortable moments of silence, she asked. "So, if you are Nahele, WHEN are you?"

Charlotte took a deep breath before she answered. "I recently met with a missionary who visited the village, and he gave me a date. It would be November 3, 1801 now. Two months and 187 years behind today." She gave out this information praying they wouldn't think she was either crazy or lying.

Brock sat back on the couch with a slump. He had a blank stare on his face. Olivia was still thinking and taking it all in. "How long has this been going on?" she asked.

"I've been going back and forth for several months now. When it first happened, I had no idea what was going on. I thought I had fallen, was knocked out, and I had a vivid dream. But then after a few days with the Osage, I realized it was really happening. I was also afraid I was stuck there permanently and had no idea how to get back. But my Spirit animal on that side is a wolf with the most amazing blue eyes, and when I followed him, I switched back to being me right in the middle of English class," she said, finally glad to be telling her story to Brock. It had never occurred to her before that Brock's mom might be more understanding.

"In English class?" Brock asked.

"Yeah, this was before you moved here. Lilly said that I had been going through the motions at school, but it was like I was sleepwalking. Then suddenly in English, I jumped as if I had just woken up."

"Lilly knows about this?" Brock asked still puzzled.

"She does. It was hard for me to describe at first, and I didn't know what was happening to me, so I had a difficult time explaining it to her. But I needed to tell someone, and she's been helping me do research and trying to figure this all out. My Uncle Jimmy knows now as well. I'll have to explain that later."

"What else can you tell us about the People?" Olivia asked.

"They're magnificent people. The men are all so tall. Many are taller than you, Brock, over seven feet. The women are all taller than me as well. They say prayers every morning to the Red Eagle, at noon to the White Eagle, and at sunset to the Dark Eagle. Their village is split down the middle by a road running East to West, on the North side live the Sky clan who are the Peacemakers, and on the South side live the Earth clan who are the warriors." Her heart raced, hoping they would believe her.

Brock stood. "Mom, do you think this is real? She could be repeating stuff from basic research that anyone could find."

Charlotte stood to face him, "Please Brock, try to believe me. I know it is a lot to ask. Imagine how I felt when it happened to me. I thought I was going crazy. I didn't ask for this to happen it just happened, and I need someone to help me figure out why it is happening. I need to know if there is something I need to do to help these people. Please, Brock, I need you." Tears began to flood her eyes as she looked from Olivia to Brock.

Brock suddenly felt ashamed for doubting her. He pulled her into him and hugged her. He held her head to his chest as the tears spilled down her cheeks. "I'm sorry, Charlotte. Of course, I'll help you and stand by you any way I can." He looked over at his mother.

"I will too, Charlotte. I think everything happens for a reason. When we found out we had to move here, we were devastated, but now I realize our purpose for being here. We're here to help you through this. I will make some phone calls and see what I can find out, okay?" Charlotte looked at her, and Olivia stretched out her arms to offer her a hug as well. She left Brock to hug Olivia, "Thank you so much, Mrs. Van. . . I mean, Olivia. I could use your support right now."

"We'll do everything we can to help you through this," Olivia said, patting her back. "Now, I suppose you should go home and get some rest. You look emotionally drained."

"I guess you're right. I have been dealing with a lot lately. I share things with Lilly, but it's hard to tell her everything that is going on. She's been instrumental in book research, but there is only so much that has been written down. Most all information was passed down through oral stories, and I'm afraid many things have been lost," she said.

"You're right. There are many things that your friend won't be able to find in books. But I may have a source who can help you and may be able to give us more information," Olivia said, looking reassuringly at her.

"Come on. I'll drive you home," Brock said, putting his arm around her shoulders.

"Thank you, Olivia. I'm so glad you moved here, and I'm so happy to have met you. You have a wonderful son as well," she said, looking at Brock fondly.

"I'm glad we're here, too, and it's nice to meet you, too. Brock is quite special." She, too, looked at her son with immense pride and joy.

Olivia walked them out the door, and they got in his truck. When they settled in, he turned to her before he started the truck. "Again, I'm sorry I doubted your story. I'm still processing it all, but I promise you I'll stay by your side and help you with anything you need."

"Thank you, Brock. You have no idea how much that means to me. I need your help and support right now."

"And when you're over there, what is it like for your body over here?" he asked, concerned.

"Lilly says it's like my personality is gone. I'm here going through the motions, but I'm not talking much unless spoken to, and then only short answers. Lilly and I call it my *shadow-self*."

"I won't let anything happen to you, Charlotte." He gently cupped his big hand to the side of her face and pulled her to his lips. Charlotte melted into him letting go of the emotions that she didn't realize she had bottled inside of her.

THE START of the Spring semester was bitterly cold. At the beginning of the school day, the students huddled closer together under the awnings and sidewalk covers waiting for the bell. Charlotte hadn't forgotten about what Kale had said to her at the basketball tournament, but she didn't know what he meant when he called her a witch. If he had been hiding somewhere spying on her and had seen her switch, she didn't think it would look anything out of the ordinary to him. She imagined that since her body stayed behind, that there was nothing to witness. On the other hand, if there had been a flash of light or if her body had blinked out for a few seconds as Scuffy and Barkley did, then that would be something strange to witness. This presented a new worry.

But, how could he tell other people about it in a way that they would believe him? If he went around telling people he had witnessed her disappearing, they would laugh at him. He could be bluffing to see if her reaction would give away more information. She decided not to react and see what he meant by calling her a "witch."

Charlotte walked into biology class with Brock's arm around her shoulders as usual. He knew the truth about her now, so if Kale tried to scare him away with whatever story he planned to tell, she had been able to explain things to him first. She was relieved to have that burden off her chest at least.

As she went to her seat, she glanced toward Kale. He sat smugly in his seat. Whatever he had in mind, he seemed confident in it at the moment.

The first week back, it seemed that Kale's threats had been empty. No one said anything to her out of the ordinary. She told Lilly about Kale's threat finally, and she was worried to know what he meant as well. She was also relieved to know that Brock knew about her alternate life now, and they no longer had to tip-toe around the subject with him. But poor Evan was still in the dark, and she knew that he suspected something. She felt sure he would never guess their actual secret.

"Do you think you should tell Evan about what's going on?" she asked Lilly, riding in the bus to Trumann high school on Friday.

"I don't know. What do you think?" Lilly volleyed back.

"I think he suspects something. I'm afraid he'll get the wrong idea, and it will influence your relationship. But, on the other hand, I don't see how we can explain it to him. It was hard enough to convince you, and the only reason Brock has accepted it is because of his experience with the Osage. Even then, Brock didn't believe me at first, and it was a shock to him."

"I know what you mean. He has given me some hints that he feels like we have something secret, and he's not a part of it. But, I'm like you. What would we tell him?" Lilly looked torn. Charlotte didn't want to be the cause of friction in their relationship.

"Maybe this will be over soon, and we won't have to keep up the charade with him much longer." Charlotte was feeling the fatigue of living two lives and hoped that there was an end in sight.

They rode in silence for a little while until one of the cheerleaders made her way to the seat across from Lilly and Charlotte.

"Hi Becca," Charlotte said to her cheer captain.

"Hey, Charlotte. I need to talk to you about something that I've heard lately." Becca's expression made her stomach sink.

"Sure. What's up?" She tried to stay calm. She hadn't done anything wrong; it couldn't be dire news.

"Well, do you think we could talk in private?" Becca asked.

"Anything you have to say, I'll tell Lilly anyway, so you might as well talk to the both of us," she said.

Becca shrugged and took a deep breath before speaking. "I know you and Brock have been dating for a while. Are y'all still together?"

She wasn't expecting her to start with this, "Of course! What's that got to do with anything?"

"Well. . ." Becca hesitated, "I heard rumors that you're sleeping around with other guys behind Brock's back."

There it is. That's what she had been waiting for all week. So, this was Kale's big plan? She looked directly in Becca's eyes and said, "That's ridiculous. When exactly would I have time to cheat on Brock when I am with him most of the time?"

"I don't know. I'm not around you enough to know how you spend your time outside of school and cheering. All I know is that I've heard it from more than one person and wanted to talk to you about it." Becca was on the defensive.

"Why? Would something like that be grounds for kicking me off the squad?" Charlotte's claws were out.

"It might be; we have a reputation to uphold. Besides, we have Regional competition to get ready for soon, and then I hope we make it to State. I can't have a member of our team spreading herself out so thin that she's not a hundred percent for competition." This hit Charlotte hard. Even though the rumors weren't true, she did have something else going on in her life that could distract her attention. Becca wouldn't care what it was that was distracting her, if it had an impact on her ability to perform; it was all the same to her. Lilly looked at her, concerned as well.

"Exactly who told you this?" Charlotte narrowed her eyes at Becca.

"Ashley heard it from Steven Huckabee, and Tiffany heard it from James Bells." Just as she suspected, Thing One and Thing Two of Kale's henchmen.

"The rumors are false, Becca. You have nothing to worry about. Someone is out to spread lies about me to get back at me for something, and that's all it is, a lie!" She made sure to keep direct eye contact with Becca so that she wouldn't doubt her. Becca seemed to accept her answer.

She turned her head and looked back at the other girls leaning over their seats to see her reaction. "I'm sorry, Charlotte. I had to verify it. But you should know, some nasty things are being said about you right now."

Charlotte sighed heavily. "Thanks for telling me, Becca. I assure you, anything you hear is pure lies. I know who started this, and I'll deal with him. But you can be confident that I'll be a hundred percent focused for competition coming up. Whatever you can do to cut the head off this ugly snake for me will help me stay that way." Becca nodded her head and went back to her seat toward the rear of the bus. She could hear the other girls questioning Becca about her response, no doubt, eager for more gossip.

She tilted her head back against the seat and let out another sigh. It was hard to convince people the truth when the lies were much juicier. People around school liked to talk about the scandalous regardless of the facts. It was more about the drama it caused; anything for the excitement.

"What do you think Brock's going to say when he hears this?" Lilly asked.

Her stomach felt like lead. "He'll know it's not true, but he'll also be angry at the person who started this." She wondered how patient Brock could be, however. He could decide that she wasn't worth all this trouble she was putting him through and give up.

SATURDAY, Charlotte invited Brock over to her house to watch movies. It was too cold outside to go anywhere. Her dad built a fire in the fireplace, so Brock and she were comfortably snuggled under a blanket on the floor watching TV when the phone rang. She jumped up to answer it.

"Hello?" she answered.

"Charlotte?" a deep voice answered.

"Yes? Who's this?"

"You mean you can't tell?"

She swallowed and looked back at Brock, who watched her curiously. She sat down at the bar.

"Kale?" That got Brock's attention, and he was immediately on the stool next to her.

"That's right, sweetheart. Sounds like you've been a naughty girl lately." She looked at Brock to see if he had heard from where he was. By the grimace on his face, he had.

"Kale, I know you started those rumors, and we both know they're not true. I've told all my friends as much. It's not going to work; whatever it is you think you're going to accomplish."

"Oh, I don't know. There are some nasty rumors out there. You sure your pretty-boy boyfriend is going to believe you?" Her eyes were big as she watched Brock's expressions. She knew he wanted to grab the phone out of her hand, but she wanted to find out where Kale was heading with this.

"What do you want, Kale?"

There was a long silence on the other end. Brock and Charlotte had their heads together, so they could listen.

"Are you as good as they say, Charlotte? When Brock dumps you, maybe you can give me some." He shocked her with this statement, and she dropped the phone. Brock rushed to pick it up.

"You listen here, you son of ..." Brock stopped short. "He hung up." He slammed the phone down. "What's this guy's deal!"

Brock looked at her, and she had tears pooling in her eyes. He wrapped her in his arms. "Don't let him get to you, Charlotte. That's what he's after. He's expecting to rattle the both of us in hopes of breaking us up. But the dude has no clue how to handle a girl. He has no idea that he is going about this all wrong. And I'm smart enough to see right through him. You don't have to worry about me dumping you over stupid rumors." This was what she needed to hear, and she sighed into his chest.

"I'm so sorry, Brock. I hate for you to put up with this as well," she said into his shirt.

Brock rubbed his hand up and down her back. "It's not your fault, Charlotte. Maybe if we ignore him, he'll realize he's getting nowhere and give up. But you can't let him see that he's getting to you." He pushed her back enough to look at her face. "Promise me. Don't let him see you get upset, okay?"

She nodded her head. "Okay. As long as I have you at my side, I won't worry about him."

"That's my girl. This'll all blow over soon, and he'll move on to antagonizing someone else." Brock hoped what he was telling her was true, but he needed to reassure her that it was. Secretly, he was worried that he was going to have to do something personally to put a stop to it.

"Let's go back to the living room and finish watching our movie. I think I know how to get your mind off this creep." He took her hand and led her back to their cozy spot in the living room.

CHAPTER TWENTY-FIVE

*T*he next week at school, it appeared Kale's plan wasn't working. Charlotte didn't so much as glance in Kale's direction. It seemed people had caught on to the fact that the rumors had been planted and were even saying how crazy Kale was for starting them. She felt better that maybe he would leave them alone finally.

Thursday, she was working out with the cheerleaders on the tumbling mats in the platform area behind the gym bleachers when Tanner came running up the stairs. He looked around for Charlotte, and when he spotted her, he rushed over, half walking half running with his long legs toward her.

"Charlotte!" Tanner tried to whisper.

"What is it, Tanner?" She suddenly worried Brock had gotten hurt during basketball practice.

"It's Brock and Kale..." Tanner started, and Charlotte gasped before she heard the rest. "Kale said something to Brock in the locker room, and they pushed each other with their arms locked together. It was like two bulls with their horns locked pushing each other back and forth. I thought they were going to destroy the whole locker room. But then coach came in and broke 'em up."

All the cheerleaders gathered around Tanner and Charlotte, listening intently to this new development in their soap opera drama.

"What happened next, Tanner?"

"Well, they stood there staring at each other like they could kill each other with their minds. They were both breathing hard, and I thought they were going to go at it again when the coach left, but then Kale challenged Brock to a fight after school off campus."

Charlotte sucked in air and put her hand over her mouth in shock.

"Where are they supposed to meet, Tanner?" Lilly had to ask because Charlotte was frozen.

Tanner looked back and forth between Lilly and Charlotte. "They are going to the cul de sac on Charlotte's street right after school."

Lilly and Charlotte looked at each other. Charlotte's heart was in her throat. The bell rang to end school, and everyone scrambled to grab their gear and head to the locker room. Charlotte had to get her books, purse, and keys from the locker room before she could go to the parking lot to her mother's car.

She couldn't get out of school fast enough. The line to pull out on the highway was frustratingly long. By the time she turned on the highway to drive the mile to her street, she was in a panic. When she made the turn onto Pinecrest, there were already so many cars parked on both sides of the street that she couldn't get past them and had to park in the neighbor's yard halfway to her house.

Charlotte hastily threw it into park and jumped out of her car. She could see the crowd gathered at the dead end in front of Isaac's house, but she couldn't see Brock or Kale. Her heart was in her throat. Not because she felt Brock couldn't stand up against Kale, but because the two of them were quite capable of inflicting serious harm to one another.

She ran down the hill, weaving in and out of the parked cars all parked carelessly and turned every which way. She could hear the shouts of the on-lookers, but her breathing was too loud in her ears to hear any sounds of the actual fight. When she passed her own house in the valley, she scarcely glanced over to see if her parents had noticed what was happening outside.

Then she ran uphill toward the dead end. Her legs felt heavy as panic zapped the energy from her muscles. She could hear the sickening thuds now as fists met bone and flesh. She heard one horrible crack and an audible grunt that made her pause in the middle of the slope to fight back the bile that came up her throat. She pushed past the people crowded around. When she reached the edge, someone held her back and prevented her from interrupting them. Those in attendance might have thought this was pure entertainment, but for her, it was her worst nightmare. How could they stand around and watch them hurt one another and cheer it on? Tears filled her eyes and blurred her vision.

Brock had a bloody lip, and Kale had blood dripping from his nose. They were both panting like wild dogs, circling each other and looking for the next chance to strike. Their fists were up, and she could see the blood on their knuckles. She choked back a sob that caught in her throat.

Kale charged Brock, driving his shoulder into Brock's stomach, but Brock dug his feet in and prevented Kale from knocking him off balance. Brock wrapped his arms under Kale's elbows and drove his knee into his stomach. Kale's breath was knocked out of him, and Brock turned him loose. Brock backed up a couple of steps to give him time to catch his breath. It was almost as if Brock was giving him the chance to throw in the towel. He could've taken advantage of the moment to land a few more blows while he was out of breath. Others around the circle were shouting for him to finish him, but he held off.

Kale was bent over, holding his abdomen. He looked at Brock from underneath his eyebrows. Pure rage and hate shot from his eyes. He wiped the blood dripping from his nose with his hand then spit more blood onto the pavement calculating his next move. He reached his hand into his front pocket and flipped out a knife. The crowd audibly gasped. Brock's eyes widened. Charlotte froze, and the scream she wanted to release caught in her throat.

Kale took a menacing step toward Brock, holding the knife out ready to strike. He swiped the knife across Brock's abdomen, but Brock jumped back as the knife sliced through the air. Brock turned the action in a slow circle watching Kale's every move. He wasn't going to back away; he would make Kale come at him.

Kale lunged toward Brock like a fencer parrying. Brock leapt to the side causing another near miss. They circled one another again, each looking for a way to end the fight in their favor. Charlotte had both her hands over her mouth, her eyes wide open, and she was barely breathing. She wanted to vomit, and she wished she could rush in between them to stop them, but she knew that, at this point, if she did, she would either be the one to get hurt or risk distracting Brock's concentration causing him to get hurt.

Brock looked for a way to disarm Kale. He took a step forward to grab Kale's arm, but Kale stepped on Brock's foot preventing him from retreating and stabbed him in the stomach. Charlotte never registered the scream that escaped her lungs. Only later, when her throat was scratched and sore, did she imagine that she must have screamed. Brock doubled over, gasping for air while Kale stood frozen, looking down at the bloody knife in his hand.

The onlookers had gone completely silent, standing in shock at what they had witnessed. No one had bargained for such a violent turn of events. Kale panted, his chest heaving and his eyes wide in disbelief. He looked from the knife to the crowd standing around. Realization dawned on his face at the severity of the situation. He dropped the bloody knife and stared at it for one more second before turning toward the woods and running in retreat. He disappeared while everyone watched him go.

Charlotte broke from her frozen state as Brock dropped to the ground. She rushed to his side, screaming, "Brock!" Tears streaming down her face, but her only awareness was of Brock. She helped lower him to the ground so that she could get a look at the damage. Without thinking, she shirked off her jacket and lifted her t-shirt over her head. She wadded it and pressed it to the spot heavily soaked with blood. Brock was already going pale. He swiveled his eyes to her face; tears filling his eyes.

"Charlotte…" he whispered.

"Shhh… it's okay. I'm here. You're going to be all right," she said to reassure the both of them. She heard other's shouting commands and had a vague awareness of Isaac running from his house saying he had called an ambulance. Someone placed her jacket over her shoulders to cover her, but her focus was only on Brock's eyes.

"Charlotte..." he tried again.

"It's okay, Brock. Help is on the way. I won't leave you. I'll stay right here," her voice sounded calmer than she felt on the inside.

"I love you..." Brock whispered then closed his eyes.

"Brock!" Charlotte shouted and shook him. "Brock, stay awake. Focus on me, Brock!" Now the panic was showing through her voice.

Brock's eyes fluttered open as she heard a distant wail of the ambulance. She leaned closer to him and kissed him on the mouth gently. "I love you, too, Brock. Please don't leave me. Stay with me. Please, stay with me."

His eyes were still open, but they had lost their focus. His breathing was shallow but fast. She wasn't aware the ambulance had pulled up until the paramedics pulled her away to reach him. She didn't want to let go of him; someone was talking to her, but she wasn't registering it in her mind. Someone had their arms around her from behind as two paramedics assessed the damage.

They moved him to the stretcher and rolled him toward the ambulance. "I need to go with him!" She panicked.

One paramedic said, "You need to stay here, miss."

But the other paramedic replied, "Let her go, Chuck. She's obviously the girlfriend."

They lifted Brock into the ambulance, and she climbed in behind. Brock raised his hand and whispered, "Charlotte?"

Charlotte clasped his hand between both of hers and replied, "I'm here, Brock. I'm here."

The female paramedic remained in the back while the other one jumped in the driver's seat. Brock looked even paler now, and his breathing was barely noticeable. The paramedic inserted a needle attached to a bag of blood. She checked his pulse and announced, "He's crashing! I'm initiating CPR." She pressed on Brock's chest as Charlotte held his hand with one hand and covered her mouth with the other. Her eyes flooded again with tears as she silently prayed for Brock to come back to her.

The paramedic placed an airbag over his mouth. "Here, help me by squeezing this. Not too fast, a regular pace like this." The paramedic demonstrated the rhythm she wanted Charlotte to maintain, and she took over squeezing the bag.

The paramedic checked his pulse again. She took some scissors and cut open his shirt. She flipped a switch on a box that revved to a high pitch. She grabbed the paddles and rubbed them together. "Stand clear, hon." Then she pressed the paddles to Brock's chest. His body lurched off the gurney. She paused to watch a monitor; no change. She rubbed the paddles again and pressed them to his chest a second time. This time when she lifted off, there was a beep on the monitor, followed by a steady beep.

Charlotte let out the breath she was holding. The paramedic replaced the bag that she had been squeezing with an oxygen mask. "He is stable for now, hon. Hold on. We're almost there."

Charlotte wasn't sure if she was talking to Brock or her. She kept her eyes on Brock's face. His chest slowly rose up and down as he laid there like he was asleep. They pulled into the ER, and the ambulance stopped. The driver jumped out and came around the back to open the doors. Charlotte sat still as they slowly rolled Brock out of the ambulance; then she jumped down behind him.

A doctor and several nurses came out of the hospital to assist them. The female paramedic began to fill them in as they rolled him into the hospital, "Stab wound to the abdomen. He's lost a lot of blood. I started a blood transfusion. He crashed on the way, and I administered CPR. BP 60/40."

"You'll have to stay out here for now, miss," one of the nurses said, blocking Charlotte from following. Charlotte stood there and watched him go through the double doors.

"Is there someone I can call to meet you here?" the nurse asked.

Charlotte stood in a daze for a few seconds not comprehending what the nurse was asking.

"Come here and sit down." The nurse took her by the shoulders and guided her to a chair. The nurse helped her get her arms into her jacket that she didn't realize was on her shoulders. She buttoned the jacket for her.

"Can I get you some water?" The nurse tried again.

Charlotte looked at the nurse focusing her eyes. "Someone needs to call his family." Her voice was monotone and automatic.

"Okay, hon. Do you know the number?"

Charlotte nodded her head. The nurse walked her toward the desk phone and placed it in her hands. She stared at the dial struggling to remember the series of numbers she needed to push. She started with a "9" then the rest of the numbers followed automatically without having to think about it.

After a couple of rings, someone answered. "Hello?"

"Hello? Mrs. Van... Olivia? It's Charlotte."

"Charlotte? Is everything all right?"

"I'm at the hospital... it's Brock."

"What happened, Charlotte? Why are you at the hospital?"

"Just get here...quickly...please." She didn't have the strength to explain.

Charlotte hung up the phone and quickly dialed her home number.

"Hello?"

"Tad, where's Mom and Dad?"

"Charlotte? Where are you? Mom and Dad are outside talking to the police. What happened out there?"

"I can't explain right now. Tell Mom and Dad I'm at the hospital. I'm okay; it's Brock."

"Okay, I'll tell 'em."

Charlotte hung up and suddenly felt like she was going to throw up. She turned to find the restroom, and then everything went black.

CHARLOTTE OPENED her eyes and looked around. She had been dreaming she was in the hut with Tetonka, cooking over the fire. She had been warm and cozy, perfectly happy. She tried to process the scene around her. She was in a modern-day hospital it seemed because she was on a flat table, and a white curtain was pulled all around. A nurse came around the curtain.

"Welcome back!" she said with a smile.

"What happened?" Charlotte asked, recalling the events that brought her here.

"You fainted, sweetie, out in the lobby." The nurse handed her a plastic cup of water.

She took a small sip, letting her thoughts come back to her.

"Brock!" She suddenly panicked. She tried to jump off the table, but the nurse stopped her.

"Hold on. Wait here a second, and I'll go check his status." The nurse left the curtained area.

Olivia came around the curtain next.

"Charlotte! They told me you fainted in the lobby and brought you in here. What happened?" Olivia's eyes were wide with worry.

She took a deep breath, "Brock got in a fight, and the other guy pulled out a knife. He stabbed Brock. I haven't heard anything from the doctors about how he's doing." Tears began to well in her eyes again as Olivia wrapped her in a hug.

"Why in the world was Brock fighting?" she asked, apparently holding back her anger because now she was more concerned about his life.

"It's all my fault." Charlotte let the tears roll and the sobs escape this time. "This guy, Kale, has been threatening me, and Brock stood up to him." Charlotte buried her face in Olivia's shoulder letting her cry for a few minutes. Olivia patted her back and waited patiently.

When she felt she could stop the crying, Charlotte sat up. Olivia handed her a tissue so that she could blow her nose.

The nurse came back around the curtain. "They have taken him back to surgery now and when they're finished, the doctor will be out to give you a report." She looked more closely at Charlotte. "Are you okay to go sit in the waiting room, now?"

Charlotte nodded her head and dropped down off the table. Olivia wrapped her arm around her shoulders as they walked back to the waiting room. When they came through the doors, Brock's dad and younger sister rushed toward them.

"What's happened?" Alex asked.

Olivia answered, "Brock was stabbed in a fight. The nurse said they have him in surgery, and the doctor will give us a report when he's finished."

Charlotte sat down in the closest chair. Brock's sister, Jessica, came to sit in the chair next to her.

"Are you okay?" Jessica asked.

"I fainted after I called you guys and my parents. I'm better now, a little." Charlotte admitted, knowing that she wouldn't be entirely better until she knew how Brock was doing.

Jessica patted her hand as they sat, staring at the floor.

Olivia and Alex stepped away and whispered to one another. Charlotte felt horrible and responsible for what had happened to their son. She worried that after this, they would prevent them from seeing one another.

Olivia came back and sat on the other side of her. Charlotte looked at her, "I'm so sorry, Olivia. I feel horrible. I didn't stop it. I couldn't stop it. This should have never happened." She felt like she was going to cry again.

Olivia put her arm around her again, "It's okay, honey. It's not your fault. We'll get through this."

Charlotte collapsed again onto Olivia's shoulder.

Alex sat down across from them as Olivia looked at him over her head. They were more worried than they were letting on. They waited for what the doctor had to say before jumping to any more conclusions.

The doors opened to the waiting room, and Charlotte's parents and brothers came in.

"Mom!" Charlotte jumped up and ran into her mother's arms.

"Charlotte, are you okay?" her mother asked.

She cried again. "Brock's in surgery."

Her mother patted her back as Charlotte cried into her shoulder.

Her dad stepped up to Brock's dad and extended his hand, "I'm Russell, Charlotte's dad and this is my wife, Rosette."

"Nice to meet you. I'm Alex, and this is my wife, Olivia." Alex gestured toward his wife. "And who are these two young boys?" Alex asked nodding and smiling at her brothers.

"This is Tad, the oldest, and Ryan." Charlotte's dad gestured to each of the boys. The boys' eyes were big, looking confused about what was going on.

"Nice to meet you." Alex nodded toward them. "This is my youngest daughter, Jessica." He gestured toward the girl sitting quietly taking everything in. "I have an older daughter, Haley, who is going to OSU this year," Alex's voice sounded less worried than his eyes revealed.

"Sorry, we have to meet under these circumstances," Charlotte's mother apologized.

"Me, too," Olivia agreed. "We're waiting to hear from the doctor about Brock's status."

Everyone took a seat in the waiting room, feeling the apprehension in the air.

"Charlotte, do you want to explain what happened?" her dad asked, looking at her sternly. She needed to answer some questions for them. They seemed disappointed in her.

"Actually, no, I don't. Not right now," she said, looking down at her hands clasped together.

She was sitting next to Olivia again. Olivia put a hand on her back as if to protect her. "Charlotte fainted in the lobby after she called us. I think she might be in shock herself." Olivia would know this, since she was a nurse.

"I'm sorry, Charlotte," her mother said, "We can talk about it later."

She didn't respond. Her stomach was all in knots, worried about Brock. She tried not to think the worst.

Everyone was silent, either sitting or pacing around the waiting room. An hour and a half later, a doctor finally entered the room.

Olivia and Charlotte were the first to rush up to him. Everyone else crowded behind.

"Is this the family of Brock Van Houten?" he asked first.

Everyone nodded their heads wanting him to be out with it.

"He's stable now. He's out of surgery and when he comes around some of you will be able to go back and see him. He's a lucky guy. The stab wound was not very deep. I think because he is young and has strong abdominal muscles, it prevented the knife from getting to his inferior vena cava."

Olivia gasped but nodded for him to continue.

"The most damage was to the colon and some of his intestines, but it could have been much worse. No kidney damage either. After we made sure there was no more internal bleeding, we sewed him up. He will be sore for a while, but he'll make it through. If you need me, my name is Dr. Scott. I'll be back a little later to check on him. I can answer any questions you have then. He needs to stay here overnight, but he can go home tomorrow. A nurse will be back to let you know when you can go back and see him." With that, Dr. Scott turned and left the waiting room.

Olivia and Charlotte turned to one another and hugged, fresh tears stinging their eyes. This time, they were tears of relief. Charlotte let out another deep sigh as if she had been holding her breath again; then she wobbled. Olivia helped her to the nearest chair.

"Are you okay?" Olivia asked, looking into her eyes.

"I'm feeling faint again."

"Here. Put your head between your knees to let the blood back to your head." Charlotte had gone completely white, and she broke out into a cold sweat.

"I'll go find her something to eat," her dad volunteered.

After he left the room, the nurse came in.

"You can go see him now. The immediate family first."

Olivia turned to her, "I'll come back to get you in a minute, okay?"

Charlotte nodded her head, fearful that he might not want to see her and blame her for what had happened.

Her dad soon returned with a box of juice and some peanut butter crackers. She didn't feel like eating, but she drank the juice through the tiny straw.

Alex came back to the waiting room. "He's asking for you," he said, looking at her.

Charlotte got up, but her legs felt numb. After she took a few steps, however, she felt the blood return to them. She felt shaky all over. The nurse directed her down the hall to his room.

The door was open, and she could see Olivia sitting next to Brock's bed holding his hand. Jessica was standing behind her mom, looking sadly at Brock. No one had asked her how she felt about what was going on.

Brock turned his head to see her when she walked through the door. "Charlotte," he whispered. A tiny smile curved his lips, and she could see that he was under the heavy influence of drugs.

Charlotte walked to his side as he reached out a hand to her. She took it, remembering how she held his hand in the ambulance.

"Brock, I—" she began but was cut off with a sob in her throat.

"Charlotte, it's okay. The doctor said I'll be all right."

"But this is all my fault," she blurted out. "I should have stopped you or him, and if it wasn't for me, you wouldn't even be here." She couldn't help the tears that flowed all over again.

"Shhh.... Charlotte. Don't blame yourself. Come here." He lifted his arms for her to hug him.

Charlotte leaned over him and let him put his arms around her as she cried into his shoulder, the third person that afternoon to receive her tears. He patted her back as he whispered in her ear, "It's going to be okay, Charlotte. The doctor said there was no major damage. I'll be as good as new soon."

She raised her head slightly and wiped the tears from her eyes. She must look a mess by now having cried all her makeup off. She was sure her eyes were red and puffy, but Brock didn't seem to mind. He still looked at her like he always did with the smile that made her happy. She tried to smile a little at him then.

"There's my girl and that beautiful smile," he said, brushing his thumb across her cheek.

Charlotte swallowed back the tears and smiled a little brighter at him. Straightening up, she looked at Olivia and Jessica, who were making an effort not to say anything.

"You look exhausted, Charlotte. You should go home and get some rest." Brock encouraged her.

"I don't want to leave you," she said.

"I'm fine now. You go home and get some rest. The doctor said I'll be able to go home tomorrow. You can come see me then." He squeezed her hand.

She stared at him, torn with what to do. She was exhausted, not just physically, but emotionally, too. She had never felt this drained before.

Brock turned to his mom, "Mom, can I have a moment with Charlotte, please?"

Olivia got up, "Of course. Come on, Jessica. Let's wait outside."

Olivia closed the door as they went out into the hall.

"I meant what I said before the ambulance came," Brock said, looking at her with his big blue-green eyes.

"I was afraid you wouldn't remember that," she admitted.

"I remember. And it's true. I would take a bullet for you if I had to. I want to always be with you and take care of you. You mean the world to me."

She was afraid she would cry all over again. Instead, she leaned over him and kissed him on the mouth. He ran his hand through her hair and gripped her tightly to him. She sighed with relief as she melted into him.

Charlotte pulled back an inch. "I was so afraid, Brock. It was like I had been stabbed, too. When you hurt, I hurt. I love you, too."

"I know. I remember that, too," he said with another smile.

She smiled at him and gave him another good long kiss. He released her so that she could straighten up again.

"Now, go home. Get some rest. Come back tomorrow and be with me."

"Are you sure?" she asked, looking back and forth into his eyes.

"I'm sure. Nothing is going to happen to me now, but you need to rest."

She let out a sigh and nodded her head, "Okay. I'll be back tomor-row." She turned to go.

"Charlotte. . ." Brock called. She stopped and turned around. "I do really love you."

She smiled a big smile at him, "I really do love you, too." Then she turned and left the room.

CHAPTER TWENTY-SIX

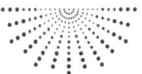

*O*n the ride home, Charlotte leaned her head against the glass window in the back of her mother's car. She was beyond exhausted. She must have dozed off because she didn't remember the drive and opened her eyes to find they were parked in their driveway. She slowly got out of the car feeling the exhaustion throughout her body. The walk up the steps was difficult; her legs felt like dead weight. She turned her head toward the cul de sac, remembering the scenes that had transpired there hours earlier. If only she had been able to stop them before it happened. But even as she thought it, she knew that if she had stepped in, it could've been her in the hospital or worse. She was glad the knife hadn't gone in very deep, and Brock was going to be okay.

Charlotte knew she needed a shower, but she wasn't sure her energy was going to last much longer. She did, however, think about Scuffy and decided to check on him. She got a scoop of his dog food and walked out onto the back deck.

"Scuffy!" she called into the dark woods. "Here, boy! I've got your food!" She walked past a few trees, whistling for Scuffy to come. Then something hard hit her on the back of her head, and for the second time that day, everything went black.

Charlotte woke with the worst headache she had ever had. The back of her head pounded. She tried to turn her head, but her stomach quickly protested. There was no light to see around her, but she knew she was in the woods. She was lying on her side on the damp ground covered with leaves. Overhead, she could make out fallen trees. She laid in a ditch or shallow depression in the ground with the fallen trees covering her. *How did I get here?* She tried to move her hands to her head to feel it but realized she couldn't because her arms were pinned behind her back.

Then a big hand came around from behind and clamped over her mouth. The hand was so big, it nearly covered her whole face.

"Don't scream or make a sound," Kale whispered gruffly into her ear. His breath was hot on the back of her neck, but she felt cold chills tingle down her spine. He smelled of dirt, sweat, and blood. He pulled her backward, and she realized he was lying on the ground behind her.

"This is all your fault, Charlotte," he continued in her ear. "You made me stab Brock. If it hadn't been for you, none of this would have happened." She searched wildly around with her eyes searching for a way to get away from him. But, like the last time he had her pinned against the wall, she was powerless to do anything against his size and strength.

"You drove me to this point. If you had only realized that we were meant to be together, none of this would have happened. I'm supposed to be the one you're with. I'm supposed to be the one you smile at and wrap your arms around, not HIM!" He spit through gritted teeth into her ear. His grip on her was getting tighter, and she was afraid he was going to suffocate her to death. Her arms and shoulders screamed in pain as they were pulled behind her, and he pressed against her.

He pressed his hand down over her nose cutting off her ability to breathe. "I should kill you right here. If I can't have you, no one will." Her headache intensified as the blood pressure increased in her head. She felt her eyes were going to pop out of their sockets. She tried to flop and squirm to get him to release his grip on her mouth and nose. Her lungs were about to explode. Then black.

Charlotte became conscious sucking in air as if she had been traveling from deep underwater and broke the surface of the ocean. She gulped air so hard that her throat and lungs burned. Her head pounded. Tears streamed down her face, and she convulsed in huge sobs.

"Stop crying like a big baby. You don't get it. Someone is going to pay, and it's not going to be me!" She tried to squirm out of his grasp, but he was too heavy for her to move. She wanted to scream; she wanted to fight back, but any energy that she used against him was wasted.

"I could take you right here! Take the one thing that he can't have all to myself." Tears streamed down the corners of her eyes. She wanted this to be over. She shook with muted sobs with his hand still over her mouth. He lifted his hand from her mouth, and he thrust his tongue in. She almost gagged and would've liked to have thrown up on him. Without thinking, she bit down on his tongue as hard as she could.

"Yow!" He growled and pulled back. He slapped her hard on the side of her head. As if her head wasn't already hurting enough, she cried out in pain. He pushed off her and pressed his hand to the side of her face, forcing her cheek into the dirt. She rolled to her side as he sat down behind her.

For the first time since Charlotte had opened her eyes in his captivity, she was free of him. But, she couldn't move. She laid there, crying into the dirt and leaves.

"I think I'm bleeding! Bitch! Quit your sniffling and whining!" He grunted at her. "You're making me sick."

She tried to move her arms, but she had no strength. "All I ever wanted was to be with you, Charlotte. You're supposed to be mine. Didn't you understand that? Didn't you know you were the one for me?" He spit his words at her like tiny daggers.

Slowly, she came to her senses. Her body still shook, but her mind began to process again. She spoke into the dirt, "How exactly was I supposed to know that, Kale?"

He spat in the dirt beside her. "I've tried to tell you so many times. I thought you knew I wanted you. You had to have known after all my attempts to show you that no one else belonged with you except me."

"Kale, I'm sorry. Will you forgive me?" She pleaded, hoping she could get out of this without further insults to her body.

He laid down again behind her and wrapped his arm around her. "You have to promise me that from now on you're my girlfriend and dump that SOB, Brock!" He said his name through gritted teeth. She was willing to agree to anything if it meant she could get out of this situation as soon as possible.

She continued to lay there looking into the dark and at the end of the fallen tree branches that must be the opening into this dungeon. She wished she could be Nahele at that moment. Next time she went over, she might be tempted to stay there. But, even as she thought it, she knew it wasn't possible.

Kale thought Charlotte was now a willing participant in all of this and leaned forward to kiss her. He stopped, just short, hovering over her lips. There was a rustling in the leaves. Kale put a hand over her mouth instinctively and froze. They remained still, not breathing, so they could catch the next sound. Her eyes searched the dark straining to make out anything among the leaves and branches. Something crawled under the fallen tree toward them. It was too small to be a person, so it must be an animal that didn't know they were under there.

It stopped once it got in, and she could hear it sniffing the air. Then it gave a low growl. Kale's body jumped back. He hadn't expected it to be a dog. Then there were two more growls outside the only place for them to escape. The animal crept closer to her, and she realized it was Scuffy. He had found her and was rescuing her!

Charlotte thought now was the time to make her move and do it quickly. She rolled away from Kale toward her dog and scrambled on hands and knees. She crawled out from under the fallen tree. Now she could see by the moonlight that the other growls were coming from her neighbor's dogs, a Doberman Pinscher, and a German Shepard. Big, scary-looking dogs. But, they weren't a threat to her. They were rescuing her, too. She scrambled her way past the dogs and stood up. She looked back at the opening to see Kale pop his head out. When he did, the two dogs snapped and snarled at him making sure he didn't move out any further. Scuffy scrambled out beside him and took off running, wanting her to run away with him while his friends held Kale back.

She understood his intention. She broke into a run, following Scuffy. She didn't know where they were in the woods and needed him to guide her back to her house.

CHARLOTTE OPENED her eyes to find Tetonka beside her. She took a deep breath of relief and smiled at him to reassure him. She wrapped her arms around his neck and snuggled into his chest.

After her ordeal with Kale and the excitement over Brock, she was relieved to be in Tetonka's arms. He squeezed her tightly into him, and they fell asleep contented to be in one another's arms.

MEANWHILE, Charlotte's shadow-self ran back to the house to find the police and her parents out in front of her house. Her body stopped once her mother spotted her and came running to wrap her arms around her.

"Charlotte, where on earth have you been? Why did you run off into the woods like that?" Her mother looked more worried than angry. Her dad, followed by the police, came up beside her mother.

Charlotte didn't speak. Her eyes glazed over in a blank stare. "What's wrong, Charlotte? Talk to us." Her mother shook her shoulders gently, trying to snap Charlotte out of it. Her body collapsed, but her dad caught her before she hit the ground.

He gently lowered her to the ground. "She must be in shock. We need to get her to the hospital." Russell said.

Scuffy began to bark as if he wanted to get their attention. He spun in a circle, barked, then ran a few paces back.

"It looks like the dog wants us to follow it," one of the policemen said. Then they heard the barking of the other two dogs.

"I think there's someone else out there," the other police officer said.

"Go see who it is. Kale may still be out there. We're going to take Charlotte to the hospital," Russell told them as he lifted Charlotte's body into his arms.

The police officers ran after Scuffy with their flashlights while Russell and Rosette got Charlotte into the back of their car.

CHARLOTTE LAID on the hospital bed wide-eyed and unfocused. The nurse looked over at her parents who were huddled together on the other side of the bed.

"I'm going to go find the doctor. I'll be right back." The nurse left the room.

Charlotte gasped suddenly and looked wildly around. She thought she saw Onaiwah leaning over her. Did Tetonka take her to the medicine woman?

"Charlotte! Can you hear us? Are you all right?" Her mother placed a hand on her arm.

She turned her head toward her mother. She blinked again to focus her eyes better.

"Where am I? What happened?"

"You're in the hospital, honey. You came running out of the woods, but you couldn't speak to us. You were in shock," her mother explained.

"Why did you go into the woods, Charlotte? What were you doing?" Russell wanted answers.

"I went out to feed Scuffy before going to bed..." She paused, focusing. "then I got knocked in the back of the head and blacked out. Kale, he..." She was so exhausted, and her head was excruciating.

Her mother and dad exchanged worried looks.

"What did he do to you, sweetie?" her mother asked.

Charlotte looked at her mother. She could see the terror and concern in her mother's eyes. "He held his hand on my mouth and nose and suffocated me until I blacked out again." She broke down into more sobs, recalling the ordeal.

Her mother patted her arm, "It's okay, sweetheart. You're safe now."

In between sobs, she continued to explain, "He...said...that...it is... all my...fault. That all ...this ...happened.... because of....me..."

"No, sweetheart. It's not your fault," her mother continued to comfort her and rubbed her arm up and down. "None of this is your fault. Kale has some serious issues, and when the police find him and arrest him, he'll be punished for what he's done today."

Charlotte tried to suck up her tears. Her mother handed her a tissue to wipe her eyes and blow her nose.

"Did he..." her dad hesitated to say it, "did he hurt you?"

She shook her head. "He pressed his hand on my mouth and pressed me down into the dirt. He might have done more if Scuffy hadn't found me. He brought Isaac's dogs with him while I escaped. The dogs were growling and barking at Kale as if they would attack him if he tried to follow me." She couldn't help but smile a little bit at the heroics of her animal companions.

Her mother sighed with relief to hear that she hadn't suffered any physical damage. But there was no denying it; she had been under a lot of emotional trauma today.

She could hear the nurse talking with the doctor outside her room. He came in to find her alert and talking.

"It seems our patient has found her voice. Welcome back." He stepped to the side of her bed and examined her eyes with a penlight. He listened to her heart and checked the monitors by her bedside. "A police officer is waiting to speak to you outside. Are you alert enough to speak with him?"

Charlotte slumped back against her pillow and closed her eyes. She nodded her head. Her head was killing her, and her body felt like it had been wrung out and hung up wet. If she hadn't been in so much pain, she might have fallen asleep that instant.

The police officer entered the room. "Hi, Charlotte, my name is Officer Bennett. I need to ask you a few questions."

She nodded her head. She felt sleepy and hoped she didn't fall asleep before he got the answers he needed.

"Was Kale Fitzpatrick the one who took you into the woods?"

Again, she nodded.

"Did he rape you?"

Charlotte shook her head, not bothering to open her eyes. She didn't want to see the look on her parents' faces, even though there had been no harm done. The saying of the act out loud was hard enough.

"Were you a witness to the stabbing of Brock Van Houten earlier this afternoon?"

She nodded, opening her eyes to look at him this time.

"Was Kale Fitzpatrick also the one who stabbed Brock Van Houten?"

She nodded, tears flooding her eyes as the images came back to her. She wasn't sure she would ever be able to get that image out of her head.

"I would like you to know that we have apprehended Kale Fitzpatrick, and he's been charged with kidnapping and assault with a deadly weapon. He's locked up in jail and will likely be there for several years once we get a conviction. You won't have to worry about him hurting you again."

She broke into sobs at this. She was even tired of crying. She needed to sleep.

"Well, that's all I have for now. If we have any more questions, we may contact you again later. I'm sorry that this has happened to you. Goodnight." The officer nodded to both her parents and quickly left the room. He looked uncomfortable at seeing her break into an uncontrollable fit of crying.

The nurse came back carrying two small plastic cups. "The doctor has prescribed you a sedative to help you sleep. You need to get some rest." She handed the cups to her. One cup had a pill in it, the other water. She took the pill and chased it down with the water. Charlotte sighed back into her pillow hoping that now she could shut all this out of her mind for a while.

"Do you want us to stay here with you tonight, honey?" her mother asked.

"Where are the boys?" Charlotte asked.

"They're staying with Mema and Papa."

"No, Mother. Y'all go home and sleep. You won't be comfortable here. Besides, I'm going to pass out here in a few minutes. I'll be okay." She tried to smile but was already feeling the effects of the sedative.

Her mother looked at her dad to see what he thought. He nodded his head slightly, so her mother got up to leave. She kissed Charlotte on the forehead as her eyes closed. Charlotte didn't have the strength to hold them open any longer.

CHAPTER TWENTY-SEVEN

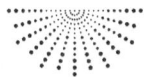

*C*harlotte opened her eyes slowly. She was disoriented, and it took several minutes for her to remember where she was. She looked at the square window in the middle of a plain wall, tiled ceiling, with a long fluorescent light. On the other side of her was a curtain, closing her off into her area. She laid in a hospital bed with metal rail sides. A machine near her head had lots of flashing lights and was beeping at regular intervals.

It came back to her in a flash, and she dropped her head back on the pillow. The door opened, and she expected a nurse or a doctor to enter, but it was Brock being wheeled in a wheelchair.

"Charlotte!"

"Brock, you shouldn't be out of bed," she said sitting up.

"Mom told me you had been admitted into a room down the hall from me, and I insisted she bring me down here." She saw Olivia pushing Brock's wheelchair. Olivia smiled, but her eyes still looked worried.

"Brock, it would have been better for me to come see you," she protested.

"Don't worry about it. They're moving me here into your room so that we can be together. Besides, we'll both be discharged by this afternoon, anyway." Brock put his hand over hers, scooting his wheel-chair as close to her as he could get. He looked anxious for her. "How are you feeling?"

Charlotte took a deep breath and let it out slowly. "I'm better now that I've had some sleep. My mouth feels like it's full of cotton though."

Olivia turned and poured her a cup of water from the pitcher on the side table. Charlotte thanked her and took a sip. She adjusted herself a little higher in the hospital bed.

Olivia took a seat on the other side of her bed opposite of Brock. "Your parents called me last night after they left you here at the hospital and filled me in. I got here first thing this morning to check on Brock and tell him what happened."

Charlotte's body still felt battered and bruised. Her headache was coming back. She rolled her head toward Brock again.

"How are you feeling?" she asked quietly.

He gave her a bigger smile than she could muster at the moment. "I'm sore. If I stay absolutely still, I don't feel the pain as much, but if I move or cough or sneeze, it feels like my insides are ripping apart."

Charlotte grimaced at the news of his pain. She felt stupid lying in a hospital bed when she hadn't been seriously injured. She had suffered serious traumatic stress. That was nothing compared to being stabbed in the stomach with a knife.

The door opened again as two orderlies wheeled Brock's bed into the space on the other side of the curtain. They pushed the curtain back, no longer dividing the room in two.

"Get the beds as close as possible, please. I gotta be next to my girl." He smiled genuinely, and she thought he was so sweet.

The orderlies had to maneuver the bed back and forth several times to get it within two feet of hers, but that was as close as they were allowed to get it. When they left, Olivia helped Brock back in his bed. Brock grimaced and sucked air in through his teeth at sudden moves, but he finally got settled back in bed.

A nurse came in next. "Well, aren't you two the cutest hospital couple I've ever seen." She smiled, but something told Charlotte she was annoyed with the situation. She addressed Brock first.

"I need to check your temperature and assess your pain level. On a scale from 1-10 how would you rate your pain? With 10 being the most severe pain you have ever experienced in your life."

Charlotte looked over at Brock to hear his answer. "It depends on if I'm moving or not."

"Let's say when you're completely still and not moving," The nurse said casually.

"Then I would say a five." The nurse looked at his stitches. She lifted the bandage carefully. Charlotte wanted to get a look too, but she couldn't see from where she was on the bed.

"Your stitches look good. You need to be extra careful about moving and not tear your stitches unless you want a longer recovery time." Brock nodded his head. He looked as if he was uncomfortable with the attention the nurse was giving him.

Then the nurse rounded Brock's bed to take a look at Charlotte. She also took her temperature, for what reason, she didn't know. "How are you feeling?"

"My headache is coming back," she admitted.

"I'll get you something for that. Let me take a look at the back of your head." She turned her head, so the nurse could exam the large bump at the base of her skull. "You're lucky that he didn't split it resulting in stitches." She shook her head slightly. Apparently, she knew more about her ordeal last night than Charlotte would have liked her to. "I'll be back with some Tylenol." She turned and left the room.

As soon as she was out the door, Brock turned to her. "So, that SOB hit you in the back of the head?" She guessed he hadn't heard every detail yet.

"Yes, I don't know with what. I went out to feed Scuffy once I got home from seeing you. Something hard hit me on the back of the head, and I blacked out. I woke up in the woods in a makeshift hideout with Kale right behind me." She shuddered a little at the memory.

Brock must have noticed. He reached his hand toward her, and she took it. She still didn't feel like retelling her trauma from last night. She knew she would have to tell him everything, but not right now. She rolled to her side to face him, but then closed her eyes in hopes he would understand and not ask any more questions.

The nurse came back and gave her some Tylenol and a cup of water. "They'll be taking you for an MRI later to check for a concussion." The nurse informed her.

"Is that necessary?" she protested.

"It is, since you blacked out. The doctor needs to make sure there's no internal bleeding. There's a small percentage that there is, but they wouldn't be doing their jobs if they didn't check to make sure." The nurse took the empty cups and once again left the room.

Charlotte laid back on the pillow and sighed heavily. Brock held her hand and rubbed his thumb back and forth across her palm in an attempt to soothe her. In a way, it did. It was nice that he was touching her.

That afternoon, they were discharged. She understood why Brock had to be wheeled out in a wheelchair, but she didn't see why she had to be. "It's hospital policy," said the orderly.

She wanted to go to Brock's house and be with him, but she knew he needed to rest. She promised she would be there to visit him the next day and every day after that until he was able to go back to school.

A light dusting of snow began to fall on their drive home. Charlotte leaned her head against the cold window and closed her eyes.

BROCK HAD to stay home for two weeks after he left the hospital. Charlotte went to his house every day after practice, and Olivia was kind enough to make her something to eat while she sat with Brock beside his bed. She still had to cheer at the basketball games Tuesday and Friday. Somehow, her heart wasn't as into it without seeing Brock on the team. The doctor said it would be about three more weeks before he'd be able to participate in athletics. That still gave him a few weeks of potential playing time leading up to Regionals and, hopefully, State.

Toward the end of the week, he was getting restless and insisted on moving to the couch in the living room. He had gotten the new Nintendo system for Christmas, and they played some of his new games. She wasn't good at video games, so she opted to watch him play instead.

Charlotte brought him his homework, and they worked on their assignments together. Mrs. Olsen had assigned a worksheet. "We have all the biomes listed on this worksheet, and we're to find the average climate, average temperature, typical fauna, typical flora, and areas around the world where that particular biome is located."

Brock tried to distract her by tickling her or playing with her hair. "Stop, Brock! We need to get this done." Although she told him to stop, her laughing and smiling meant she was enjoying the attention.

Olivia walked into the room, and they straightened. "Are you getting your work done in here or do I need to sit down and watch over your shoulder until you finish?"

Brock looked at her sideways and gave her a guilty look. She nudged him on the shoulder as if to say, *I told you.* They settled down long enough to finish their assignments. Brock was probably learning more working with her on his assignments than he ever actually did in the classroom.

"Maybe I need to stay home permanently, and you can come over and teach me every day." He snuggled into her shoulder while she sat putting her stuff back in her backpack.

"Something tells me after a while we wouldn't be getting much done." She smiled back at him.

Brock decided to turn on the TV to see what was on, and he happened to catch the news.

"A local teen accused of stabbing another teen, then kidnapping the victim's girlfriend is still behind bars tonight. The prosecutors say he will be tried as an adult and could face twenty years in prison. The teen is also under investigation in connection with two other separate incidents of arson and vandalism. No other suspects have been named at this time."

There was a mug shot of Kale in the corner of the TV screen. Brock quickly turned the TV back off. He and Charlotte sat in silence.

After a few moments, Brock spoke to her, "Do you wanna talk about it?" He touched her lightly on her back.

Charlotte shrugged her shoulders. "I wake up at night feeling like someone's suffocating me all over again, and I can't breathe. I have panic attacks at school for no reason. I think part of it has been because you aren't there to make me feel safe. I feel so vulnerable. That's how he made me feel, vulnerable and helpless. I couldn't do anything against him. If it hadn't been for Scuffy and the other dogs, I don't know that I would have gotten away from him." Tears ran down her cheeks, and Brock wiped them away with his thumbs. Then he pulled her to him. She was careful not to lean into his sore stomach, but having his strong arms around her made her feel safe again.

"I dread having to testify at the trial," she moaned.

"We both do," he added.

They sat staring into space, thinking about what it was going to be like in court facing Kale again. Brock felt a red-hot anger deep down that he tried to suppress and not let it consume him. Whereas, she felt panicky and thought she would lose her sanity if she had to face him again. Both were attempting to be strong despite their inner conflicts.

Brock tried to change the subject, "How are things in the Osage village?" It was still strange to him to talk to her about this separate part of her life. She told him everything that had happened over there as well, and it didn't comfort him any, knowing that she was living as a married woman doing what married women do with their husbands. He felt sick to his stomach now thinking about it. Then the incidents with the bear and Hula being bitten, he wished he could somehow be over there with her to protect her there, too.

"Quiet, for now. I watched several of the people play a game like Lacrosse. It was brutal. You would have loved it." She tried to smile at him and shake her thoughts of Kale.

"I get worried about you crossing over or whatever you call it," Brock said.

"I refer to it as switching because I'm switching bodies. But that's not true either because Nahele doesn't go into my body when I'm in hers."

"Where does she go?" Brock asked.

"I'm not sure. It's like I'm her. No other person is talking to me in my head; it's only me."

Olivia came back in, "Charlotte, I'm afraid it's getting late."

"Yes, Mrs. Olivia." Charlotte had decided, since she didn't want to be called Mrs. Van Houten that she would put the Mrs. in front of Olivia so she could still seem respectful toward her. "I was getting ready to go."

"Did you get all your assignments finished, Brock?" Olivia looked at her son.

"Yes, Mom. We finished." He grimaced as he swung his legs over the side of the couch. Charlotte helped him as he tried to stand. He still couldn't stand straight; he had to walk hunched over instead.

"Oh, I almost forgot," Olivia said. "I talked with a friend of mine back in Oklahoma who did some digging around about Spirit Travelers, and they wanted me to pass on some vital information to you." Olivia looked concerned at her. "He said not to let the body of the person you're in die while your spirit is with it, or your spirit will be left to wander the earth in between worlds."

"Oh, my goodness! I didn't know that. What would happen to my body here?" She was shocked to find this out.

"He said, at first, your body would sit and stare into nothingness for a while, like being in a catatonic state. That's how many lost spirit travelers' bodies end up in mental health institutions. They're detached from the world, and no one can reach them, but then the body eventually goes comatose and dies. But it could take years for a spiritless body to wither away like that." Olivia looked carefully at Charlotte to see her reaction.

"Thank you for telling me. I've been wondering about that, but now that you've told me, it feels like somewhere in the back of my mind I knew that already. The longest I've been gone was six days, and even then, Lilly said my body was becoming unresponsive. We both agreed that any longer and it would be obvious that something was wrong."

"Charlotte, are you sure you need to continue doing this? You still don't know what you're supposed to be doing over there and what if something does happen to you?" Brock looked more worried.

"I need to keep going back so I can figure out what my purpose is. Besides, I have my spirit animal guide there to protect me. He's already saved me once. That's what he's supposed to do, keep me from dying while I'm there, so my spirit isn't left to wander."

Brock didn't look convinced. "I guess we can talk more about it later."

"Yeah, I need to get home. Thanks again, Mrs. Olivia. Tomorrow, we have another basketball game, but I'll be sure to check in on Saturday, okay?" She kissed Brock briefly on the lips and left.

On the way home, Charlotte had a lot to think about. She felt more exhausted lately every day. It was all she could do every night to shower and go to bed. It seemed as if she could never get enough rest. Maybe it was because she wasn't sleeping consistently through the night and was waking up from nightmares. The only time she felt she honestly got enough sleep was when she was Nahele. It was probably because she slept with Tetonka's arms wrapped around her all night. Come to think of it, that sounded like a marvelous idea.

CHAPTER TWENTY-EIGHT

*A*s it turned out, Tetonka had left the day before to go on a deer hunt. However, Charlotte felt she did sleep better. She assumed that maybe Nahele's pregnant body helped her sleep deeper. She decided to begin the day and grabbed the kettle to get water. It was a beautiful fall day, and many women were out at the stream smiling, full of happiness.

Charlotte walked back to the hut thinking she needed to visit with her sister today and spend some time with her. She hoped Hula was adjusting to her new circumstances. She wanted to encourage her that she could still have a productive life.

She set her kettle of water down when she heard a woman scream from somewhere within the village. She rushed out to see where the scream had come from and heard many other noises of people running and yelling. She crept behind the huts careful to keep an eye out for signs of danger. Without having seen any visible threat, the sounds of the people told her that something was wrong.

Charlotte finally came to a hut toward the west end of the village and peered around to see several white men. She counted the number of men she could see and thought there were about ten of them, ransacking some of the huts. One man dragged a woman by her hair as a child cried and tried to pull the man's hand off his mother. The man backhanded the child. She gasped then quickly covered her mouth so that they wouldn't hear her.

The other men threw things out of the hut, rudely touched some of the young girls, and ate the food that had been stored away for the winter. A young boy about twelve came straight down the road to face the men head-on with his bow and arrow. He shot at a man, grazing his cheek. This only angered the vagabond, so he pulled out a musket rifle and shot the boy dead in the middle of the street. Now there was a flood of screaming and crying women and children running away from the men as quickly as they could.

She needed to get to her horse. She had a general idea where the men had gone hunting and felt that if she could somehow slip past the men to the other side, she could mount Cornsilk and ride to find them. She crept behind one more hut and carefully peeked around the corner to see if any of the intruders were visible. She was about to take a step when she was grabbed suddenly from behind. A dirty, rough hand covered her mouth preventing her from screaming.

"Well, now. What do we have here?" The man said grotesquely in her ear. He was French. She had no idea what he said, but she was reasonably certain it wasn't good. She fought as hard as she could to get out of his grasp. She had a terrible sickening feeling in her stomach. If she couldn't free herself, this wasn't going to end well.

"Henry, keep this *donzelle* low for me!" The man screamed to another man, apparently named Henry. That's all she knew. Another dirty man who smelled worse than the one behind her came to help.

Then suddenly the man behind her froze, and she heard a gurgling sound. Then the man in front of her arched his chest forward as if struck in the middle of the back. She was immediately freed and pushed the man in front of her off as he fell forward. The man behind her fell to the side. She quickly turned to see who had come to her rescue.

She saw her mother standing a few feet away, a bow in her hand with Hula clutching the quiver of arrows and pressed against her mother's back. Both women had a look of terror written all over their face. Charlotte stood frozen in place. She was in shock at how closely the man had come to raping her. Even so, she still had been grossly violated. She saw a movement out of the corner of her eye and screamed as she turned around ready to strike at another assailant.

It was only another young boy retrieving his tomahawk from the back of the other man. He, too, looked frightened but had had enough courage to bury his only means of defense in the other nasty man.

Her mother ran to her as she lost all strength in her limbs to remain standing. "Nahele, you must get to your horse and ride to the men for help," her mother said.

She was in shock and felt numb all over. She wasn't sure she could make her body move. Her mother and Hula got their hands under her arms and helped her to her feet. She stood wobbly for a few seconds willing some strength back into her body. Even the little boy tried to help her stand.

"Nahele, you must go. You know how to ride, and we need to alert the men who went on the hunt. I will take your sister and this boy, and we will hide in the woods until they are gone. Please, Nahele, do you hear me?" Her mother shook her, bringing her out of her shock.

Hula slapped Charlotte across the face, and she blinked some recognition back to her present situation. "Yes..." she stammered. "Get horse... must ride." It was hard to make her mouth work.

"Go, Nahele. I think the rest of the men have moved further into the village, and you are clear to get to the pasture now." The two women and the boy began to help her move and shoved her in the direction of the pasture. She took a couple of wobbly steps, and then, realizing she could stay upright without collapsing, she ran for the pasture.

Charlotte ran into the pasture spooking some of the horses that remained. She called out to her horse, and it turned its head in her direction. She caught the reins. First, she had to lean her forehead against her horse's neck to gather her strength for one more second. She said a silent prayer to *Wah'Kon-Tah* to give her strength and to help guide her horse to the men that she needed to find.

Grabbing a handful of the horse's mane, she swung herself onto her horse as Tetonka had taught her to do. She clicked her tongue to get her horse into a run, and they took off as fast as they could out of the village. She followed a small hunting trail that she knew the men had taken. But, how far and at which point had they left it, she didn't know.

Then out of the woods burst Barkley, running ahead of her horse, leading the way to where she needed to go. Charlotte almost burst into tears at the sight of her animal spirit guide. Once again, he was there for her in a time of danger, guiding her to where she needed to go.

They raced at full speed for some time. She panted as much as the horse and wolf were from the exertion and desire to get there as fast as possible. She leaned down on the neck of her horse, breathing behind its ear. Tears stung her eyes and streamed down her face as she tried to push the thoughts of what happened in the village out of her mind and concentrate only on finding Tetonka.

Finally, Charlotte came over a small rise and saw a group of wigwams with smoke floating from the center. She almost broke out into sobs at the sight of the camp but managed to hold back until she could find her husband.

She slowed her horse as they came into camp and jumped down yelling for Tetonka or anyone who might be in the camp. The first person to appear was Kajika. She stopped short realizing that this was the last person she wanted to see right now.

"What has happened?" he said, in a way that sent a chill down her spine. "Why have you come running into our hunting camp all the way out here?"

"There are intruders in the village," she began. "They are raping, stealing, and killing our people." She choked on the words and wished she could find Tetonka as soon as possible.

"Come into the hut and get a drink of water. I will go find the men to bring them back to camp right away." He had a strange look in his eyes that told her not to trust him, but she went into the hut anyway, feeling like she might collapse again, needing to sit down.

Charlotte had barely gotten into the hut when he grabbed her and forced her to the ground. He fell on top of her like a dead weight. She struggled under him, not believing that this could happen to her twice in one day. She thrust her knee up doubling him over. He gagged as if he was about to vomit. Charlotte got to her feet just when Tetonka burst into the hut.

When it registered in her mind that he was standing before her, she flew into his arms, almost knocking him over. He held her tightly to him, processing the scene before him.

"Your wolf found me in the woods, and I followed him back to the camp. When I saw your horse, I knew something must be wrong." He said into her hair still looking puzzled at Kajika struggling for air on his knees.

She pulled him outside to tell him what was happening back in the village. She didn't have to say much before he began to turn to get the others still in the woods.

"Wait!" she screamed hysterically, "Don't leave me here. Take me with you!"

Not waiting to ask why and, furthermore, afraid he knew why, he grabbed her hand and pulled her behind him, running toward the woods where the others were still out hunting.

After a few minutes, she had to pull him to a stop. He ran much too fast for her to keep up, and she had a sharp pain in her side. "I can't keep up with your long legs," she gasped in between sharp breaths. He knelt pulling her onto his back and began to run again.

Only a short way further, they came upon the others. They saw Tetonka follow the wolf back toward camp and decided they should go back as well to see what was happening. As with her, he only had to tell them that there were intruders in the village before the rest of them were running again back to the camp. She rested her head on Tetonka's shoulder as she bounced up and down while he ran with her on his back. He was strong and had good endurance to be able to run and carry her at the same time. She could feel his strong legs as they took long strides climbing the small hills and running around the rocks and trees. After today's events, she wasn't sure she would ever let go of his back.

It seemed like they got back to the hunting camp faster than the outbound trip. Kajika had gathered the horses, ready for the men to ride out. Tetonka slid her off his back but held onto her hand keeping her close to him. Tetonka hadn't asked her about what happened in the hut before he had arrived, but she saw from the look he gave Kajika that he wanted explanations when this other situation was over.

The men mounted their horses, ready to ride back to the village. Kajika and another young warrior would stay behind to roll the wigwams and other hunting gear and follow as soon as they could.

"I don't think I have the strength to stay on my horse to ride back," she told Tetonka.

"You will ride with me, and Kajika will bring your horse back with the rest of the camp supplies." He said this more as an order to Kajika, who merely nodded his head in obedience.

Tetonka swung up on his horse then reached down for her pulling her up behind him. He kicked his horse to run and yelled, "Ya!" as all the men followed him racing up the hunting trail. Charlotte began to relax a little now that she had her arms around her strong, brave, and formidable husband. Even though the men who had assaulted her personally were dead, she wouldn't rest easy until all the Frenchmen, who had plundered their village were caught and punished.

The men slowed as they neared the end of the village. The sun was setting low and only a few more minutes of daylight were left. They stopped their horses outside the village. They dismounted and grouped to decide their next move. All the men looked to Tetonka for instructions.

"Nahele, you stay here with the horses. Some of the men, you go quietly around this side of the huts while the rest of us go around the other side." The village was eerily quiet. They didn't know if the intruders were held up in one of the huts or had left the village. She didn't want to stay behind all alone, but she didn't want to go into the village and come face to face with those dirty men again either.

Tetonka wrapped his arms around her and whispered into her ear,

"You will be safer here for now." He touched his forehead to hers. "Your wolf is here to protect you."

She looked down, and Barkley was sitting beside her panting from his hard run back with them. She hadn't seen him once Tetonka had found her at the camp. She thought that he had probably stayed hidden in the woods out of sight, keeping an eye on her the whole way back. She suddenly felt much better. If Tetonka wasn't with her to protect her, at least she had a backup protector for whom she was very thankful.

Charlotte hugged Tetonka and told him to be careful. He turned to the group that was to go in the direction he had indicated, and they crouched down moving silently, but swiftly, out of sight. She knelt to Barkley hugging him around the neck and burrowed her face in his fur. He continued to pant as if smiling and proud of himself for being a suitable protector.

"You deserve a good juicy steak when this is all over," she said, and he licked her cheek in agreement.

Soon, they were waiting in complete darkness, and she shook from the cold. She huddled up to Barkley attempting to stay warm next to his fur. She saw a figure of a man walking straight down the village road toward her. She couldn't see his face, but from the outline of his body and the way he walked, she knew it was Tetonka. She breathed a sigh of relief. If he was walking out in the open, then the threat of danger must have passed, at least for now.

He approached her again and wrapped his arms around her. Rubbing his hands up and down her arms he said, "You are cold. We need to get you back to our hut. But first, we need to take the horses to pasture."

He helped her gather the reins of the horses, and they led them to the pasture and released them. She looked around for Barkley, but he must have gone back to wherever he stayed when she didn't need him. She would've liked for him to stay so she could reward him, but she supposed he would show again unannounced, and she would reward him then.

Tetonka took her hand and led her back to the village. "Did you find the intruders?" she asked.

"No. They have gone. But we found their trail, and at first light, we will set out to track them and hunt them down." She looked over at him as they walked side by side. She could see in the moonlight that his jaw was still tense, and his brow scrunched forward.

"What else did you find?" She already knew of some of the damages but was afraid to hear more. Tetonka bent over to pick up a thick stick that would make a good torch when they came to a fire.

"We found three women and two children dead. One young boy was dead in the road. Only two of the men were killed." His jaw muscles flinched, and she wasn't sure if it was because he was holding back his anger or tears.

"I saw the boy get shot after he tried to shoot one of the men with his arrow. He only grazed the man on the cheek. The other two men were the ones who attacked me." Tetonka stopped suddenly at this and turned to face her. "My mother shot an arrow through the neck of one and a young boy buried his tomahawk in the back of the other." She rushed out fighting not to burst into tears.

Tetonka pulled her into his chest. "Did they hurt you?"

"No," she said not wanting to replay the scene in her mind.

"Did they..." he trailed off.

"No. One was about to if Mother hadn't shot him before he did." She felt a sob catch in his chest as he squeezed her tight against him.

"What of Kajika? Why was he on the ground in the hut before I came in?" He continued to hold her against his chest as if afraid to hear her answer, yet already knowing the truth.

"He forced me to the ground and pinned himself on top of me." She squeezed her eyes shut as tears rolled down her cheeks. Tetonka growled deep in his chest, and it vibrated in her own. This was a grave insult to Tetonka, and she knew that he would sever his bond with his kola over this.

"I assume from the position he was in, he didn't succeed either," he said through clenched teeth.

"No, he did not. I kneed him in his stones."

Tetonka let out a short chuckle at this then bent his mouth to the top of her head and kissed it. "You are a brave and fierce woman, my love. My heart breaks at the thought of what you have been through today. I promise you I will avenge the death of our people and the attack they have made on you and others."

They turned to walk back to their hut. She pulled on his hand slightly and said, "First, I need to check on my family."

He nodded and changed direction.

❧

WHEN THEY DUCKED into the Nahele's family hut, everyone turned in surprise. When they saw it was Tetonka and her, they rushed to hug them. Charlotte hugged her mother and sister, as her grandmother and aunt hugged her from the back. Her two small cousins clung to Tetonka's legs. There were many more tears of relief and sorrow over the events of the day. Finally, she was able to peel herself away from everyone enough to look around to see who was accounted for. Her father, grandfather, and uncle had gone to the big council meeting at the main village at Marsh of the Swans. Charlotte was thankful that Tetonka had not gone with them, or he would have been too far off to contact and come to their rescue.

The hunters' pursuit of the intruders in the morning would give them peace, knowing they would likely not be returning.

Tetonka put his hand on her shoulder. "I need to go and check on my family. You stay here, and I will return soon to stay here tonight." He kissed her quickly and left the hut.

All the women sat around the fire, still clinging to one another and staring into the flames. Finally, her mother asked, "Does anyone want anything to eat?" Everyone shook their heads except the two little ones. Her mother got up to get something for them. Charlotte hoped they didn't know what actually happened today.

The others might not feel like eating, but her mother knew they at least needed something to drink. She poured some warm water into small bowls with some soothing herbs to help calm their nerves and hopefully help them sleep.

Charlotte sat holding the warm bowl in her hands and smelled the sweet aroma wafting above it. Off in the village somewhere, they could hear the wailing of those who had come back from hiding in the woods to find their loved ones dead. Hula told her of how they had hidden, staying out of sight of the intruders. When the rest of the men saw the two who were killed, they decided to leave the village.

She had to tell them the horrible news of the other women and children Tetonka had told her were dead. This brought fresh tears to her sister. Grandmother rocked back and forth and began to whisper prayers to *Wah'Kon-Tah*. The others followed her example, and each of them whispered their prayers. It sounded like the moaning and wailing that was going on outside the hut only at a lower decibel.

She prayed for the spirits of the villagers whose lives had been taken. She prayed that *Wah'Kon-Tah* would receive them and guide them along the Milky Way to the land beyond, where they would meet their other loved ones who had gone on before them. She prayed for the families who had lost their loved ones. She prayed for the strength and safety of the other men who were at the Big Council meeting and that they would have a safe journey home. She prayed for the men who were going to track down the rest of the vagabonds and that none of them would be further injured or killed. Finally, she tried to pray for the spirits of the men who had assaulted her and lost their lives as well. She found it hard to say the words even though it was the custom of her people to pray even for their enemies. She was only able to pray that their spirits walked along the path in the sky and found suitable judgment in the eyes of *Wah'Kon-Tah*.

Tetonka returned to their hut reporting that everyone was well and accounted for in his family. His younger brother was there to stay with the women and children, so he could stay here to watch over them. All of them were deeply grateful for his presence and felt they would sleep better, knowing he was there among them. But none of them were as thankful as Charlotte to have her husband with her while her mother, grandmother, and aunt were undoubtedly worried about their husbands.

It came time to sleep, and everyone rolled out mats and blankets around the fire. One of the little cousins slept huddled against his mother while the other one slept underneath the blankets with Grandmother. Hula slept next to her mother, and of course, Charlotte was comforted by the warmth and security of Tetonka spooning behind her. He was so big that her entire body was cocooned inside his. When she was snug in his embrace, she felt the full exhaustion of the day wash over her. Her body still ached, but she suspected that in the morning, she would feel the pains from today even worse.

It was still dark out when she felt the rush of cold hit her back when Tetonka left her side. She pried one eye open to see where he was going. She noticed her mother had gotten up as well to put together some food for him to take with him. He thanked her, then knelt to kiss Charlotte goodbye. She wrapped her arms around his neck, tempted not to let go. She kissed him hard and as long as she could before he finally had to pull away.

"I will be back with the scalps of those who raided our village and killed some of our people. And I promise you, I will come back to you," he said breathing into her ear.

"You are my heart," she told him.

"You are mine as well." He ducked out of the hut to join the others in tracking the vagabonds.

Charlotte felt a sudden sting of panic in her stomach but then quickly tried to reassure herself that he was quite capable of handling himself; he was bigger and stronger than any of the men she had seen the day before. She knew their men could outwit them and overcome them quickly in hand-to-hand combat, but the fact that the French, as well as all Europeans that traveled the wilderness, carried guns was all too worrisome. She snuggled back into her blanket, feeling his warmth still inside and tried to go back to sleep.

CHARLOTTE NERVOUSLY WAITED for Tetonka's return to the village for two days. Toward the end of the third day, someone came shouting that they spotted the group of men returning. She jumped up and ran to the end of the road to meet them. They looked tired, and a few of them were wounded. When they got close enough, they slid off their horses as the younger boys ran out to get their horses and care for them.

When Charlotte saw Tetonka walking and favoring his right side a little, she gasped and ran out to meet him. She pulled his right arm around her shoulders and wrapped her arm around his waist. "You are hurt," she said, stating the obvious.

"Nothing that won't heal." He tried not to wince. Many of the other wives and mothers ran out to greet the rest of the men. Everyone gathered in the Peacemaker Chief's lodge to hear the news of what happened, and Onaiwah began to check over each of the men and attend their wounds. Someone began wailing and crying outside the lodge. Charlotte moved to get up and see what was happening when Tetonka caught her by the hand. "We lost two of our men. We had to build a travois to carry them back."

Understanding the situation, she slowly sat back down and said a little prayer for the dead, their loved ones, and the fact that her husband wasn't one of them. Onaiwah came over to Tetonka to check his side. She made him lie down to get a better look. He had a very dirty and heavily bloodied bandage wrapped all around his ribs. Charlotte winced at the sight of so much blood.

As she suspected, once Onaiwah removed the bandage and cleaned the dried blood away, she saw a deep gash that went almost front to back along one rib.

"The white man's metal must have struck right at the bone and traveled along the bone tearing the flesh," Onaiwah assessed. Charlotte knew that it needed to be disinfected and stitched, but she knew from her people that they didn't believe in stitches, or surgery, for that matter. She needed to convince the medicine woman of what she knew and how to do it.

Onaiwah dug around in her bag and produced a silver flask. Charlotte's eyes went wide. She hadn't expected that.

Onaiwah winked at her and said, "Strong drink is not good for the people, but I keep a little in supplies for such an occasion as this." Then she leaned down to Tetonka and said, "This will sting a little."

She quickly poured a generous amount along the wound. Tetonka growled low in his throat in response. Charlotte had to suppress a giggle at how animal-like he sounded. She knew it had to sting a lot and it worried her to see him in pain like this. If it got infected, it could kill him.

Onaiwah extracted a curved bone. She lifted it and said, "A rib bone from a little bird."

A tiny hole had been drilled in one end. She threaded deer sinew as thin as string through the hole and began to stitch the wound together. Charlotte sat and watched in awe and held Tetonka's hand as he breathed fiercely through his nose fighting hard through the pain. When she finished, she spread an ointment over the stitches and wrapped his midsection in a cloth.

"Take him to your hut and see that he gets some rest. If he has a fever, come to me immediately," she directed her. Charlotte nodded her head and helped her husband up. They walked rather unsteadily back to their hut. It was a rare occasion for her to be the one supporting Tetonka, but she was glad to have him back in her arms.

Once Charlotte had Tetonka settled in their hut, she set about making the fire. "Did you kill all the men?" she asked while she worked.

"We came back with seven scalps," Tetonka replied still wincing a little.

She hesitated, "Only seven?" She thought a minute. If two had been killed in the village that meant nine in total. Was she sure there had been ten? She decided not to make an issue of it. What could one man do? He was a vagabond, an outcast from his people. But there were many marauders and intruders coming into their lands every day. There was always a possible threat to her people, this was no different.

Then she asked, "Did Kajika join your men when you were tracking the intruders?"

Tetonka winced as he tried to find a comfortable spot, "I have not seen Kajika since the day he assaulted you. If he knows what is good for him, he will stay away from me and this village until my blood has cooled."

Charlotte agreed. Most importantly, now that Tetonka was severely injured, he would have a challenging time fighting Kajika if it came to that. But, knowing Tetonka, he would be stubborn enough to try. She prayed Kajika had found a place to hideout far away and not come back.

She made a stew for Tetonka to drink and cleaned up when he was finished. She made sure the fire was strong and sat down at his head. She gathered his head into her lap and smoothed her hand over his hair to ease him to sleep. When he breathed easy, she slid out from under him. Charlotte eased herself down next to him and reached out in her mind like Onaiwah had taught her for her other self.

CHAPTER TWENTY-NINE

*B*rock had been back at school for two days. He could stand straighter now and only winced now and then if he moved suddenly, coughed, or sneezed. Charlotte had been distant the previous week, and Lilly had informed him that she was her shadow-self. He could tell the difference now. What did she do when she was over there? Why was she doing it? He hadn't had much time to think about it before his run-in with Kale. At first, he just thought it was her imagination. That she had gotten caught up in researching his family history and had somehow made up this whole story about going back in time. It was too impossible to even think about.

But when his mom confirmed the story with stories from some of the older ones at the reservation, he got a little spooked. He had grown up hearing all kinds of stories from his elders. They believed his people came from the sky and landed in the trees and that the animals spoke to them. He always thought that was just their primi-tive way of explaining the world as they understood it. They didn't know how else to explain their existence. For all he knew, his people had been aliens from another planet and had forgotten their original world.

Now Charlotte claimed to have this magical ability to leave her body and go back in the past into someone else's body, the body of an Osage girl. How was he supposed to feel about that?

But she came back to him smiling brightly this morning before school, and he thought he never wanted her to lose that beautiful smile ever again.

All the students were apologetic to him wherever he went. They were sorry for the part they played in witnessing the fight and felt partially responsible for his stabbing. Even Kale's closest buddies apologized to him. They went to the police and told them everything Kale had done and their part in it. They were having to do community service for their role in burning her car and smashing his dad's Impala. They would also be testifying at Kale's trial as witnesses to all he had done and had been saying about her over the past few months.

Brock was only slightly relieved that Kale was behind bars and was facing a long time in jail. It didn't feel like closure to him yet. He thought maybe it would be final in his mind once the trial was over. He especially hated to think that Charlotte had to testify as well. He knew the pain and anguish Kale had caused her and didn't want to see her have to relive all that over again at the trial. But it had to be done, and when it was all over, he hoped he could help Charlotte heal from her internal wounds. Physical wounds were much easier to heal than emotional ones.

Even though Charlotte was back from the past, Brock noticed that she wasn't as bouncy and bubbly as she had been. He hoped it was simply the Kale situation still hanging over their heads, and she would bounce back once that was over. But, he also worried that something else was on her mind. He needed to talk to her but didn't want to do it at school.

The basketball team had a home game that night. Even though he wouldn't be playing for a couple more weeks, he wanted to at least be on the sidelines with the team. Since there was a game, Charlotte didn't have to stay after school for cheer practice, and she invited him to her house to get something to eat before they had to be back at the gym for the game.

"Charlotte, can we talk somewhere in private?" Brock asked after they ate in her kitchen. Charlotte's little brothers were hanging around, and her mother was always walking in and out.

"Sure. I need to feed Scuffy. Come out back with me." Charlotte found Scuffy's water bowl and filled it at the outside tap.

"How are you holding up?" Brock watched her carefully as she sat the water bowl down.

She straightened to look at him and sighed heavily. "I'm okay. I try not to think about it. I spent the last few days as Nahele, and there was an incident. . ." Her eyes shifted to the woods, and Brock wondered what she was thinking. Was it the other guy in the past or what Kale did to her out there? He felt a pang of jealousy for one and anger for the other.

He took a step forward and held her hand. "I wish I could somehow erase your memory of everything he did to you and spare you the pain I see in your eyes." He reached with his other hand and tucked a strand of hair behind her ear. She smiled at him and rested her head on his chest. When she did so, she saw that her brothers were peeking out at them from behind the curtain of the sliding glass door.

"Let's move a little further out away from prying eyes." She stuck her tongue out at her brothers before she turned with Brock and walked off the back porch. Scuffy came out from under the deck and walked ahead of them.

"What was the incident?" Brock asked, holding her hand and looking at her carefully. She was looking down at the ground as they walked past some of the trees.

CHAPTER THIRTY

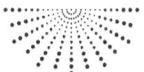

*C*harlotte felt the unexpected switch. She opened her eyes as Nahele in her hut. Tetonka stood at her side. The look on his face was utter astonishment. Did he see something change in her when she switched? He looked at her, eyes wide open and mouth hanging down.

"Husband, are you all right? What happened?" Charlotte tried to remain calm to determine what he witnessed. She had never seen him look like this. He was always very stoic with his facial expressions.

"Charlotte? Is that you?" Tetonka asked.

Charlotte sucked in a breath. How did he know her other name? Then it hit her. "Brock? Is that you?" Now she was quite sure she had the same look on her face as he did on his.

He looked around the hut taking it all in. Charlotte put her hands on his chest and looked into his eyes. He looked down at her, examining her closely. He took a step back from her and examined his own body.

"Brock?" Charlotte asked again.

He looked up at her and a wide grin spread across his face. "Charlotte?"

They stared at each other for a moment. "I was holding your hand, and we were following Scuffy." She paused. "How do you feel?"

He closed the gap between them and took her hands. "It was the weirdest feeling I've ever had. One minute I'm walking with you, then my body seemed to be floating in outer space, and now I'm here looking at a beautiful Indian girl." He looked at her mischievously. "So, I'm your husband?"

Charlotte nodded, still smiling up at him. "Tetonka," she whispered as if saying it too loud would make it untrue.

"So, if I'm your husband, then we can..."

She knew exactly what he meant. But when he bent down to wrap his arms around her, he stopped short, wincing in pain.

"I didn't expect to have my stomach pain still." He grimaced, grabbing at his side.

She caught him by the shoulders. "Tetonka was shot a few days ago. That was part of what I was about to explain before we switched."

She helped him sit down by the fire. "Close your eyes for a minute and let the memories come back to you." She rubbed his arm up and down to comfort him. He did as she asked and after a moment, he gasped.

"Oh! This guy's a bad ass!" Brock was impressed, and a little intimidated. But now that was him, and he didn't know what to think about that. "I remember now. Oh, god! How awful!"

She was relieved not to have to repeat all the events back to him.

He reached over to her and moved her to sit in his lap. "Now I understand what was on your mind today at school. But it's over now, right?" He kissed the top of her head. Charlotte sighed and rested her head against his collarbone.

"I hope so. But. . ." she hesitated.

"But what?" He pushed her away a little to look in her eyes.

"I thought I counted ten men who came into the village. Two tried to rape me and were killed, and you and the others killed seven. That makes nine. What if there is still one more out there?" She laid her head back on his chest as he wrapped his arms around her.

"I don't think one man can do any more harm to the village. He wouldn't dare come near us now knowing what we did to the others. If he knows what's good for him, he will get as far away from here as he possibly can." They sat next to the fire listening to it pop and crackle.

Brock's stomach growled, and Charlotte slid away from him. "I need to make us something to eat." When she got up, Brock watched her amusingly.

She saw his look and asked, "What?" She grinned, still feeling a little uncomfortable with the way he looked at her.

"It's so amazing to see you like this. We're husband and wife playing house together." He chuckled a little.

"Tetonka would never say anything like that. If you want to stay over here a while, you better get in touch with your inner Tetonka, so no one suspects something strange has happened." She came over to give him a quick kiss, but he grabbed her instead and brought her down into his lap again to kiss her more thoroughly.

"Something strange has happened, and I think I like it." His breath was hot against her cheek as he brushed his lips across her skin. He bent his head lower to kiss her neck.

How could she resist? She melted into him as he cradled her in his lap. "You bet I want to stay over here a while." He whispered into her ear. Then he winced again when a pain shot through his side.

She took advantage of his momentary discomfort to stand up again. "Your performance might be a little hindered seeing how you're hurt over here like your other self." She grinned at him mischievously this time. "First things first. We need to eat and take care of things before we're settled in for the night."

As she moved about the hut, Brock asked, "What about our bodies...you know...back there?"

"Your body will go sit on the sidelines and watch the game and my body will cheer like always. I've never seen what I look like when I'm over there, so I don't know. I only know that Lilly says I'm still doing what I normally do; I'm just devoid of personality, you could say." She didn't look at him while she said this but continued to busy herself around the hut.

He sat, thinking about what his shadow-self must look like. He hadn't paid attention to Charlotte's shadow-self enough to understand the difference. He wondered if his parents would notice.

Charlotte made a stew, and they ate quietly by the fire. When they finished, Charlotte took the bowls and rinsed them out. Brock was dusting the animal skins and "fluffing" up the bed, so to speak, when a messenger announced outside their hut that the men from the council meeting at *Marais des Cygnes* had come home. Charlotte looked pleadingly at Brock.

He looked at her for a second then slumped. "Okay, we can go for a little while, right?" He looked dejected to have his plans put on hold yet again.

She gave him a big smile and kissed him on the cheek, then took his hand to lead him to the Peacemaker Chief's longhouse.

The longhouse was packed, and they had to push their way in to see the men who had returned. Brock looked like a kid in a big toy store; his eyebrows were up, and his mouth was slightly open. Charlotte got his attention and pointed to her face. She scrunched her eyebrows down, telling him to change the look on his face. After a second, he got it and quickly turned his face to a frown. She thought it was a little too much on the opposite extreme, but at least it wasn't as apparent as before. She chuckled, thinking about Brock in Tetonka's body. How strange this must be to him, and then she remembered her first experience and knew exactly how he felt.

They found a space in the corner to observe the elders and listen to what was being said.

"We have known that the Spanish tribe and French tribe have tried to keep us from trading with the white men across the Great River," her father, Chayton, was saying, "and they have declared to only trade with us if we are in good standing with their chiefs. But others of our tribe in the southern *A kan sea* bands have been rebelling and causing great trouble. I am afraid this has reflected badly on all members of our tribe even though not all of us are willing participants in their acts of violence.

"We all know that the main trading posts that have been set up for our people are either at the place the French man calls Saint Louis or the *A kan sea* post. We, however, have been secretly trading with the white men to the east on the river the French call the Saint Francis. The Spanish Chief in the south has learned of this and wants to put a stop to it. They are afraid more white men to the east will move into this land. We, also, do not want the white man to move into our territory.

"The only white men our people trust are the Chouteau brothers, Auguste and Pierre, from the French tribe. They have been good to us in maintaining trade even when the Spanish chiefs have denied us. We will continue to be loyal to Pierre Chouteau. Now there is another white man who wants trade with us. He is called Manuel Lisa from the Spanish tribe. He is stirring up trouble with the Big Chief in a place they call New Orleans to stop us from trading with our white brothers, the Chouteau. We will not abide by this and will stand by our trusted friend.

"This is the consensus of the tribal council in the Big Osage village of *Marais des Cygnes*." Chayton finished speaking and put the speaking stick in the center of the circle so someone else could have a turn at speaking or ask a question.

Another man picked up the stick. "What do the Little Old Men in the Big Osage village have to say about us rejoining the village in the north?" He put the stick back in the center of the circle.

A man sitting next to her father, who she recognized but couldn't recall his name, picked up the stick to address the question. "The Little Old Men are losing their influence over the southern *A kan sea* Bands. The chiefs and warriors down south are not listening to the words of the Little Old Men. They have pleaded with us to come back to the north so that our numbers will be great, and we can defend ourselves against the northern tribes that are also waging war against them in the north. Many of us here have enjoyed our separate peace away from both the northern tribes and the southern bands. Some say we should stay here and become our own people. Others feel it is our duty to return to the north and stand up for our homeland."

Charlotte looked over at Brock to see his expression. He looked back at her. Brock knew what the ultimate fate of his ancestors would be. Could he say something to influence them? He was a respected warrior among these men and might have a more significant influence than her. As if understanding this, Brock looked down at his feet thinking this over. What would be the right thing to say at this point?

Then Charlotte squeezed his arm so that he would look at her again. She shook her head ever so slightly telling him this wasn't the right time still. She wanted to talk to him privately so they could work out their best course of action in this case. He nodded his head in agreement understanding her intention. Then she tilted her chin toward the door indicating she was ready to leave. Brock pushed his way back through the crowd, and they exited the longhouse.

Once outside, they took a deep breath of fresh air after being in the crowded, smoke-filled house. "Can we take a walk?" Charlotte asked.

He nodded his head and put his arm around her shoulders, as Brock always did when she was Charlotte. They walked into the cool night air.

"What are you thinking?" she finally asked after she was sure they were far enough away from any of the villagers.

"What year did you say this is?" he asked.

"It's November 27, 1801."

Brock thought for a while, then spoke, "When will the United States buy this territory?"

"It will be late 1803, close to Christmas time."

"Do you know what happens to the Osage once the US gains control?"

"My Uncle Jimmy sent me a letter with some information and Lilly has been doing more research."

"Wait. Your Uncle Jimmy knows about this, too?" Brock stopped walking.

"Oh, right. I forgot to tell you about my conversation with him over Thanksgiving. It turns out that these abilities, such as spirit travel, are passed down from generation to generation and my family has a history of abilities." Charlotte was embarrassed she hadn't told Brock about this before now. So much had been going on lately in their other life.

"So, since I'm over here, does that mean I have this ability, too, or is it because of your ability that you brought me over?" Brock was confused.

Charlotte shrugged. "I don't know. I haven't been given much guidance this whole time. I'm still piecing it all together. Anyway, back to the historical research. We've discovered that they will build a fort closer to Saint Louis called Fort Osage in 1808. Once word gets out that the US has purchased this land, many settlers will pour in from the East. The Osage will respond by stealing horses and putting as much of the white man's possessions on those horses as they can carry and take away. And anything else that they cannot, like furniture, they will smash and destroy. Fort Osage will be built with the intention of curtailing these attacks, but it won't help much in the long run. President Jefferson will make many treaties with the Osage regarding their land. He will send them plows and looms and attempt to convince them to become farmers. The Osage won't want to become farmers because it means they will have to give up their traditional buffalo hunts. There will also be an increase in other tribes from the East, like the Cherokee, Creek, and Choctaw, moving into this territory, and we will be at war with tribes, like the Pawnee, Shawnee, and Apache, in the West." She paused and sighed heavily. She was beginning to see the bigger picture.

He thought this over as well. He remembered the stories he heard growing up on the reservation. He knew all about the promises that the United States government would make and then break over and over. He knew the horror stories. These people were his ancestors. A part of him wanted to mount a vast rebellion and work to change the course of history so that his people wouldn't be pushed to the reservation in Oklahoma. He wished with all his heart that the Osage people could unite and fight the white bullies in the East. He wanted to carry a message to all the Indian tribes in America and get them to stand as one people to create a new nation of Native Americans. What if he could prevent the slaughter of millions of Natives across the land and turn the tide of history in their favor?

He was quiet for some time thinking this over. She brought him back to reality by saying, "I know you want to fight for your people."

"Yes, I do. With my memories as Brock, I see the reservation that my people will be reduced to. With my emotions and warrior spirit as Tetonka, I am filled with anger and hatred for the white man for doing that to us. I want to raise up a great nation of my people and free my people before we're slaughtered like cattle." He fought to keep his voice from raging.

She could feel the tension in his body. She took his hands and felt him shaking. She wrapped her arms around his waist and laid her head against his chest hoping to calm the storm that she knew wanted to burst out.

Charlotte was alarmed to find his whole body shaking, his skin was hot, and he had broken out into a sweat. This didn't seem a typical response even if he was outraged. "Brock? Are you all right? Why are you sweating? The air is cool?"

Brock continued to shake, and his teeth rattled. "I'm not feeling good. I need to lie down."

She turned him in the direction of their hut, but then thought maybe she should get him to the medicine woman instead. She altered their course praying it wasn't serious.

THEY WALKED into Onaiwah's hut to see her lying on her pallet breathing softly. Charlotte hated to wake her. She gently shook Onaiwah's shoulder, and she opened her eyes.

"Yes, my dear. What brings you to me so late at night?"

Charlotte turned her head to Brock/Tetonka and Onaiwah

followed her gaze. He stood in the middle of the hut with his arms wrapped around his middle. He looked like he was holding something in to keep it from escaping.

Onaiwah jumped up and led him to sit on her pallet. She moved to the fire pit and stirred the embers, placing more wood in the center. It blazed back to life. Onaiwah set about gathering things from her supplies. Charlotte lit a torch in the fire to give Onaiwah some light over her husband.

Onaiwah pulled back the bandage over his stitches and saw they were red and swollen. She pressed around the stitches but saw no signs of pus under the skin. She quickly made a poultice and dressed the wound with fresh bandages. Then she covered him with a buffalo skin.

"I need you to get some water from the stream," Onaiwah handed Charlotte a kettle. She quickly exited the hut. No sooner had she gotten away from the light when she wished she had grabbed a torch to help light her way in the dark. She stepped carefully through the grass while she moved as fast as she could.

She reached the edge of the stream and fell to her knees. Her hands shook as she dipped the kettle into the water.

She heard a noise and jumped, dropping the kettle in the grass and spilling most of the water. Out of the dark, emerged Barkley. Relieved to see him, she forgot the kettle and ran to hug him.

"Oh, Barkley! I'm so happy to see you. Something awful has happened. Tetonka has a fever." She buried her face into his fur. Barkley whined a little to show his sympathy.

Then she remembered her urgency to get back and refilled the kettle. With Barkley by her side, she felt more secure on her walk back to the hut. She left him to stand outside as sentry while she went in.

Onaiwah took the kettle from her and placed it over the fire. When the water was boiling, she scooped a bowl full and placed a concoction of leaves she had prepared in the water. After she was satisfied it had steeped enough, she poured the liquid into a clay cup.

"Nahele, help me set him up."

Charlotte sat and helped raise his head and shoulders. He didn't open his eyes. Onaiwah set the cup to his lips and instructed him to drink. He managed to swallow a couple of tiny sips.

"I will need to give him this drink every few hours. You can lie down next to him, and I will make a bed by the fire."

Charlotte maneuvered herself under the buffalo hide beside her husband. Occasionally, he would shake, and she would hold him tightly as if she could make it stop and go away. This was exactly what she had been afraid of after Onaiwah stitched him up the first time. Modern day medicines seemed like a miracle compared to the remedies they had in this time. A simple infection could spread and turn fatal quickly.

Suddenly, it occurred to her. *What if Tetonka dies and Brock is still in his body.* Olivia had warned her about dying as a Spirit Traveler. He would be caught between worlds, left without his body in either time.

Charlotte squeezed him a little tighter and whispered in his ear, "Brock don't die on me. I can't lose you. You have to fight through this." He didn't respond. All she could do was hold him and comfort him and pray that his body fought off the infection.

She needed to switch them back. Onaiwah had taught her how to do it in her mind, but how could she do it for the both of them? *This wasn't supposed to happen. You aren't supposed to be here.*

She remembered Barkley lying outside the hut. *Maybe he is here waiting to take us back.* Relief washed over her as she realized this. *As soon as he can walk, I'll take him out to Barkley, and he will switch us back.*

Feeling better at ease with this plan, she drifted off in a light sleep until Onaiwah woke her again to check on him and give him more to drink. He had stopped shaking, but his skin still felt hot to the touch.

The third time Onaiwah woke her to administer to Tetonka, the sun was peaking over the horizon. Charlotte was so tired she could hardly open her eyes. At last, it seemed his fever had broken. His skin was cooler, and he wanted to roll onto his left side away from his injury. She helped him roll over then decided she needed to make a trip to the stream.

She exited the hut to find Barkley still lying outside. "Barkley! His fever broke." She rubbed his head as he wagged his tail. "I think Tetonka is going to be okay. Once he wakes up, I'll bring him out and you can switch us back."

Barkley followed her as she walked through the wet grass to the stream. She washed her face, scraped her teeth, and relieved herself. She felt better about Brock's condition now. She would make sure Tetonka was doing better, then switch her and Brock back to their own time.

She was walking back to the hut when she heard men shouting on the main road in the village. Charlotte ran to the big Mother tree. At the edge of the village, there was a gathering of people and some men arguing on past them. She worked her way through the onlookers to find Kajika and several French soldiers arguing with Tetonka's father and brother.

Kajika saw her and pointed to her. "There's his wife! She will know where he is."

She froze. *They must want Tetonka. But why?*

Kajika came up to her and grabbed her by the arm. She tried to jerk away, but he tightened his grip making her wince. He pushed her toward the Frenchmen. "Here is his woman. She will take us to him."

Charlotte looked at Kajika. "Kajika? What are you doing? Who are these men and why are you hurting me?" Tetonka's father and brother came to stand next to her.

"Kajika? What is the meaning of this? We have never seen you act this way!" Chaska, Tetonka's father, demanded.

One of the Frenchmen spoke up instead. "We have orders to bring back the man responsible for killing seven of our countrymen."

Charlotte turned to look at the man who spoke. He wore a blue and white soldier uniform complete with black hat and red plume feather, knee breeches, and black knee-high boots. He carried a musket with a bayonet. He had a long, thin mustache with a pointed beard on his chin.

He looks like a Three Musketeer, Charlotte thought. She wouldn't have been surprised if he announced his name was D'Artagnan and raised his sword shouting, *All for One, and One for All!* Then she realized he didn't have a sword, and that era was older than this time period. She looked at the other twenty or so men standing further back who were dressed the same and carried the same weapon. Standing next to the French soldier who spoke was the dirty vagabond who she saw the day of the raid on their village. He had a fresh red scar across his cheek.

Charlotte felt a cold lump drop in her stomach, and she fought back the bile at the base of her throat. She opened her mouth to say something, nothing came out. She tried to swallow, but her throat was too dry. After a second attempt, she found her voice to speak, "What is your name and on whose authority are you here?" Her voice cracked a little. She tried to hide her terror by looking straight at the leader.

The Frenchman seemed taken aback that an Indian woman would address him that way. At first, it seemed he wasn't going to answer her question, but then he replied. "I am Brigadier General Edgard Etienne Colbert. I have a witness here that says one of your men killed seven Frenchmen, and another one of your men here has informed me that this same man is responsible for stealing horses and raiding in Saint Genevieve. I am here to arrest this man and see that he stands trial in front of a judge in Saint Louis."

It took a little while for her to understand him through his thick French accent. When she comprehended what he said, she turned to Kajika and narrowed her eyes at him. "You are his kola! And you would hand him over to these men as if he were a dog!" She was so furious she almost spat on him. The other villagers were catching on to her outrage.

Chaska and Takoda stood next to her with equal stares of contempt. Kajika didn't seem moved by their looks. Something had been brewing in Kajika; she had been witnessing his increasing antagonism over the past few months. *What happened to him to make him turn on his people, his kola?*

Before she had time to think about how she was going to get Tetonka out of this situation, there was a commotion coming from the back of the group of villagers. She turned to see the group splitting in half to allow another group of men to pass. Then she saw two French soldiers dragging Tetonka by the arms toward them. His fever might have broken, but he was still weak. He apparently didn't have the strength to stand or raise his head. Then she realized with a shock that the men had knocked him out.

Charlotte cried out and tried to rush toward Tetonka, but Kajika held her back.

"Is this the man?" The Brigadier General asked the vagabond standing next to him.

The vagabond walked to Tetonka, grabbed him by his hair and pulled his head back. Charlotte winced.

"That's him," he said and let his head fall back.

"Do you agree this is the same man who raided Saint Genevieve and stole the horses?" The Brigadier General addressed Kajika. Kajika nodded his head. His face was like stone, neither happy nor angry.

The Brigadier General motioned for his men to bring Tetonka along.

Charlotte screamed, "NO!" and once again made a move to reach him. This time, she was held back by her in-laws.

"We have to let him go, *Me nah*," Chaska whispered. "We can't fight them."

She didn't or wouldn't hear him. If she didn't get to him to switch within the week, Brock would be stuck here, and his body in the future would go catatonic.

She fell to her knees crying and screaming, "NO! Don't take him! NO! He can't go!" She felt a growing hysteria within her. She couldn't breathe. She pressed her hands to her chest. This can't be happening. She can't let him go like this. She can't lose both of them. This was not supposed to happen.

She watched helplessly as they tied his hands and threw his limp body over the back of a horse. She couldn't believe they were treating him like this. *Why didn't someone do something?*

The Brigadier General mounted his horse. Every part of her body wanted to run after him, beg him to let him go, tell him there must be some mistake. Not Tetonka, not her husband. Take someone else, anyone but him.

The further away they walked with him the more she felt as if they were sucking the life right out of her. It was like a vacuum pulling at her inner soul. She felt the world closing in on her from all sides and her vision narrowed to one singular point. Charlotte's only thought before her world went black was, *I have to rescue him.*

EPILOGUE

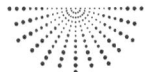

Book Two of The Spirit Traveler Series

*I*f you liked *The Forest Beyond*, then you'll love my next book *The White Stag*. Here's a sneak peek.

HIS BODY ROCKED BACK and forth as his awareness slowly returned. He winced as the full force of his headache hit him. It felt as if someone had stuffed rocks into his skull. It pounded with such force that for the moment all he could hear was the throbbing of his heartbeat. He winced again as a sharp pain pierced his side. He tried to open his eyes, but he was immediately assaulted with the brightness of the day making his head throb even more. When he tried to reach with his hands to shield his eyes from the glare, he realized they were tied together with rope.

He squinted cautiously, only opening his eyelids with the tiniest of cracks. He made out rocks, dirt, grass. He could see his hands and arms dangling down in front of him. As his eyes adjusted a little more, he noticed the hooves of a horse walking across the ground that seemed to be his sky.

How did I get here? Brock thought. He tried to think about the last thing he remembered. He remembered being with Charlotte holding her hand behind her house and walking into the trees. He remembered the realization of being in Tetonka's body.

Oh, no. Am I still in the past? It came flooding back to him now. He remembered going to the meeting in the Sky Lodge and listening to the men who had returned from the Big Osage village. He remembered walking out with Nahele/Charlotte to talk and how angry he got wanting to change the course of history. Then he remembered the fever and being in the medicine woman's hut.

Are they taking me on horseback to get better medicine? Tetonka's caution told him to wait and listen. He tried to relax his body so he wouldn't give himself away by appearing conscious.

He heard beyond the throbbing of his heartbeat in his ears and noticed others walking both behind and in front of him. He heard men's voices speaking French. He felt hungry and thirsty, and he was anxious to discover why he was in this situation. He slid off the horse and collapsed in a heap to the ground.

Someone yelled, "Halt!" and a rush of feet surrounded him. He continued to feign weakness until he could assess his situation and possibly make for his escape.

No one touched him until the apparent leader of the group rode up beside them on his horse. "We will take a rest here." The leader announced. "You, there. Get him up and set him by these trees. And you, go find some water."

Rough hands grabbed him and forced him to his feet. He was weaker than he had imagined. They shoved him down next to a tree as he continued to keep his head hanging down in fake delirium.

A few minutes later, someone shoved his head back and poured water into his mouth. He tried to drink as much as he could without choking. The cold water ran down his chest, making him shiver. Out of the sun and under the shade, it was cold. The sun on his back had kept him warm enough while on the horse, but now he had goosebumps on his flesh as he fought to control the myriad of thoughts running through his mind.

Someone wrapped a blanket around his shoulders. He chanced a peek at the man squatting in front of him. He seemed to assess his condition. The man didn't look at him with hostility, just passive concern.

The man addressed him. "I am Brigadier General Edgard Etienne Colbert. Do you know why you are in my custody?"

Brock raised his eyes slowly to get a better look at the man speaking to him. He glared at him for a few seconds then slowly shook his head.

"Do you recognize this man?" The general pointed to a man standing further back to his right. Brock shifted his eyes toward him, then immediately narrowed them like arrows shooting toward the man with the scar on his cheek.

"Apparently, you do." The general quickly surmised. "He claims you killed seven of his men in an ambush and took their scalps."

Rather than dignify the statement with a defense, Brock spat on the ground in Scarface's direction.

"Told you he was a nasty bugger," Scarface retorted. He kicked the dirt at his feet and sent it flying into Brock's face.

Quicker than anyone would have imagined, Brock jumped to his feet and in one leap had his arms looped around Scarface's neck choking him. It took four men and another knock on the head to get him off. Brock was head and shoulders taller than all of the men holding him captive and probably twenty to thirty pounds heavier. Their only means of keeping him under their control was to keep him unconscious.

Brock came to a few minutes later, sitting against the tree. This time, they bound his hands behind him, and his ankles as well. His head hurt so bad he had to fight hard not to vomit. Daggers of pain pierced his eyes whenever he tried to open them. He rolled his head back against the tree trunk and squeezed his eyes shut.

A harsh whisper in his ear made his body tense, "I'm gonna enjoy watching you hang, Injun." Brock froze, keeping his eyes tightly shut.

The nasty vagabond spat into Brock's face and pushed himself off the tree leaving Brock with nothing to do but bite his tongue and plan his next move.

When the men were ready to move, General Colbert gave orders to untie Brock's feet and tie his hands back to the front. He ordered him to walk behind a guard on his horse. The guard secured the rope to the pommel of his saddle with a lead making Brock walk a few feet behind.

Brock's head pounded with each step. His stomach rolled with hunger, but the thought of food made bile lurch up to the base of his throat. The guard kicked his horse into a trot, but Brock's long legs easily kept up with the pace.

Seeing that the tall Osage man had an advantage, and the pace was not punishing enough, the guard urged his horse to run. Brock had no choice but to run behind the horse. With his hands tied together, his gait was awkward, but he was undaunted. They had left the rest of the company behind. Only two other guards were on horseback keeping pace behind them; the General stayed behind on his horse with the walkers.

The guard pulling Brock urged his horse to go faster and faster until finally, Brock was moving his legs as fast as he could to keep from falling. He stumbled over rocks, roots, and holes in the dirt trail. Eventually, his foot caught on a tree root, and he stumbled to the ground. The guard never slowed his horse and continued to drag Brock along the ground like a sack of potatoes.

AUTHOR'S NOTE

I first came across the idea that Native Americans might have lived on Crowley's Ridge in the course of researching my ancestry. I was reading *Greene County: A History* when it told of Benjamin Crowley and other area leaders using abandoned log buildings in the area until they could build stronger structures of their own. Therein, it also contained a map indicating that the Little Osage lived in the area before white settlers.

I then began an online search that revealed several different opinions as to who might have been the actual original inhabitants. Whether they lived on Crowley's Ridge is not supported by any evidence that I have found. They might have built some temporary lodges there during their hunting seasons. The Quapaw are most commonly believed to have lived closer to the area but further south near present-day Helena.

Another source attributed the early structures to some Delaware Indians as a result of moving westward away from the Colonists in the 1700s. Lastly, the buildings could have been built by Cherokee who had already begun to leave Georgia and South Carolina before their forced removal in 1830. They could have settled in the area in the early 1800s.

I chose to use the Osage in my fictional story because their physical descriptions and their way of life intrigued me, and I felt they would make for a great romance story. The descriptions of their physical characteristics are based on facts that I have found to be true about them. Their general way of life, hunting, religious beliefs, ceremonies, agriculture, and local food gathering are all based on my research. However, the family way of life I altered to fit more romantically in a fictional story and, therefore, to be more relatable to a reading audience. I tried to stay true to the Osage People as best I could to honor these people for the great people that they were and those who still are.

I don't doubt that some of the people living in these areas today are descendants of Native Americans of various tribes. I am a descendant of Cherokee and other unknown tribes. Although I did not retain the skin coloring (I am also of predominately Scots-Irish descent), I do remember several individuals who I went to school and church with who could have easily been close descendants due to their darker tan skin tone. My maternal ancestors in Greene County can be traced back to as early as 1851 with even earlier ancestors coming from Missouri and other parts of the South.

AFTERWORD

I want to make the reader aware that I use the terms *Native American* and *Indian* interchangeably. Some Native People's use the terms interchangeably as well as the term *Native Indian* occasionally. I realize all these terms can be politically sensitive, but my use of them is with the utmost respect and no racial bias is intended in any way.

In the preface of *The Adventures of Tom Sawyer*, Mark Twain wrote: "Most of the adventures recorded in this book really occurred; one or two were experiences of my own, the rest those of [characters] who were schoolmates of mine. ...but not from an individual—[they are] a combination of the characteristics of [people] whom I knew, and therefore belongs to the composite order of architecture.

...Although my book is intended mainly for the entertainment of boys and girls, I hope it will not be shunned by men and women on that account, for part of my plan has been to try to pleasantly remind adults of what they once were themselves, and of how they felt and thought and talked and what queer enterprises they sometimes engaged in."

I read this quote (with substitutions to fit my narrative) after I had written this book. It fits for this story as well, with a little added fantasy for extra imagination. I hope you enjoyed reading my book.

Christine DeYoung 2018

ACKNOWLEDGMENTS

There are many people that have helped me in writing this book that I would like to thank. I am grateful to my former students Marisa A. and Jackie C. for their input and relative look on today's teen. You were a great inspiration. I want to thank my daughter for giving me advice when I needed it. You helped guide me in the right direction when I was struggling with the next step in which to take the book. Thanks to my two sons for listening to Mommy's crazy stories and long-winded explanations. Thanks to my parents for showing enthusiasm to read the finished product. Most of all, I want to say thank you to my long-suffering husband for putting up with my crazy ideas and supporting me and my children while I stayed at home and worked on my research and writing when I should have been cleaning the house. Thanks for talking it up with everyone you met to generate an interest in the book before you had even read one page, and thanks for editing my awkward sentences even when it hurt my pride a little. Words cannot express how grateful I am and how much I love you.

I have included in this work of fiction some stories that were authentic to the Osage people and other Native American tribes, so I want to give credit where credit is due. These references refer to the corresponding asterisks within the text.

* from *A History of the Osage People,* by Louis F. Burns.Copyright © 1989 The University of Alabama Press.

** adapted with permission from *Traditions of the Osage: Stories Collected and Translated by Francis La Flesche,* by Garrick Baily. Copyright © 2010 University of New Mexico Press.

*** Story taken from:
Http://www.nativeamericanembassy.net/www.lenni-lenape.com/www/html/LenapeArchives/LenapeSet-01/feedwich.html

Horse, Follow Closely: Native American Horsemanship, by GaWaNi Pony Boy. Text Copyright © 1998 by Bow Tie™ Press

Indian Medicine Power, by Brad Steiger. Copyright © 1984 Whitford Press, A Division of Schiffer Publishing.

INDEX

Index of Native American names and terms:

Kola— warrior-brother
　Me nah— older daughter (sometimes spelled Mi-na)
　Itancan— leader
　Waunca—imitator or follower
　Tsi shu— Sky clan (Peacemaker's)
　Hun ka— Earth clan (War-maker's)
　Ni u kon ska— People of the Middle Waters
　Wa sha zhe— Osage
　Marais des Cygnes— Marsh of the Swans
　A kan sea— Arkansas
　Wah'Kon-Tah— Great Spirit or God

In case you read the first edition of my book, here is a list of character names I changed and their meanings:

Nahele (formerly known as Indigo)— Forest
　Tetonka (formerly known as Stomping Bull)— Buffalo
　Hula (formerly known as Violet)— Eagle

Niabi (formerly known as Yellow Flower, Indigo's mother)— Young deer

Takoda (formerly known as Kicking Calf, Stomping Bull's brother) — Friend to everyone

Onaiwah (formerly known as Sunewah, medicine woman)— awake, alert

Nayati (formerly known as Cutting Knife, Kicking Calf's kola)— One who wrestles

Kajika (formerly known as Elk Horn, Stomping Bull's kola)— Walks without sound

Chayton (formerly known as Red Falcon, Indigo's father)— Falcon

Chaska (formerly known as Buffalo Tail, Stomping Bull's father)— First born son

Mahpee (formerly known as Sunset, Stomping Bull's mother)— Sky

Wande (formerly known as Eagle Feather, Indigo's uncle)— White Eagle

ABOUT THE AUTHOR

If you would like to know more about the author or her upcoming books, visit www.christinedeyoung.net or you can reach her by email at christine@deyoung.net.

Connect with her via social media:
https://www.facebook.com/xylanderspirit/
https://www.facebook.com/writerchristinedeyoung/
https://twitter.com/christinedeyoun

amazon.com/author/christinedeyoung

Be sure to leave a review and tell all your friends about the book. Your continued support enables the author to continue writing more stories like this one.